V KNOX

Time

falls like snow

A blue door, black sand – red flurries in the age of Gemini

for Sarah and David

Time
falls like snow

ISBN: 978-0-9937380-9-8

Editor: Silent K Publishing
Cover design: Veronica Knox and SpicaBookDesign
Cover and interior illustrations: Veronica Knox
Typeset at SpicaBookDesign in Times

Printed with www.createspace.com

Silent K Publishing:
Victoria, British Columbia, Canada

www.veronicaknox.com

Hadrian's Wall – Northumberland

TABLE OF CONTENTS

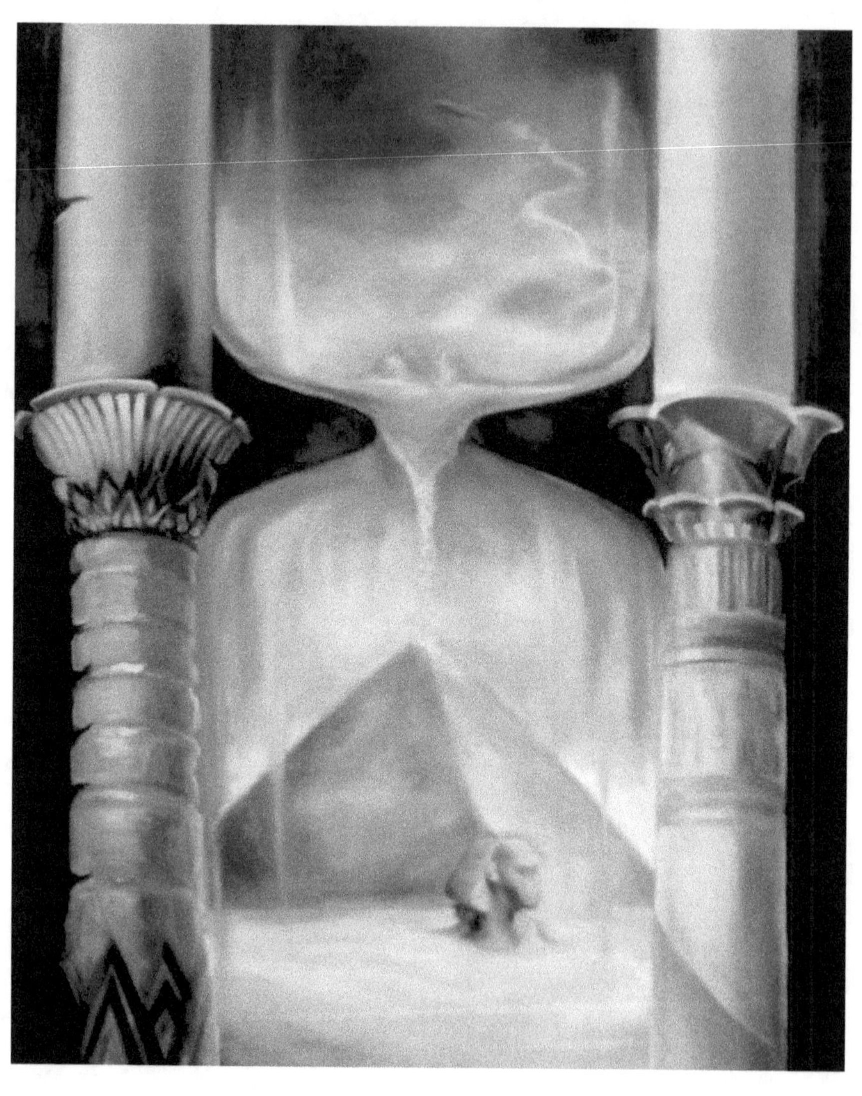

"To see a world in a grain of sand"

~ WILLIAM BLAKE

'TWINTER – the first portal' – *an extraordinary time-slip story where ghosts, time-travel, a dozen terrible secrets, and a curse of snow takes a pair of telepathic twins on an adventure in ancient Egypt and into the future where the safety of earth's ecosystem lies in their hands.*

Twins Christopher (Kit) and Bathsheba (Bash) Stratford-Smyth who live in a suburb of greater London, are twelve when their Egyptologist father goes missing from his dig in Egypt.

Meanwhile, Bede Hall, their grandmother, Lady Nan's stately home in Northumbria, is in danger and not a little angry. It feels cruelly abandoned at its hour of need, put up for sale while its matriarch, oblivious of her old home in danger of being sold to shady developers, has intentionally distanced herself from responsibilities by retreating into a fog of distracting memories. While the Hall faces being turned it into a commercial venture, or demolition, Lady Nan dreams on about a previous life she remembers in ancient Egypt.

But the Hall has no intentions of being sold without a fight. In desperation, it summons its considerable powers and orders Lady Nan to wake up and return home.

Lady Nan hears but fails to comply until the voice of her childhood playmate, a ghost child who lingers in the Hall's unsettling 'cold spot' behind the blue door of an abandoned room in the attic known as the 'winter room', joins the Hall's request.

Lady Nan regains consciousness, her old eccentric vital self, to discover her son-in-law still unaccounted for. She takes control by rallying her family's flagging energies in a resourceful threefold plan to save the Hall, free her lost friend, and provide a home for her daughter's grieving family.

To save money, Mrs. S, a former teacher, recalls her eldest son from university, homeschools the twins, and takes in a private pupil for extra income. Unfortunately, her pupil is a snooping bully, the son of a greedy realtor intent on acquiring the Hall by any devious means he can.

His son is sent in to spy and sabotage the Hall's sudden reversal of fortunes, because after watching television with its new residents, Bede Hall hits upon a money-making scheme that leaves its shameless predators out in the cold.

The twins turn thirteen and adapt to life in Bede by finding the Hall's resident ghost. But Kit uncovers the village of Bede's darkest secret when he spontaneously stumbles into one of several time portals in and around the Hall. Kit glimpses an imminent ice-age and receives an implausible shock with devastating personal consequences.

The miraculous rescue of Mr. S, brings an addition to the family of an adopted teenage brother, a street kid from Cairo who is naturally aware of the Hall's strange influences even though the twins' parents and older brother remain unresponsive, oblivious of it's supernatural powers.

At the end of book one, Lady Nan passes away. She takes her place as the head ghost of Bede Hall, picks up the gauntlet of protecting the world from disaster, and recruits her enchanted childhood toys, a snow globe and hourglass, to help unlock the past.

In a plan to save the Hall, the family, and the rest of the world, the twins, their newfound mentors, and several ghosts, unite to form a team called the 'Twinters', a name comprised of the words twins and winter.

Three years have gone by since the twins first arrived to live in Bede Hall. Kit has had enough of the Hall's games. He has several disturbing secrets to keep and an impossible decision to make.

BEDE HALL IS ALIVE BUT ALL IS NOT WELL.
Turning sixteen isn't going to be easy.

TWINTERS
Carpe Diem

*Venture into Bede
by way of this prologue –
and welcome.
But remember…
once through the portal,
you may have to stay!*

THE VENERABLE BEDE HALL
Northumberland, Great Britain

There are three generations of Stratford-Smyths 'living' in Bede Hall. The fourth is the ghost of a nine-year-old girl, which makes them four generations spanning four dimensions.

Bede Hall hovers in and out of this world, visiting its past and future which means that even in the blistering heat of August it could snow at any time. It was old. The word ageless barely covered it, and the word timeless was an outright lie. Older than time was closest to the truth. But even then, strictly speaking, the Hall was older than history.

When she was alive, the elder Beryl Stratford-Smyth, the Hall's matriarch, and Lady Nan to her grandchildren, had frequently pointed out, that under the playful laws of serendipity, words often contained hidden messages. For a start, the family name contained the word myth. For another, two highly significant words, venerable (esteemed) and vulnerable (frail), perfectly framed the Hall's present mindset.

While mortified by its precarious state of disrepair, Bede Hall fancifully celebrated its majestic future restored to its former position of power. More than once, its haughty delusions of grandeur had saved it from ruin. And now, being sold to local developers was simply not an option.

And while the Hall mulled over a last hurrah to save itself and the world from an embarrassingly defensive position of diminishing power, Lady Nan's transition from life to death strengthened her claim as its presiding queen.

Lady Nan's passing set her body free to shape-shift at will from old-age to childhood, and her playful nature of alternating from wise-woman to precocious nine-year-old without warning, made her seem even more eccentric. 'Beryl the younger' habitually retreated into her fanciful childhood. 'Beryl the elder' maintained a firm hold on the knowledge gained from her recent sojourn of seventy-odd-years and mined her previous lifetimes to reconcile the past and balance the trying times ahead. In so doing, Lady Nan embraced being slowly absorbed by the future but her childhood home refused to gently crumble into the landscape without a fight.

As a child, little Beryl learned to swim with the stone mermaids who lived in the fountain. Fairies taught her the language of the flowers, woodland spirits showed her how to read the changing seasons, and old Mr. Parks the gardener, gave her botany lessons, praising her as a natural 'green thumb'.

Beryl was proud of her thumbs; nevertheless, she remained unbearably lonely for human companionship after her twin brother was sent off to school. She played alone in the manicured flowerbeds that spread in a scented skirt around the great house and hid in the garden maze to daydream.

As a daughter, Beryl was assigned a series of governesses who routinely fled in tears after experiencing frights in the cold spot outside a room near the attic nursery. It was dubbed the Winter Room because wintry wind emanated from the keyhole of its blue door even when the rest of the house sweltered in the extreme heat of summer. And sometimes, when a crying child was heard, the wind took the shape of a blue mist and drifted through the nursery wall… or so Miss Beryl, said.

But then, grownups dismissed Beryl as a strange child whose moonbeam mind was filled with featherheaded notions. She remained bored and out of sorts until she made friends with Bede's resident child ghost – a kindred spirit, her own age, who 'lived' behind the locked door of the Winter Room.

The two were inseparable for nine years until the tragic loss of Beryl's brother pushed happy memories of childhood aside. Beryl grieved for a long time, refusing to be happy, and Bede's young ghost, feeling abandoned, retreated into her room, only showing herself the same day every summer in the hopes her friend would return. But Beryl focused on growing up, and it wasn't long before she married and her responsibilities as a young mother and chatelaine of a grand estate, consumed her entirely.

Beryl's busy jangle of housekeys rang through the hall's corridors louder than any ghost dragging chains. And much later, after the joys of being a grandmother waned, Lady Nan lapsed into a fog of pleasant daydreams to block her painful memories in a retirement home in a town called Withering.

In desperation, Bede Hall summoned her like an angry father to stave off the predator developers keen on turning it into an hotel, but it was the plaintive call for help of her childhood playmate that stirred Lady Nan into her old self.

In generations past, Lady Nan would have been branded a witch, considering she claimed her favourite old toys, a snow globe and a brass hourglass, and her brother's beloved replica of King Tut's throne, transcended the laws of chronological time. And while her grandchildren were small, and with her reputation as a grand storyteller, there was no reason for them to doubt her.

Teenagers Kit and Bash, short for Christopher and Bathsheba, respectively, had always experienced the natural telepathic bond of identical twins, but in no-way had their idyllic school holidays spent enraptured by Lady Nan's time-travel japes prepared them for the cold reality of moving to Bede Hall after their Egyptologist father went missing on a dig in the Valley of the Kings.

Fond summer memories framed in blue skies and fluffy clouds soon faded when confronted with poverty and camping out in a deteriorating ruin of damp rooms and dusty dreams. To distract themselves, they made a game of seeking out the rumoured ghost of a lost girl who Lady Nan, the reinstated, often dithery matriarch, assured them was real.

Confronted by the timeless 'Winter Room', the frosty skeleton key to its blue door, and the child who still lived behind it, was daunting, but it seemed ordinary after Kit blundered into a time portal and discovered that Bede Hall was frozen, buried to its rooftops in snow in the year 2020, and it was revealed the twins were the pair of champions prophesied to resolve Bede's old score with an ancient curse.

Unlike his sister's continual growing delight, following her grandmother's calling as a green thumb, Kit was loath to embrace his new home as a wonderful adventure. Bede Hall and its village were puzzling, but he'd formulated a scientific theory to explain the phenomena in a world that was beyond strange. It must be the exotic plant-life surrounding the Hall that caused an oddly selective mass hallucination. The notion that Bede Hall was manipulating its new tenants in its obsession to survive, was extraordinary as much as it was *extraordinarily* dangerous.

Searching for answers with his mentor, Dr. Peregrine Brooks, led Kit to experiment with the practice of stilling his mind for a few moments each day, sitting in his great uncle's throne chair. But steeped as the chair was in the tradition of mindful relaxation, to Kit, it was nothing short of a dodgy time machine, and his will-power blocked any progress.

Emptying his mind always ended in horrific visions of earth's future, akin to impact winter. The very words were chilling. He'd witnessed it first hand. He had *been* there.

When it proved impossible to dismiss the haunting images of earth landlocked in a freak ice-age, a newfound detachment over-came him. Kit turned a blind eye to the bizarre events he'd begun to suspect may be true and focused on saving his family.

But the worst part of Kit's refusal to cooperate with Bede Hall was that it caused a stalemate between once devoted siblings who now faced each other as opponents, scowling over a chessboard the size of Bede Hall's vast lawns. And chess, not being a friendly game at the best of times, neither of them particularly wanted to make a move to unseat the other.

BEDE'S TIMELINE

History comes and goes. Empires rise and fall, civilizations flourish and cultures collide. The laws of probability converge and stir up trouble. Geological time advances. Volcanoes explode and cool, seas flood and subside and turn to ice. Ice melts. Species evolve and mutate. Land rumbles into hills and valleys, and grass grows over everything. And in spite of the flowering of art and the inevitable clashes of war, science advances and retreats, and Bede's heart continues to animate each new age, according to its true nature.

From first to last, Bede Hall reigns over the ashes of its ancestors: from a sacred henge built of trees to the great hall of a Saxon lord and a succession of fine houses each grown more grand with human progress.

But before all of it… before Bede Hall inhaled its first thought as a stone pyramid, it was a primordial hill emerging from a timeless sea. A mound of muddy memories, sheltering the seed of a dying civilization where the human race could sprout anew.

Each of the Hall's successive constructions have grown phoenix-like from the energy of its previous bones. Which means its latest incarnation is both ancient and new – the oldest and the youngest at the same time. But then, figuratively speaking, everything happens at the same time in Bede.

Within its mystical boundaries, the hamlet of Bede forms an island without a sea. Hadrian's Wall defends the Hall's back, the Green Lady's forest safeguards its eastern border, an Iron Age ditch protects it to the west, and a low fence of robbed stone from a medieval monastery defined the southernmost cottage of Bede Village, marking the edge of the old world.

Saltwater breezes from the west and the sweet scent of Lindisfarne's holy isle to the north, sweep through breaks in the ancient wall to play in the Hall's gardens. Lady Nan told her grandchildren, that on the solstices, it's possible to see a candle burning on Lindisfarne if you put your mind to it.

Bede thrived in its isolation, separate from the bustling world of London, three-hundred-miles to the south. From the air, the old Roman road, Dere Street, still cuts a straight grey swath through the forests where Saxons and Normans once traveled as the falcon flies.

Long ago, Vikings had pillaged from the eastern shore and Scots had raided from the north, yet a serene pocket of calm flourishes, protected by energies older than the pyramids.

If time stands still anywhere, it's at Bede. If ghosts haunt anywhere it's in Bede Hall.

Faint traces of prehistoric circles, lines, and squares lay etched into the fields. Phantoms of early Bronze Age ditches encircled mounds and barrows that shimmered to life after the rains, and the hillocks of Iron Age settlements played hide-and-seek in the long nettles. Saxon gold shuffled deep under the earth with Neolithic flint arrowheads, dagger blades made of iron, and mosaic tesserae from Roman villas. And all the while, the tips of abandoned cairns poked their noses from mossy hillocks into the sunlight.

For thousands of years, crude dwellings and settlements crumbled into ruins until a maze of grassy banks sectioned the landscape of Bede into a creased map of curious lumps and bumps, covering the secrets of the ancestors.

Long ago, Bede's natural water features, the sources of ancient power, had been stolen by the Romans for their formal spas and new temples. Springs and streams were rededicated, displacing the old guardians, renamed to merge with a pantheon of Roman gods – immortals 'borrowed' from the Greeks without permission. They built forts over the shrines of the green gods and clogged the sacred wells with sacrificial animal bones and amulets, vanquishing the local water spirits to trickle away underground in disgrace.

In time, their abandoned pagan settlements were absorbed by the dark ages and subsided into shallow impressions left in the clay underbelly of the rich topsoil. Stone circles tilted out of kilter in tired fields, straining valiantly to mark the solstices. Hadrian's great wall stood as a gallant reminder of the long-gone glory days, keeping out marauders while Bede remained steadfast under an ancient spell of protection.

Left to themselves, the old nature gods silently returned to Bede from the netherworld. The face of the Green Man, overseer of the growing seasons, and lord of the harvest festivals and woodland creatures, began appearing again in the barks of trees. Chloris the Green Woman, consort to Jack-of-the-Green, gathered the scattered fairies into colonies and fanned the waning magic into sacred fire.

The elementals rallied their weakened whorls of energies into vortexes of great power. Comets, falling stars, and solar flares revisited the skies above the rumble-grumbles of the earth as it stretched and cracked its skin. Fresh waters bubbled anew from sacred springs. Bede's Sprites sent forth its water-beetle messengers, the Egyptian scarabs' distant cousins, to rally the twice-borns. Comeuppances long overdue blew hot and cold out of season.

Vengeances lying dormant for eons, slithered from the withered skins of mummified enemies in a fresh colony of eager snakes in the grass. The Green Man retreated, and Bede Hall, savvy to the magnitude of old scores and subtle reprisals, trained its youngest champions and prepared itself for war.

In spite of Kit's denial of all things supernatural, Bede Hall's topiaries wandered over the lawns like a herd of giant green animals, faster than human eye could detect, meeting secretly with the trees to discuss the return of their absent master, the Green Man, comparing omens and portents with the forest's colony of trickster fairies.

Head of security, Anubis the cat, guarded the gates and portals with his scurrying army of grapevine mice and beetles that relayed progress reports across the forest floor to the twice-borns in the village.

A network of honeybees kept a close buzz on the local developers, continually plotting the Hall's future incarnation as an hotel. And the resident ghosts of Bede Hall and a contrary chair conspired to stabilize the warring factions within the Hall by gaining Kit's trust.

Meanwhile, erratic events swirled ferociously in Lady Nan's snow globe. There were days her hourglass was encrusted with frost too hot to touch.

Kit privately toyed with the idea of using the time portal in the maze to slingshot himself back to 2013, but all things considered, the prospect terrified him, and the ostrich approach of burying his head in sand, mocked the real dangers of the Egyptian desert.

And so, it falls to Bede Hall's time corridors, the Great Sphinx of Egypt, the rules of twindom, the power of nine, and its chosen champions to save the planet from becoming a ball of blue ice orbiting the sun.

With time running out, the chair is misbehaving again. And as determined as Kit is to ignore his supernatural experiences in favour of scientific proof, he's learned the hard way that all memories and dreams are inhabited by ghosts of one kind or another. But now, lives are at stake.

Besides, Lady Nan's wisdom continually haunts him: *If you really want something enough,* she liked to say, *a little thing like dying won't stop you.*

I

THE ART OF FREEZING

Bede Hall, Northumberland, England
OCTOBER 22, 2016

The chair was misbehaving again. Kit tapped his fingers on the armrests, arose with a sigh, and stood back from it, thoroughly disgruntled. He rattled it's frame, none too gently. *Rotten piece of junk. You're supposed to calm me down!* He stretched his cramped muscles, and walked off in yet another huff. Regrettably, huffs were becoming all too frequent.

There was no need for special powers to see a few hours into the future when Kit was honour-bound to report yet another clash of wills. He could picture it now. His friend Dr. Brooks, would be silently miffed, smiling encouragement as always, with an even-tempered expression.

Kit rehearsed what he would say: *Look, I tried. It just doesn't work*. He would be sure to maintain eye contact for a full minute and then deliberately look away. Averting one's eyes at the appropriate moment often got him out of trouble.

Brooks would counter with an offhand 'you're trying too hard, lad. You're meant to sit and wait. The answers will come if you open up and let go', and tell him for the zillionth time to be patient. 'Not 'kidding around patient', he'd add, reminding Kit, yet again, that he'd been granted a special gift. *Humph…some gift.* Kit would stand mute, eyes riveted to the tops of his mentor's shoes, looking appropriately chastised. *Yeah yeah yeah.* He'd been chosen for a reason, and everyone… *everyone*… was counting on him to save the world. So, no pressure.

Kit lobbed his mobile phone at the chair, with equal parts frustration and malice. It was, truth be told, aimed at himself – a projectile of self-punishment. *I don't know why I keep this stupid thing. It never works.* His thoughts accelerated inside the round tower like a super-collider until the phone hit the seat of the chair squarely on target with a sickening crack. Plastic met wood and bounced onto the floor spilling its innards, sliding towards wolfhound Jack.

The dog sniffed it suspiciously but otherwise ignored it. Flashes of temper came and went with humans. His guardian skills were best left for real enemies. He'd been getting signals all day. The chair was upsetting but it meant well. It was a friend, but a foe lurked nearby, and the curious black box was nothing he could eat. The tone of his master's voice meant he, Jack, would be called upon for comfort, any time now. No matter, Jack had been primed by Anubis the head feline security officer, and was ready.

Bored with the ongoing chair game, Jack barely raised his eyes from his ruglike position on the floor, but something covert arrived. The dog's nose detected an odourless scent. His ears detected silent voices. Canine instincts shifted instantly from mild concern to high-alert. With hackles raised and ears flattened – a low growl rumbled in Jack's throat. He lifted his head and emitted a single sharp yelp that trailed off into a skinny whine. Kit de-twitched the dog's ears. "It's okay mate. I'm not mad at you. I'm just a mad scientist."

Black soulful eyes gazed lovingly into the boy's. *"That's what we're all afraid of,"* he whimpered.

A faded tapestry of a fanciful forest scene hung to Kit's left. If he'd examined it with the scrutiny of his inner scientist, he would have noticed the barely visible image of an Egyptian princess holding a white cat. And if he'd looked closer still, he would have seen the ghostly image of a man with pale green skin and leaves for hair who peered from the bark of a tree while fairies frolicked below him in a garden of sunflowers.

Fanciful images failing to register was no coincidence. Kit deliberately blocked such things. Plants were particularly unwelcome in his domain. Plants were the cause of all his troubles. Even the picture of a flower made him queasy. His best course of action to neutralize a bizarre situation gone to seed, was to remain constantly vigilant. One had to be wary of any plant growing in Bede.

Other than the happy photos of his father at the Great Pyramid of Giza, the artwork that adorned his walls told a grim story. A menacing picture of the face on Mars was pinned to a corkboard with diagrams of volcanoes. He'd drawn an angry X over it. And a framed poster of earth seen from space, hung over an iron cot.

The poster resembled an abstract painting. Hot colours radiated from the centre gradually progressing from red and orange to cold blues and greens at the edges – a revealing map of heat-sensitive topography that exposed the heart of a gaping wound under the earth's crust. It had a large X drawn over its central red blob in magic marker. Underneath the image, in handwritten black letters, were the words 'Yellowstone Caldera' followed by the date 2020 and an exaggerated exclamation mark. The same poster of the Yellowstone Caldera also hung in his bedroom, but it hadn't been defaced with a marker.

As Kit made his circuit, he passed a coatrack, a torch sconce, several wobbly piles of books stacked on the floor, and a large blue wall-clock with no hands. His soft-soled slippers shuffled over a pattern of griffins and flowers bleached with time that gave the impression of an old sepia photograph woven into a threadbare carpet. He was grateful that it absorbed the chill off the slabs because, even in summer, the tower maintained the frigid temperature of a medieval stone church. But it's walls were damp in a nice way. They smelled like history.

Jack no longer shadowed his master around the small room. Kit would be back soon enough.

On the third pass of the coatrack, Kit grabbed a fleece hoodie in midstride and wriggled it over his head. Sometimes, even on scorching-hot days like this one, which were freakishly out of season, an extra pullover wasn't enough to compensate for the lack of a modern heat source inside. Fingerless gloves completed his tower-gear.

He checked his rumpled hair in his reflection in the clock's crystal and combed it back into shape with his fingers. The dramatic shock of silver in his forelock showed white in the hazy image. His head of prematurely-grey hair registered less in the dim light. So much for sibling genetics. "Identical twins, my arse," he muttered under his breath.

Bash's hair remained light brown. She called Kit's 'look' portal hair, after his untimely run-in with one of the so-called temporal anomalies positioned in key locations throughout the countryside and within the Hall. And because Lady Nan reported the gateways as 'equal opportunity time portals', Bash constantly reminded Kit of his 'portal panache' whenever he tried to convince her that witnessing supernatural occurrences in Bede was an illusory state of mild hysteria.

Bede Hall pushed his science buttons. "It's a reversible dissociative condition," he'd cautioned, "that alters one's perception of reality. I believe… no, I'm *sure*, it's triggered by the presence of some rather potent botanicals in the Hall's gardens, thus enveloping the area in 'a deceptive continual flux of confusing stimuli." Although, even he had to admit, scientific jargon aside, his brief glimpse of the future had been remarkably lucid.

Kit had some ruder words for traumatic stress, but there was enough tension between brother and sister. The feedback from

Bash's friends after last year's surprise appearance of 'the new look' had been instant and unanimous. In a word, the final consensus was 'different'.

Different, Bash had elaborated, was the new sexy. Great, Kit thought, who knew that looking old before one's time was girl catnip. Playing hard to get made it worse. The fact that he was deadly serious was irrelevant. Kit's salt and pepper panache had a magnetic effect on the very creatures he recently determined to avoid. Apparently, being wiser 'before one's time' didn't rate tuppence. Not than any them would reach middle-age, let alone old age, if his catastrophic vision of the future was accurate. And especially not, if the Bede Prophecy was true. Even on Kit's most skeptical days, he couldn't quite shake his terrifying waking-dream of planet earth completely engulfed in ice and snow.

The lack of climate control with its indoor-outdoor extremes of freezing and baking was as tiresome as it was ominous. Weather reports forecast the normal chill and rain for the approach of November, but Bede languished, apart from the rest of the country, stuck within a dream of summer. Yet another desperate measure to escape to cooler climes. The weather was becoming as much of an enemy as the plant kingdom.

Back at ground zero, the chair was just a chair. Kit's phone sat, face up and flashed a weak blue signal between human eye-blinks, but Jack saw.

Kit did a doubletake. "Hey, wasn't that on the floor?" He pocketed the phone after a cursory examination followed by an unscientifically-thorough shake.

The realization they were all doomed hit harder each time. Kit choked back a strangle of rude words that died in his throat – a weird cross between anguish and hysterical merriment. He collapsed beside Jack and buried his face in the dog's wiry fur. "It's just you and me, mate. I hate this stupid place. Why did we have to come here."

Jack nuzzled his cold nose into Kit's hand and thumped his tail on the flagstones.

Kit raised his eyes to a nebulous shape forming on the ceiling. "It's not fair. I'm just a kid. I can't possibly save the whole bloody world."

The chair was no ordinary chair. It was a replica of King Tutankhamen's throne, a family heirloom – an object of some significance in his family's history. It scuttled an inch sideways with a grating sound and froze, awaiting further instructions while Kit was preoccupied with a white blob slowly manifesting arms and legs above his head.

Ancient Egypt loomed big in their lives.

Unwinding his anger at the top of a Saxon round tower meant Kit was confined to tracing its circumference, constrained at the end of an imaginary ten-foot-length of string that seemed tethered to the centre of the earth by a wilful chair.

The grey cylinder of cold stone amplified Kit's restless mood, and while he sulked, the chair, brooded too, out of sorts within a crackling of increasingly oppressive static. *"The boy is not ready,"* it sent to its master. *"His admirable rebellious streak will do him credit later. But for now, it won't do. It won't do at all!"* The air snapped with unruly sparks. *"It won't be easy to train him in time. We can only hope the sister will make him see sense."*

Sandaled feet and hands with fingers slowly took shape on the ceiling. "Taraq," Kit said, mildly piqued, "if you're going to pop in you may as well POP. This dawdling performance art is a getting a tad theatrical."

"I didn't want to intrude," came a childlike voice.

"Well, that'd be a first."

"Then I shall pop out."

Taraq's form disappeared abruptly in a melodramatic exit, popping sound-effect included.

"Ruddy ghosts," Kit said to Jack. "What're they like, eh. C'mon mate. We're done for the day. It's time for a walk. I don't care how insanely hot it is outside, I need some fresh air."

As was the untrained rule, Jack descended last. How his four feet despised spiral staircases.

II

TOWERING PLANTS

A shimmering mirage met boy and dog at the door and tagged them over a green lawn the texture of straw to a shade tree. Once outside, Kit peeled off his hoodie, already sticking to him from the unprecedented October heatwave.

Jack immediately sprawled on his side, panting to counter the severe temperature. He raised his head an inch and growled, sensing danger a millisecond before his master, as a colourless ripple distorted the air surrounding them. An odorous wave of lavender undulating over the lawn brought him to his feet in mid-bark. Before descending, it came to a stop and hovered menacingly over Kit's head, retreating only slightly from Jack's demented barking.

Its soft impact sent Kit reeling. Jack charged at it, teeth bared at a hazy bubble of nothingness.

The scent, fused with oxygen, entered Kit's nostrils, filling his head like a balloon. He tried to expel it with a cough, but it shimmied down his throat, staining his insides purple. His automatic gag reflex failed to dislodge it but he caught his breath as his arms evaporated. He examined his left arm as it reformed, half-expecting his skin to be mauve. "Go away. I don't accept you!"

The tinny voice of flowerets giggling, came back. "You have no choice little Kitty. WE have accepted YOU."

Dizziness arrived fast, cloying and sweet. Lavender perfume filled his body like helium, invading the world he was meant to save. It was everywhere. Sickly—creeping—permeating.

Anubis crossed the lawn in a black and white streak and arrived hissing. He flew at the luminosity now shaped like a wasp's nest, batting what looked like a sugary piñata with his razor claws reminiscent of a grizzly bear's.

"Surrender little Kitty," the plants whispered.

"Never," Kit shouted back. He cracked open his eyelids and squinted through slits, warily sniffing the air. Pungency nil. Normal to normal-ish atmosphere. But his throat begged for water and he felt strangely buoyant. "C'mon Jacks, race you to the house." Misjudging his equilibrium, Kit stood too quickly. Lightheaded, he had to spread his legs apart for balance. His knees hit the hot grass seconds before his forehead. Individual needle-sharp blades scratched at his eyes. *Take deep breaths…no, hold your breath…no, breathe normally. This isn't real. It's not happening. Look at Jack…pant like a dog… get to the kitchen… nice and slow… walk nice and slow… you need water…find water.*

He waited, folded in half, and counted to ten until the queasiness passed. Jack's whine whistled in his ear, reminding him he had an ally. Kit clung to Jack's neck and pulled himself to a wobbly standing position, thankful for having a dog sturdy enough to support his weight.

His face buried in Jack's hairy coat momentarily grounded him. He breathed in a welcoming doggy musk. Its earthiness eclipsed the stifling sweetness he could only describe as an undesirable abomination of quintessential floral-ness.

Before he made it to the house, the banished scent congealed into a spiky monster behind his eyes and split his head with a miniature fairy axe. A stab of pain arrived, intimidating and royally purple. "Jack, come here boy."

Jack obeyed without hesitation and allowed Kit to lean against his body, and together they limped towards Bede Hall like conjoined twins.

Kit fell headlong into the kitchen, neatly tripping over Jack, intent on getting there first. The thud when his foot connected with the wolf-hound's ribs shocked him out of primal thoughts of water. For a split second it occurred to him that maybe his problems would be over if he dehydrated into a mummy. The prospect had its advantages.

Kit stooped to massage the impact point. "Sorry mate. I didn't mean to. I'm dead thirsty," he gasped, already at the sink. The tap turned full-blast, sent a refreshing gush of spray in his face.

"Slow and steady wins the race, moron," the voices chanted.

With the stream of water adjusted, Kit filled the largest glass he could find to overflowing and gulped it back, hoping to drown their presence, but they gurgled and threatened to regurgitate. He refilled the glass and poured it over his head which silenced them. At least, they receded, temporarily chastised into a damp echo.

Kit shook his head like a wet dog, but a final slap of perfume threatened to unseat him again. The word 'unseated' brought Kit to his senses. *Go to the chair. Go now!* Once again, the lavender neatly pole-axed him from behind. He swayed, clutched the sink, and stared into the white porcelain. *Stay conscious…fight… stay focused… count the cutlery waiting to be washed… that spoon is encrusted with marmalade from breakfast.* He counted each piece to distract himself from being attacked by a vapour. *I love marmalade… three butter knives… lavender is disgusting stuff…four spoons… it's inside me… of course it's not… this is an illusion… one breadknife… stay calm… two forks and a ladle… do not cave. Hold on… how can a voice sound purple? Never mind, it just can, that's all. That's the gravy ladle… I love gravy.*

Kit sponged a soaking tea towel over his face from mouth to forehead, hid his face in the crook of his arm, and inhaled his sweat. It was strangely comforting. He listened. Silence. His stomach quietened before he slumped to the floor, burying his nose into Jack's fur, the texture of a rough doormat that smelled of home. An earthy welcome mat. And for a moment, embarrassment reigned. He was ashamed of his panicky overreaction. "Jack, I know it's mental around here, but that's the first time meditating made me feel I was going to be sick."

The kitchen door swung wide as his adopted brother, Tut, swaggered in. After scanning Kit's wet hair and flushed face, his first words hit Kit like the attack it was meant to be. "You look like you've been in a fight. Who won?"

"I was attacked by some lavender."

"Wow! And you lived to tell the tale?" *Zing.*

Kit was dizzy, but not about to cave in front of his adopted brother. "It was touch and go, smart arse," he zinged back. It was hard to tell they'd once been best pals.

Tut left the room with a final well-aimed arrow. "Time travel should be a doddle, tough guy."

Kit slid to the floor and cooled his face on the kitchen tiles. The distance from the kitchen to the top of the tower was formidable but it was a sanctuary of sorts. He'd need more than Jack to get there. *Stay on the floor. Call for help. Damn. My phone is useless. Concentrate. Call Bash.*

Her telepathic message came in loud and clear. *'Kit what's wrong? Can you make it to the sundial? Meet me there pronto. Tut says you're having a dizzy spell. Suck it up Superboy… and bring a bottle of lemonade, please and thank you.'*

Jack was pressed into service. Back outside, the tower loomed once more, a fat obelisk against the sun, his personal sanctuary, and in twenty-four-hours he would be ready to fight another day. Ready for another heroic attempt to channel Einstein, Superman, and his hero Carl Sagan. He headed for Bash, burping lavender all the way. *Everything's cool. This isn't happening. Not happening… not happening.*

The floweret's voices resumed, stalking him, giggling in unison. *"We think it is."*

Bash was waiting for him at the sundial, looking mildly concerned, breezy in a white cotton dress and sunglasses. She shaded her eyes at Kit's approach. "What's up? You look as sullen as ever," she said casually. "You seemed a tad… um… engulfed. I thought you were dying or something."

Kit looked out of sorts, finally upright with his hands in his pockets. For telepathic twins, his listless energy cloud was palpable to Bash. "So did I."

"Have you had a run-in with another phantom of your imagination?"

His reply was deliberately evasive. "I may have."

"AND?"

"And science won the day. Thanks for asking."

Bash stared at his empty hands. "Did it drink my lemonade?"

"Sorry, I forgot. Are you aware that Bede lavender has thorns?"

Bash faced him as she always did, a self-assured wordsmith, notorious for her own grandiose vocabulary. Choosing flamboyant words for their poetic effect and speaking them without flinching (but with an edge of pity) was her personal stamp of panache. Even so, it rattled her that her identical twin was blind to the delights of the mystical world she loved. Realms she blissfully described as 'numinous'.

It was a sad puzzle, and one she had no intention of ignoring. How could they be so different? Somehow she had to win Kit over to Bede's plight and their shared responsibility. Their duty couldn't be more clear. Heritage begged allegiance, especially in their present state of crisis. Kit was beyond wrong. His 'olfactory confusion theory' was his melodramatic way of burying his head in the sand. Pure subterfuge… *yes*, she thought with smug satisfaction, *that was the exact word. Mild hysteria indeed. Kit could stew inside this stifling heat and be as pretentious as he liked. Sooner or later, he would have to admit the truth… that his misguided diagnosis of euphoric captivity was utterly bogus. He WAS Bede Hall's chosen time traveller, and Bede Hall was ALIVE!*

"Okay Mister Science," she said in one of her superior tones, "then please explain, in rational terms, why Mum and Dad and Rupert never perceive anything out of the ordinary around here, that is, apart from this manic heatwave. They breathe too, don't they?"

"Maybe *none* of us are breathing," Kit said. "Maybe we're all ghosts who've been haunting this place for centuries."

Bash's grin radiated surprise. She clapped her hands. "Now you're talking. Hold that thought. There may be hope for you yet."

Three years prior, floating in a state of shock after their father's disappearance, Kit had tried to maintain a logical belief in mind over matter. But now, enough was enough. The time for foolish fantasies was over. The whole idea of an inanimate object's ability to transcend time and space was preposterous, and more specifically, the throne chair's function as a biological trigger for achieving extrasensory perception was rubbish. Besides, the chair continually denied him access. He'd failed. He was done. Almost.

Dr. Brooks, his mentor, had dared to equate prolonged meditation with psychological time travel. He called it an intuitive gateway to an altered state of reality. But back then, Kit was vulnerable. Anything irrational that might locate his missing father was worth pursuing. This was the only explanation he could give of swallowing Brook's premise that certain heirloom's were embedded with a family's genetic code. Even Brook's certainty that physical objects possessed the ability to transcend time, had made sense. But that was the sign of a good mentor and the result of Kit being suspended in a state of grief and shock, not to mention the backlash from a series of lucid dreams and a spontaneous 'chair incident' that Brooks casually labelled a natural out-of-body experience.

For Kit, continuing to harness the chair's supposed talismanic powers had become a guilty preoccupation with responsibility – a desperately-futile occupation. His thoughts continued to punish him. *How was I suckered into such embarrassingly pseudo-scientific nonsense?* Even more incomprehensible, *why am I still dabbling in the possibility it might be true?* The answer arrived instantaneously. *I've seen too many strange things. And sometimes, Hydrogen forgive me, I almost WANT them to be true.*

With his father safe home, he resented the keepsake that had once felt like a precious gift from a trusted teacher. It galled him that his lack of emotional progress could be measured by a persnickety piece of furniture. Furthermore, dabbling with the subconscious mind was, in his opinion, an unforgivably *un*scientific experiment.

III

SEEING IS DECEIVING

The remains of a Saxon tower adjoining the manor house on the Bede Hall estate, was Kit's hideout – bequeathed to him from his grandmother on the twins' twelfth birthday. Bash's legacy was a walled garden with a greenhouse, her own retreat nestled in a grove of topiary animals that, she had insisted to Kit, moved imperceptibly when no-one was looking.

That argument had been the start of a difference of opinion regarding Bede phenomenon that eventually blossomed into an ongoing feud.

Kit had stared hard at the green animals grouped around them, comparing angles with his fingers. "I can't see any difference," he concluded. "They haven't budged."

Bash had crossed her arms in defiance. "Their new poses are too subtle to be detected without a camera," she'd said.

"I think you've conveniently forgotten that Lady Nan made up that wandering topiary story about her childhood to entertain us. Maybe even scare us a little."

"Spoil sport."

Kit used common sense as a last resort. "Look it was fun when we were five. I believed her topiary adventures too. Even the names she gave them."

"They do have names. Parks told me."

"Geez Bash. You scare me sometimes," Kit shouted.

"Keep your voice down. There's no telling who's listening."

A quick scan of the area proved they were alone. "I mean, you're a little addled, not brain dead. Mental suggestions are a subconscious form of wish fulfillment. The brain has a *mind* of its own, but the mind has a *will* of its own. Optical illusions are its language."

A smile twitched the corners of Bash's mouth. "Are you saying…"

"Look, I *know* you talk to plants. So, think of them talking back the only way they know how, on your wavelength." He tapped the top of her head. "In pictures *you* imagine in there. That shouldn't be too hard for you."

Bash did one better and punched Kit's arm in victory. "This is wonderful. You're saying plants think. I do believe you've come over to my side. What is it you call Bede?"

"Cloud Cuckoo Land."

"Welcome home. At last, you're one of us."

"Hardly. All I'm saying, is that words aren't the *only* form of communication. The brain reads pictures in everything."

"Hence the term EXTRA-sensory, which… I believe is science for *paranormal*."

Stalemate.

Facing each other now, in the intense heat of October, squinting at each other across dazzling green grass that should have been stubble, Kit's view was the same, and the rivalry continued.

Bash looked glamorous wearing designer sunglasses under a wide-brimmed straw hat.

Kit squinted into the sun. "Nice shades."

Bash grinned. "Yeah. I nicked them from Rupert's collection."

"I should grab a pair. He won't notice. He's lost count of how many he's got. His obsession with imagined celebrity knows no bounds."

"Sometimes, I forget what Rupert looks like. It's always a shock when he takes them off."

The day roasted silently between them. The lazy drone of a bee cut through the daydream they were sharing about Egypt and burning sands.

"I'll give you one thing," Kit said, as if continuing a previous debate. "It's true that scientists dream stuff up… at first."

"Why professor. Stuff and dreams? Whatever next. Will pigs fly?"

Kit wrinkled his nose in disgust. "But afterwards, the scientific mind relies on pure mathematics. Logic is a discipline that serves humans far better than living in the clouds, cuckoos notwithstanding."

Bash gently rapped Kit's skull. "If, for one second, you stopped thinking like a robot in there. I'd…"

He blocked her hand from rumpling his hair. A thing they both did to make each other crazy. "Excuse me, Princess of Everything. I'm a calculator. I form premises. I test them. *Ergo*…"

"*Ergo*," Bash interrupted. "Your mind is programmed to ignore supernatural phenomena. Like *you're* not just as fixated on proving academic hypotheses." She curtsied by bowing her head. "O' King of Science."

Kit tickled Bash's hand with a blade of grass and whispered. "Look, kiddo, you've wanted to live in a fairy tale since you were old enough to wave a toy magic wand." He brandished the grass like a sword and tapped her nose. "*Principessa*, it's no wonder you see bizarre things here. You expect them. You've programmed your brain to interpret Bede as a mystical place. And your nose isn't much better. But, inhaling heady scents can mess with real-time memories. Kings outrank princesses. King takes princess. Checkmate. Princess concedes defeat."

Bash's stared blankly, looking through him. "Lucky for you there's no princesses in chess… *matey*."

Kit scowled. "We used to think in sync. There was a time when it was always a win/win with us. I miss that. I miss my best friend. That's *you* Princess."

Bash broke free from his emotional outburst, nodded a feeble "Me too", and quickly changed the subject. She purposely inhaled a deep breath for effect. *"Aaahhh."* Her eyes widened with a sudden realization. "So… my nose is dreaming. Nice. Very nice, Professor." She sniffed the air a second time. Her face lit up with a grin. *"Mmmn, très odiferous."*

Kit laughed while pretending to pull out his hair. *"Aarggh!* All I'm saying, is that certain exotic plants can create toxic hallucinations. Take this green grass. It should be burned to a crisp?"

"Lavender is a common garden species."

"The eyes are unreliable, your majesty," Kit said, widening his own for effect. "One sees what they want to see. It's called pareidolia. That, and you're hopelessly ensorcelled."

Bash removed her sunglasses and copied his stare. "Yeah, like that face on Mars that *still* freaks you out. But great word usage, Einstein. I'm impressed."

"I was just a kid. We're nearly sixteen now. And by the way, seeing faces in patterns is natural. Even babies do it. At least I grew up."

Eyes closed, Bash tilted her head back and fanned herself with her hat. "Oh really. So, why do you still have a poster of the Martian face on your wall?"

The tower room had first served as the wannabe lab of a kid wild for science, but three years later, its only room had become Kit's place of refuge away from the overly critical eyes of siblings and friends, growing evermore sinister by the day. A heated bedroom awaited him inside the house proper, but the temporary sleeping arrangement in the tower was handy for power naps because even a stolen hour spent there had the habit of stretching to half the day or night. Time was funny stuff. On several occasions, he'd dozed off for a few minutes and dreamed entire lifetimes.

For the past six months, Kit further distanced himself from his extended family in a desperate attempt to remain sane in a world, in his words, gone *doolally*. At least, that had been his intention. But lately he felt more like a mad scientist railing against irrational humans who'd been hoodwinked by local folklore, the odd trick of light, some decidedly eccentric villagers, and a sinister garden perennial.

Being ensorcelled by superstitious gibberish topped common sense, with the exception of three people and the occasional drop-in guest. How they, his parents, or his older brother Rupert remained unaffected was a mystery. He'd had no such luck. And now he was talking to chairs.

From day one, living in 'Wonderland' had been too compelling to dismiss. Not only too good to be true but completely over-the-moon-crazy. For the first year, he too had been a besotted moonbeam, but that was before he wriggled free of the hallucinations. Before it got dangerous.

Fortunately, he was obstinate enough to regain his powers of reasoning in a baffling environment he could neither accept nor leave. Supernatural phenomena were plain out of the question. But some unknown influence still affected his judgment. Perhaps if he held out long enough, the ghost of little Anna would disappear and all the attending fretfulness with her. Science would save him and he would save everyone else, and then he could get on with being a normal teenager. At least, that was plan A.

IV

THE GHOST OF REASONABLE DOUBT

The chair was where Kit left it, stranded after being pulled into the centre of the room. As always, when it was in service, Kit glanced about slightly embarrassed before sitting down. This time there was no gingerly lowering himself into its power. He fell into it, desperate to win a battle of wills, nearly knocking it over. It was a case of mind over matter, and a lot mattered.

A jolt of power surged up Kit's spine and flushed his insides with electrical sparks. His blood effervesced like Coca-Cola. A feeling akin to a sugar rush coursed from his toes into his fingers, gripping the chair's arms and his knuckles turned from white to purple and back again. Jack whined loudly, his head cowered in Kit's direction. Kit pulled himself free. "No more games," he shouted, jumping up, contorting to rid himself of the tingling sensations. "It's okay Jacks. We're okay, boy. No worries. Enough is enough."

He circled the chair like a wary animal, facing it as if it might bite, assessing the situation with faked calm. "I am *not* afraid of you," he whispered.

What happened next, surprised him. He involuntarily lashed out, delivering a vicious kick to the leg nearest him. His voice reverberated off the walls. "USELESS WASTE OF TIME!" He was not as in control as he'd thought. Now he was in for it. Bede Hall didn't take kindly to criticism.

An imperceptible fluid ribbon of red energy snaked from the leg and coiled itself around Kit's ankle as he continued to circle the chair. The stream of colour intensified with each pass, dragged into an orbit, ever-increasing in speed until it lightened and spun into a protective cocoon of white light that gradually enveloped him, unawares.

He glanced at the clock and shuddered. How appropriate that it had no hands or gears – an inspired gift from Bash that symbolized his obsession with temporal space-time, back in the day when the prospect of time travel was still a subject for jest.

But there was nothing remotely amusing about the real thing. Time was coldblooded stuff. After digesting a ghastly trip to the future, emotional torment had become his natural state. The words he'd so recently uttered, 'waste of time', came back to haunt him as much as Anna.

The chair, was symbolic, given to Kit in trust by his aging mentor Dr. Peregrine Brooks, a psychologist with the heart of an Egyptologist who passed it on to Kit. It had been more than a bequest from Kit's Great Uncle Bentley to his best friend. 'Never mine to keep', the doctor had insisted. "It will always remain a Stratford-Smyth family heirloom."

For fifty-two years, as its appointed guardian, Brooks awaited the chair's rightful heir, and for all that time it had become the embodiment of his deepening obsession with Egypt. But it had come at a terrible cost, and after the throne passed from his hands to Kit's, Brooks' sense of duty increased tenfold.

Brooks once explained: 'the most trustworthy vehicle for mentally transporting a chaotic mind is a meditation chair that evokes an idyllic state of well-being.' That's how he spoke when he was in teacher mode, as if delivering a lecture. But at other times he mellowed to conversational tones. The throne was declared the ultimate visual aid befitting the mindset of the leading family of Bede, an area with powerful links to archaeology. In Brooks' view, a meaningful touchstone could anchor a mental traveller during a bumpy inner journey. Molecules, however, were never meant to follow.

Taraq watched Kit from the ceiling. He recoiled from Kit's tantrum, and when his friend's walkabout took on the urgency of pacing, Taraq dropped down behind him to offer his ethereal support. He reached towards the throne, warmed his hands on its ancient heat and spoke lovingly with awe and a hint of surprise. *"Since you forgave him, then I must, also."*

The power emanating from the throne washed through him in a wave of homesickness, and his eyes closed to savour the memory. It was past understanding how the living failed to prostrate themselves in the presence of such overwhelming power. It was inconceivable that they were oblivious to the colours binding the shadows of tomorrow and yesterday together.

In his own astral journey, Taraq had travelled the required 'night of a million years', transcended the corridor of judgements, and reached the mouth of morning. And now, as his reward, he resided in Bede Hall, the house of reincarnations, steeped in the memories of forever, reunited with his sister, Anu, even if she did call herself Anna.

A flash of living gold caught Taraq's eye as the carved winged goddesses of the four directions quivered from the corners of the throne, calling up a soothing breeze to cool the carvings of King Tutankhamen and his queen, *Ankhesenamen*.

The figure of Tutankhaten lifted his arms in supplication to the sun god, Aten, causing his false name Amun, to wink wickedly from its cartouche, blinding Taraq as painfully as a shard of glass. The impostor's name stalled for time, in wait to fight any future champion who dared to reverse its power. And in that moment,

Taraq decided he was the one destined to safeguard the sacred seat of the Aten. "I wish to serve you, now and in my next life," he said.

"I accept your request," the chair said. *"As it was, so it shall ever be, my child."*

The echoes of remembered prayers opened Taraq's heart as he inhaled familiar incense and perfumed unguents, mystically transporting him thousands of years to the Valley of the Kings where he breathed again the unmistakable fumes of the valley's rituals. He tracked his progress as a hologram, repeating an endless loop of precession, following the trails of spice and natron through the royal valleys to the underground holding tombs that froze time.

In a waking vision, Taraq watched himself kneel, offering bread and beer to the Aten, engulfed in the heady weightless feeling from the perfume of a thousand lotus petals scattered at his pharaoh's feet. He remembered his delight, beguiled by a swarm of tiny half-human creatures that danced from the fragrance into his head, where they popped like the fragile soap bubbles he'd observed in Bede's kitchen.

Buried alive with his twin sister had been a welcome sacrifice for his pharaoh, King Smenkhare, but Taraq's last memory was heart-breaking. After his sister Anu's brave utterings of farewell, her life-force drifted from the tomb along with the perfumed creatures that Bede Hall called fairies, to be reborn as Anna.

Taraq had curled up beside his sister's bones for three-thousand-five-hundred-years. In all that time, he took comfort from the radiant green face of Osiris, shining from the painted wall. From time to time Tutankhamen's golden sarcophagus took on a lustrous tinge as if a shroud of translucent emerald silk had floated from the wall, to rest over the king's face like a mask.

Kit slowed to a stop and faced the chair as if it was the enemy, and Taraq, lost in time, walked through him.

Kit startled awake like a sleepwalker. The white light around him blinked out as he straightened. He folded his arms, scowling.

Brooks was wrong. This whole place was wrong, and now he was more frustrated than ever. Doubts invaded the logic he'd once been so proud of. Intoxication was real, so perhaps the increasing hallucinations were real. Even chairs weren't just chairs in Bede. Three years ago, he'd been a sane kid, happily acing his science exams for fun. He ran his eyes over the chair – a tourist studying a fascinating exhibit in a museum. The chair sat there smirking. The gold was too bright. It hurt his eyes. "You're a colossal waste of time," Kit burst out. "Do you know that!"

A tiny spark of trapped sunlight detached itself from the chair and whizzed past Kit's ear. He heard it giggle. Another illusion. He should be used to them by now. He was losing his mind, not calming it. He considered the benefits. Less school and more time to... The words *more time* mocked him. Time was running out; he was running out of excuses. Kit closed his eyes and spoke. "I know you're there, Taraq, so you may as well show yourself."

Taraq materialized, eyes first. "May I be of assistance, Master?"

"For the love of Hydrogen, I'm not your flaming master! How many times do we have to go over this? You know it creeps me out."

"That's why I said it."

"You ghosts are..." he searched for one of Bash's snooty words... "perverse."

"Thank you," Taraq said proudly, "Dr. Brooks says I'm a promising therapist."

"I think there's far too much training going on around here. You are what you are, an Egyptian slave-boy from the eighteenth-dynasty transported to twenty-first-century England. What's promising about that? Was that you giggling just now?"

"I believe it was a fairy."

Kit snickered. "How silly of me, of *course* it was. They're everywhere. And for Pete's sake, please stop appearing like the Cheshire Cat!"

"I'm here to assist you... as a friend... I have a new plan."

Kit squinted at Taraq, taking in what appeared to be a boy in a long white nightshirt with a shaft of moonlight shining through his body. What could possibly go wrong?

The two stared at each other as they often did when sizing up an awkward situation. Finally, Kit's shoulders relaxed. Maybe going crazy wasn't so bad. Except for stirring up emotional pain, meditation was just a mind game, after all. Kit leaned over, gripped the chair by its arms, and gave it a shake. "Stupid – rotten – pointless – games!"

Taraq gasped and would have stopped breathing altogether had he been alive. He positioned his semi-transparent body to shield the chair, and concentrated. His shade became slightly more solid. It was hardly formidable but he hoped it signalled a more substantial threat.

Kit noted his efforts and issued a sigh embedded with a trace of amusement. "Seriously? Dude?"

Taraq's form relaxed into the thickness of fog.

For a full sickening minute, before it ceased, Kit heard the blue clock ticking. After deliberating several minutes more, he slumped to the floor. "I'm a terrible brother," he blurted.

After a rather long silence. Taraq gave an involuntary splutter of protest.

Kit shushed him with a single raised palm. "No. I wasn't talking to you. I had to hear it said out loud. You've known me for a few years. It's true, isn't it? I'm a useless brother."

More awkward silence.

"Bast got your tongue then?" Kit said.

"It's not *entirely* true," Taraq said carefully. Although, I have to say, you aren't much of a father figure."

"I'm fifteen, Taraq. What do you expect? And you needn't look at me like a lost puppy. Technicalities aside, and as insane as things are around here, I'm *not* your stepfather."

Taraq surrendered, both hands in the air. "There's still time."

"Are you deliberately being perverse again?"

Taraq's sandals disappeared up to his knees which made him more ghostlike. His robe floated like a white sheet with a face and arms. "I think so. But what does perverse mean? And who is Pete?"

Kit shook his head and suppressed a chuckle.

With this slight release of tension, Taraq's feet returned. He stooped to inspect the gilded wood. A slight crack in its gold skin shed nine miniscule flecks of gold to the floor. He cupped his hands around the leg and intoned a prayer to Osiris, the god of regeneration. As the throne's self-appointed guardian, he would have to anticipate Kit's temper tantrums and take future precautions. Master or no master, Kit should respect his elders. And even a replica of an ancient chair of power deserved allegiance.

"Please do not take your anger out on the throne," Taraq said in his clipped accent. "It hurts… it hurts everyone."

A furiously buzzing headache sent a flash of pain behind Kit's eyes. "Do you hear bees?"

Taraq's eyes squeezed shut. He shook his head. "Not bees. Never bees. I know that sound. They're wasps!"

"It's probably the electrics," Kit said, rubbing his temples. "They're always buzzing. Taraq, are you okay? You've gone white as a ghost."

"Back in my time, we were beset by a plague of wasps. They killed many. They killed my parents." Taraq laid his hands over the hairline crack in the chair and recited an Egyptian prayer.

Kit's tactless remark registered as a shocked intake of breath. "Sorry, Taraq. I didn't think. That white-as-a-ghost remark. I wasn't trying to be clever at your expense."

"Whatever it takes to make you stop harming this chair and yourself. Can you not sense the life-force inside it?"

Taraq placed his ear to the throne's back and heard the faint ticking of a clock. "This damp country can't be good for…"

Kit resumed his walk around the chair. "Trees creak, Taraq, *ergo…* wood does too," he said over his shoulder. "Wood expands and contracts all the time."

"It is *breathing*," Taraq insisted, and listened again. The ticking paused and in its place, he heard a gentle sighing as the wood shrank inside its gold shell.

Kit wheeled to face Taraq. "Oh, for heaven's sake. IT'S – A – CHAIR! … and, by the way… it's only a COPY… a clever fake, I admit, but still a fake. Chairs aren't alive. Buildings aren't alive. Sometimes old buildings like Bede Hall have an atmosphere but they can't talk or issue instructions. And CHAIRS CAN'T BREATHE!"

Taraq looked up from the floor. His expression saddened. "It *is* a voice. You are wrong. And you are afraid of the Hall because you've heard it speak. I know you have."

Kit pulled Taraq to his feet. "It's the ruddy wind, my strange little friend. Bede wind gets into everything, like sand at a picnic, or…" he paused to jab Taraq in the shoulder, "like ghosts who don't mind their own business."

"Exactly," Taraq said. "It's pink."

"Sorry? What's pink?"

Taraq shut his eyes and stood once more in his beloved desert, its sandy floor shifting through time and space. A wistful smile played about his mouth as he remembered the changing faces of sand. It was moody. At certain times of day and at certain angles, it teased the eyes. Sand was rarely yellow. It had a subtle color for each hour of the day and night. When the waning sun wanted to play, it shimmered pale pink. And now, after three winters spent in Bede, he understood that when the moon wanted to play, sand looked like blue snow.

Kit, growing tired of debating a sentimental ghost, clapped his hands together to wave him away. "Fine. Okay. Have it your way. I don't know what's got into you, but something's stirred you up and no mistake." He raised his palms in protest. "And please, don't try to explain. Truly, I don't want to know." He rubbed his toe. *Why was it sore? Oh yeah, I kicked a stupid chair. I'm truly losing it.*

The first time Kit 'travelled' out-of-body had been the innocent experiment of a boy-scientist, eager to follow a few alpha waves to a brief wander in a familiar room, especially since he was coached into a safe landing by a responsible adult.

The second event had been spontaneous. He'd retreated to Bede Hall's maze, one of his favourite sanctuaries, to read a book in peace, and losing his concentration, he took a walkabout to unwind, but making a wrong turn brought him back to stand over his sleeping body – an odd sensation somewhere between panic and curiosity. Anna had been waiting for him.

Being alone with the ghost of Anna was unsettling but Kit overcame the instinct to wake himself, and in the spirit of scientific investigation, he dared himself to explore without a net.

Flying over Bede Hall like Peter Pan had been a bit of a lark until time shifted beyond the natural order of things and the future exploded into snow and fear. Time travel was a darker game. Time travel changed the stakes. Time travel made a liar out of him. Made him a worrywart. *'what if the door to my body had locked behind me? What if I hadn't been able to get back in?... and worse, what if it happens again when I'm on the edge of sleep? If it was sneaky once, what would stop it a second time.'*

Kit lied to protect his sister. But most of all, he lied to cover his shame because the terrifying prospect of being abandoned alone in a time that wasn't his, was as ghastly as Taraq's story of being entombed. It eclipsed any sense of feeling responsible.

Pleas against his better nature strengthened his resolve that the supernatural was a load of old rubbish but everything he believed about modern science was blown to pixels. Everything he'd heard about betrayal was true.

Kit's thoughts gravitated between running away and literally putting down permanent roots. Except the season *wasn't* changing. It was stuck on summer, with temperatures exceeding anything recorded in living memory. The thought of roots was disturbing enough, but the nightmarish image of him turning into a plant was horrifying.

A third trip was never going to happen no matter how hard they begged.

V

THE LITERARY BUG

'Penny for your thoughts,'' Bash sent Kit. *'What on earth's got into you? It's like you to scribble bits and bobs in your journal thingy, but something's different. You're always stuck in your ivory tower. Do you need to be rescued?'*

Kit snapped his notebook shut and peered around, expecting to see his sister with her arms crossed, baiting him. He was alone. Bash was only in his head. *'You shouldn't sneak up on a person like that.'*

'Then you shouldn't leave your mind open. Are you ever coming out of that tower?'

'It's cooler up here.'

'Okay... and the real reason is?'

'I think I'm going to write a book. That is, I NEED to write a book. That is…um…I think it's for the best, to document…things.'

She snickered. *'Good luck.'*

'To make sense of things.'

'Ooh, a fairy tale then. I thought you didn't believe in fairies.'

'I don't. But I do believe in documenting things.'

'How droningly dull.'

'Think of it as a science log. Like on Star Trek.'

'Your wannabe life's story?'

'Something like that.'

'What's it called? Observations of a Geek? Mythology Deconstructed' A Geek Odyssey?'

'Funny.'

'Will I be in it Mr. Spock?'

'Rescue would be a fine thing.'

'Mum says it's time for dinner. It's your fave. Winter food. York-shire pudding with lashings of gravy.'

VI

MESSAGE IN A BOTTLE

THE BEDE CHRONICLES
by Christopher Carter Stratford-Smyth
OCTOBER 31 – ALL HALLOWS EVE, 2016

My name is Christopher Carter Stratford-Smyth. This is my account of the bizarre events unfolding in 2016. It's appropriate I begin this account on October 31st because every day is Halloween, here. Bede Hall declares it so. But I've come to my senses.

If what's going on is true, I'm a time traveller. And if that isn't weird enough, the human race may be living on borrowed time. Which is a dicey thing to say for a time traveller. It's not what I wanted to be. And perhaps it's all a terrible joke. Except, something crazy is happening. And soon, I may not be able to think straight. So, I'm hoping that words laid out on a page will clear my head. But hope is wishful thinking, and, science geek that I am, it's not nearly good enough.

Albert Einstein tried to tell us time was sticky. I'd have to say, he may have understated its properties a tad, but then, he never lived in Bede or met Anna or the ghost of my grandmother. If he had, it would explain his mad electrified hair. I'm fifteen. My hair turned grey with a streak white as snow, this year.

Weather warning. There's a snowstorm brewing around the corner of the year 2020. To be more accurate, it's an ice-age behind the blue door in the Hall's Winter Room, and it's stranger than anything Einstein ever dreamed of.

Logic singled me out for immunity, as if, as a kid, I'd been vaccinated against fantasy. But Bede has this hypnotizing effect, and even a dedicated wannabe scientist like me was temporarily hoodwinked. It took a year to come to my senses and two more to build up a resistance to what I now recognize as local mythological hogwash.

Let me be clear… I firmly believe that science is the ultimate litmus test for truth. But after yesterday's events, I feel compelled to leave a paper trail of these strange times heading from bad to worse.

From the little I know about drugs, my family and friend's symptoms point to a mass hallucination wrought innocently enough by the perfume of a seemingly innocuous flower.

At least, that's my scientific conclusion. I mean to discover a cure.

But first, I must further document my belief system because the scientific method is my chosen field of discipline. I consider deductive reasoning the highest authority over a measurable world. I maintain that logic overrules speculation. The element of hydrogen with a capital 'H', reigns as true-north in my personal sky. It's a symbolic entity that personifies the source of universal power. Hydrogen is the mathematical proof that explains the supreme energy that rules the cosmos. It's more than a dynamic force. It was the first whimper and it will be the last big bang. I've seen the future, so I should be proud to have something to do with hydrogen's final sendoff at the end.

The truth is, I've time travelled… that is, I've *been* an unwilling time traveller. A spontaneous one. And I mean to survive by staying put… if that's even an option.

I've always been in awe of astrophysics, and honoured Hydrogen as the father of the elements with no agenda save the creation of planets – all the more ironic, since I've been singled out to outwit its imminent and catastrophic appointment with the Yellowstone Caldera in order to save the world. And here's the biggest irony… I don't have much time.

My father encouraged us children to use our imaginations. To that end, my sister and I practiced our natural telepathic abilities into a superpower and indulged in creative mind-play. Bash became a voracious reader of fairy tales and I studied encyclopedias that blew science-fiction out of the water. In my version of the rock-paper-scissors-game, waking erases dreams, reality shreds fantasy, and science eclipses fiction.

'Professor Dad', an eminent Egyptologist, taught me to be mindful of data – the miniscule and the obvious. Especially, the obvious.

Christopher, he used to say, *interpreting the obvious requires a focused mind*, and then he'd wink mysteriously and warn me that pure science rarely suffers a paradox. I had to look up the word paradox, but when I questioned him further, he'd only say *seeing isn't always believing*. It turns out I'm *living* in a paradox. A most contrary conflict between quantum mechanics and the general theory of relativity. A logically unacceptable situation of having to time travel in order to prove time travel is impossible. A contradiction that, despite my efforts, and according to the dictionary, may prove to be true.

The definition of a paradox as a seemingly absurd contradictory statement that when investigated may prove to be true, was the opposite of what I wanted to hear. So, I asked Bash who was over the moon to, in her words, finally dazzle me with the science of language.

First, she set me straight that my problem was more of a personal dilemma, and relished proclaiming me an absolute oxymoron. I countered by calling her a regular moron. She warmed to the challenge and more or less won the day by calling me a conundrum with incongruous qualities. Apparently, I have flaws.

But what if it's my logic that's flawed. What if my conclusions are wrong? What if my investigations prove that supernatural activity is real? As a scientist I have to remain open to that possibility. Am I prepared for that?

For a kid like me, aligned from birth to the exacting disciplines of scientific principle, my father's untimely loss in 2013, when I was twelve, and his return a year later, was especially devastating.

Our grieving family, minus our paternal backbone, ironically sphinxlike for an Egyptologist, had been forced to land in Bede Hall, smack in the centre of an enchanted fairy ring three miles in diameter. A formidably-purple fairy ring. Bede lavender takes prisoners. Bede Hall is holding my sister hostage for its own ends. Mum is a bit of a lovely muddle-head; my older brother Rupert is an idiot, despite the fact he's studying at Oxford University; but it's particularly vexing that Dad remains unaware of anything out of the ordinary. Which leaves me, the objective twin, scanning the horizon for a rescue party.

Bede is definitely otherworldly. Let me repeat… it is *not* of this world.

We're closed off from ordinary society, and outsiders rarely visit, including big brother Rupert, a celebrity in his own mind, who keeps to his university as much as possible. Word has it, he swaggers his toffee-nosed lord of the manor persona over anyone impressed with that sort of thing, wearing sunglasses day and night. He isn't anything resembling a lord of the manor although he lords it over the rest of us whenever he can.

Lady Nan's estate had been on the market since decrepit old stately homes were too expensive to take on. It was about to fall down until bad luck compelled us into a surprising business scheme. But even that is suspect.

The Hall had an idea that was translated by one of the most extraordinary members of our extended family – the ghost child of Bede Hall. My sister and I went searching for her as a bit of a lark during a time when any ridiculous adventure was a welcome distraction. Sadly, we found her. I've done my best to help her grow up emotionally, but she's an unstable needy little girl.

I say to anyone who reads this: be forewarned. DO NOT come here without serious backup.

I've sensed an elite group of the local population in the main village who know more than they let on. So far, they appear harmless, but I'm cautiously paranoid. It's not easy to trust anyone when you can't even trust a building.

It seems the Hall itself is in charge. It's like living inside a science-fiction movie where aliens blend in with earthlings to gain control.

Throughout our childhood, Bede Hall had been a glorious retreat during summer breaks where Bash and I ran wild, shedding the cement dreariness of school and life in greater London. Driving through the gates of our grandmother's crumbling estate meant entering a delightful portal to another world – a playground where we were free to indulge in the absurd for a few weeks of fun. Truer words were never spoken because Bede Village and the Hall appears to have a network of time portals. I've been through three. Deliberately surrendering is madness, but that's what is expected of me. I'm still fighting. Holding out that I've been dreaming crazy lavender dreams.

There was a time when Bash and I wished we could stay in Bede all year round, but when that wish came true, the circumstances were ones of forced desperation, and for me, it's still a waking nightmare. Now it's a case of chickens coming home to roost. Be careful what you wish for.

My whimsical twin is a walking contradiction of a teenager blissfully full of herself but never bashful. But then she loves the word paradox and uses it as often as she can. As the newly-appointed overseer of the Hall's lush gardens, she was quick to declare her fealty to the Bede dynasty. But there was nothing supernatural about big brother Rupert flaunting his renewed status as heir presumptive, oblivious as ever to all things beneath the radar of his increasing self-importance.

Did I mention, there isn't much time.

*An unprecedented December heatwave
drizzled hot rain over the ancient hamlet of Bede,
nestled in the shadow of Hadrian's Wall.
Its stones steamed under the struggling sun
as a puff of hot air traveled downwind
to stir the thirsty treetops surrounding Bede Hall.
But the raindrops fizzled before reaching the earth
and left a thin blanket of vapor hovering near the
scorching hot ground.*

VII

AFTER THE CIRCUS

Bede Hall, Northumberland, England
DECEMBER 1, 2016

Bash's favourite rowan tree provided the only decent shade within hearing distance of the kitchen. Even so, she shielded her eyes behind a pair of big brother Rupert's designer sunglasses, left behind on his last visit. Kit lay next to her, spread-eagled underneath the canopy, feeling like a deflated balloon. As he blocked the sun's glare with his arm, a barely perceptible tongue of flame issued from its surface and delicately licked outer space.

Such activity, visible to the naked eye, used to be rare but solar flares were becoming more erratic. This one was so much more. There was no mistaking a coronal mass ejection. The thought crossed Kit's mind that he should record this event in his journal if only he had a way of knowing what time it was, or if he could be bothered with standing up or walking or lifting a pen ever again. Just staring at the sky, wondering at an absurd purple cloud floating ridiculously out of place against a small window of fierce blue, sapped all his energy. It was easier to close his eyes and blot out the never-ending questions science demanded.

Besides, in his opinion, earth being consumed by the sun wasn't all bad. It would free him from his present responsibilities, and all things being equally insane, he could float off to a new planet as ghostlike as he pleased, all neat and tidy. Ghosts were real enough – a recipe of indiscriminate electrons, microbes, and protein molecules of undetermined composition and temperament.

Bash leaned against the rowan's trunk, enjoying its energy tingle-mingling in her spine. Parks taught her it was the easiest way for trees to talk to humans but even Kit felt her mind wandering behind her shades to romantic thoughts. She was too enamoured to listen to trees.

Every now and then, their thoughts slipped sideways into each other's. Usually it was like dipping one's toe in a strangely familiar pool. Today was typical.

Bash answered Kit's earlier thought. "It's 5 o'clock," she said, dreamily, long after his question had evaporated.

Kit stirred and peeled his arm from his forehead. "Thanks." He relished the false sensation of a cooling fan as a faint breath of wind met the exposed sweat on his skin.

It took all his effort to roll over on his side and stare over the vast empty lawns surrounding Bede Hall. They looked bleak, now that the movie people had gone. With no snow in the forecast, the film crew had travelled to Iceland to shoot their winter scenes. Considering all that Kit knew, it was ironic.

A listless grey haze draped itself over the grass, all the way to the horizon. "The circus has left town," Kit announced, solemnly. He wasn't even sure if it was a thought or he'd managed to find his *'outside'* voice.

His words echoed flat against the heat. It was far too bright for late afternoon. It felt like high noon. As a rule, skies darkened early this close to Christmas but the leaves hadn't turned colour or shed their leaves. Even the trees were lethargic.

Bash brushed a sticky green Rowan leaf from her cheek and followed Kit's gaze. "A nice long calm after the storm," she said.

An untimely vision of Six, shirtless, digging in the garden, flashed across Kit's mind, interrupting his observations of the weather. Bash was daydreaming her usual romantic fantasy of late.

The image vanished as soon as it came; they had rules about invading one's intimate thoughts. *"Sorry, Sis,"* Kit said. *"My bad. No worries. I didn't see much. Consider yourself blocked."*

Six, short for 'Stanley Parks the sixth', a nineteen-year-old whippersnapper apprentice gardener, was fast becoming the local teenage heartthrob. But he was shy as a deer and shunned the spotlight.

Bash ignored any discomfort. "I find the solitude quite lovely but you're far too languorous," she said, smiling.

"Six is never languorous, is he?" Kit said out loud. "He's far too..." he coughed theatrically behind his hand, "you know... diligent."

Bash took a deep breath to defend this obvious bait, but it caught in her throat as if she inhaled soot. Her eyes watered. Something was wrong. "Do you smell anything strange?" she spluttered.

Kit sniffed the air. "Yeah. It's 5 o'clock and dinner isn't ready. Mum's far too *languorous* a cook for my liking."

Bash clutched her throat, sunglasses askew, and jabbed Kit in the ribs. She sent him a look of exasperation. "Hopeless... *cough* ... you're absolutely... *wheeze*... hopeless."

Kit thumped her back. "Did you swallow a bug or something?"

Miraculously, Bash's normal breathing resumed as if nothing odd had happened and she waved him away. "It's a sign," she said, adjusting her sunglasses. "Parks will know."

The treetops sighed overhead. A low branch reached down and tickled Bash's arm. This was a normal occurrence but it never failed to unnerve Kit who quickly looked the other way. "If it *is* a sign and you're as powerful as Parks says, shouldn't you know without having to ask?"

"Some scientist *you're* going to be," Bash said, examining her manicure. "For someone who spends so much time in a batty old tower you don't seem to have assimilated any bat senses."

Kit rolled his eyes – a reaction she sparked a lot. His sister's fondness for snooty words could be irritating. "Assimilated? Really?"

Only close family members knew Bash wasn't showing off. Neither of them were. Kit spouted as much science as he dared and Bash used fancy words as a matter of course. He'd teased her once by asking if she'd swallowed a dictionary. She replied: no, it was a thesaurus, and silenced him with her well-rehearsed expression that Kit called 'the stare of pity'.

"It means learned... picked up," Bash explained. "One day, I expect *you'll* pick up. And by the way, my preoccupation for fancy words is me *assimilating* lessons from Lady Nan. Nowadays it's fun for messing with my baby brother's head. Consider it my *penchant* for scientific experimentation with vocabulary."

"Well, lah-dee-dah. And yes, I *do* know what languorous means. You've told me several times. And I'll have you know that being languorous is basic prep for scientific thinking. It gives wild ideas a calm place to land. It's called being open... as in *receptive*. Scientific fact one: you're barely *three* minutes older than me. Scientific fact two: in four months and five days *both* of us turn sixteen."

Bash flashed an easy smile and linked the fingers of her right hand in Kit's left. "Behold the power of words. One word and POW!... you blast off into the statistic stratosphere."

"What do you expect from a rocket scientist. Besides, I happen to like measuring things."

"And I, your *older* sister, happens to enjoy winding you up."

"Rabble-rouser," Kit snapped.

"Incendiary," Bash snarled.

Kit made a derisive sound in his throat. "Whatever. I grow languorous with this conversation."

Bash pushed her sunglasses onto her forehead and squinted into Kit's eyes. A sure sign she meant business. "Experiments are your thing, right? Wait until you're a real scientist. They use a special lingo all of their own. And I'm not talking *big* words. I'm talking *gigantic* words. Words that spin off into cosmic-babble. Pretty much white sound to the rest of us lowlifes. Just wait until you have to explain something advanced to us. You'd better get used to it. Experts have to live on their own private planets or they'd have no-one to talk with. You'll see."

"Bede is definitely a strange planet but Planet Bash is a tad environ-*mental* if you ask me," Kit said. "And aren't you a high princess of the greenwood or something? Although, I have to say, talking to plants can't be all that exciting. Unless you have serious self-esteem issues."

Bash prodded his arm. "Like you don't."

This remark brought Kit to his elbows. "Touché."

"There's no need to scowl, Mr. Science."

Kit's scowl deepened. "I can't help it. You provoke me."

"Parks says learning the Latin names for plants is a required new language for a landscape designer like me. For instance, I bet you weren't aware that this rowan tree is from the genus Sorbus Domestica."

"I absolutely wasn't."

"And its sub-genus Rosaceae, is related, by the way, to the *rose* family... old English name, Quickbeam, and it was known as a bird-catcher."

"You don't say."

"It was especially revered by witches, which, is why Charlotte visits it so often."

Kit made a cross-eyed crazy face. "Charlotte is a fruit loop with a wild imagination."

"Charlotte is a florist."

"Pardon me... Charlotte is a *florist* with a wild imagination."

Bash patted the tree trunk, affectionately. "Scoff all you like Mr. Statistics, but this tree is magical and known to protect against malevolent beings. In your position, you should have more respect."

"Unless it takes the sting out of time-travel it's of no use to me."

"Okay, clever clogs. Have your fun, but it's also called the Way-farer's Tree because... wait for it... it prevents people on long journeys from getting lost. Ring any bells?"

Kit looked up into the boughs heavy with the red berries of summer and addressed the tree as if they were old friends. "Thanks Rowan. Next time I'm stranded in the future I'll know who to call."

"The exciting part is when the plants talk back," Bash said.

"I would think."

The breezy nature of the twin's conversation upset the Rowan tree. It grew impatient. One of its branches poked Bash harder. It whipped a thin branch against Bash's arm and dropped a clump of sticky leaves onto her shoulder.

Bash was right. Bede *was* a different world. It would be an under-statement to say the last three years had pushed Kit completely out of his comfort zone. But there was no denying that seeing was only a small part of believing. He was now friends with several ghosts and had travelled into the future. Stumbled into it more like. He'd astral-traveled to modern Egypt and met the teenager who was now the twins' adopted brother. He'd investigated the eerie cold spot in Bede Hall – the Winter Room where the laws of physics went haywire, and discovered things he'd rather not know. Two were serious enough, but a third kept him awake at night and uncharacteristically owly during family get-togethers.

The logistics behind the blue door evaded Kit, but now more than ever he intended to unravel science-fiction into logical explanations.

"Well, good luck with that," Bash said, hearing Kit's thoughts. She rabbit-punched him in the arm. "No secrets between twins, mate."

Kit let out a deliberately low sigh so he wouldn't show he was upset.

"You wish," Bash sent.

But it was odd how Bash hadn't been able to hear his two worst fears. "Here's a newsflash from Planet Kit," he said. "We'd better get eco-friendly very soon if we're going to save *this* one."

"And speaking of experts, Parks showed me how to test the wind for signs of trouble," Bash said, rubbing the red mark on her arm. "Weather warnings and such. That man can smell a storm that's weeks away. He's a true phenomenon. He says clouds are stories."

"Newsflash. That *man,* by the way, is a *ghost!* So, he doesn't exactly operate in the same realm of consciousness as you or I. And, by the way, I can smell a Sunday roast beef and all the trimmings, well enough." Kit grinned and tousled Bash's hair to make her crazy. "Anyway, what do I need bat senses for when I have you?" He gestured over the expanse of deserted lawn, his arms outstretched like a dowser. "Besides, if I'm so thick, why can I still feel… them?"

Bash smoothed her hair, took a deep breath, and cleared her throat. "What? Feel who?"

Kit shook his head. "And *you're* the sensitive one." He opened his arms to encompass the grounds and gazed absentmindedly towards the lake. "The ghosts of circus past, that's who. Lady Nan can still see them, you know… the actors and the crew. She says they never left."

Bash perked up and closed her eyes, all the better to listen. "Well, do you at least *hear* something strange?"

Kit copied Bash by scrunching his eyes, and gave up. "Not a sausage."

The mention of sausages made him extra hungry. When would Mum call them in? She'd promised no more hot-weather salads. Already visions of Yorkshire pudding holding a pool of savoury brown gravy turned Kit into one of Pavlov's dogs. Comfort food nearly always involved gravy.

"It's a *lack* of sound really," Bash said. "All the birds have stopped chirping." But as soon as her words were out, a wave of birdsong burst from behind the purple cloud, now indigo, and filled the sky. The cloud vaporized with a loud popping sound as if it had imploded.

"I heard *that,* right enough," Kit said. "So, what's the story in *that* cloud?"

"It's too dark for words."

"If I don't eat something soon I shall faint." He searched his pockets for a last granola bar and automatically broke it in half. Whatever one twin had was equally shared. Twin's Law.

Without notice, the grey mist lifted from the grass. Bash announced the toxic chill had left her throat. The sky sparkled clear blue and the branches above them became thick with every sort of bird native to Bede. *Spooky. Now where had they come from?*

"I'll ask Parks," Bash said. "He knows everything."

Mrs. S' voice rang out, carried on the feeblest of winds. "DINNER'S ON THE TABLE!"

Bash jumped up with a single leaf as a jaunty beret clinging to her hair. "Bloody hell, is that the time? I was supposed to mash the potatoes and set the table. Come along egghead. Sit next to me. I'll cut your meat up for you."

Kit countered with "Come along birdbrain. Sit next to me. I'll explain how photosynthesis works. You *do* know that this grass shouldn't be even remotely green."

Bash listened intently as the birds swayed the branches. Usually, the trees whispered reassuring thoughts to her or hummed soothing tunes, but today the rowan was clearly moaning. Definitely not a good sign. She swallowed hard to stop from tearing up.

Kit paused to examine the name 'bird-catcher' for all of three seconds, pulled Bash to her feet, and shouted the most important word of the day to the empty sky. "GRAVY." He brushed the leaves from Bash's shoulder. "Hold on. You have a wee chip, just there."

She crossed her eyes at him. "Funny."

The tree groaned with the heaviness of its winged visitors and shifted its weight so its toes in the earth caused a mole to pop out of one hole and run to ground into another. It shook itself as the twins departed, and sent a telegraph to Parks through its roots. *"You might want to have a word with your apprentice. It took me twenty minutes to get through to her. And please tell her I'm very sorry for the bruises."*

VIII

FLOWERS BEFORE GRAVY

The scent of flowers mingled with roast beef filled the kitchen. A vase of white carnations made a cooling centrepiece. It was the regular first of the month delivery of a memorial bouquet for Lady Nan.

Kit sniffed the air with suspicion. "Are those Bede carnations?"

Bash's eyes flashed defensively. "Of course they are." She selected a stem and waved it threateningly at Kit. "They won't bite."

Kit recoiled. "Says you."

"Gravy eclipses smelly flowers," Tut said, smirking at Kit. "No worries, I shall protect you if they attack."

"Too right, mate," Kit mumbled, his mouth stuffed with bread and butter.

Bash grimaced at Lady Nan and shook her head as if to say 'boys are hopeless'. She corrected Tut's dodgy English. "That's *fragrant* flowers, Tut. Delightfully – *fragrant* – flowers. Not smelly."

There was a time when Lady Nan would have stepped in to enlighten her wayward grandson on speaking with his mouth full. But since her death, she wandered into her past glory days, staying close enough to eavesdrop but far enough away to be on her own, 'coming to life' when danger was afoot or there was a plan that required her approval. She still maintained her position as chatelaine, and in case anyone had forgotten her authority, she made sure she kept a set of housekeeper's keys on her belt and smiled knowingly when her grandchildren cited them as the clanking chains of Marley's ghost. And although she took their teasing with good grace, she made a habit of rattling the impressively large keychain from time to time, whenever she wanted to interrupt a conversation with something to say that couldn't wait.

Kit shot Tut a look of disgust with a crooked smile. "Tosser."

Bash deliberately traced her cheek with the head of the carnation while staring at Kit, before clumsily replacing it so it nearly toppled out of the vase.

Anna drifted in to adjust the wayward stem and buried her face in the white flowers while Mrs. S walked through her to stand over Kit with a ladle suspended over his plate. "Where do you want your gravy?" she said.

"Everywhere," the teens said in unison. It was a family joke and expected. They performed a high-five to celebrate their solidarity.

Tut grinned. "I almost said, none for me, thanks."

Kit pointed his fork at Tut. "I find it sadly distressing that in two years *you* haven't cottoned on to the fine art of mashed potatoes and gravy."

"I guess we're not the only ones who require advanced training," Bash said.

Mrs. S, hoping to join the conversation, asked innocently, "What training is that?"

"Oh, nothing," Tut said. "It's some silly contest we've got going with Parks about which one of us can recite the most Latin names for plants."

Bash pointed to the carnations and winked at Anna. "*Those* are gillyflowers."

"They were your grandmother's favourite," Mrs. S said. "Dr. Brooks still sends them like clockwork. Sweet man. I expect it keeps her memory alive for him."

Kit blew on a steaming fork of mashed potato. "That's *not* Latin."

Lady Nan shook her head from her chair by the fireplace. Her favourite cat, Anubis slept in her lap, one ear tuned to the conversation.

"It's old English," Bash said.

"I don't know how you keep so many loose ends in your head," Mrs. S commented.

"I didn't," Bash said. "Lady Nan just told me."

Mrs. S was only half listening. "*Hmmmn?* Oh, I almost forgot. Rupert called. He's coming for Christmas after all."

Kit inclined his head towards Mrs. S and gave his sister a nudge. "Watch it, soot for brains. Try not to upset the apple cart."

"Why are you all so short tempered today? Even Parks is out of sorts. And I don't know where your father is. I need the car this evening."

Lady Nan overheard and held her hands out to warm them on a fire that wasn't there. She smiled a distant smile. "Peregrine never forgets," she murmured to Anubis.

IX

ELEPHANTS UNDER THE CARPET

DECEMBER 2, 2016

Kit Stratford-Smyth hot-footed it down the spiral stairs, narrowly escaping a turned ankle.

"What's the hurry?" Taraq said, floating through him, hand outstretched as if he was directing traffic, which he was.

"Bug off, you insubstantial wee phantom," Kit said, brushing him away. "And I say that with real affection. You can accompany me but don't try to lecture *me* on physics. You're not exactly on solid ground in that department."

"You know, I *have* grasped some aspects of English sarcasm."

"Have you been spying on me and Brooks?"

"How else am I going to keep in the 'loop' as you call it?"

"I want to get Brooks alone before the others arrive."

Taraq crossed his arms – a miniature genie blocking Kit's escape route. "Since when has storming-off ever amounted to anything *substantial*?"

"Touché. Now move, runt."

"You're too angry to be alone with Brooks right now. I'm helping you by stalling for time."

"That's actually very funny. What do you think I've *been* doing? My entire mission for the last year has been stalling for time. What else would you call putting a permanent kybosh on the time portal of no return? But right now, you can help me by getting out of my face."

"You can walk all over me," Taraq said. "Walk through me if you want, but I'm doing you a favour. You'll thank me."

Taraq watched Kit fume and stomp his way back up the stairs. He was pleased. In fact, he was so pleased with himself that he'd forgotten to ask what a kybosh was.

Brooks' living room swarmed with eight people. To be more precise, four people and four *former* people. Brooks was in the kitchen surrounded by Anna who was trying to help. Kit ducked from her sight. The best he could do was join the others and position himself so he could watch his fellow Twinters, the team formed to save the Hall, and scan them for any cracks in their resolve to believe a prophecy on a bit of paper that no-one had ever actually seen.

The Twinters, a combination of the words winter and twin that, unbeknown to those involved, reflected a far-distant but significant age of Gemini impacting on Bede Hall's present challenges. Naturally enough, after his misadventure into the future, in Kit's mind, the Bede Prophecy was always the *Winter* Prophecy. Two years had passed since the twins' fateful encounter with the blue door that opened to more than the abandoned attic bedroom of a long-ago housemaid.

Kit had reluctantly come to terms with ghosts. There were reasonable explanations for such phenomena. The human body was not entirely explored. The phantom essence of a person could be explained rationally as an ethereal shadow of particles in a state of flux. A cluster of rogue molecules. Most of science existed in unseen realms, so a complex system of flesh and bones could hardly be expected to tell the whole DNA story.

In the microscopic world, humans were essentially a configuration of atoms, and beyond that it was anybody's theory, so it was possible for an element of life-force to remain earthbound for the purpose of taking care of unfinished business or even new business.

His grandmother, Lady Nan, was proof. And then, there was 'the child' Anna. Her presence set Kit's nerves on edge because he knew her secret. Anna would be nine-years-old forever if nothing intervened to send her home. Another of Kit's 'no pressure' responsibilities.

Places that looked like Bede Hall cried out for haunting, but Bede Hall had cried out for saving. The house had a mind of its own. It had plans. Bede Hall was alive but all was not well. It had flat out ordered Lady Nan to return. The timing being critical, she'd brought her daughter and her twin grandchildren with her. Her son-in-law was believed dead after going missing on his dig in Egypt. Lives were in transition. Emotions ran high and expectations remained low. Histrionics aside, the situation was volatile and the Hall took advantage.

Neither twin had volunteered as the champions of Bede cited in the prophecy. Their acceptance, according to legend, as defenders of the Great Hall were taken for granted; their predetermined assigned duties were clearly defined. Neat and tidy, according to a far distant plan.

Bash, being wholly enchanted with her role of grounding the land with the whimsical title 'Mistress of the Green', meant she was not only on-board, but the highly-motivated captain of the 'Good Ship Lavender'.

Kit, who loathed the very word supernatural, had major qualms. He'd been cast in the dubious role of time traveller. Clearly, it was not in the prophecy's best interest for him to stay home, tilling the soil, growing giant vegetables, and refining a strain of lavender that beguiled the locals, and perhaps spread south to the markets of London to pacify and enslave an entire population. Who knew what Bede Hall had in mind.

He would be tossed into the backwaters of time, landing alone in unchartered locations with the obscure mission of seeking out the loose ends of 'what had been' that may or may not untangle Bede

Hall's present predicament, and in so doing, maybe, just *maybe*, preserve the time portals for future generations who, ironically, actually required an alternate future in order to survive. An ice-age was hardly conducive to preserving the human race.

Closer to home, closer to the year 2020, the ice-age Kit had glimpsed spelled the demise of his beloved sister. It was a detail best kept to himself. He'd immediately informed the Twinters of the natural disaster. The word 'natural' rendered that his duty, but sharing the rest served no-one. So, in the interests of martyrdom-by-default, Kit kept the goriest details to himself.

For the time being, there had been six years to work on a solution, so staying afloat relied on keeping the time portals intact. Timing was critical the Hall said. Which was rich coming from a building crumbling into imminent bankruptcy. The orders were to wait until further notice on a calendar that only the Hall knew. The volcano detail was put on hold. Bede Hall's financial status was given top priority. Fortune smiled. And now, fortune frowned and now there was less time to perform a geo-illogical miracle.

Sadly, as in most cases, time marched on more quickly than expected, and now D-day was fast approaching. D for decision, counting down to the below zero temperatures of 2020, and the final decision was Kit's. The term 'now or never' stalked him, dreaming and waking. Postponing the inevitable was rapidly closing-in, and he was losing face. Everything hinged on him being a superhero and blasting off into inner space. He could tell by their expectant expressions, the Twinters were growing impatient.

Bash, once his closest ally, and the person he wanted to protect the most, was becoming hostile. It wasn't lost on him that by saving her from mental anguish he'd doomed himself to the role of coward. Cowardice. All he saw were the words coward + ice. Was there ever an end to the irony.

Tonight, he meant to face his mentor and, if possible, make an end to the madness. If he could wake everyone up from the lavender nonsense, then perhaps there'd be a chance to redeem himself.

Kit had started out as a founding member of the group committed to saving the planet from the very ice-age he'd witnessed on his first trip through the time portal. It was logical. They were the only ones privy to inside information. But being in the loop eventually sounded increasingly loopy, and Kit's internal science bug finally hatched from a naïve caterpillar to a butterfly with the wingspan and temperament of an angry Pterodactyl.

His change of heart hadn't been overnight. And yet it was the nighttime that gnawed at his resolve to be the sole representative on the side of logic. Night terrors became normal, if that is, anything in and around the village of Bede could be described as normal. It was surprising, even to Kit, that certain individuals were exempt from the mass hallucination affecting the community. Exceptions to rules negated good science. And so, nightmares wandered into the dangerous territory of anxiety attacks during the day.

In hindsight, regular school might have saved his sanity, except any local school would have been tainted under the same influences. But Kit and his sister and the recent addition of an adopted brother were educated under the home-school rules of their mother. Mrs. S, was herself, innocent to the weirdness that kept growing weirder under her very nose.

It seemed ridiculous to cite lavender as the culprit. But to Kit, not being the green thumb his sister proclaimed to be, it was the most obvious offender. Its suffocating scent impregnated everything. It was surprising that the buildings weren't several shades of purple from prolonged exposure. He was sure, if he ever visited London again, he would suffer the jeers of passersby as a teen inexperienced in the subtle application of cologne. The whole thing was too ghastly to think about.

The 'mammoth in the room' that no-one admitted to seeing, was the prolific species of exotic plants that luxuriated in the hothouses of Bede Hall, and that the Hall itself was the biggest 'green house' of them all.

Bash had been perfecting Bede's own strain of lavender as a lucrative sideline.

Her mentor, Parks, Bede Hall's head gardener, stepped into the shadows and let her shine. Charlotte Findhorn, herbalist extraordinaire, spoke of a breakthrough species rumoured to induce even greater heights of intoxication. Pampered and encouraged to ever-expanding levels of aromatic seduction, lavender was turning into a viable business of its own. Its reported side-effects, from the villagers, were dizzying altered states of perception and vivid lucid dreaming.

Kit recalled the last meeting of the Twinters. He had been making notes of a new manifestation. The sound of a ticking clock began following him from the tower, a shadowy companion, accompanying him everywhere. Timing him. Shaming him. Sometimes he listened to music on headphones to be rid of it. After he'd accused Taraq of mischief, Taraq had feigned offense and denied it, but the Tinnitus stopped.

The Hall was testing him again.

A bouquet of Bede lavender glowed like neon from the centre of Brooks' table. All eyes rested upon it while thoughts of D-day consumed all the air in the room. The grandfather clock chimed eleven. "Time for elevenses," Lady Nan said, ever punctual when it came to the ritual of mid-morning tea and chocolate biscuits. "And then, we decide."

"Hang on," Kit said, "since I'm the one who's going, shouldn't it be *me* who decides?"

"It *should* be," Bash replied. "But it's obvious, you are unwilling or can't."

Ben raised his hand like a kid in school. "Has the Hall given us the go ahead?"

"The Hall says it's to be next year," Brooks announced. "But don't get complacent. Next year is only a few weeks away."

Lady Nan called for order by clanking her keys at the clamour of voices vying for attention. "Mark your calendars. The Winter Solstice approaches in three weeks. The *beginning* of the end will start then. There will be significant signs. These things don't occur to the minute. It's not clockwork, it's calendar work. But there will be a gradual decline of energy. So, fair warning. Kit will have to go during the first year of the beginning time. It's an open invitation to explore the solution we require to survive."

Kit sighed audibly and relaxed into his armchair. He'd get complacent if he wanted to. Other than his departure time expanding comfortably, there were no surprises. The key dates were always seasonal. The solstices: summer and winter; and the equinoxes: vernal and autumnal, and the harvest festivals: May Day and All Hallows. He made a quick calculation. He had possibly eleven months' reprieve. Time was on his side for once. He would make it count. Hadn't Brooks' clock just had confirmed it nicely. Anything could happen. A lifetime could happen. An asteroid could hit the earth. In his mind, he saw six dates on a calendar circled in red. "Elevenses it is," he said. "I'm famished."

There were three teapots. Clear Pyrex glass for herbal tea, Blue Denmark patterned china for Earl Grey, and a 'Brown Betty' for the strongest blend, English Breakfast.

Charlotte gave her report casually, leaning back on flowered cushions. "The French countryside boasts an extraordinarily powerful variety of lavender." She paused to wink at Parks. "The regions south of Paris produce many other unprecedented hybrids and botanicals. Hardy species, by all accounts," Charlotte continued over her poised teacup. "I already have Mr. Leoni from the village sourcing out a supply of healthy seedlings. Unfortunately, the modern use of pesticides and the increasing levels of industrial pollution make it difficult to obtain the rarest specimens. But I have every confidence we can attain new heights in our gardens, and boost our yield, if we're vigilant."

Kit studied Charlotte's face as she spoke. There was something about her. She got under his skin. As if she knew a secret. Well, fair enough, he had more secrets than anyone. But that wasn't it. She controlled Bash which was odd because to even attempt such a feat was nothing short of pointless. No, it wasn't control, it was influence. She had captivated his sister.

He recognized it as Magnetic Entrancing, which made it scientifically creepier and set him on edge. Her look set off warning bells. Pixie hair, hypnotic eyes, always dressed like a garden in flowered prints. She was the embodiment of 'garden-ness'. No doubt her choices were influenced by being a florist. A subtle confirmation of her higher purpose. Subliminal advertising. After all, she *was* around flowers all day.

Charlotte challenged his gaze. It was thunderbolt clear. Those riveting eyes were lavender. She was enchanting. As she smiled, the colour of her eyes deepened into spellbinding. Goosebump time. If he had to describe her, she was lavender made flesh.

Charlotte cosied up to Bash keeping her gaze level with Kit's. "More sugar, Kit?" she said, without moving her mouth. The woman never blinked.

"Nothing less will do," Bash was saying. "Not if sales will keep us afloat as well as the movie business. We can't hope for a harvest that would come anywhere near to revenues of that kind. But it's all we've got. People will buy it. If it's powerful enough they won't be able to stop themselves."

Lady Nan poured her second cup of Earl Grey. "We will need all the power they possess."

The sprig of lavender tucked into Parks' hatband emitted a faint giggle as it wriggled free. Parks heard and reached up to secure it tightly. "Oh no, you don't," he said amiably as a tiny mauve creature, the size of a mosquito, spun away.

Kit deliberately busied himself, concentrating on keeping a third heaping teaspoon of sugar from spilling, and stirring it into his tea. He stirred long after it was dissolved, examining a hole in the toe of one of his socks so no-one would ask his opinion. He savoured the hot tea trickling over his tongue and recoiled from its sweetness. *What the… I never take sugar!* He looked up to find Charlotte smiling at him, so he drank the rest of his 'syrup' in one long gulp, burning his tongue. He choked quietly, and crashed his cup into its saucer.

Charlotte raised the glass teapot high as if in a toast. "Herbal tea, Kit? It's not so sweet. This one's elderflowers and mint. Very refreshing."

Kit tried not to blink. "Thanks, no," he managed, his eyes watering.

The conversation in the room drifted into a background lull and Kit thought back to the time he and Bash had moved to Bede when they were barely thirteen.

After the first year of initial upheaval and shock, events had subsided into the veneer of business as usual. The Hall had maneuvered itself into a going concern as a rental property for movie sets. One production had taken hold, and the series 'The Curse of Pryde' had grown into a regular source of income. But then the prophecy reared its ugly head. It took precedence, eclipsing financial security, at least in the lives of the Twinters – a gathering of the hoodwinked plus one better-late-than-never, dissenter, himself, Kit Stratford-Smyth.

It was hardly a stroke of luck that Bede Hall was hired out as a movie set. The idea had been contrived, delivered, accepted, and activated with uncanny speed. Mrs. S and big brother Rupert had more-or-less complied. Swift success followed, as if the entire project had been masterminded by the Hall itself. Bede had that effect.

When Kit was thirteen and devastated by the loss of a parent, it had been easy to regard the Hall as sentient. And after decades of financial famine it was uncanny how its fortunes miraculously reversed in a few months. But there were no such things as miracles.

Reaching the winner's circle in that kind of time scale was unprecedented. Not without a few hiccups or some underhanded 'hands'. The aura of a fixed lottery win made Kit uneasy.

It was as if a permanent state of mild hysteria had sealed everyone under a glass dome. As if the moon had remained perversely full in order to create tension.

Being in such close proximity to commercial melodrama made the strangeness of Bede-like goings-on seem relatively subdued. So, it was inevitable that the family would be enamoured with the fantasy of 'The Curse of Pryde' – an ironically, parallel saga modelled on a fictional family of Egyptologists.

Bash likened movie magic to technical fairy glamour and was roundly criticized by Charlotte who, along with Parks, was the only one unmoved by all things Hollywood.

The paid actors were encouraged to stay in-character off-screen in order to maintain a sense of continuity between takes. But this had planted show-biz promises under the family's skin until even the Twinters began to accept Bede Hall and the fictional Pryde Manor as twin locations.

The family had been coping in a delusional fug long before 'the biz' descended on them. And yet, there was no denying, the movies had been a godsend for saving the Hall, and it brought Taraq the younger into Kit's life. Taraq, an unlikely companion for a teenager like himself who decried the paranormal, had become a useful sounding board in a world in need of ethereal navigation. And… happily, Taraq took the edge off Anna sightings.

The twins' recently-adopted brother Tut (Taraq the elder) and the others had no such excuse. And how was it their parents remained immune to the madness? They drank the same water and breathed the same air. What toxins could be so discriminating? Science held a distinctly impartial view of the situation. Half the village were sleepwalkers and the other half, possibly quite mad. Eccentric but delightful, Mrs. S called them. And it was true they were an affable lot. And the most affable of all was his own mentor.

The distinguished psychologist Dr. Brooks, tailored as a country squire in immaculate tweeds, had been nothing but kind and helpful at a time Kit needed a father figure. He'd been thrust into the head of the family even though Rupert was older by ten years. It was Kit's struggling logic that had grounded the family throughout his grandmother's ravings and his brother's snooty theatrics.

Tut had gone over to what Kit called the 'purple' side, rather seamlessly. Plucked from the violent streets of Cairo to the heady safety offered in the countryside of Bede, he'd slipped into Bede Hall as easily as a new set of clothes.

Likewise, the sweet smell of success lulled everyone but Kit into a false sense of security.

X

LETTING GO

Dr. Brooks' plush sitting room pulsated with background Mozart played at the lowest volume. It was meant to nurture the few plant species dotted about the house as well as soothe his guests, but it created a sense of suspended animation. Maybe they were hypnotized. Brooks could do that. The power of suggestion was a form of therapy that psychiatrists used. And what was the difference between self-hypnosis and meditation anyway.

Kit surmised everyone had been ordered to keep calm just to placate him. That was a surefire way to put everyone on their guard no matter how much they wanted to believe they were safe. They were ganging up on him. The walls were closing in. He'd have to stay alert and not drink anything. Was he imagining things? Well, of course he was… he lived in Bede.

The room felt stuffy, muffled from the real world. Even the TV, when it was on, and it seldom was, was always muted. The news was softer. The tables had no sharp edges but perhaps that was due to the dulling of his senses from the lavender. Great fields of the stuff encircled Bede like a moat. Perhaps it was a lack of sleep. He found it hard to breathe through a lavender fog.

Expectant faces floated in every corner. Forced cheer, Kit suspected. The events that were coming were far from comforting. Even now, Brooks was about to ply them with sugar. Surely the lowest form of persuasion on the planet.

There sat Anna with her waiflike expression, staring wistfully into the future. Her blue eyes pinning him to the wall whenever he let them. And Taraq, literally hovering over her as only a ghost can, protecting her as if she were the crown jewels of Egypt's eighteenth-dynasty.

Brook's easy-chairs were filled with the various stages of fear masked as hope. At least, that was Kit' hypothesis. And theories were reasonably dependable. Weren't they?

Kit had learned a thing. He didn't like people that much. The realization came over him as his gaze drifted over, of all things, Brooks' mantelpiece. A mirror hung above. Framed photographs were arranged below. They showed villagers smiling and waving as if nothing untoward was amiss, flanked by portraits of famous psychiatrists and archaeologists. Their faces swam before him, full of secrets and terrifying ideas. And lies. One photo was a close-up of the underside gills of a mushroom. It had the distinct earmark of a Vincento Leoni original, although the local chemist never signed any of his limited-edition prints. Force of habit, he told everyone. What did *that* mean?

Brooks was off in the pantry clattering about amongst a tower of biscuit tins looking for a sponge cake. Imagine putting one's molecules in the hands of a man who had misplaced a 9-inch diameter cake in a closet with only three shelves. Incredible trust. Incredibly shortsighted. No. It was simply not on.

Kit startled the others' fake optimism. "You know, I don't actually *like* people all that much," he confessed suddenly to the mirror.

This wasn't entirely true because he liked a lot of people, but given the years of isolation and living in a constant state of skepticism at Bede Hall, he'd lately come to the conclusion he'd just as soon retreat into his observations and science experiments alone. He reckoned he'd be gone in the near future. Removed in a snap of the fingers. Likely, erased. Any day now, he was scheduled to be zapped to goodness knows where. But somewhere bad.

He ran a finger over a silver Art Deco picture frame and examined his fingertip. There was no dust. "Entering a time portal will be the end of 'now' as I know it," he said out loud, continuing as if talking to himself. "As I *think* I know it. But it's all so subjective, isn't it?"

Multiple voices contradicted him, protesting overmuch, murmuring hollow assurances of safety and encouragement. All but one. Bash crossed her arms and radiated her displeasure. The word 'coward' echoed from her mind into his.

Kit, worn down against a sea of opposition, often doubted his own sanity. But the others hadn't seen the future. He scrunched his eyes to blot out the recurring image of a snowbank as high as the moon.

"Have you got a headache," Anna asked. "Can I get you anything?"

Kit rested his head on the mantelpiece and softly banged it against the wood. At least he wouldn't be around to witness the end of the world because the imminent future loomed just as precariously as the far distant past. He was hardly spoiled for choice because the not too distant future was equally catastrophic. He'd *seen* it – bleak as living in the sub-zero whiteout of Antarctica. He'd resorted to what many humans did in such a position; he built a wall around himself and surrounded himself with abstract busyness.

But Kit's worst disgrace, his guilt of guilts, was knowing he'd become a vehicle of the very thing he despised. At some point in the future, if his vision was true, he'd turned his back on pure science and become, perish the thought, a writer of science-fiction. The knowledge left him embarrassed and ashamed. He'd caved.

The only reason he even *considered* relenting to time travel was the chance he could bypass his unfortunate literary phase and re-emerge, firmly dedicated to science.

He'd immersed himself in study but astrophysics confirmed the universe was crazier than anyone could imagine. Surprisingly, as time went on, his physics text books read more and more like science-fiction until he often doubted his own sanity.

Kit pushed his toes into the thick pile of the Turkish carpet to prove he was there, anchored in reality. He turned away from his anguished expression in the mirror and unleashed his hostility on the room. "I feel like I'm the volcano about to explode. Why have I been selected, eh?" His gaze briefly alighted on the ghost of his Great Uncle Ben and slithered away to the carpet. "Why doesn't Brooks let someone go who's already dead? *Hmmmnn?*"

Tut, the usual vote of reason, was quick to reply. "We're all being tested," he said.

Kit looked up from the pattern of sphinx that decorated the carpet's border. He'd counted them the first time he was in this room. Counting sphinx grounded him. He'd been nervous. Now there was only one sphinx to worry about. THE Sphinx. "Rubbish," he said.

The notion of the room being as silent as a tomb freaked him into stuttering.

"A-a-a-and speaking of dead," Kit continued, "why is all the grass still green? Photosynthesis should have stopped. Everything should be brown by now. A desert of purple sand perhaps, but I guess that would be too close to the truth. That wretched lavender has something to do with it. The scent is everywhere. It's an hallucinogen, isn't it? We're all zoned out under a kind of an olfactory spell."

Tut wrinkled his forehead. "A factory? I don't understand."

"Olfactory means the sense of smell," Bash said.

Kit brightened and addressed his grandmother. "Maybe Tut's onto something. Maybe Bede Hall *is* a factory. We sort of manufacture lavender, and the fact is, we do sell the stuff. Is it one of your puzzle words with clues? It would fit because in science, a factor is part of an equation. It means a reasonable cause."

"Of course it fits," Lady Nan replied, her expression softening. "Kit, if it has special meaning to you then it's definitely a word to explore. Listen… a flower's essence is its scent. And the words scents and sense are homophones."

"I love those," Bash said.

"No wonder the English language is so hard to learn," Tut declared.

Kit raised his eyes in disgust and Lady Nan continued. "The sense of smell is the fact or essence of the matter you're worried about. Commonsense equals a common garden flower's scents. Do you see how it works? And we have Tut to thank for bringing facts, factors, and factory to our attention."

"No problem," Tut said. "Glad I could help."

Kit's frustration returned. "Yes, that's all very well. But this isn't some parlour game. I'm trying to establish a sane line of reasoning."

Taraq and Anna, in his peripheral vision, were sitting with their heads together as usual. Next to them was Ben, Lady Nan's twin brother, who kept alternating between age five and nineteen. Kit rounded on Lady Nan who was smiling to herself, still sorting out the word scent. "In fact, *some* of us aren't even here at all. Are you!"

Lady Nan sighed and crossed her arms to match her granddaughter's. "Oh, Christopher, my dear child."

"My name's Kit and I'm not a child. Please don't pat me on the head to silence me. I'll be sixteen in a few months. I'm not the spineless kid who arrived here. I've had time to…"

"Grow a spine?" Bash said.

Kit thrust his hands and his pockets and glared. "To think."

Bash rolled her eyes. "Ooh. Clever clogs."

Kit turned away from her and spoke to the ceiling. "One of us has to be."

"It's the dew," Bash said. "It's different here."

Kit made a strangled sound in his throat. "Don't be stupid. Can you hear yourself?"

Bash wriggled excitedly in her chair. "No. Charlotte once explained."

"Oh, this is going to be good. Go on then. Magic, is it?"

"It's not *actual* science."

"You surprise me."

"Charlotte's on duty with Parks, or she'd be here to tell you properly."

"Magic covers just about everything," Tut blurted. He looked shamefaced. "I'm just saying."

Kit let out another harrumph. "Yeah, a multitude of sins, more like. Look. Guys. There are definitely medicinal plants that have miraculous properties. Well, not *miraculous*. That's the wrong word. Some of them mess with your mind."

Tut checked the troubled faces of the others. "You need to seriously chill out, mate," he said.

Kit thumped his fist on the wall. "All of you keep telling me to relax. Now here this: relaxation never fixes anything."

Tut held up his hand a few inches above his knee. "*Um…* excuse me, no. Dr. Brooks told me that relaxation stills the mind so that solutions to things in need of fixing can occur. He called them presentiments."

Kit felt a pang of jealousy tinged with anger as the stirrings of a green monster coiled around his innards. So, Brooks had taken another apprentice under his wing. *I guess he'll need a replacement for when I get zapped inside the portal. Doctors were practical people.* Trained, he'd heard, to distance themselves from their patients. *Well fine. He was done anyway.*

"Why are all of you tiptoeing around the lavender, ignoring the dirty great elephant in the room?"

"Describe it, Anna said. "Go on. If you can see it and we can't, then help us."

"It's a figure of speech," Bash said. "It means an important issue too big to ignore but everyone does, so it invades the room to get attention."

Anna's density thinned into a wisp. "Like a ghost. Like me?"

"Actually, it's a massive purple blob with tusks, waving a red flag in its trunk with time travel written on it," Kit snarked.

Lady Nan continued to sew without raising her eyes from her embroidery sampler that read 'believing is not seeing', and shrugged. "The ghost of an elephant wreaks no havoc," she murmured to her sewing basket.

Lady Nan's remark left Kit feeling trampled by pachyderms? Where had *that* word come from?"

Bash grinned knowingly and raised her eyebrows. "*Elephants to you*" she sent.

Kit ignored her and took a deep breath, that the others recognized as the precursor to a science lecture, addressing no-one in particular. "Technically, molecular deconstruction, time travel to you lot, is possible. I know that. It's called a magnetic polar flux within an area of geological dissonance. Einstein wrote about it." He sighed and kicked a plant pot that contained what looked like a large gnarled twig with red leaves. "To be more accurate, it's called Bede, but I'm not buzzing off to 'Whenever-land' because of a fairy story or a plant. And by the way, isn't Parks another figment of our imagination? Aren't all of the Parks family, to some extent!"

Six put up his hand, gingerly. "*Um… I'm not!*"

Bash, upset for the tree, changed the subject. When it came to Six, she wanted no suggestion he might be just another ghost-Parks in a line of ghosts. "Steady on. That rowan sapling is going to be planted at the gates. It could save your life someday."

"It has to be ready in eleven months in order to be planted at the most auspicious time on the next eve of All Hallows," Lady Nan said.

"Right," Kit sniggered. "I feel safer already. Sorry, I momentarily blanked out. That stick's a baby rowan tree, protector of, what was it? Wayfarers?" He appraised the tree lovingly. "Ah, yes, my soon to be best friend." He righted the pot with a quarter turn and shook hands with a branch. "Sorry pal. I lost my head. Didn't mean to disturb. But you're going to have to toughen up a bit if one little kick upsets you."

Six drummed his fingers on the arm of a leather armchair. "I reckon everything happens the way it's supposed to. Any road, that's what my grandad says, and…" he paused to look sheepishly at Bash. "Being dead for hundreds of years means he knows a thing or two about life."

"I'd go in your place," Taraq said.

Anna chimed in with a slight variation. "I'd go *with* you."

"It's karma," Bash said. "Maybe we should all go."

Lady Nan spoke wistfully to her brother, Ben. "Perfume is time travel in a bottle."

Kit looked at his fellow Twinters with incredulity. "You've all gone mad!"

The New-Age instructions from Kit's first encounter with Dr. Brooks came flooding back and bounced the logic from his brain. Three-years-ago he was still a gullible child, upset after losing his father. He'd wanted to believe time travel would find him. And his first lessons in meditation came exactly at the time Bash's first lavender crop was harvested. Even Bash admitted she found it intoxicating.

"I was barely thirteen," Kit shouted, startling Pigeon, drowsing in his cage.

"Where did *that* come from?" Dr. Brooks said, entering the room, triumphantly carrying a cake platter aloft. Kit, his serious apprentice, was not usually subject to emotional outbursts.

XI

PHILOSOPHY 101

Kit cornered Brooks in the passage. "Can I stay and have a private word after this charade is over?"

"A heart to heart? You look like you could use one."

"I'm beginning to unravel."

"Beginning? My dear boy, you're a mass of nerves."

"Okay, I've been falling apart ever since I followed Anna to the freaking ends of the earth!"

"But have you figured out what's *really* bothering you?"

"Yes, Dr. Freud, I have. It's the flipping chair!"

Brooks steered Kit towards the kitchen. "Keep me company while I tidy up. I've got to unload the dishwasher. Just take a seat and cool off. We can chat."

"The last flaming thing I want is to take a *seat*. I can't sit still."

"Right then, put on a pan of milk for cocoa."

"You said the throne would help me relax. You said I'd find my way. But meditation is rubbish. I get so wound up I even scare Taraq. He thinks I'm going to throw the thing out the window."

Brooks peered around to read his apprentice's body language. "Look, if you don't want it."

"No worries. I would never do such a thing. It's beautiful but it's, for want of a better word… dead."

"Keep stirring that milk. It's mesmerizing in a good way. Breathe the steam, watch it swirl clockwise for a bit and then reverse and stir it backwards. That split second, when the momentum changes, is neutral. Time ceases to matter… literally. It's the Zen of milk. Aim for feeling like that. You're running north and south. Change directions and listen. Watch yourself arriving."

"So now boiling milk is meditation practice."

"It is. Grooming Jack, is. Washing dishes, is. Mowing grass, is. If you let it, the chair will be your guide. It will support you. It literally has your back. Surrender your fears. I know you despise the concept of alchemy, but when you float in a river of churning thoughts, mediation transmutes them into a still pool. Leaden thoughts turn into gold."

For a moment it looked as if Kit had swallowed Brook's poetic philosophy, but his gaze wandered past his teacher to settle on a persistent memory. *The winter of death is coming and I'm powerless to stop it.*

Brooks touched Kit's shoulder and he startled with a look of surprise. His teacher seemed to be speaking without moving his mouth. *"What?"* Kit swallowed audibly and refocused. "Taraq is all freaked out about some buzzing we heard," he said without hesitation. "It seems out of order to me, that a ghost can be afraid of something."

"Taraq is young but he isn't flighty. He's devoted to his old life. That throne represents a great deal to him. He was a servant, remember." The level of the milk rose dangerously close to overflowing. "Watch it. That milk's going to boil over."

Kit removed the saucepan from the heat just in time to see it froth and subside. "He heard me threaten to chuck it, that's all. He has no concept of English humor."

"You ought to know," Brooks said.

Kit banged the pan down hard so milk slopped onto the counter. "You wouldn't be so flip if you'd seen what I did. It was awful. Imagine the sight of Anna near death, clutching a teddy bear. Well, almost a teddy bear. It was a rabbit doll. And almost-dead is just as final when you can't *do* anything, and then you find out she's dying because *you* left her. And by 'you' I mean me, obviously. Even if it's a fantasy brought on by that purple menace Bash calls a lavender crop, it's a hell of a thing."

"You're trying too hard. Relaxation is letting go."

Tut's earlier expression jeered at him. "Yeah, so Tut said." The sulkiness of a whiny little kid in his voice was embarrassing. *Control the milk. Stir both ways. Froth and subside…froth and subside.*

"You can't force slowing down the mind. But keep going. You're onto something. Follow it back. Remember not too long ago when you were a tyke, visiting the Hall? You used to find your way out of the maze, blindfolded, for fun. Accept what's going on and..."

"Look, I know it's your profession, but you can't analyze me out of this."

Brooks led Kit to a kitchen chair, recently vacated by Anna and pushed him down. "I'm not supposed to. That's not how psychotherapy works. My function is to be a mirror. *Your* mirror. I've explained that many times. And it's not a job; it's a responsibility. I need hardly explain it's what your grandmother wants. And she's a force to be reckoned with. Right?"

Brooks poured scalding milk over a paste of powdered cocoa and sugar. For a while he followed his own advice and stared into the vortex of swirling liquid as he stirred.

Kit put his head in his hands. "I'm doomed. This summer will never end. I'll die of sunstroke or heatstroke or a plain everyday stroke. I'm that stressed."

Brooks pursed his lips. "You're being melodramatic."

"That's a bit rich, isn't it, considering this village and the Hall has diligently served and been served by the movie fantasy industry for the last three years?"

"I guess you learned a few tricks, then."

"Not enough, apparently."

"Look kiddo, Dynasty Films saved Bede Hall's bacon… at least for a while. They'll be back when this ridiculous summer moves on. You told me yourself that the planet's weather is haywire. *That's* not an illusion, is it? It's global warming. Nothing to do with lavender."

"What do I know. Maybe I was wrong. I'm clearly not cut out for science. In case you hadn't noticed, I'm a smartass geek. Just ask Bash."

The pressure of denying his future consumed Kit with anger. "All I ever wanted was to be a scientist who discovered great things."

There followed the clattering of clean plates and cake tins being returned to their shelves.

"Excuse my ignorance," Brooks said, tugging his ear, "but isn't being a time traveller a pretty amazing opportunity to discover a serious strain of forgotten science? You know as well as anyone, recorded history is only five-thousand-years-old. A dozen civilizations could have come and gone before that without a trace. So, who's to say time travel wasn't the norm at one time, eh? And then, somehow you end up writing about it a few years from now, presumably with a positive take, to inspire a future generation of scientists. Now *that's* a future worth traveling for, isn't it?"

Kit blew on his cocoa and sipped it from a teaspoon. "I never thought about it that way."

"Not bad for a thousand-year's work in the blink of an eye. You'll be back in no time. Pun intended."

"That's a tad euphemistic, isn't it? Not to mention ironic. I go back to… what? some obscure 'when' and no time will have elapsed when I return? Now who's delusional."

"If it's all lavender fluff, then you'll have had a nice psychedelic trip. I believe I mentioned those."

"You did, but you forget. You also told me about a few *bad* trips."

"You can't have one without the other. That's life being life. Besides, even a bad trip is fuel for those books you're going to write."

Kit scraped the chair back from the table. "You had to remind me about *that*." He sneered at the chair he'd vacated. No more sitting. He abandoned the spoon, cocoa, and chair, and paced the room.

He came to rest against a tiled wall and leaned against it, his eyes burning a hole into the floor.

Brooks stared unfocused over his cocoa. "You could do worse things," he said causally with raised eyebrows.

"Yeah. I could dive into the portal again."

"Look," Brooks said. "Consider this, if you're wrong, the time portal is only a necessary experiment. Lad, you have… *may* have, the ability to change the present, and the repercussions of that are infinite. By changing what was, by putting things to rights, just maybe the ripple effect…"

"Is what? Actually worse?"

A floorboard squeaked as Kit, pumped up with indignance, shifted his weight against the wall. "Time shouldn't be meddled with. This place should be destroyed. Okay, maybe not destroyed, but purged. I should just shovel Bash's death and all that snow out of my mind, right?"

"That's an awful lot of shoulds."

Kit shrugged. "As many as it takes."

"And, here's one more," Brooks said. "You should stop hypothesizing. If you truly want a career in science, stop speculating. Take it from a psychiatrist, cogitation is overrated and surmising is just bad science. Second-guessing is futile."

Kit looked skeptical but he wanted to believe his mentor. "Spoken like a true Borg."

"Conjecture is a dead end. Scuze my bad joke, kiddo. Get some sleep. Sit in the chair for an hour, take a deep breath of lavender, and call me in the morning."

"Great, I'll be assimilated."

"Kit, my boy, you were assimilated the first day you set foot here."

"I remember. It was right here in this house. You…"

"No," Brooks interrupted, patting Kit on the back. "It was on the driveway of Bede Hall."

Kit repressed a smile at the memory. "If I may, I'd like to reopen the discussion about inanimate objects with unlikely powers," Kit began.

"Say a certain chair? I mean you studied philosophy, so, when *is* a chair more than a chair? Bash says it's existential, whatever that is."

"Chair philosophy ends in a kafuffle of thoughts. Why go there?"

"Well maybe if your blessed meditation chair *had* relaxed me, I wouldn't need to ask."

"That old chestnut. Look. All chairs are *not* created equal."

"I beg to differ. They're all made for seating. Anything more is all in the mind of the sitter. Uncle Ben's chair was supposed to be *more* than a chair. And like a muggins, I believed you."

Brooks wiped down the kitchen counter, folded the wet cloth neatly, and hung it over the faucet before stretching his back. "Ever heard of the placebo effect?"

"Yes. It's a medicinal lie told to unsuspecting guinea pigs, a.k.a. mugginses. Case in point, a messed-up kid given instructions to meditate in a chair with healing 'vibes'. I believe that's the word you used."

Brooks placed a hand on Kit's shoulder and left it there. "You know son, skepticism is a fine thing in a scientist but cynicism is an enquiring mind gone too far."

"So… about Great Uncle Ben's inanimate old chair."

"Are you sure it's inanimate?"

Kit nailed Brooks with a vicious look of contempt. "It's a CHAIR!"

"What about a building?"

"Don't be cagey. You mean Bede Hall."

"How do you explain that it wanted to watch television?"

"*Hmmn*. Let's see. I can, in one word… Anna. SHE wanted to watch television."

"And how do you explain Anna?"

Kit's face crumpled. His back slid down the wall as if he was slowly deflating until he sat like a human puddle on the floor. His voice came muffled from between his knees. It was no longer angry. It came like the wail of an injured animal. "It's not my job to explain Anna. I'm just a kid. Nobody ever thinks of that. Doc, I'm only a kid!"

XII

A FURY OF WASPS

PANGEA – PLANET EARTH
175 million-years-ago
The FIRST AGE of GEMINI – THE TWINS

The feathery ghost of a full moon hung over the pyramid of Bede on a ceiling of blue daylight – a paper-thin peppermint disk almost completely dissolved on the sun's tongue. Aligned to the nearby circle of obelisks, it rested on the fingertip of the central monolith. And for a single heartbeat, time ceased to be.

Meanwhile, the planet Mars minded its own business and pulsated silently, a beating heart in space. Under the cover of earth's spring equinox, it breathed in and out without detection.

In its decaying outbreath, gravity compressed its equator, distorting its shape into a slightly elongated sphere. It was at this point that it held its breath for a frantic day and night – a red wasps' nest hanging in the cosmic blackness of time. And after it settled into a rarified atmosphere of discontent, it inhaled.

The most powerful Starscopes on earth missed the display of red sparks orbiting Mars in concentric rings. Oracles appeared reluctant to translate their divinations as significant portents that boded ill. Scientists barely detected a minor surge of energy that nudged their world off-centre and duly noted a slight polarity shift but they failed to predict the clusters of baby earthquakes that plagued the region under showers of falling stars. Nor did they map the newly created fault lines that crisscrossed the coastal provinces in patterns like the running cracks on an icy pond.

So, when the population awoke to an overwhelming buzzing of wasps, it came as a surprise.

Astrologers frantically cast new charts. But astronomers never observed the rings of Mars dissipate and swarm into a ball that collided with the surface in an explosion of disturbed lava. In hindsight, only one shaman, deep in a dream-quest, witnessed the impact that resembled a giant drop of blood splashing upwards into a liquid crown, and saw it collapse into the rim of a living crater.

Blood spatters of molten rock flecked the exposed left cheek of the ancient stone face emerging from the windswept Martian plain. It stared blindly into the past as a fury of powdered rock rolled towards it across the Desert of Tranquility. The incensed wall hissed to a stop, rose into a column, and inspected the icon, respectfully circling the monument in a mounting vortex of veneration before it swirled into its ears and nostrils and polished its mouth with scorching sand.

A flow of liquid glass circled the empty eye socket like a drain, willingly sucked into an agitated caldera of hate. As the shockwaves subsided, a low-density pall settled over the scene, covering the face in a shroud of red dust for a Martian winter that lasted twelve-thousand-five-hundred years.

And while earth's epochs rose and fell according to their season, the landmass of Pangea divided and fragmented into the submerging continents of Gondwana, Avalonea, and Laurasia, like the abandoned pieces of a discarded puzzle. And a far-distant pit of red demons on Mars simmered in hibernation, seething under a banked fire of stinging sand.

Only a single magus in the province of Bedea assembled a gathering of 'The Nine' – the sages of each territory, to deliver a prophecy of far reaching certitude. And then, after a stroll in the exotic Gardens of Artifice, Goswold Mundi had the presence of mind to place the prophetic scroll in the capstone of the Bede pyramid.

PROPHECIES UNDER GLASS

BEDE HALL – the SUMMER of 1940

Nine-year-old Beryl, the future Lady Nan, spent her first precious hour in the library, poring over the three-foot-high globe, tracing the contours of the continents, mentally piecing the ragged shapes together like a puzzle. But the best globe she had was hers alone, small enough to hold in her hands, made of glass, and it was full of pretend snow.

Everything in the room seemed designed for a giant. Armchairs were big enough for two, and the family's ancient dictionary took both hands to turn the pages. It stood chained to a pedestal as if it might fly away. She pulled down a smaller version from the shelves and curled up to read as if it was a story. Words contained stories. Some were born from foreign tongues and had burrowed their way into the English language over time. Every morning she chose one word at random and used it as many times as she could during the day. This quirk meant she was ignored a great deal of the time. It was one of Miss Beryl's games, they said, and went on about their business, but Beryl delighted in being a 'seen and not heard' child.

There was a lot of busy-ness in Bede Hall, and for that Beryl was thankful. Her library hours were never idle but the days were lonely. With her twin brother Ben away at real school, her governess, Miss

Prentice, had put aside academics and resorted to lessons 'more suitable for a young lady', assigning her time to read and draw and sew.

Geography was best self-taught anyway. The library's many atlases meant traveling to other countries in the comfort of a deep velvet armchair where tea, cucumber sandwiches, cake, and an extra saucer for cream, was served precisely at four o'clock.

The chair was the best place for a catnap. Big enough for two. Big enough for a girl and a cat named Unicorn to travel to Africa and back before teatime.

Beryl escaped to the library whenever she could. Today her mother and father were nowhere in evidence. Their car had made that lovely crunching sound on the drive as it drove away. Lovely because it meant she had the Hall to herself. Lovely because she could gaze into her snow globe without being reprimanded for lollygagging. A crime for which she was particularly known.

The clock struck three times. Unicorn stirred from washing his face and patted Beryl's arm. It was his job to alert Beryl to the impatient snow globe, now emitting gold sparks in a beautiful halo. It was time to go. She had a whole hour to travel before one of the housemaids brought tea on a silver tray with legs.

The wind changed direction, and the scent of Bede's lavender crop breezed in from the open window bringing in a stray honeybee. To Unicorn's amusement, it alighted on the snow globe, dared him to play, and buzzed to the top of a tall shelf. He nattered a half-hearted meow and returned to washing his face. Small flying creatures were plentiful, always distracting, and he'd learned that some wings were less friendly than others. Best to ignore the lot of them and concentrate on the extra saucer and the cream Beryl took in her tea.

Beryl closed her eyes and took a deep breath of the fresh lavender sprig pinned to her dress that Parks had given her that morning, and closed her eyes.

When she was ready, she turned the globe upside-down to make it snow. Slowly, she opened her eyes and peered in. Strangely, her breath fogged the glass as if it was truly a winter's day inside and she had to wipe a small window to see in.

But what she saw was amazing. She was no longer outside looking in. She was inside the globe looking out at the library, and Unicorn was batting the glass with a paw the size of a car. She heard his muffled cries and tapped her fingers on the glass. "It's all right, I'll be out soon."

Moments later, after she returned to the chair, an apology was in order. "Sorry Corny, it's this chair. It has a mind of its own. And it's nearly teatime."

The bee buzzed frantically about the room in a frenzy to escape, and Unicorn growled. "It's okay Corny, it's only a bumblebee." But it wasn't a bee, it was a wasp. Unicorn arched his back and hissed until it soared out the window.

Beryl watched the snow inside the globe turn to rain. Torrential rains soaked a verdant earth over a miniature Hadrian's Wall until the light from the desk lamp broke through the gloom and the gentle droning of bees and birdsong filled the library. Rain splashed off Hadrian's Wall and Beryl imagined herself flying over Bede Hall. Below her rested the lake where she visited the mermaids, and the manicured gardens with the maze and her topiary friends. She spiralled into the centre of the maze, her special hiding place. Something new was there. A small statue of a unicorn with a plaque. But she was too high up to read the words.

She burst out the entrance into a sunlight reflecting off a dripping topiary sphinx, she hadn't seen before. It turned to watch as she circled past. Tiny rainbows flashed inside the prism-like droplets. A white kitten slept between his paws. Even the garden looked different. "Take me to my own time," she whispered. These future glimpses were sometimes uncomfortable no matter how often they happened.

Once she was assured of being home, Beryl took a turn around the Saxon tower. She swooped across to the Hall, covered in ivy wriggling over the red brick walls where the movement of a curtain in an attic window several floors above momentarily distracted her. A girl's sad face appeared behind the curtain and a hand waved, but was withdrawn quickly. The curtain fell back into place, undisturbed. No-one ever left the attic windows open. The housemaids who slept there were too busy to stare out of windows. She wasn't allowed up there.

The ivy surrounding the window turned white with frost and it began to snow.

And as it did, the snow inside the globe stopped fluttering. Bede disappeared and rain fell on a large sphinx. But it never rained like that in Egypt.

Beryl ran to the window where snow had collected on the sill. A bee floundered on its side, making a circular clearing in the frost where blue paint showed through. The library windows were never blue. They were never wood either. This was a different window. Peering out, she made out the library window far below her with its mullioned glass and stone sill.

She closed her eyes and wished herself into the garden where snow dusted the sun dial and a patch of tall yellow sunflowers she hadn't seen before. Parks promised he would surprise her. As she watched, the head of one sunflower slowly crystallized into ice.

Beryl took a deep breath, and landed back in the library, staring at a glass paperweight. The sunflower was trapped inside, frozen into glass ice that held down the edges of an open map of Bede on her father's great desk.

A faint voice called out from far away. "Rain, where are you?"

It was the girl who everyone referred to as her imaginary friend. A ghost her own age, named Snow who had given her the pet name, Rain.

Beryl's hands still held the snow globe, but they were the hands of an old lady.

Lady Nan answered shakily. "I'm just reading." Beryl, at seventy-six, recognized her own voice, enfeebled with age. "I'm nearly done, luvvy. Wait there," she called back. "I'll be up in a minute." ...or did she mean next August?

XIV

ALIVE-ALIVE-O'

DECEMBER 12

Kit stared at his stark admission glaring from a fresh page of his science log under the heading December 12, 2016. *I believe in ghosts.* Seven stinging words followed. *I'm just not cut out for romance.* Cleaning up one's 'affairs' was nasty business. More cleaning would have to follow if he was going to set himself free. Six more words: *Running away is the only solution.* Eight words: *But at least, I'll be thorough about it.* More deep thinking. Seven words: *Someone's bound to ask questions in the…* his pencil paused. Short bursts of self-incrimination wanted to be recorded. One last word. He pressed the pencil harder into the paper and scribbled the word *'future'*. He stared at it a long time before adding an exclamation mark. He stabbed the dot underneath it savagely, until the lead snapped. He grabbed a pen and wrote *I do <u>not</u> believe in prophecies* in black ink. He paused as a dust mote burst into white flame and disappeared. Had he seen it? Two words of finality had to be said: *or fairies.* Take *that* Tinkerbell!

After he retrieved his notebook flung to the other side of the room, Kit turned to a blank page and inhaled a deep breath. *I have to leave this paper trail. Even though it's unlikely that anyone will be able to find what's left of me. The scary thing is, maybe there will be no-one left to look.*

He tried to force a clever Dickensian first line of his memoir but soon abandoned it in favour of the plain facts as incredulous as they seemed when captured in black ink. And then his words wrote themselves and wouldn't stop.

THE BEDE CHRONICLES
by Christopher Carter Stratford-Smyth
DECEMBER 12, 2016 – Bede Hall

I've made several attempts at documenting the happenings at Bede Hall. Today is a new page and a new start, writing from scratch because today things seem clearer.

The other day I was lax. I ignored the sun, and the sun never lies. Earth is in for a doing, but even that is eclipsed, pardon the pun, by the astounding events from famine to feast in 2014, and then, during this year's autumnal equinox, the weather stood still and the sundial sealed winter in a narrow wedge of icy mauve shadow.

Time and the movie biz moved on to greener pastures, and by that I mean white, in order to shoot their season finale requiring snow and icicles dripping from skeletal trees.

A deluge followed by a blistering drought left everything green in a spectacular reversal of photosynthesis that effectively drowned our chances for financial survival. Meanwhile, Bede bakes in a rogue December heatwave, in a state of stasis, heading towards the greenest Christmas on record.

The chance of a summer shoot waits in the wings unless a perverse spring decides to blanket us in frosty red leaves.

I may have more than a slight case of sunstroke. I may have fallen victim to the hallucinogens. There are hundreds of exotic botanicals thriving out of control in Bede Hall's gardens and greenhouses. Or, I may have simply lost my mind.

Bash, Tut, and me formed a team with Dr. Peregrine Brooks (a psychiatrist friend of my grandmother's), Charlotte Findhorn (a local herbalist), and my grandmother. The thing is, my grandmother Lady Nan was deceased at the time. As was her brother Ben, our gardener Parks, and a pair of unlikely children who joined us. There are times I think I may have died as well.

There are ten of us in all. We called ourselves the Twinters – a jazzy name, less flippant than it sounds, that connects the words twin and winter. But now it doesn't matter. If we'd had badges made, I would willingly hand mine in.

But I've leaped ahead into quantum Bede. The walls of the Hall not only have ears; they have mouths. Mouths with voices attached to a mind, and the sentient willpower to dwarf the notions of all the Leonardo da Vincis, Sir Isaac Newtons, and Albert Einsteins rolled into one.

I do not make the following claims lightly because logically, they can't be true:

BEDE HALL HAS A MIND OF ITS OWN. BEDE HALL IS ALIVE. BUT ALL IS NOT WELL.

That said, I ask you to proceed as if they *are* true or nothing will make sense. Stated simply, Bede Hall literally ran its own show for a while because that's what the estate became – a lucrative cornerstone of British show business. It was hired out as a movie set to a particular television series, 'The Curse of Pryde', that mirrored our real lives in parallels too precise to be entirely coincidental. Their addition of fanciful time portals were beyond uncanny.

The screenwriters of Dynasty Films, a subsidiary of Hollyworks Productions, were briefed on our family's historic links to ancient Egypt by Edgar Tweedy (a school chum if you ignore the chum part). As a result, they thinly disguised our private secrets into a runaway theme of heroic adventures. We were a perfect match until the writers seized upon the local rumours of hidden treasure in Bede Hall, and fanned a frenzy for pharaoh's gold into a solid storyline.

To sum up: in 2014, the Hall's chances for continued existence were initially sabotaged by a local realtor with big ideas, and then by his son, Edgar. It didn't help that Bash and I made Edgar look like a fool. I guess, in the end, revenge was inevitable.

The syndicate of developers still lay in waiting. It covets Bede Hall more than ever, since its worth has trebled. But then, so have our financial woes. According to Lady Nan, the Hall says it can feel the developers breathing down its neck. She acts as the Hall's ethereal translator, and likes to remind us, with her philosophical resolve, that 'fortune is as fortune does'. Ours are mercurial… business turned out to be as changeable as the weather. No winter equalled no movie business equalled no income.

And Bash was right. My dilemma is personal: there ARE time portals in Bede Hall, it still refuses to be sold without a fight, and I've been volunteered as one of its warriors. Commandeered is more accurate.

My given mission is as incredulous as it is foolhardy. And if Charlotte is to believed, pixie dust is also involved. I've been coerced, prompted to do the right thing, and bullied, and by that, I mean bamboozled.

I am outnumbered but I still refuse to be canon fodder in a supernatural war with a building as my commanding officer.

That said, if I *am* to be a warrior, then it's to personally survive an internal battle of doubt. If only logic was an effective weapon. Science at fifty paces suits me.

There are days I doubt my sanity.

If it's possible to believe and disbelieve at the same time, then that's my present state of mind. I may be writing this in a dream within a dream. A dream brought on by the close proximity to hallucinogenic plants. Bash and I will be sixteen in April, and, dashing as it may look according to my sister's friends, my prematurely grey hair is a result of constant stress distilling the natural from the supernatural.

In a NUTshell (as in crazy) Bash has surrendered and I resist. There were days, when the film crew were here, that I snuck a copy of the latest television script to stay ahead of the truth. Because that's what life in Bede turned out to be… a wild fantasy fanned by gossip and lies. The developers who were left in the dust remain far from harmless. Edgar Tweedy made sure of that. More of him later.

The 'Curse of Pryde' enjoyed unprecedented success. It seemed as if, on a financial basis, Bede Hall's ship had come in. My older brother, Rupert had found his true vocation, sucking up to celebrities; my father, missing on an archaeological dig in Egypt and believed dead for over a year, came home, no worse for wear; and Taraq, who we affectionately nicknamed Tut, the Egyptian boy who saved his life, was welcomed into our family.

For a while, the seamless addition of a new brother meant Bash, Tut, and me, essentially became triplets. I used to think he was the only person on my side. It's hard to tell, every day he's becoming more Bede-ified.

We had another Taraq living with us at the time. I say living, but he's a ghost. Taraq, the wandering ghost of an Egyptian slave, was already in residence when the living Taraq arrived. Two Taraqs in one house was confusing, even if only one of them was visible to my parents, so he had to be given a new name. Tut seemed appropriate and in keeping with our own abbreviated nicknames. Mom and Dad still have no inkling of any ghostly presences. So far, so good. But I use the word good, loosely. I think the situation may be worse than I originally thought.

Our grieving family had been recalled (summoned, actually) from boring suburbia in the south, to do its bidding, and now we're firmly established in the haunting countryside that boasts direct links to the enchanted isle of Lindesfarne and local folklore steeped in superstition, old wives' tales, and old fashioned traditions.

We're here, roots and all, for good or ill, readily and grudgingly drawn into a cause larger than life. I say 'we' but as for the supernatural goings on, my parents and older brother are as in the dark as Bede Hall when the electrics go wonky – a regular occurrence that unfolds like clockwork. I'm sure for equally dark reasons.

Bede Hall saved us from living on the street after my father was declared missing on a dig and believed dead. We, in turn saved the Hall from demolition because, as ridiculous as it sounds, it liked to watch T.V. The full truth is, Bede Hall liked to watch TV with Lady Nan, Bash, and Anna (the Hall's resident child-ghost and Lady Nan's invisible childhood friend).

Together, they hatched a creative plan to raise enough money to save it's walls and restore its dignity as a proud historical land-mark. But even a commercial operation with heart is a Band-Aid. Bede Hall gained some time, but its biggest fight, according to an ancient prophecy, is a future battle that requires its time portals to remain stable.

When we were children, Lady Nan would give her snow globe a shake and peer into the miniature blizzard for a new story, the way a seer uses a crystal ball. She enchanted us with her own versions of history.

She was our personal fairy-godmother and gypsy fortune teller rolled into one. The snow globe was often interchanged with an hourglass, a similar storytelling prop. Twin crystal balls. Sand and fake snow stood in nicely for hot and cold, entirely in keeping with the ancient Egyptian doctrines of duality and balance. I've studied these concepts in-depth to understand my dad's obsession with that time period.

Lady Nan once recited a poem entitled 'Antigonish' that terrified me but delighted Bash. I had so many nightmares that Lady Nan made a word-game out of it, adapting it for my sake. And in the end, it came true. A mini prophecy before the major one. No wonder prophecies freak me out.

It turns out, Lady Nan is even more unusual in death than she was in life – as ever, the annual Queen of the May, matriarch of the Stratford-Smyth family and devoted to Bede Hall that (or should I say 'who') overrules us all.

Our family crisis took a turn for the worse after Bash and I stumbled into the Winter Room's secrets, chasing down Bede Hall's shy ghost-child. One secret has been too uncomfortable for me to think about, let alone share. But here, I offer a brave assertion: Facts are facts until disproven.

Dr. Brooks became a much-needed father figure who brought balance into my life. He offered me an apprenticeship of sorts, and introduced me to the art of centring the mind. But it opened my heart like a door and invited me into the unexpected consequence of out-of-body experience. And now I believe I was unwittingly hoodwinked. Even if it was for the right reasons, he played me for a fool. He had me believing a chair could bring me peace of mind. Before I go. IF I go. I intend to make mincemeat of this notion.

Astral projection and extrasensory perception are subjects I'd previously sidestepped for lack of their ability to be measured. I'm still assessing the dimensions of accompanying space-time, obsessing and weighing the damages against the benefits. But exploring this phenomenon has gone terribly wrong.

Not exactly brainwashing but brain deception… spontaneous mind control… and by that, I mean OUT of control. Not even calculated substance abuse because the countryside around Bede is steeped in exotic plants. You might say it's a specialty of our eccentric head gardener. He's a ghost too. My theory is that we're all in the same lucid dream. What else does one call being ruled by hallucinations?

The crack in my theory is this: the actors who worked here and other visitors were never drawn into the dream. Why were they immune? Something set them apart. What?

If I go along with the mad consensus of time travel, it's not because I have to *know* the truth. I have to *change* the truth.

There are days I wish I'd remained in the dark. Reading that admission shocks me. It's nothing a scientist worth their salt should wish. But when a hidden door opens, the entrance remains known even after it closes.

I've learned that a door is more like a gate. One can see through the bars on the other side even when it's padlocked with a thousand keys. Science exists beyond the gates on either side of Bede Hall.

And now I'm ruined for an ordinary life. Not ordinary, exactly, but steady. The firmer ground of science is agitated into quicksand. And I'd always planned on being a scientist worth my salt. But science is still the magnet that pulls me into the mystery of Bede that lies hiding in the woodwork and the landscape and deep under the ground.

Ever since our family retreated here to wait out that cold father-less time, our lives have been turned inside out. I can no longer deny every strange thing I've seen but I can't admit I'm wrong. Hallucinations mean I can't rely on what I see. I have to appear to be in control. For this reason, I welcome Bash's romantic infatuation with Six. Distractions aside, faking willpower isn't easy when Bash can read my mind.

Bash often reminds me that the word myth is embedded in our family name, Stratford-Smyth. She asked me how I could be so utterly disenchanted by a landscape alive with myth-o-logical beings? My answer was a simple fundamental truth… the words myth and logical are as incompatible as oil and water.

And so, for most of our 15.999 years, Bash and I have ping-ponged our opposing points of view, all the time blindly devoted to each other. I once pitied any person who tried to come between us, but now, I have to admit, that person is me.

Our older, self-important brother, Rupert, had a go at us once-in-a-while, but even he had the smarts to back off when we confronted him together. But that was in the good old days when innocence was bliss, summer morphed into fall, and telepathy could be understood as a natural firing of neurons from a central matrix. Simple biology.

And now the two of us are three. Tut, the latest addition to the family, was adopted two-years-ago. He fits in. Parks says Bash and I are no longer double-trouble but a solid triple-threat to vanquish what's coming. He's referring to something relating to the Bede Prophecy… the Winter Prophecy. All I know, is that it's no small event. He's been waiting for it for hundreds of years, biding his time until the eleventh hour.

According to Charlotte, the town clock reads a few minutes to eleven… but no pressure. The days tick by with a mounting sense of dread on my part and excitement on Bash's to meet Pan, the legendary lord of the forests she swears is on his way. Did I mention she's a romantic?

Naturally, we keep Rupert and the parents in the dark. Rupert would go all high and mighty on us and create what he would call an intellectual review of the situation. Alternatively, it would not be entirely out of character for him to go to pieces and panic. No doubt, Mum and Dad would move us back to greater London if they knew how dangerous this place is.

I hope that Bash's specter of some omnipotent 'Green Man' will micromanage the business from afar because Rupert runs the whole shebang. He's not so much in charge as charging ahead for his own glory – one more future challenge to worry about. If the movie business fails to return, Bede Hall won't be able to financially support itself and the developer wolves will howl down the door which is a disaster of a different sort, and one with greater consequences.

Money from the business bought us time. And time is bankable here. If we're thrown out of Bede Hall, and I can't believe I'm writing this, there will be no access to the time portals and we may as well all invest in snow shoes and thermal underwear. In this spirit, one way or another, I intend to remove myself from the equation.

I've visited the bad news of the year 2020, a number ironically regarded as describing perfect vision. It's the direct opposite of today's heatwave. If what I saw through the time portal is true, an ice sheet will cover the earth in a few years unless a way is found to confound the law of geophysics. Again… no pressure.

According to Bash and her co-mentor (more like co-mental) Charlotte Findhorn, Parks anchors the sacred landscape of Bede and its latest hall against an event that's been hinted at but not fully explained. It seems a little farfetched, but I sense there's more than a 'Roman road' between ancient Egypt and the impending winter disaster.

It's not that I don't *want* to know. The truth is, in everyone's best interests, if I'm to save them, it's healthier *not* to know. And with even more irony, even as a seasoned time traveller, I can't turn back the clock and un-know something. Between then and now there's an ugly knot to untangle, and lucky me, I've been volunteered to unpick the ghastly ghostly thing.

All I know for sure, is that Parks may have never shirked his responsibilities, but I still can.

Kit stopped and drank an entire bottle of warm ginger-ale before scribbling:

BOTTOM LINE TIME

According to legend, I'm the designated time traveller and my twin sister Bash is an agent training to ground the earth's magnetic core. But for now, we're a couple of teenagers who, along with our adopted brother, and several ghosts, are a team meant to form a stable pyramid, waiting for higher instructions.

We're a bit like Lady Nan's snow globe – we hold the future in our hands… correction, the past holds it, which is why I intend to drop the ball.

Once it seemed that my sister and I made up one normal person between us. Being a practical boy-scientist I like to measure things. Being a romantic girl, Bash loves to dream things. And being identical twins, we share more than a birthday; we share each other's thoughts. But lately I'm happy to report that some of the terrible secrets I've discovered in Bede are mine alone.

Somehow, I've been able to block Bash when it suits me.

But here is the craziest part. The ghost of Anna is my future daughter who is only seven years younger than I am, and I know the exact day my sister is going to die.

I want to leave here and go home, but I *am* home.

'ANTIGONISH'
- William Hugh Mearns – 1899

Yesterday, upon the stair
I met a man who wasn't there
He wasn't there again today
I wish, I wish he'd go away...

When I came home last night at three
The man was waiting there for me
But when I looked around the hall
I couldn't see him there at all!

Go away, go away, don't come back any more!
Go away, go away, and please don't slam the door.

Last night I saw upon the stair
A little man who wasn't there
He wasn't there again today
Oh, how I wish he'd go away.

LADY NAN'S VERSION OF 'ANTIGONISH'

- based on the original by William Hugh Mearns – 1899

Yesterday, upon the stair
I met a girl who wasn't there
She wasn't there again today
I wish, I wish she'd come to stay...

When I came home last night at three
The girl was waiting there for me
But when I looked around the Hall
I couldn't see her there at all!

Stay, please stay, don't leave me any more!
Stay, please stay, and please don't slam the winter door.

Last night I saw upon the stair
A little girl who wasn't there
She wasn't there again today
Oh, how I wish she'd come to stay.

XV
NOBODY'S BUSINESS

THE BEDE CHRONICLES
by Christopher Carter Stratford-Smyth

2014 had been a year of upheaval, uncertainty, and terrifying loss, so when the movies showed up it was a welcome distraction. It was like having a permanent festival in our backyard.

Production crews set up camp in a portable sea of mobile trailers and tents. Movie stars and extras swanning about made life exciting. The manor gates had to hold back a throng of onlookers clamouring for a glimpse of the rich and famous. Inside the gates, catered food and camaraderie flourished. Bash learned some unsavoury new words, and, paradoxically, I became enthralled with special effects.

The reversal of deaths in the family ended the year on a bitter-sweet note. Tut increased the family by one. Dad returned to the land of the living and Lady Nan passed over the same threshold to a finer molecular state, absorbed into the walls of Bede Hall. Her continued presence maintains the family members at seven.

Bash says Lady Nan is a human bookmark, keeping her place at table, climbing the stairs to bed, and discussing the gardens with Parks. She patrols the thresholds with Anubis, her right-hand cat, and after they were reunited, she grew closer to her beloved brother, Ben.

The following year, Tut became quietly enamoured of Imogen Banks, a child star; and Rupert was transformed from a persnickety bully into a swaggeringly obnoxious one.

But, here it is, the tail end of 2016 and still the Hall instructs the Twinters to bide our time. Lady Nan translated: *'Bede Hall wants us to conserve our energy and above all, remain patient. Enjoy the calm while it lasts. There will be time enough to address our mission when a clear path asserts itself. The portals have a mind of their own. In the meantime, the training will continue at an even pace. But not to worry, the Hall assures me that everything is unfolding perfectly, according to a higher calendar.'* Then, as usual, she smiled sweetly and ordered the partaking of tea and cakes.

The Hall remains plagued by eternal summer. It seems we're always under the weather. It should be the apex of business as usual but the present heatwave anomaly put a halt to Dynasty Films production schedule. The television series 'The Curse of Pryde' is on forced hiatus. And we are on high alert to fight a new battle in an extremely old war. The truth is, it's our proud family that's under a curse.

Bede is the epicenter of weird. The extraordinary is commonplace in and around Bede Hall. The ordinary turns tail and runs. I envy them.

By Tut's first English Christmas, Bash and I had only begun to unravel an entire village of secrets kept hush-hush by a surprising network of eccentric locals, Parks calls 'the twice-borns.'

The Twinters felt obliged to investigate the outlandish discoveries I'd made when I'd been coerced into a time portal that links the Hall to Bede Village. Likely it connects to other parts of the world and time. Everyone but me is curious to find out.

I know three things for sure: one – the Hall says the solution to prevent or survive a future disaster lies in Egypt's ancient past; two – it's literally an earth-shattering event, and three – no way can anyone breathe a word of this to my parents.

At least four ghosts, one time-traveller, a quirky professor of psychiatry, and a singularly obstinate and possibly unhinged parrot named Pigeon that answers to any name beginning with P, comprise the original Twinters.

And Parks says the twice-borns will join us along with, and I can't believe I'm saying this, a colony of problematic fairies at the bottom of the garden, and a camouflage network of sentient animals that have been watching our backs since my sister and I came here as children.

I keep two crazy secrets locked in a box because some things one discovers at the business end of a time portal are best kept to themselves. But the strangest thing is, that by protecting the 'trio', I became the odd one out. It's a lonely business knowing terrible truths about the future.

The ghost 'traveller', Anna (the persistent child, once called Snow) still 'haunts' her old Winter Room under the eaves once a week, but she spends more time with Lady Nan in the old woman's bedroom, left intact after her death as an informal shrine. The two of them while away the hours discussing new plans to help the Twinters save the future.

Lady Nan is content to remain the figurehead matriarch, and Dr. Peregrine Brooks who still courts her, his childhood sweetheart, was the obvious choice of leader since he projects an aura of authority over the proceedings that, left to itself, all too often degrades into to a squabble of ideas where members are reduced to speculation and guesswork.

But Bede Hall and its appointed gardener, Parks, are the only ones with any authority. Even so, neither seem entirely sure how to proceed with the daunting superhuman task of stopping a volcano from erupting in the year 2020.

Charlotte Findhorn, Bash's second mentor, Parks' companion, and proprietor of the local florist shop, never fails to deliver Dr. Brooks' regular order of white carnations for Lady Nan on the first of every month. But then, 'passing on' at Bede doesn't necessarily mean *moving* on. It often meant *staying* on in a less solid form. Lady Nan is as present as she ever was to her chosen few, but invisible to anyone she deems too sensitive to accept her apparition.

Our family brought new life into the Hall after a bleak first winter. After we shook ourselves, we shook out dusty old curtains and bad vibes, and reopened bedrooms in the east wing with the option of moving upstairs. That said, Bash, Tut, and I have remained permanently 'grounded' on the main floor. I enjoy the freedom of my draughty tower but I also like having a comfy bedroom with carpets and a fireplace and electricity.

Tut's bedroom remains next to mine – an extension of a labyrinth of servant's halls no longer necessary for a small family forced to huddle in the far corners of a great mansion. And given the squeaky nature of Bede Hall's staircases it's also easier to sneak out to the midnight Twinter meetings in the tower.

Bash chooses to stay close to her beloved plants, so her bedroom opens onto a garden via French doors. Being a 'green thumb' she feels happiest close to growing things. Nature is invited in whenever weather permits. Flowered wallpaper and chintz armchairs give the impression of sleeping in, what Bash calls, her bower. A grass-coloured carpet makes a seamless path into the great outdoors to a patio under a vine-covered lattice roof that she insists everyone calls a loggia. *Her* loggia to be exact.

Torrential rains drowned the beginning of the third season of Bede Hall's new business, hired out as a movie set. The sickly drought that followed, may have put a permanent end to it. 2017 is shaping up to be a spectacular failure. No portals = no reversal of fortunes.

I cracked a joke once, that Bash was a 'budding' botanist and she in turn, kidded that I was a mad scientist who can barely match my socks when working on a new theory.

My new theory is this: all the green thumbs and matched blue socks from here to Timbuctoo pale by comparison to the pent up hostilities of warring factions poised on the edge of an angry volcano, several thousand years past its 'best by' date.

I reacted to the Bede Prophecy with defiance. It was all right for some. Apart from Lady Nan, I am the only one harbouring a ghastly premonition and Anna's true identity. I'd experienced the freezing wasteland of snow that covered my shrouded body and Bede Hall clear up to its eaves. But that was the future. Perhaps I will discover some scientific answers so it will never happen.

Drinking a bottomless sea of tea, and biding one's time polishing off an endless supply of cream cakes inside an hourglass where the sand has slowed to a trickle of grains, are non-essential activities. All I want to do is to sprint away to someplace where life is normal. Normal in that the future is a relatively safe place for exciting teenage plans and dreams.

XVI

WHEN CATS FLY

DECEMBER 13, 2016

Bede Hall gathered its troops in the ways only a sentient building could – using stealth and trickery and calling in favours handed out long ago against a history of siege and treachery.

The previous three years, fraught with bizarre discoveries, required increasing secrecy. Not only was Bede Hall the centre of extraordinary paranormal activity, but the battle foretold in the Bede Prophecy's, looming earlier than expected, threatened to destroy the time portals.

All the while, the fuse of the planet's impending catastrophe had barely three years to burn while earth's volcanic energy brewed a dirty spell within the Yellowstone caldera.

The Twinters faced an idyllic future, if one could call saving the planet a casual responsibility.

"It's always a matter of time," the Hall imparted casually to its head feline guard, Anubis – a black cat named after the quintessential canine Egyptian Jackal god. "Some things never change. The greatest battles are forever won and lost at the same time."

"I can smell them. This is the year they arrive, isn't it?" Anubis said. *"Some of the trickster fairies are rallying. I think Lady Nan's 'wordsmith rules' are correct: listen for the subtle similarities in*

pronunciation, follow a pun into a labyrinth of meaning, be aware of 'a war of' shared letters, change one or two letters in a word, and it reveals all. She calls the rogue fairies 'furies' – once friends now fiends, she says. And don't get her started on anagrams."

The Hall rattled its windows in a bad temper. "Trust Lady Nan to know." It chuckled. "She's always spelling and *spell-ing* if you understand the twin meaning. She rarely misses a trick, although I've kept her in the dark about a few things. She'll know soon enough. This is the chance we've been waiting eons for. We must have a victory. I only wish we'd had more time to train the twins. Neither of them is completely ready."

Anubis yawned, circled into a sleeping position and dropped gracefully. *"Tut's a good lad. His street smarts may be the example Kit and Bash need to grow up fast."*

"That's what Charlotte says. We'll see."

"We'll see what the cat drags in."

"Case in point my dear Watson: feline wisdom and lifelines reflect the ankh of life and the essence of feline. Pray notice the words life and feline woven together to prove the point. The arc of life. Kitty literacy, if you will. Kitty <u>litter</u>-acy. The art of reading kitty litter. Litter being the sands of time. Yes, yes, you needn't give me that look. Littermancy is a real thing. Not an art humans gravitate to or find appealing. But there it is. Laid out so to speak, for all to see."

"And don't forget canine. The rule of nine… 'Can nine?' The question begs to be answered." Anubis lifted his head and sniffed the putrid air with disdain. *"They always smell like a building after a fire or worse. Most unpleasant. Even more ghastly than that dreadful will-o'-the-wisp stuff."*

Bede Hall's voice changed to one of authority. "Will you 'go back' if necessary? If I command you?" If I ask you as an old friend?"

"If given a choice, I'd just as soon 'fly in the air', thanks all the same. Entombed or 'En-timed', it doesn't make much difference. They're both nasty. But you are my master, and I will obey."

XVII

ANOTHER TRICK IN THE WALL

Hadrian's Wall paled in comparison to the one Kit built around himself. The one that guilt built – a project as massive as the construction of the great pyramid.

Banks of wild thistles held the roman wall upright. A dozen species of moss growing between the stones held it together. It was an appropriate setting for a stony goodbye.

The term divide and conquer had inspired him but standing there with Lily's doe eyes brimming with tears, he felt far from victorious.

Lily reached for his hand and he pulled away as if burned.

"It's best I go. I am sorry if… if I…"

Lily interrupted to save face. "I know you're only being cruel to be kind… but I'd rather be on my way than hear excuses and reasons. Besides, I can't tell the difference anymore."

Kit distanced himself from the sweetest girl he knew. He had carried an increasingly bright torch for Lily Butterfield for over a year but recently stopped making eye contact with her. Wild notions of running away to sea consumed him. Logic dictated that a clean break was infinitely better than a game of starry-eyed passion that could blossom out of control.

The possibility of any romantic attachment rang alarm bells. To be safe, Kit gave the frosty treatment to every teenage girl who crossed his path. Other than his sister, he remained unapproachable. He retreated into his tower, away from giggles and flirtations.

Becoming known as a science snob served him. It gave him an edge – time to incubate a sincere curiosity of the supernatural. And that curiosity was the only thing, apart from phantoms of nagging guilt, that kept him from running away.

On the surface, he acted belligerent, and he was genuinely hostile from feeling manipulated, but the scientist in him survived to fight, and a game of 'pride and seek' resulted that caused him to deceive his sister.

Bash believed Kit's act, which was strange because normally she could read his thoughts.

It hurt Kit that his own twin came to regard him as insensitive and selfish. It was as if he'd become two people in a Jekyll and Hyde performance that often fooled himself.

He convinced himself he was only being cruel to be kind. Perhaps, after all, it had been one of Bede's fairies who had covered him in a flimsy glamour that Bash couldn't see.

He told Bash he couldn't see the fairies, when he could. He heard them as well. They knew and kept his secret which is why he never trusted them. Some of them were deceitful little muckrakers. They all looked sweet, and annoyingly most of them giggled, but some sniggered. The cats swatted the ones that made rude noises.

Fairies were a symptom of an unsound mind. Seeing them was dangerous. None of them could be trusted. He raised his toothbrush and sniffed. *Even this toothpaste is organic.* Mr. Leoni, the chemist, and Charlotte made it using Bede-grown mint.

"I mean," Kit reasoned, talking to his reflection in the bathroom mirror, "I've been exposed. So, how can I tell if I'm under the influence of botanicals?" He paused brushing. "My senses are compromised. Logic dictates I'm too far gone, mired in Bedian physics where a building has me doubting my own sanity. Therefore, it's impossible for me to discern the difference between the science of horticulture and magic tricks. The only possible way is to get out of here. I need distance. But where?"

He looked like a stranger in the steamy mirror. Someone entirely bereft. His mouth stung from the peppermint toothpaste under his tongue. Toothpaste infected with lavender. He spat out the offending froth and watched it swirl down the drain. He flushed the last of it with a fast stream from the hot water tap and continued to rinse his mouth with handfuls of hot water and then his face with more frantic splashing. When the water ran too hot for comfort, he soaked a face-cloth, ignored the pain as he wrung it dry, applied it to his face, and pretended to disappear. Escape. Time travel would at least get him out of here, even if it was in a mental institution. Perhaps that would be a blessing. He hid under another compress of hot terrycloth.

When he emerged, his reflection in the steamed mirror was as insubstantial as Taraq's when the boy was upset. "I'm upset too," Kit said.

"You can't stay here," the reflection replied. Kit's terrified expression stared back, daring him to take immediate action. "Run," his reflection said. "Get out. Go to the police."

Kit buried his face in a dry towel and emerged with an even crazier thought. Tell Dad. Have him speak with Dr. Brooks. He wiped the mirror and faced the smeared distortion of his desperate lookalike. "Would that constitute betrayal or be the smartest thing you've ever done?" he said.

"You're talking to yourself again," the reflection said.

"Tosser," Kit said. "No returns."

Kit opened his bedroom window and leaned out, inhaling lungfuls of toxic Bede air. For once it smelled delightfully fragrant. "If you're listening," he said aloud to the horizon, "I'm not going to betray you. I may as well tell Pigeon as tell my parents for all the good it would do."

Down in the kitchen, a restless Pigeon gnawed the bars of his cage. He already knew and needed to warn Parks. *"Beryl!"* he shrieked. *"Here kitty kitty… nine lives… time for action… tick tock."*

For the second time that day, Kit retreated into a welcome fog of sanctuary. He relished the protective steaminess of the hot kitchen and the silent washing-up ritual after supper.

The ticking of the mantel clock seemed oppressively louder than usual. Bash washed while he and Tut took turns drying. Pigeon was reasonably subdued, nattering to himself, and Jack was spread flat under the table, chasing dream rabbits.

"It's coming pal, Kit said to Pigeon. "I think the Pidge is ready for his game."

"In a minute, Pollyanna," Bash said. "This water's too greasy. I'm making you new bubbles."

Pigeon rejoiced in one of his favourite P names. *"Polyanna… goody two shoes."*

Bash drained the sink and added a squirt of washing-up liquid under the tap.

"Goody goody," Pigeon cackled.

A few ghosts read by the fire and paid the living no mind. Luckily, Mrs. S couldn't sense them at all, which was good because one of them was her mother, the twins' grandmother, Lady Nan.

Taraq was at Lady Nan's knee, hearing 'Winnie the Pooh' for the first time. Anna, perpetually nine, stared out the window looking for her father, but she'd been doing that ever since Lady Nan was a girl.

The peace shattered when Tut left to put the bins out and Mrs. S retired to another room.

"Where did she go?" Bash asked. "Can she hear us?"

Kit ducked his head out the kitchen door. "It's kind of ironic. She's gone to the living room," he quipped.

Bash, spoiling to have a go at Kit all day, exploded like an old scold. "Christopher Carter Stratford-Smyth. You've been in a right old snit for ages, but ever since you dumped Lily Butterfield, you've outdone yourself!"

"I didn't *dump* Lily. She just wasn't the one. I saved her."

Bash smacked her forehead melodramatically, sending soap bubbles flying. "Of course! What was I thinking?"

Pigeon, a longtime bubble enthusiast, performed his happy dance when Bash dropped his regular blob of suds on his perch. *"Be nice you two,"* he squawked in Mrs. S's voice.

Kit gave Bash his most earnest look. "Well, I did."

"Hi. My name's Bash. I'm your telepathic twin. Have we met?"

"Have we met?" Pigeon cackled. *"Beryl!... where is that girl?... more and more."*

"Neither of us can afford to be distracted right now," Kit said. "Isn't daydreaming about Six irresponsible?"

Bash's eyes flashed. "That's *different*. Six and I have to *work* together!"

"Hi. My name's Kit. I'm your telepathic twin. Have we met?"

"Six is my friend."

"Distractions -- are -- futile," Kit replied, mimicking the expressionless voice of a drone.

Bash cocked her head sideways. "Observed with all the sensitivity of artificial intelligence. Are you going to stay semiconscious the rest of your life?"

"You mean the rest of my soon to be cut-off *short* life? Yes, I am."

She pushed a large china platter dripping with water at him. "If you're not careful you'll stay a sad lonely android-hybrid-thingy forever."

Anna drifted by and blew another handful of soap foam into Pigeon's cage.

He lifted one talon gingerly and touched it. *"Lonely forever,"* he crowed. *"Forever blowing bubbles."*

"I'm fairly sure that being an android is probably best when one's molecules are about to be zapped through time at the speed of light," Kit said. "Or haven't you thought about *that*?"

Bash flicked him with soap and water. "Look, I know you're terrified... *flick*... but I happen to think... *flick*... the more... *flick*...

human you are, the better you'll function as our… *flick*… go-to historian-mediator."

Pigeon flapped his wings in a frenzy. *"Bubble fight. More… more,"* he demanded and received a last generous dollop of white foam on his talons.

Kit flicked a wet tea towel at Bash's legs in a feeble attempt to deflect the formal lecture he sensed coming.

Nothing could stop her. "Our logistics of survival may well depend on super-scientific analysis," she ranted, "but it also hinges on crucial emotional timing. And I believe it was you who said the best scientists relied on dreams and intuition." She stood facing Kit, hands on hips. "Well?"

"Well, I guess I'll see you in my dreams, then," Kit replied.

Pigeon let out a shriek. *"Anna's dreaming… there there child, it's only a bad dream."*

XVIII

GHOSTS OF SUMMERS PAST

Bede Hall, Northumberland, England
DECEMBER 16, 2016

On the morning of December 16th, after watching the family eat breakfast, young Taraq and Anna huddled together a short way off composing a Christmas wish-list. The name Rain was at the top and circled three times in red ink for luck. As always, nine-year-old Anna made sure Kit was never out of sight. But Kit was determined to hold on to his sanity in spite of what he saw, solid as a brick wall, so he spoke over them as if they weren't there because, technically, they weren't.

Bash sat beside Kit on the lawn, her thoughts wide open. *Be nice to her,* she said.

Kit turned to glare at Anna, whose presence angered him although she'd done nothing to deserve it.

Anna smiled back wistfully in a way that made it difficult for Kit to breathe. "Some days are simply too hot for science-fiction," he announced. "That is my latest hypothesis. You can take it to the bank. The truth is, we live in a place where quantum physics can only dabble."

Bash tickled a ladybug with a blade of grass. "We've had to adjust. People do it, all the time."

"Right. Tut's lost his senses over a stupid teenage actress and you're over-the-moon all the time, drooling over Six."

Her answer nearly bowled Kit over. "*What part of 'Six and I are friends' don't you understand?* We have to *work* together."

"You never tire of saying how wonderful everything is," Kit replied. "I say, no way can this place be real. Sometimes I think you and I have been brainwashed. I mean, aren't we dreaming all this?"

"So what? We've always been able to share lucid dreams. What are you trying to say?"

"I'm saying, I want to wake up!"

Anna hugged her knees looking miserable.

"I'm real," Taraq said, "and so is Anna. What does quantum physics mean again?"

Kit gave a derisive chuckle. "You still don't get it, do you? You're a couple of GHOSTS. You're vapours. Insubstantial." He dismissed Anna and patted young Taraq on his shoulder, taking care not to swipe through the boy's body that looked solid but was more of a cloud that could change density at will.

Today, Taraq was almost transparent from shock which signalled he was either upset or confused. Anna's sad form flickered like a candle. The two of them held hands to ground themselves but it did little good.

Kit stifled any brewing remorse and brushed their feelings aside. "Just so you know, I'm not proud of my behaviour," he said to Bash, "I'd run away if I had somewhere to go. If I could change the past I would never have opened that damned door to the Winter Room because once something's happened the first time, that's it – for *all* time."

He shoved his hands into the pockets of his jeans and mumbled an excuse at the ground. "I know what I know." When he looked up he bumped into Bash's disapproving expression. "That is, I…"

Bash held up her hand to shush him. "No, no, stop. No explanations are necessary. Foretelling future details would disrespect the time portals. They're not meant to be used as a Magic Eight Ball."

"I wouldn't. I haven't. Give me *some* credit."

The ladybug launched itself with a whir and flew through Anna's forehead. "Fly away fly away fly away home," Anna said, blowing it a kiss.

"You're safe here, Anna," Bash said. "Make a wish."

Kit groaned. "And what good, pray tell, will *that* do?"

Bash scowled at Kit and sent him a telepathic message. *She adores you. Would it hurt you to be nice to her?"*

"She needs to grow up," he sent back.

Bash's thoughts rushed at her brother, making him dizzy. *"She can't grow up, as you well know."*

"Ladybugs are lucky," Bash said out loud for Anna's benefit. "That's one of the first things Parks taught me."

Kit tore a handful of grass and threw it at her. "Have we been hoodwinked by fairies, then? You're the one who sees them. Will we wake up and find five-hundred years have gone by? According to local folklore, that's what they do. Isn't it?"

Anna started to cry.

Bash hugged both children and glared at Kit over their heads. *"Monster."*

"By the way, where *do* fairies go in this heat?"

"One day you'll see them. Charlotte said so."

"Supertacular!" Kit checked his watch. "Gosh is that the time?" He nudged Jack, with his foot. A grey hairy rug moved in the grass. "Gotta go. I'm late. C'mon Jack."

Anna perked up and brushed invisible snow from her winter coat. "Can I come too?"

Bash's thoughts rattled inside Kit's head. *"It's her wish. Don't be a jerk,"* she said.

He countered with a private, *"I've got wishes too. And I wish I'd never met her."*

Kit spoke with his back to Anna. "Sorry, Anna. Not this time… Guy's stuff. Tut and I… we… well, I said I'd meet him."

Bash chastised Kit once more. *"Run away to your chair then."*

Anna broke away from Bash and pulled at Kit's sleeve. "I won't get in the way," she sniffled.

Kit turned away, refusing to make eye-contact with Anna who was fast evaporating. His sudden anger surprised him. "JACK… GET UP… NOW!"

Anna dematerialized completely and Taraq's form popped like a balloon.

"Nice work," Bash said.

That's when Lady Nan appeared. Immediately, Anna reappeared, a small figure standing alone by the sundial, waiting. Lady Nan waved to her that she was coming, and by the time she reached Anna, she'd become her nine-year-old self as Beryl.

Jack raised his head, sniffed once, pretty much ignored Kit, and decided to stay.

In turn, Kit ignored Bash's dirty looks, and texted their adopted brother Tut. There was no answer. The phone genie repeated what he already knew: *we're sorry, the person you have called is not available*. Phone texts had a mind of their own, working when a message was deemed important to the Hall.

Tut's phone was usually switched off unless previously arranged. Kit ended the call and pretended to leave a message: "Sorry I'm late. I'm on my way. Five minutes."

Jack whined a little to save face. "That's okay boy," Kit said. "You stay here and protect Bash from the fairies."

"Tosser!"

Tut was actually thrilled to leave his sad identity behind in Egypt. Other than the year, he had no recollection of the date of his birth and was happy to hitch his birthday to April 6. He was a year older than the twins but having never gone to school, he felt considerably younger.

Despite the fact he was computer savvy, Tut had never been comfortable with owning a cell phone – a throwback from his life as a street kid in Cairo. He often said he preferred to be out of reach now that he was free. He'd been too accessible in his old life, permanently on-call under the control of a black-market gang who acted as if they owned him because they did.

Rescue from slavery was a dream come true, even though England's damp climate plagued him. He was presently delighting in Bede's heatwave, but it made him melancholy for the desert he loved. Like his ancestors, he was closely tuned to the sun. Lately, he could be found basking somewhere on the roof – an exposed hideout where his bones absorbed the heat and he felt at home.

Tut took his freedom seriously. He was grateful for his new life with the Stratford-Smyths and idolized Mr. S, but he sought out places of refuge where he could hole up alone. Especially since, given the chance, girls followed him around in the village like lost puppies. His exotic good looks were magnetic and his disinterested attitude made him more desirable. Girls were as perverse as ghosts.

Kit took his freedom seriously too, but there were complications. He was a named partner in what he called a senseless idiotic prophecy. "Talk about a rock and a hard place," he shouted to Sage, the topiary sphinx.

He was stuck between guilt and his sister, so there was no hope of escape.

Sage never moved a leaf.

The more it snows (Tiddely pom),
The more it goes (Tiddely pom),
The more it goes (Tiddely pom)
On snowing.

~ A.A. MILNE
'THE HOUSE AT POOH CORNER'

XIX

AND SO IT GOES

"Prophecies are dashed tricky," Parks said. "Erasing them is trickier." Kit had this fact drummed into him as part of his 'special' education.

Visiting the past confirmed what once was, but the act of observing it could still violate a sacred trust between man and nature if a time traveller wasn't careful. The future was a taste of what *would* be but with care it may be changed at a critical juncture. A slight shift may create a massive change, so treading history's footsteps required a cool head. "Think robot," Kit reminded himself. "I'm gearing up to be a human computer. And artificial intelligence is a branch of emerging science and therefore, *a la, vis a vie*, as a logical consequence, an interest worth pursuing."

Kit's mission, as outlined in the Bede prophecy, was to redress a wrong by uncovering a human glitch (possibly a faux pas), amend it, collect data, assess, cross-reference everything, and formulate a perfect solution in order to prevent a volcano from triggering a rogue ice-age. Then, loop home a few minutes after he left. Simple. Very scientific. No pressure.

He'd prefer to have remained blissfully ignorant of the future catastrophe he inadvertently witnessed when he was thirteen, but he reminded himself that if he failed to act, in a few years, Bash

would die. Ironically, to avoid that and resolve a few disturbing personal glitches, he would have to travel back to the blistering sands
of Egypt. Way back. The year 2020 was shaping up to be what it
represented, a perfect hindsight vision. Perfectly awful.

Kit would never admit it, but the sound of Anna's laughter spilling
down the stairs cheered him. He followed it to the open door of
Lady Nan's old room and peeked in.

Had they been looking over his shoulder, his parents wouldn't
have heard or seen either of the girls sitting in the window seat. But
they would have wondered why Pigeon's cage was in the window of
an abandoned room and why he was squawking the words *tiddely
pom.* The reference had long-since been forgotten.

Although his grandmother's voice was young, her words were
familiar. She'd read 'The House at Pooh Corner' to three generations, and taught her grandchildren to recite the snowy day song.

Pigeon was squawking the tiddely poms which brought on fits of
laughter from both little girls. There was Beryl, the twin's grandmother age nine, reading to Kit's daughter, also age nine, while
he watched in a state of wretchedness. It was a surreal moment
considering Kit was not yet sixteen. Such were the fluctuating irreg-
ularities of time travel. Such was the timeless fluidity of country
life at Bede.

"The more he looked inside the more Piglet wasn't there," Beryl
read. When she covered Anna with a crocheted blanket Beryl had
reverted to an old Lady Nan again. It was Lady Nan who continued
to read aloud to the sleeping girl. She was aware of her grandson's
presence, and without turning to look at him she motioned him over.
She patted the bedspread. "Sit here, luvvy."

Never letting the story slip, she read for Kit's benefit:

> *The wind had dropped, and the snow, tired of rushing
> round in circles trying to catch itself up, now fluttered
> gently down until it found a place on which to rest,*

*and sometimes the place was Pooh's nose and some-
times it wasn't, and in a little while Piglet was wearing a white muffler round his neck and feeling more
snowy behind the ears than he had ever felt before.*

Kit, restless as ever, rose up and wandered over to the dressing table where he picked up Lady Nan's hourglass. As he examined its underside, the sand changed from white to pale pink. It trickled in a steady stream – a pink thread that froze like an icicle, the width of a darning needle.

Lady Nan's voice returned to the voice Kit remembered. "Time has to stand still sometimes," she said. "So we can catch up."

Kit caught a glimpse of himself in the triple-panelled mirror. Dozens of Kits receded down a corridor of gloomy boys to infinity. Pooh's observation had been spot on. The more Kit looked, the more he wasn't there. Multiple sad faces confirmed he was tired of rushing around in circles.

Lady Nan smiled over his shoulder but only a single image of her reflected back. "It's time you told everyone," she said.

113

XX

SIX REASONS

Bash plunked herself between Kit and Tut at the breakfast table. "Did you hear the rumour that Parks and Charlotte are getting married," she said reaching for a piece of toast.

Kit gave her a sympathetic smile. "Don't be daft – you know I never listen to that pesky fairy gossip. Besides – a ghost bridegroom can't marry a living bride. Charlotte isn't in love with a man three times her age. She's in love with the idea of Parks. The Parks, who by the way, is a dead ringer for …. sorry, I meant to say, who looks an awful lot like Six."

Tut shook his head and scraped back his chair. "I'll leave you two to it," he said, removing the knives from the table. "Try not to draw blood, will you." He returned the butter knife. "I need some time to myself. See you later, Kit… or what's left of you."

Bash spooned jam onto her unbuttered toast. "They were together all those years ago."

"That's *their* story."

"You know Parks is a ghost, so why can't you understand that they bonded. It's romantic."

"Parks died young. We only see the Parks he wants us to see. We only *saw* the man he *wanted* us to see."

"You're telling me Parks is also Six. You're saying that I'm in love with the same guy as Charlotte? Is Charlotte in love with Six?

"Technically, yes"

Bash recoiled, her eyes wild. "How is that not the worst imaginable situation? How is it even possible?"

"Parks reverts to the appropriate age for Charlotte. It's a personal thing. We see Parks as ancient but Charlotte sees him as her true mate. In a way, they're growing old together in a fairly unique way wouldn't you say? Six is also Parks... *ergo*...."

"So, falling for Six is a big lie."

"Six *may* be alive. But how can you be sure? Parks says he finally decided to reincarnate as Six. If that's true, then Six is as real a descendent as any of us. He'd be a separate entity. Right? In any case, Charlotte is not interested in Six, other than he's the spitting image, so to speak, of her beloved – a 'might have been' great-grandson or as many 'greats' as necessary to make it here."

"So, Six is a whole new person, then?"

"He resembles the young Parks as anyone of us might take after a distant relative. You see. It's all relative. Absolutely relative."

Bash's terrified expression relaxed.

"Of course," Kit added, "there's no telling if he actually fancies *you*."

Bash's panic face returned. "I have a chance. There's plenty of time." Her eyes met Kit's and faltered.

"Yeah, not so much. Talk about your unlucky number six. You have three-ish years, not even, and in the meantime, I love how you're speechless around him. It gives me a breather... or should I say, a new brother."

"You can be right cruel."

"It's tough-love Sis. Apparently, I'm quite good at it. It's a science. Six's hands are tied. And, like it or not you're the boss's sister."

Bash flinched. "Nice. Thanks for that."

"Well, you are."

"Rupert is *not* the boss."

"He kind of, *is*."

"Parks runs the estate. Parks and Charlotte and me… and…"

"And Six. Don't you just love circles. Maybe you should think of him as another new business partner or a replacement brother after I go AWOL."

"Maybe *you* should think of Anna as a new sister. What do you know that you're not telling me? Give me one good reason why I don't have a chance."

Kit sighed from his narrow escape with the truth. "I can give you six."

Bash crosses her arms "Go on then."

"One: maybe he *isn't* real. Two: his family is insane… bad genes and all that. Three: he's not nearly smart enough for you. Four: he's probably not interested. Five: he's high on lavender or some weird plant all the time… and, by the way, so are you."

Kit uncrossed Bash's arms and placed them at her sides. "Number six is that we're all going to die in a terrible ice-age so there's no point… Okay, I can't actually tell you *all* of number six. It's a secret… I can't possibly divulge a fairy confidence."

"You're full of rubbish."

"But I *can* tell you, number seven."

"Go on then."

"I think he fancies Tut."

Bash rabbit-punched Kit's arm.

"Sorry, I couldn't resist. Well, it's your own fault. You're so moony and melodramatic." He rubbed his arm. "That's going to bruise."

"Good."

"Look, don't listen to me. I'm not cut out for romance."

"No kidding, Sherlock."

"No-one is. Romance is merely a biological trigger from an olfactory exchange of spontaneous natural body musk, scientifically known as pheromones. We humans are as organic as your plants. Basically, were conscious bags of skin filled with nerves stimulated by hormones. Love, my dear Watson, is an hypnotic trance triggered by scent."

"Mock all you like, wise apple, lavender is a business. And seeing's how it's the only business we've got, it may just save our bacon."

"Yum, lavender-flavoured bacon. I'm so glad I won't be around to witness it."

"You're going then?"

"Seeing's how I'm the only time traveller we've got, I may have to save your lavender-scented bacon."

"I'm not sending Six signals. Am I?"

"You should know all about the powers of smell, living here with the wretched lavender or whatever it is that has us under its thrall. You told me about the side-effects of perfume once. If you recall, it was Lady Nan's empty perfume bottle that triggered her memories of Brooks. In fact, you called it time travel in a bottle. Multiply a sprig of lavender by an entire field in bloom, and voila, here we are hijacked by plants, besotted by the first person we see, thinking it's more than it is. Lovey-dovey is for books. Get a grip."

Bash grabbed Kit's sore arm. "Two bruises are better than one," she said.

XXI
BUSINESS AS UNUSUAL

THE BEDE CHRONICLES by Christopher Stratford-Smyth
DECEMBER 18, 2016

Why does the word mental jump out at me? Judgmental, fundamental…

Bash, short for Bathsheba, is a romantic earth mother. She says the scent of history wafts its way to Bede Hall the way a homing pigeon makes a beeline for its dovecote. She talks like that all the time, having been mentored by our eccentric grandmother, her witchy friend Charlotte Findhorn, and Stanley Parks, the most bizarre gardener in the world.

Parks was the first and last groundskeeper at Bede Hall. I use the word 'was' because he's been dead a long time. And not just 'ghost dead'. He's no vapour trapped repeating his old steps in some movie replay that loops forever. He's a solid 'citizen' who wields a serious shovel. My mother can see him fine, but not 'see through' his act. His actions are present. Everyone in the village sees him. It's challenging enough to keep six gardeners all named Stanley Parks in order, let alone two Taraqs. But then it's bizarre enough to continue living with my deceased grandmother. Bizarre barely explains Parks' true identity.

My 'late' grandmother still refers to Parks as a living institution even after we discovered he'd died centuries ago. He has appeared in solid form over countless generations as his own descendants to continue his sacred duties without arousing local suspicions. We've adopted his system and assigned his incarnations numbers because he's always insisted on being called Stanley Parks.

Parks 6 is the only Parks who is truly alive. From what I've pieced together, after having to accept the fantastic concepts of reincarnation and ghosts, is that Parks finally chose to be reborn properly to begin a new family tree.

Trees loom big in the landscape of Bede, and Parks' kinfolk have populated a veritable forest of continual occupation. His prehistoric line of descent is so far distant it can't be traced past a brief mention in the Domesday book. I've tried.

Six is the culmination of Parks wisdom. His true apprentice and heir. He features heavily in my sister's diaries. Not that I read them. I don't need to. She dreams unguarded. She carries a torch for him as sure as the statue of liberty.

When Bash asks me for a second opinion on the state of the clouds over Bede, I never know what I can add to her wild conclusions. She looks for portents and signs in everything. This morning she found a message in the cornflakes at the bottom of her cereal bowl. I'm a teenage science geek, not a meteorologist or a teacup reader.

I accept some things are beyond the norm around here, but humouring pseudo-science goes against the flimsy threads of logic that bind me to the truth.

Being late, in the traditional sense of dying, has nothing and everything to do with time. Theoretically, when you travel back in time, no-one ever dies. In a perverse way, they die over and over again. But History really does repeat itself. *After* an event has occurred, nothing can change it. We can bend time but we can't break the universal laws of physics. The flaw is that I can die in the past... and that's the hard science of it.

I've had my atoms flung into a time portal and glimpsed a future I wish were untrue. The Yellowstone Caldera is going to blow in a few years. It causes a new ice-age. There are no gardens and canned food only goes so far as supplies allow.

And this is true. Anna, the ghost of Bede Hall is only sort-of dead. When I left her in the Winter Room in 2023, she was in a cryogenic state which *is* dead but not. She's a natural time traveller. She visited Lady Nan when my grandmother was nine-years-old. They were best friends. She is the child ghost of Bede Hall.

Anna was my grandmother's invisible childhood friend. Beryl, Lady Nan as a child, thought she was a ghost because she had all the qualifications of being one.

Anna frequented a particular room and brought the chill of the ice-age with her because that's the room in the future where she lies in some 'Sleeping Beauty' curse. I've been in that room only once or twice in the last three years.

I can't shake what I saw. How it looks in the future. Bede Hall is buried in snow up to the Winter Room's window. That window becomes a door. When I first saw it, Bede Hall looked like a ski chalet and I thought I was dreaming. But, lucid dreams are normal for me so going along for the ride was amusing until I discovered I was dead too because Anna said I'd gone on an expedition to find her missing mother and never came back. That was the tip of an extremely ironic the iceberg.

Anna had recognized me the day Bash and I cornered her in the old servant's quarters. She had been waiting for me. Staring out her window-door looking for me and waiting for my return which if it does happen, will be too late.

Anna, Taraq's sister in a former life and Lady Nan's ghostly childhood friend, is my daughter – a physical impossibility when one does the math because she was born in 2014 when I was fourteen. Bash is buried in the village cemetery. And according to a recurring dream I've been having since I turned nine (the number nine is significant in Bede-World for some reason) I froze to death on an expedition of mercy. I failed to rescue Anna's mother, whoever she is.

120

I never saw Tut or my parents in the future. Pigeon was there, still a family icon with a smart mouth, but unless he's a phoenix in disguise, he's not going to last. I have no idea who Anna's mother is, and the mystery is a constant anxiety. Is she a girl I know here? If I don't meet her can I change the future where Anna won't exist and maybe the caldera will stay bubbling out of sight for another million years?

Or is everything I do predestined? If I run away, do I run into a girl or away from a girl? Not that a human relationship has any influence over a geological force thousands of miles away, but in the tiniest shelf of my mind, it's all connected. So, I'm damned if I do and damned if I don't. And so is the planet.

My future scientific career is doomed. Anna showed me the science-fiction books I'd written in the future. An entire shelf of them. So, I must have caved at some point (in time). Woken from this mass hallucination of insanity and accepted truths I refuse to believe. I live in a pocket of time inhabited by Bede fairies and ghosts and magic gardens. I live inside a conundrum. I am a sphinx tying to solve my own riddle.

The responsibility is pressure cooker insane even without the wretched Bede Curse that hangs over us all. The legendary Bede Prophecy predicted the arrival of miraculous twin energies (Bash and I). Together, by grounding the present and the past we're capable of saving the Hall from a permanent winter that's somehow connected to ancient Egypt.

That's where the Twinters want me to go – through the second portal in the maze to save the world.

Some days I want to tell my parents. They would put a stop to living here and I could bury my head in the sand instead of a ghastly snowbank of forever.

I can't undo what I know; I can only learn from the past, return to influence the present, and hope for the best.

My problem is, if I had my druthers, I'd just as soon never scramble my molecules again, but I know too much for the Hall to let me stay.

XVIII

THE CHRISTMAS GRAPEVINE

THE WINTER SOLSTICE – DECEMBER 21 – 2016

The sap in the rowan tree quickened as a welcome voice breezed through its branches. "He's almost returned," the voice announced.

The branches quivered humbly, "yes."

A dryad slithered under the bark, twisting in an upward spiral as it travelled, its high voice tinkling like a bright wind chime. "It's time."

The rowan shook the dew from its leaves to be sure it had heard correctly, and gently sighed a family of baby robins into the sky.

"The master says not to expect too much from *her*," the wood nymph continued. "She's a little green."

"Well, precisely. She was *born* a green-thumb."

"Quite so."

"And the boy?"

"The boy will be fine."

"He's not ready."

"He's a fighter. When the time comes…"

The rowan's trunk creaked and snapped. A few branches rattled to the ground before it composed itself. "But my dear friend, I thought you said it *was* time."

Green tendrils combed a twig from the tail of a passing grey squirrel. "Time is an inexact science as you well know."

A few red berries bounced on the grass below. "And *that's* what worries me," the tree deva murmured. "The boy favours *pure* science."

"He *will* be ready," the dryad commanded. "The master charges you with gifting him a talisman."

The tree's crown rustled like a lady's silk gown as it bowed in deference, as low to the ground as it could. "Yes, of course."

XXIII

FLOWER POWER

Bash lay on a grassy slope behind the maze, squinting at the weird display of flashes emitted by the sun, wishing she had a pair of Rupert's powerful designer shades. Where were brothers when you needed them. Kit ought to see this. The liminal boundaries were thin enough for him to slip through.

A loud v-shaped flock of Canada geese passed overhead, momentarily blocking the display. The sound of them honking out of sync made her dizzy. She closed her eyes and steadied herself by clutching the grass either side of her. It took ages for their cries to fade. And even after she was sure the sky was empty, she heard the humming sound of stilled harp strings.

When Bash looked again, the sun pulsated like a beating heart and fragmented into a thousand miniature yellow planets. Balls of animated light fell to earth.

Parks and Charlotte had taught her well. The solstices brought new dimensions into focus, so she allowed the strange anomaly to unfold with curiosity rather than fear. Sometimes she felt she might be even more of a scientist than Kit. She giggled and fell back in the December grass, delighted as the discs landed gently all around her. Each one with the sound of a muffled fairy bell until the green field glowed with yellow spheres.

"Nimue," she called out. "Are you here?" And then, after a new thought. "Are you *doing* this? Thank you. It's extremely... *um*... effervescent of you. Sorry, I can't think of a better word. Magical hardly covers it."

Silence. No tinkling of fairy laughter.

No matter. All was well because the earth's vibrations radiated from the ground into her back as a healing massage. It was the clearest of signs. Contact with the soil was an organic thermometer if you knew how to read it. Today the temperature was in accord with the season of midsummer even if it *was* the midwinter solstice.

Bash thanked the Green Lady Chloris and opened her arms to the glorious sensation of a sphere shower. Baby suns landed like soft lightbulbs. Pop pop pop. The brightness dimmed as the sun's children cooled into the earth and the music of straw rustling in the wind lulled her deeper into a new season.

Globules of liquid honey burst on impact in slow-motion and pooled into golden puddles before sinking into new cracks in the soil. She sent Kit a message: *Come to the back garden you'll want to see this. I think the sun's burning out. Please hurry."*

Kit heard and sent back. *"Yeah, thanks for the heads up. I'm kind of doing something important right now. I'll catch you later."*

When she woke, Bash found herself in a field of wild sunflowers waving at their mother, still shining whole in a fierce blue sky. The landscape was unfamiliar, fields of grain as far as the horizon at the edge of a straggle of farm buildings. Definitely, nowhere near Bede Hall, but there was Feathers, mewing around her feet, grounding her to safety.

Kit is sleeping, she thought. This is his dream. Was it the future or the past or just a quantum leap in real time to a remote location? Whatever it was, it was a message of considerable importance.

Parks had warned her. "Pay attention. I am your master-teacher. Listen for my voice in all things. Situations may arrive out of the blue, but I prefer to call it 'out of the green'. Fluctuations of the timeline are triggered by each birthday. Take note: this coming April you'll be sixteen, a milestone year, and now, with the added energies Charlotte, Brooks, and I are weaving around you and Kit, you'll be overwhelmed at times. Your natural abilities are growing exponentially, speeding within a slipstream of space, racing against time. When in doubt, I will tell you what to do." He had shushed her questions with a smile. "The Stratford Smyth line runs true," he said. "Never doubt you and Kit are its rightful heirs. May you feel, from time-to-time, the presence of your ancestors and descendants who travel to and from Bede with the lightness of a true heart. Time must be held captive in an hourglass in Kit's keeping. The earth will be protected inside a globe of snow, in yours."

Bash closed her eyes and messaged Kit. *Are you there?*

I heard him too, Kit said. *"No worries. I'll say one thing. Dead or alive, Parks is a born storyteller."*

Sometimes, one of the twins was the forerunner of a new experience and the other had to catch up. Bash suspected Kit's ability to travel through the portals was such a phenomenon.

It was dark. Her watch showed she had been there for nine hours. It was suppertime. *Save some gravy for me*, she messaged Kit. *I think I've just seen the future. I don't know what you've been going on about. It's quite lovely.*

I'm going to bet you haven't gone too far ahead, then, Kit sent back. *Mum and dad have gone out, so there's plenty of gravy.*

The future suddenly felt too hot and too cold, and as menacing as the sound of geese on the wing, honking as if their lives depended on flying to the moon.

XXIV

CHIMERA

Bede, Northumberland, England
DECEMBER 23, 2016

Bede drifted towards Christmas as it always did. Aligned to the pole star, it continued to move steadily towards the appointed green rites of regeneration eons before the feast of Mithras had eclipsed it. But this year, the absence of winter predicted an extended summer holiday. Parched green grasses thirsted in the dehydrated soil. Birds too listless to fly built temporary nests near the edges of the shrinking lake and kept to the trees. The butterflies had fanned themselves into early cocoons, months ago. Only the bees bumbled erratically from flower to flower at dawn, to share the precious rations of dewdrops with the dragonflies and moths.

The ghosts of Lady Nan, Ben, Anna, and Taraq listened dreamily to the discussion of Christmas presents as Tut, Bash, and Kit made a guessing game over the brightly wrapped packages under the tree. They speculated, albeit distractedly, sipping bedtime cocoa, the traditional winter beverage regardless of the baking hot nights. The seven children passed as a normal cosy family.

The four youngest sat on the floor beneath the Christmas tree, hugging their knees. Lady Nan had reverted to Beryl, her nine-year-old form, as did the twins' Great Uncle Bentley. Beryl shook her snow globe and stared intensely into the snow. Feathers and Snowball lay sleeping while the ghost of Unicorn batted the lowest tree ornaments to no effect. Jack was alert with his eyes on a plate of shortbread cut into stars.

The coloured fairy lights reflected the innocent expressions of bygone times, each 'child' lost in their memories. Every now and then one of the blue lights spun out of the tree and flew into the garden. Anubis, sitting guard at the open door, watched them go, scanning the evening for similar-sized red lights that sounded like wasps.

The three teens sprawled on overstuffed armchairs pulled together in a huddle for privacy. Mr. and Mrs. S were still sequestered in the kitchen discussing finances. Their raised voices filtered into the, ironically named, 'living' room. But, nothing about the scene was innocent.

"Kit sniffed his cocoa. "You know, this drink reminds me of the good old days, ten years ago."

"We were younger than all of you," Bash said, smiling at the children.

"Old traditions almost makes things feel safe," Kit continued. "It wouldn't be quite right sipping lemonade, listening to Christmas carols, surrounded by holly garlands, which by the way, with these temperatures, should be artificial." He sounded more like an old man reminiscing about days gone by.

"It *is* safe," Bash said, smiling reassurance at Anna. Beryl burst into tears and disappeared, taking Ben with her, but she left her snow globe rolling on its side.

Kit stretched his toes towards the cold fireplace where Beryl, newly manifested as Lady Nan, knitted by a fire that wasn't there. The windows and French doors were open to create a through draft which was too weak to affect any movement in the curtains. "That's because you've been bewitched," he said to Bash. "You're Parks' darling teenage protégé. For three years, he's filled your head with romantic stories how the sites of the old ones' sacred springs were reduced to wishing wells filled with amulets. Plus, he gave you the swanky formal title: 'Daughter of the House of Bede'… which, you have to admit, has the ring of a fairy tale about it. And speaking of fairy rings, how *is* the lavender? Still purple is it?"

Bash fanned her face with a Christmas card. "They're *not* stories. I call it being enthralled with historical facts."

"You do know what a thrall is, don't you?"

Lady Nan sighed audibly, and knitted faster. "Kit, have you had too much sugar or are you going to stay jealous all your life?" It was not meant to be answered.

Kit's blank expression stared through Bash, ignoring his grandmother. "A *thrall* is a captive slave… I'm just saying." He focused on Tut's face. "The groundwater table is drastically low, so, you have to ask yourself how the local holly managed to remain perfectly green and healthy."

Tut smiled wanly, raised his cocoa in a toast, and gently clinked mugs with Bash. "Maybe it's the holly that's bewitched, then."

"It's *some* people and *all* of the plants," Kit said after a long pause.

Tut tipped his head towards Anna and Taraq – a gesture that said lighten up there are kids present. "What about you, Kit? What do *you* want Father Christmas to bring you this year?"

Kit snickered. "You will be surprised to know that all I want for Christmas is a magic wand. A weapon to fight fire with fire."

Lady Nan dropped her ball of wool, and Unicorn pounced on it, making Jack bark at the ball that seemed to be moving of its own accord.

Bash clinked her mug to Kit's with extra force and sent him a telepathic message: *Lighten up for Anna's sake. She's extra fragile at this time of year. A weapon? really?* It's something *with which* to fight fire with fire," Bash corrected out loud. You know for the last few years, you have undergone a few changes of heart."

Kit sent back: *Anna has to grow up… and yes, I do know how that sounds. And really? Is grammar important at a time like this? Taraq is a ghost too and he accepts life-changing… I mean, new things.* "If you mean," he said aloud, staring pointedly at Anna, "that while navigating the murky seas of reality and illusion, I remain dedicated to renouncing all things, other than the residual fourth-dimension traces of human atoms, as supernatural, then your observations are correct."

Taraq manifested between Kit and Bash. "Give it a rest, you two. It's Christmas. You're upsetting Anna. One of the first things I learned here is that Christmas is the season to be jolly."

"In spite of your non-physical state, Taraq, after three years, you know me better than anyone," Kit said.

Taraq bowed formally to Bash. "Daughter of the House of Bede, mystical phenomena actually causes your brother physical pain. I have witnessed his suffering many many times. He has made it clear that he finds metaphysics a bore. His exact words were a crashing bore."

Bash punched Kit's arm playfully. "Having a science-minded brother is a bore. And Taraq's spot on. We need to invoke an atmosphere of jollification."

"But I will say one thing about observations," Kit persisted, "and it's scientific."

Bash feigned melodramatic shock, turned away from her brothers, and tickled Anna's arm with her foot. "So much for Christmas surprises," she said, blocking Anna's view of Kit. "What do you want in your stocking?"

Anna righted the snow globe and polished the glass with her sleeve. "Real feet would be nice," she replied, older than her ghost years, and promptly evaporated. Lady Nan suppressed a sob. And as expected, Taraq followed his sister.

Tut leaned forward. "Go on mate, you can tell me. Anna's gone."

"Contrary to popular belief," Kit said solemnly, "seeing is mostly *disbelieving*."

Bede Hall was, in Kit's opinion, a chimera – an absurd creature with a lion's head, a goat's body and a serpent's tail that he'd heard about in the stories Lady Nan read to him as a child. The Hall had fused its body, head and tail from a variety of architectural sundries to create a monster of a house that Lady Nan lovingly called a hodgepodge of perfect mishmashes. Cross-pollinations of the botanical kind rooted its purpose. It also boasted a history that reached back, as Lady Nan loved to repeat: beyond the seven seas, the ancient Greeks, and time itself.

Lady Nan was a born storyteller, prone to the art of exaggeration, which made her best stories all the more thrilling, particularly after a brief glance in her snow globe – a childhood toy she referred to, in her lighter moments, as her crystal ball. She loved the tales of Greek mythology as much, if not more than, Grimms Fairy Tales, indeed, she was proud to point out that the word myth was encrypted within the family name Stratford-Smyth. It proved her point, she said, that occult meanings resided in words and their pronunciation. Secrets in the open air for all to see and hear.

Strangers always made the mistake of pronouncing Smyth as if it had an 'e' at the end, rhyming it with scythe, but even that held the echo of a cipher because it was a smithy who forged such for-midable weapons. Lady Nan never tired of correcting them all or to admonish, with a pointing finger, to also never *overestimate* the power of words. Interpretation resided in one's solar plexus. And much to Kit's everlasting humiliation, intuition overruled analysis.

But even as Kit fervently disavowed the power of wishful think-ing as delusional, there were days his determination flagged, and to keep the peace, he reluctantly conceded to possibilities that he knew couldn't be true.

Still, for all the concessions he made, Kit was stalwart about one thing. He repeatedly rejected the ridiculous notion of being the designated role of warrior-messenger, predestined to travel the worm holes of time that were embedded throughout the countryside and in the walls of Bede Hall. It was simply, not on. And if by some miracle it *was* true, holding time in one's hands was too big of a responsibility for one teenager.

On the days when the budding physicist failed to explain the inex-plicable, he clung to the faint hope that perhaps the fanciful Bede prophecies had expired. But the word 'future' always stopped him cold. In any case, turning sixteen at Bede was not going to be sweet or a breeze.

XXV
POSTCARD FROM MARS

DECEMBER 24 – the morning of CHRISTMAS EVE – 2016

Bash wandered through the kitchen in search of chocolate biscuits. Pigeon looked despondent in spite of his new cuttlebone. "Hey Pidge. You look very down in the beak. Feathers got your tongue?"

Pigeon muttered to himself. *"Chocolate,"* he said.

"Did she take the chocolate as well?"

The parrot rallied a little, sidling towards Bash on his perch. P words being his passion and fancy words being hers, she tempted him. "Preponderance," she said stroking Pigeon's feathers.

He closed his eyes and leaned his head to one side which always made him appear cat-like. He seemed genuinely pleased, if not a little hypnotized. One of Charlotte's wee spells: the human trick to train creatures is in the tone of one's voice.

"Um... Paleolithic. Now, how's that? One good turn deserves another. What wise words do you have for me?"

"Pride and Prejudice," he squawked.

"Thanks mate."

"Charlotte says... Charlotte says... dilly dally," Pigeon muttered into his feathers.

"Sorry? What does Charlotte say?"

"Christmas is coming... the goose is getting fat... please put a penny... in the..."

Bash finished the nursery rhyme in sing-song tradition. "In the old man's hat."

Pigeon squawked *"NO"* in his best pigeon-ese. *"In the goose neck lamp."*

"Silly Goosie," Bash said. "Pleasantly Plump Christmas Goosie."

Pigeon flapped his wings and let out a maniacal shriek.

Tut and Kit strolled into the kitchen in search of potato chips.

"Now, according to Charlotte, that was parrot laughter," Bash said. "And she knows all manner of bird and animal languages." She rubbed Pigeon's beak and he settled down. "That's more like it, my sweet little Pineapple."

Charlotte's voice mentally summoned Bash, interrupting their parrot moment. "Come at once, my dear. Someone is here that you should meet. Don't dilly dally, there's a good girl."

"I've got to run," Bash announced suddenly. "Tell Mum I'm off to Charlotte's."

Kit picked a handful of nuts from a bowl. "Tell her yourself. She'll have questions. She always does. Any idea where the nut-cracker is?"

Tut spoke from inside a cupboard. "She won't even know you're gone."

"Um… No chance," Kit said, winking at Bash "Mothers have a peculiar sixth sense for these things."

"I doubt that," Tut replied. "If you ask me, pretty much everything gets by her. You know perfectly well that she has no sixth sense at all. If she did, we'd be living in London right now."

"After all the times we've disappeared, Mum likes to know when we go out. It's a formality we've learned to respect, if not honour… sometimes. Ever since Dad's little adventure, Mum worries about us being kidnapped. She's a nervous Nelly when she doesn't know exactly where we are. If she really knew what we were up to she would need therapy. And if she could see Lady Nan as we do, she would need a straight jacket."

Bash eyed the potato chips. "Don't be giving Pigeon any of those. Salt could kill him."

"Potato," shrieked Pigeon. *"One potato two potato three potato four."*

Bash left Pigeon in high spirits, chortling over his new favorite tongue twister: *"Peter Piper picked a peck of pickled potatoes"*, animatedly bobbing up and down in obvious glee, fluffing out his scarlet and lime-green feathers.

The noise coming from the pantry told Bash that her mother was in a sorting frame of mind, taking a last inventory of Christmas provisions.

"Mum, I'm off to the village for a last-minute Christmas shop that can't wait. Can I get you anything?"

The sound of shifting tin cans stopped while Mrs. S pondered her answer. "What time is it?"

"Nearly time for elevenses."

Mrs. S made a low remark Bash couldn't quite make out. "Maybe pick up the post. Thanks darling. Don't be long, there's a good girl, we've got Christmassy things to do."

When Bash arrived at the corner shop, the post office section was crowded with villagers picking up parcels. A wreath strung with silver bells jingled merrily with the frequent comings and goings. Mrs. Spoondance, the postmistress was flushed pink and breathless from too much seasonal bustling.

"Well, look who it is," she said, fanning herself with an envelope. "Funny you should drop by just now." She handed Bash her 'fan' – a red envelope decorated with Christmas stickers. It was addressed to Bathsheba Stratford-Smyth c/o Bede Hall. "This was just left for you." She tapped the worn wooden countertop. "Right here, barely a moment ago. Must be a local. There's no stamp.

Well, someone's drawn a wee face where the stamp would be. I didn't see who left it."

An impatient customer pushed her purchases in front of Bash.

"Happy Christmas Bash," Mrs. Spoondance called out over the woman's head. "There's no other post for the Hall, today. Give my best to your parents."

Bash examined her name written in a formal calligraphic hand on the front of the thin envelope. For some reason, she sniffed the ink and recoiled from the musty smell of coal dust. A yellow smiley face surrounded by petals had been drawn in the upper right corner. She turned it over. The back flap was unstuck, sealed only with the same flowery face imprinted in a blob of red sealing wax. Beside it was a clear black thumbprint.

It opened easily with a crisp pop. Inside was a postcard. Clearly an outer envelope had been unnecessary, apart from privacy. The front was a reproduction of an old-fashioned movie poster. The title 'They Came From Mars' was emblazoned over a flying saucer and a few people with frightened faces. Odd. Not very Christmassy. The reverse was written in the same elegant handwriting: *Dearest Bathsheba. I'm red with envy. I can't wait to see you.* It was signed with a single letter 'M' embellished with a sweeping ornate flourish. Someone had practiced their penmanship. Again, the inside ink reeked of a damp fireplace.

Bash reran a fleeting impression of herself and Kit lying in the grass, a swarm of birds, and the painful whip of a branch. The day she'd choked on a cloud that smelled of soot. Bash rubbed her arm where a yellow bruise still lingered. Who was M?

Charlotte's florist shop was decked out in holly and poinsettias. Orchestral waves of Silent Night and the delightful scents of a cinnamon and clove potpourri met Bash at the door.

Charlotte's pet marmoset monkey, Beegle, was unsuccessfully helping her attach a Christmas angel to the top of a small pine tree. Bash managed to right it while Charlotte distracted Beegle with some crinkly cellophane.

Charlotte greeted Bash warmly with a spicy mug of hot milk in her hand. Drink this," she said. "It's... *um*... a special blend of mine. You could say a special-tea of the house."

"Mmmn. Hot eggnog? Very traditional."

"That depends on where you call home." Charlotte said, tipping her head to one side, keeping her eyes on Beegle. "I call it Christmas Tea."

Bash sniffed it with some trepidation. "Do I detect a hint of marzipan? Gosh, it doesn't have mistletoe in it, I hope. That *would* be a specialty."

Charlotte shrugged. "It might," she said with a wink, and got straight to the point she'd summoned Bash to hear. "Did you know that Kit sees Bede Hall as a chimera," she said, casually extricating a porcelain cup from Beegle's fingers. "Not very respectful. He doesn't consider a mutant house worth saving. And he seems to have forgotten all about the consequences of the caldera."

"He hasn't. My brother jumps every time mum or dad so much as mentions winter, and only the other day, when Anna smiled at him, he scooped the ice-cubes out of his water and hurled them into the fireplace. It surprised Lady Nan so much that she retreated into little Beryl. Uncle Ben had to calm her down."

"If Kit refuses to use the portals, Bede Hall will fall. He's our traveller. But his fears have cost him his sense of purpose."

"He thinks it's being a scientist. His theory..."

"Mastering time and space *is* science. Deep down, he doesn't believe in his hallucination theory. It's an excuse. Something else is bothering him. If anyone is hallucinating, he is. The worst of it, is he's beginning to believe his own lies. If he doesn't turn around soon, his anger will turn to hate and nothing will save him or the future."

Bash rubbed her arms as if chilled. "He's my twin. My equal in stubbornness, and *he's* trying to turn *me* around. So, it's a bit of a stalemate."

"Nimue tells me that Kit is writing down his thoughts. She's alarmed at what she reads."

Bash's eyes focused. "You're spying on him?"

Charlotte pressed a fresh cup of tea into Bash's hands. "Whisht, dearest girl. Do not trouble yourself. Sip this. We're not controlling Kit; we're monitoring him. The prophecy stipulates he must remain free to decide. But he feels abandoned. He's experiencing a crisis of conscience, and so he's trying to work out what he should do by having a conversation with himself on paper. Yesterday, he wrote that the Hall is possessed by the rampant collective unconscious of ghosts with a perverse sense of entitlement."

"Sounds like something I would say."

Beegle leapt onto the tree from Charlotte's shoulder, shattering a glass ornament in the process. "I believe he got the notion from your grandmother," she said.

Bash suppressed a chuckle. "Good old Lady Nan. She still tries to hone Kit's language skills, as if science-speak wasn't enough."

Bash grabbed the dustpan and brush in the corner but when she looked for the shards of red glass they were gone. "I distinctly heard broken glass."

Charlotte changed the subject. "It was nutmeg and cardamom."

"Sorry?"

"That you tasted in the eggnog. A traditional infusion, you might say."

"Why does that sound ominous when you say it?"

Charlotte played the 'follow my line of thought game'. "According to the Nimue, your brother is planning to run away."

"I have to walk with that idea awhile before I confront him," Bash said, "I hear his innermost thoughts, but that's news to me."

Charlotte shook her head in slow motion and avoided her eyes. "Not always."

"I would know if he was hiding anything big like that."

"Some things you shouldn't know. And deep down you don't *want* to know."

"I should give him the benefit of the doubt. He deserves that."

Charlotte's eyes met Bash's over the Christmas brew. "Quite. And *you* deserve to be in the dark for a while longer. Humor him. It's his Christmas wish."

"Should I be worried?"

"Sometimes, a state of worry is essential for survival."

"You're being a tad melodramatic, aren't you?"

Charlotte drained an entire cup of eggnog before she answered. "It depends. How much is a tad?"

Charlotte's swished the full skirt of her flowery summer dress. Its pattern of sunflowers on a blue background swirled into a blur and her emerald earrings flashed. Bash had to close her eyes. Sometimes one of Charlotte's sudden dancer pirouettes dazzled her without warning.

It was then Bash noticed a woman standing nearby, filling a stand with greeting cards. A petite redhead with stripes of turquoise blue and yellow in her hair that escaped from a wide-brimmed hat. She brushed her hands on her green cape and held out her hand. "Allo," she said with a French accent. "*Je suis* Hannah Johns, and you must be Meez Bash. I av eard so much about you."

Hannah petted Beegle with one hand but the monkey was more interested in the plate of croissants behind her. Hannah invited Bash to sample with a sweep of her spare hand. "I made zem fresh zis morning. Please." Beegle strained to reach the plate. "Take one." She gestured to the counter set with a teapot, plates, and an open jar of lavender honey. "Zair is the compote of Charlotte as well." Beegle's wiry figure inched closer to Bash. "*Non,*" Hannah said, blocking Beegle's long arm reaching for a pastry. "Zey are not for leetle monkeys."

Bash eyed her drink warily. 'Special blend' could mean all

manner of concoctions. Over the years, she'd been mildly affected by a few of Charlotte's potions of herbs and spells.

"Hannah is here to brighten up the shop," Charlotte said quickly. "And Beegle is here to eat all her croissants if we take our eyes off him."

Since Charlotte owned a florist shop full of colourful flowers it seemed an odd thing to say. Bash turned her attention to the display of framed sunflower prints hanging behind the cash register. "I'm familiar with one of them but I didn't know there were so many different versions."

Charlotte inclined her head to her art gallery. "Obviously they're Van Goghs. Hannah sells them and the matching cards as well. I have a special print to show you. It's in the back."

There's that word again. "Charlotte, why does 'special' make me nervous whenever *you* say it?"

Charlotte grinned. "I can't *possibly* imagine."

"Vincent… now ee was *spécial*," Hannah said. "*Exceptionnel, non?* His work is my *obee*."

Bash nodded but raised her eyebrows and looked to Charlotte for clarification. "Sorry?"

Charlotte translated. "She said hobby. But she's wrong. Van Gogh is her *passion*. Now, about that special surprise. But first, drink that tea to the last drop."

Bash drained her cup and held it upside-down to prove she'd surrendered. "It tastes a bit like… Christmas trees," she said.

Hannah nodded. "Go you two, go, I will stay here weez ze Beegles and guard ze croissants. But you must urry."

Charlotte was true to her word. The art print was incredibly special. It was brimming with magic. Its colors pulsed like an erratic heartbeat balanced on a large easel in the scene of a bedroom that appeared to be melting. At first it showed Vincent's famous bedroom, and then, as the light played upon it, the painting changed into the unmistakable interior of Kit's tower.

A simple wooden kitchen chair with a straw seat, painted canary yellow, was placed beside the bed instead of a table. It's companion chair, closest to the viewer, morphed into Kit's meditation throne. Twin chairs.

Kit perched on the edge of the single bed cradling a strange black cat, with enormous paws. He waved hello from the painting. "Hey Sis. Hello Charlotte."

Being completely tipsy already, Bash lost her balance. "How? What on earth," she squeaked.

"You mean *where* on earth. Vincent painted his bedroom in Arles, France, a hundred-and-thirty-years ago. In 1888."

Bash's knees buckled as she hyperventilated. "Omigod. Is Kit there? Back in time? Has he time travelled? He's not supposed to do that yet. I have to get home. I feel quite dizzy."

"What can I say, Bede is a woozy kind of place. Very *woo woo woozy* if you understand my meaning. I like to think that my special infusions are also special *confusions*."

Bash giggled uncontrollably. "Very droll. "Lady Nan would appreciate that. Did you know… that… that we play… *um*… with words, her and I?"

Charlotte nodded. "Yes, I know. By the way, Kit's home safe and sound in 2016," Charlotte said. She looked up and to the left. "He *is* sitting on his bed though. And he's thinking of *you*."

Bash sniggered. "I doubt that. He's got Mars on the brain these days."

"He's a scientist boy-wonder. They're easily distracted."

"He's been obsessed by, or I *should* say, terrified *of* the face on Mars ever since he was nine-years-old. After some nightmare he'd had. I was fortunate not to be invited into that one."

The curtains swayed like wild flags and Bash had to grab onto Charlotte to keep from falling. "What on earth was in that tea? Did you add spirits?"

"In a manner of speaking."

Bash smiled for the both of them. "You never lied to me before."

"Lying is the lowest form of manipulation."

"I'm either having an hallucination or does Beegle have wings?"

Charlotte did a double-take at the bruise on Bash's arm. "Where did you get that?"

"I don't remember. It appeared over a week ago. Maybe… Perhaps… I think."

"Is it still sore?"

"A little."

Charlotte examined it closely under a goose-neck lamp. "I'm not surprised; it's magic – an unheeded message." She plucked a leaf from a nearby plant and pressed it over the skin. "It should stop hurting now. Really Bash, you should pay more attention. Especially since your brother is so easily distracted. Part of your training is to remain constantly alert for signs. I'm counting on you. I have… plans."

"What plans?"

Charlotte blushed and busied herself extracting a croissant from Beegle's grip. "Well, you received *my* message loud and clear. How's the dizziness?"

Bash squinted at Beegle's wings. "*Hmmnn?*"

"Are you feeling better?"

Bash heard herself mumble from across the room. "So, what does the message say?"

"I have no idea but it bears the ethereal signature of a rowan. So, it's powerful magic. Think back. Did you bump into a branch or something?"

Bash put her hand in her pockets and closed her eyes. She touched the edge of the red envelope and pulled back as if burned. "Oh… wait. I *do* remember. This envelope just reminded me. It was a day when Kit and I were laying in the grass under a Rowan tree and I felt a tinge of… well, it was strange. I was choking and then I wasn't. And there was a sooty smell in the air." She cleared her throat in remembrance and produced the red envelope for Charlotte to see. "This postcard was delivered today. It has the same musty smell."

Charlottes's eyes widened at the red seal. "Great Goddess, where did *that* come from?"

"Sorry, no return address. Someone left it for me in the post office. What on earth is wrong? You've gone quite pale. It's that tea of yours."

"Charlotte lifted the envelope gingerly, holding it by a corner and slipped it into a plastic bag. "Nothing on this earth," she murmured in a grim tone. She turned the sign on the door to 'sorry we're closed' and grabbed her purse. "Hannah, would you please lock up for me? I need that delivery of poinsettias watered. Thanks." She winked. "I wouldn't ask but it's *très* urgent."

Hannah's mouth was a terrified 'Oh'! *"Oui. Je comprendre.* You must urry. *Allez.* Go."

Beegle abandoned his croissant caper and jumped to Charlotte's shoulder in one leap.

Charlotte gave him a handful of rose petals. "We've got to tell Parks and the others."

The Beeg stuck his nose into his rosy snack and made a chirping sound.

Bash managed to shout "Nice to meet you, Hannah. Joyeux Noel." as she was unceremoniously pulled out the door.

"Joyeux Noel, appy Chreesmas," Hannah called back. But her mouth hadn't moved. It was still the shape of a startled O.

Charlotte punched a number into her phone before her car keys jangled open the doors of her delivery van. She jammed Bash's bike into the back with several plastic containers labelled miscellaneous, mistletoe, and ivy, and headed for the Hall. They were on the move.

Bash, astonished that a cell phone worked in Bede, discovered how much hearing only one side of a distorted conversation revealed.

Charlotte wasted no words: *"Brooks, I'm calling an emergency meeting… I know it's Christmas Eve… no, it has to be this afternoon…Parks does know…yes, an hour…I'll bring the kids… of course they're kids… Parks is rounding up the others… sandwiches and tea…one hour."*

No hello. No goodbye. No preamble or thanks. She was a different Charlotte. General Charlotte with no time to dilly-dally.

"Call Kit," she ordered Bash, "and tell him we're picking up him and Tut in fifteen minutes," she said. "Tell him it's an order and to drop whatever he's doing. Tell them to be outside."

The cloud growing inside the van obscured Bash's view of the road.

"And open a ruddy window," Charlotte said, "or we'll asphyxiate before we reach the gates."

The smell from the postcard wafted from Charlotte's handbag and out the passenger window, leaving a putrid trail of black smoke as they travelled.

Bash clung to her seat as the van skidded around a tight corner. "We're going to be stopped by the police," she shouted over the grinding of gears. "They'll think the van's on fire."

"No-one can see or smell that filth but us," Charlotte said. "Hang on. I have to drive as if we're *going* to a fire."

"Are we?"

Charlotte glanced over at her passenger. Her eyes were wild and kind of happy in a weird sense. "Too bloody right, we are," she said.

XXVI

'THE NEVER NEVER'

DECEMBER 24 – the afternoon of CHRISTMAS EVE – 2016

Kit sprang mid-daydream from his meditation chair as if he'd received an electric shock. What on earth! He stomped about flapping his arms as if to rid himself of a wasp, and Jack followed his lead by spinning in a circle, barking as madly as the time he'd cornered a squirrel in the stables. The commotion snapped Kit into action. "Crazy dog. Don't mind me. I'm just having a bit of an upset."

Something had happened.

Worse yet, the chair had been clear about one thing. *Pay attention. This is important.*

The vivid scene Kit had relived, seconds ago, lingered like a nightmare, as fresh as the day it happened. It had been Christmas Eve, eight-years-ago. He was seven, small for his age. The twins had been taken to London for their annual excursion to see an afternoon pantomime of 'Peter Pan' and the Christmas lights.

The fantasy of living in Neverland was their favourite story. Bash was infatuated with Tinkerbell and the concept of fairies in general. Kit said he wished he could fly and never grow up, and was curious to know how the backstage mechanics of pulleys and wires worked that enabled Wendy and her brothers to levitate above their beds.

He was hooked on aerial theatrics, determined to unravel the mysteries of how the actors' invisible safety harnesses held them suspended.

The theatre – an ornate cavern, lit with huge glass chandeliers and seasonal decorations, bedazzled the twins. Balconies lined the walls. Red velvet stage curtains trimmed in gold braid and tassels, parted briefly as a face emerged to scan the crowd.

When the footlights came up, Kit had a clear view of the stage. Part of the contraption of flight simulation could be made out dangling from beams in the ceiling. It was natural for him to pause and study stagehands working the system of winches and pulleys and cables.

"Stay together," Mrs. S said. "Follow me. We may have to go single file, so Bash, hold my hand, and Kit you hold Bash's. She led the twins into the aisle where they squeezed into a procession of overexcited children and exhausted parents. They inched their way down the grand staircase as part of a congested traffic jam.

An impatient woman with a group of children in tow elbowed past Kit, shoving him hard enough for him to lose his grip on Bash's hand and knock him off-balance. The witch of a woman had hissed 'get a bloody move on, time-waster. I haven't got all day.'

When Kit righted himself, Bash and his mother were gone. He was left, beached from a human river of pushing and shoving.

Kit stood his ground, following Mrs. S' instructions, that should they be separated, to stay put and wait. Kit planted himself – a human traffic island within a stampeding herd of parents and their single-minded children spurred on by sugar overloads and the anticipation of Christmas morning, eight hours away.

The theatre emptied of life and Kit was left alone on the stairs, reeling from the nauseating smell of stale popcorn and lady's perfume. The chilling realization that no-one was coming for him finally hit twenty minutes later. He remained standing for another ten, his pulse slowing, feet nailed apart to stop the truth from killing him. He'd been abandoned.

The palatial interior closed in, dwarfing him. It had morphed from lavish to garish with threadbare carpets, faded red velvet upholstery and hangings, framed by the overall impression of dingy gold paint. Kit surrendered, collapsing amongst the abandoned clutter of paper cups food wrappers, feeling motherless, sister-less, and helpless. The overwhelming creepiness made him sniffle but he swallowed his tears until the echoes of an ominous voice mocked from the rafters: *Boys don't cry,* it said. *Boys do NOT cry!*

Back in the present, Kit was unnerved but curious. He chose to analyze the experience with the throne as far away as possible. From the safety of the cot, thankful for Jack's company, he tried to recall how the replay began. Had he accidentally asked the chair a question? He thought back. No. I was giving it another chance. We parted in anger. I sat in the stupid thing, not to 'have a go' but to overcome my mistrust of Brooks. Missing part of the equation, he tried again. Why today? The answer came back so clearly he sighed with relief. Of course, it was Christmas Eve. No big deal. Anniversaries triggered past events. He checked the clock and sensed the hour as it had no hands. It was the exact time he'd been lost, alone on the stairs. But why this year? He hadn't felt like this last year.

There was only one person who might have picked up his fears. Bash would understand. He sent her a telepathic call. *"Hey."*

"What's up? I'm with Charlotte."

Kit nearly signed out. *"Brooks' chair is misbehaving again but I think it was supposed to. I had this déjà vu thing about that time when we went to Peter Pan and I got left behind. Does that ring any Tinkerbells for you?"*

"Yes, clever clogs."

"Will I like it?"

"You will when you accept that Bede operates within its own rules of quantum physics. With your present attitude, you're lucky the chair worked at all. Nimue says the chair has a special plan for

you. For us, really. It simply delivered a message that you needed to hear, in a TIMELY manner."

"Now who's being clever. But I did ask it why I was intimidated by a theatre."

"Hmmn?… intimidated by a building. I'd say that was an obvious clue."

"You're saying I'm scared of Bede Hall."

"Formal questions are never the real questions you want to ask." There was a pause. *"And it's not Brooks' chair anymore, it's yours. It's giving you a second chance."*

"Funny, I thought I was giving the chair a second chance."

"Take it, and don't forget to say thank you."

"Who's that talking in the background?"

"You don't want to know."

"You're having a pow wow with fairies again. You know, I talk to Jack all the time but he doesn't talk back."

Bash groaned. *"Of course, he does. He is right now. I can hear him. He's asking if you're okay. He's really upset."*

"Yeah, he looks a bit antsy."

"I'm not surprised. He's around YOU all the time, and you're not exactly Mr. Sensitive. She took a deep breath that sounded more like a pained sigh. *"Kit?"*

"Yeah?"

"Parting in anger is unworthy of a scientist…It wasn't the chair. You were giving YOURSELF a second chance."

Maybe she was right. *"Bossy britches!"*

"The chair sees through your disguise. It recognizes you, Peter Pan. You always said you wanted to fly. That's time travel isn't it?"

"And you're scared of growing up."

"Geek."

That time she was right for sure. Bash knew things. *"Freak!"*

Bash's voice softened. *"You do know, don't you, that we both got our wish. We wanted to live in Neverland. Gotta go."*

Kit rubbed the sudden soreness in his upper arm with a terrifying thought. Oh God. Maybe I WAS there! The encounter with that rude woman gave me a nasty bruise.

He didn't dare look.

Jack's ears were overly alert, his breathing, whiny. "What do you reckon mate? Are you worried? Did I disappear?" He flopped onto the cot and patted the blanket. "Up you pop Scragamuffin, there's a good chap. No worries. Everything's okay. I didn't mean to scare you."

Jack leaped easily, clearing Kit's legs, landing with surprising agility.

Kit allowed his emotional memories to replay at will with no anesthetic. The intensity stunned him. He recoiled back from the chair in a state of shock, gut-punched and winded from an eeriness so familiar.

He'd been a boy when he'd been terrified enough to double over with sick, stunned at the size of his life against the world. It was how he'd felt the day, not long since when he'd travelled to the future, trapped at the business end of a time portal with the blue door locked against him.

Jack cowered, moved to Kit's side, and nudged his nose into Kit's hand.

"That's odd," Kit said. "What do you make of that?"

He witnessed again the shock of seeing a sad ring of stones poking a few inches above the snow's crust like a miniature Stonehenge, all that showed of his tower's crenellations. Bede Hall's roof and top floor in a similar state, the interior an empty shell inhabited by ice and snow and death. He used his lucid dream technique of controlling threatening images and reduced the scene until it fit inside Lady Nan's snow globe.

Being lost in time was no different than being a small boy lost in a theatre. He felt like a fish gasping out of water. *Boys do cry!*

As an outsider in a strange land, aliens would push past him, uncaring and disconnected. But this time, he'd be irretrievably lost for the rest of his life in a lonely state of terrifying anonymity amongst strangers.

Once unleashed, other memories came fast. A slideshow of memories grouped under the heading abandonment. One wasn't even his own. Taraq's ordeal, buried alive in an Egyptian tomb was particularly claustrophobic. It seemed he'd been lost countless times, the worst being the times he abandoned himself. There was Bash at twelve, crying over a dead bird and he, dry-eyed, with the cold eyes of a neutral passerby-twice-removed who probed it with a stick while Bash dug a grave and lined it with grass and leaves. *Back in time, I will be no better than a dead bird with the blank eyes of strangers probing me with sticks.*

He saw himself, a heartless boy, bird's plight forgotten, moving on without a care to a hot supper and a warm bed. That evening, the twins sat side-by-side to draw, something they loved to do together. Kit drew the lifeless corpse of an insignificant bird; Bash sketched birds in flight. She'd set the sparrow free. Kit, ever the scientist apprentice, had treated the sparrow like a specimen to dissect. *Guilt… fear… guilt.* Removed from feeling. Logic ruled. Kit was all about diagrams with labels; his twin cried over every crushed flower or fallen bee. He remained neutral or mildly curious.

Fair enough, I'm a freaking coward. Maybe I deserve to be stuck in time like a fly on flypaper. Anger flared into self-pity and shame. *No-one cares now and no-one will care in the past. I may as well go. Not that I'm going to own up until the last possible minute.*

Jack's wet nose nuzzled his hand.

I'll be helpless and friendless as a homeless dog.

Kit cradled Jack's head and scratched the dog's ears. "I'll miss you old thing. But in time, you'll forget me too, won't you, boy."

The words 'in time' hit hard. "You've got to hand it to Lady Nan. She knows her stuff. She always says words are ciphers. No worries, Jacko, my Anna will see you right."

'MY Anna!' the words brought Kit up short, embarrassed enough in front of a dog to correct himself. "What I meant to say was, Anna is a bit like a guardian angel as far as you're concerned." More guilt. As if Bash's future wasn't enough. Guilt plus shame ended in confessing the worst of oneself to a dog.

XXVII

ONCE UPON A TWINTERS' EVE

DECEMBER 24 –
the late afternoon of CHRISTMAS EVE – 2016

A sour stench radiated from the postcard in the centre of Brooks'
dining table. The Twinters huddled around it as if they were
roasting a demon on a campfire which in some sense, they were.
Charlotte reached into her pocket and threw a handful of crushed
mistletoe berries onto it as if to douse it. It coughed, in the way
an enchanted postcard might, and the smoke fizzled out enough to
expose the words 'It Came From Mars'.

"I've seen that movie," Kit said. "It's rubbish."

Parks turned the blighted postcard over with the handle of a
teaspoon. "I know that handwriting."

"Wait until you see this," Charlotte said, keeping her eyes level
with Bash's face. "Show them your bruise, girl. Go on, now."

Bash rolled up her sleeve. To her horror, the irregular bruise had
grown into a familiar shape. It was bright yellow with a brown scab
at the entre. Unmistakably a sunflower.

"I have one too," Kit said, rolling up his sleeve. "But it's only
psychosomatic, from a vivid memory I had earlier of a woman
punching into me when I was a kid."

150

Charlotte sniffed. "So, you believe *thinking* about being bruised caused yours?"

"Let's not dismiss the facts," Brooks said. "Twin bruises on twins a few minutes apart. That's not a coincidence."

Brook's garden sweltered outside on a freakish Christmas Eve. He drew the curtains to block out the non-autumn colours. Inside, the Christmas tree glittered with fairy lights, and seasonal music swelled from the radio. He clapped his hands loudly and addressed the teens. "Right, come to order. Your parents will be here soon, and we can all play the game of 'Christmas inside your grandmother's snow globe' to our heart's content." He gestured towards the smouldering image of a flying saucer. "But for now, we have this to contend with."

"Maybe we ought to let the parents in on... you know... things," Kit said. "Developments."

Lady Nan's snow globe manifested on her lap swirling with a red snowstorm. "Absolutely not. We've been through all that. What they can't see can't hurt them. They wouldn't believe a word of it anyway."

"But the curse. We know it's going to show up bigtime soon. This postcard is just an invitation to the party. Wouldn't it be fair if they knew?"

"And what about the future?"

"There's nothing they can do other than worry and that would turn every day into a bigger nightmare. We need to be free to save them. That's what the Hall says isn't it Lady Nan?"

"It is. Bede Hall has enough to worry about other than the family moving away for safe keeping."

"There's no such place."

"We don't know that for sure. Maybe this whole ancient curse business will be over by spring. If spring ever comes."

"That's the thing about old curses," Dr. Brooks said, pouring himself a generous snifter of sherry. "They show up as future ones." The sound of the glass decanter stopper clinked into place. He lifted his glass in a cheerful toast to Lady Nan and Ben. "To absent ghosts."

"To Good King Wenceslas," Bash said, raising her sherry glass of Coca Cola.

The voice of Bing Crosby filled the room: *'I'm dreaming of a white Christmas.'*

"The rest of the country is at least experiencing bare branches and rain," Tut said.

"There's still time. It *could* snow tonight," Anna said, she being the least likely to wish winter on anyone.

The snowstorm in Lady Nan's globe settled down to pure white. "We're all together. And that's the main thing." She smiled at Ben who had reverted to his youngest self and was the only one present who looked appropriately excited. He sat with Jack, staring at the brightly coloured packages. Anna's mouth quivered, wistful as always, reminded of the last Christmas with her parents.

"Mom and Dad will be here soon."

Another strange but commonplace family dinner was about to begin – a table set for the living with the adjacent sitting room filled with lounging ghosts. Tut was confused. "How many do I set for?"

"Mum and Dad, you, me, and Kit, Charlotte, and ..." Bash giggled. "That makes seven dwarfs counting Doc here."

"And me, I'm Snow White," Anna said, clutching a rabbit doll as if it was a teddy bear. She buried her nose in its fur, and suddenly her old red mittens materialized on her hands.

"Hang on, Kit said, pointing to the doll. "Isn't that Pookie?"

Bash replied quickly, smiling at Anna. "The very same. I gave it to Anna. It always comforted me when I was her age."

"Ghosts eat outside," Kit announced.

Taraq got up from the table and headed for the door.

Kit pulled him back. "Come here, runt. I was only joking."

"Parks will manifest later after the food's gone. He's got the perfect excuse for being delayed. The Hall is always cranky when we're celebrating away from home."

Charlotte returned from the kitchen to catch the inference that Parks had to pretend he was alive. "He can manage a wee dram," she said.

Lady Nan, Ben, Taraq, Parks, and Anna kept each other company and tried to speak in semi-whispers, not because they would be overheard by Mr. and Mrs. S but lest their private conversations could divert attention from the one at the table.

Kit sipped his cranberry punch and Tut savoured his hot chocolate, his go-to favourite during every season... seeing's as the English summer was infinitely milder than his Egyptian days.

"You better not use the name Doc in front of Mum. She'll have a fit."

"I'm dreaming of a red Christmas," Bash sang. "Parks you'll have to be the *red* man now."

Parks scowled. "Not even in fun, minx," he said. "They'll be no disrespecting the old ones while I'm in charge."

"I thought the fairies were in charge."

Parks spluttered, too offended to speak.

Kit caught Bash's expression of horror. She shook her head slowly and mouthed the word stop.

"I'm only having you on, Parks," Kit said. "It's a joke."

"There's nothing amusing about what's coming' young master. They're powerful trouble and they've been saving up their anger for a few thousand years or more, so introductions won't be a pretty sight. A bit of black snow's nothing at all. You'll see. You lot had better prepare. I'm long-dead but you young ones aren't. Nor are your parents."

Kit held up his hand. "Excuse me, Parks... who's *they*?"

Jack whimpered in his sleep. His paws twitched. A tremor rippled under his fur.

"Even Jack has the good sense to be worried," Parks said. "He's not dreaming about rabbits, either. Just look at him. He's having his own private earthquake. Jack's got his nose to the ground. He can smell what's coming. You'd best be watching the animals. Especially Anubis and Feathers."

A rumble of agreement filled the room.

Parks tapped his cane on the floor. "And Pigeon may have a few insightful things to say and all," he said.

Charlotte banged her fist on the table for quiet. "Let's get some things straight concerning fairies, shall we," she said, her many bracelets jingling like bells.

"Charlotte has the floor," Dr. Brooks shouted over the din.

Parks 2 popped in suddenly and gazed at her with affection.

Charlotte waited until the room was ready. "Always consider the brightness of fairy light," she said. "And you'll appreciate this, Kit, fairy light is like a litmus test – a thermometer to measure human weakness. And logically, anything that measures weakness also measures strength by default. Truth is gauged by their lightness of being. Therefore, assess any situation involving magic by asking them a question and notice the colour of their answer. Use the obvious clues of light and darkness. Fairies will try to deceive a human with the red spectrum, but they cannot conceal their moods for long. The brighter they glow the more powerful they are. A dim or flickering light means they're thinking and you have a chance for escape. Yes, *escape*. A dim or flickering red light means they're in the mood for mischief. Some of them can be a little devious when they're bored."

Charlotte settled herself comfortably in her armchair upholstered in floral chintz. Her flowered dress merged with the pattern of pink and white cabbage roses.

"Where did Charlotte go?" Kit said.

"I'm right here," Charlotte replied, directly opposite him.

He startled. "I didn't see you there."

"It's my special glamour," Charlotte said, sitting forward. "I'm pleased it worked. I call it Christmas camouflage with a twist of nutmeg. This dress is my regular combat uniform. Reporting for duty."

Kit scanned the room for Parks. "Now Parks has gone. Does he have a glamour too?"

"It's leaves," Bash said. "He just blends into the trees."

Parks dropped by for the family supper Christmas Eve carolling. He brought small gifts for everyone wrapped in twists of brown paper, but Bash's was a leather pouch inscribed with fairy runes that looked like Egyptian hieroglyphics. He winked. "It doesn't do to open a gift before its time. Timing is everything. Christmas morning is magic," he said.

Kit passed a glass of something strong to Parks. "Charlotte can be a little devious with presents. But I expect you know all about that."

Parks drank his shot of whisky, and winked at Kit. "Aye, Miss Charlotte keeps me in line, right enough," he said.

XXVIII
CHRISTMAS PRESENT

DECEMBER 25, 2016 – Christmas morning

Christmas morning there was no stopping the new Stratford-Smyth master of ceremonies. Tut handed out the presents. He announced each gift tag as a proclamation of the good life. "To the Green Princess from Parks." He passed a small leather pouch to Bash, "I reckon that's you," he said.

On cue, Kit pulled a small package from his dressing gown pocket and pretended to squint at the tag. "To my brother, Sherlock Holmes," Kit said. "I reckon that's you, Tut."

Tut grinned and gave it the customary shake. "Is it a pony?"

Tut, who was continually cold, was thrilled with his electric blanket and went to bed early with cocoa and a mince pie, minus the usual hot water bottle.

Charlotte had smuggled her present into Bash's room. The print of Vincent Van Gogh's bedroom hung on the wall where it could be easily viewed from the bed, and there was a jar of leaves on her dressing table labelled SPECIAL TEA – *drink me*.

The 'Alice-in-Wonderland-like' message reminded Bash of Lady Nan's empty perfume bottle. It had been special too, its remnants so twined to its distinct scent that it acted like a passport to one of her grandmother's old memories. In a playful moment, Bash had dubbed it time travel in a bottle.

Bash sniffed the pouch. "Remember that memories are oddly olfactory," she said to Tut by way of explanation.

Parks' Christmas pouch for Bash contained a handful of sunflower seeds and cryptic instructions to keep them dry and wait for a critical planting time – namely: midnight New Year's Eve under the full moon. *These are potent seeds,* the note advised. *Not to be confused with regular seeds. Keep them under your pillow. Pleasant dreams, little apprentice.*

XXIX

MAGIC JACK

DECEMBER 26, 2016 Boxing Day

The Sunflower seeds called Bash just after midnight. *"Mademoiselle,"* they whispered. *"The moonlight she is ready. We have ze message from Jacques."*

Bash answered without opening her eyes. "What does Parks want at this hour?"

They giggled. *"Not that Jack... Beanstalk Jack."* They giggled like her lavender plants.

"Nimue, is that you?" she mumbled. "I'll see you tomorrow. Please let me sleep... off you go, get out of my dream and let me ..."

"Non, not zat one, eh. Madame Charlotte, she tell Monsieur Jacque to show you... c'est surpris. Now, urry up. Come weez us before the light she is too bright. The lady of the moon, she is a cousin of hers, oui? She say her beams zey are parfait, oui?"

Bash separated from her body and sat up in bed. The French doors had blown open and the billowing net curtains waved like two giant hands. Behind them, the old rowan tree's familiar muttering joined the voices of the sunflowers. *"This way, Mistress."* Had the French doors been speaking to her? Silly thought, but she heard singing in the distance. An old French nursery rhyme about Brother Jack. *"Frère Jacques, Frère Jacques, dormez vous? Are you sleeping? Are you sleeping? Sonnez les matines, morning bells are ringing, Din dan don."*

Bash pulled on her slippers and robe. "Of course I'm sleeping, as you well know," she replied to the empty room. "At least, I *was*."

A gentle breeze blew the floor-length curtains into a shimmering veil, and the scent from her walled garden was intoxicating with the perfumes of midnight. Eagerly, she followed it. Was something wrong with the seeds?

A far-off glow illuminated a tall tree by the far wall that hadn't been there the day before. But when she reached it she found a sunflower stalk that reached to the stars. The ridiculous image almost caused to wake but she remembered an important lesson from Parks. Lucid dreams called out for a reason. They begged to be heard. They always required further investigation.

Charlotte too, had made a point of dreams being serious messages. Signs are everywhere she'd said. And never closer than your subconscious mind. Never ever dismiss the significance of a seemingly obscure sign. Often their meanings are hidden in 'familiar archetypical memories'. Bash remembered because of the word archetype, one of her favourites.

So, on second lucid thoughts, the very fact that a 'beanstalk' loomed at her feet was invitation enough. Magic seeds called for magic plants, and now the underside of a giant sunflower beckoned her. She climbed it without hesitation. This is going to be a lark. I wonder if Kit will show up.

Dream-climbing posed no obstacles. And as she grew closer, the head of the sunflower resembled a green flying saucer perched on a pedestal. Tendrils at its base allowed her to pull herself hand-over-hand through a crown of spiky green leaves. She parted the golden petals, and what she saw amazed her. She expected to see a landscape of brown seeds. Instead, she stood facing a vista of fields in a crazy-quilt of green and gold coloured shapes under a vivid-blue kaleidoscope sky. Wherever she was, it was midday. The yellow field, in which she stood, rustled with sunflowers.

A man's cheery voice agreed hailed her. "Bonjour Mademoiselle, *bienvenu...* welcome."

"It's about time," the sunflowers sang.

The man agreed. "Isn't it always?"

Bash nodded. "I know that feeling only too well."

"Don't mind them, they're saucy little minxes. But always cheerful and friendly. I come out here to lift my spirits."

The voice belonged to a man wearing a blue coat and a crushed wide-brimmed straw hat, seated at an easel. The sunflowers bowed into a clear pathway, inviting her towards him.

Bash searched her vast vocabulary for schoolgirl French. Good morning *Monsieur... um...* hello... *bonjour*," she said.

The man checked the sky and smiled back at her. "It's afternoon, *non?*"

Bash felt like Alice behind the looking glass in some aerial version of a rabbit hole skylight. "Wherever this is, I expect it's always like this."

"Non Cherie, we have some, how do you say, glorious... *c'est magnifique* starry nights."

She pointed to the ground. "It was a starry night where I just came from." She bent and patted the earth like an old friend. The soil was friendly. "Somewhere below here."

"You are *Anglais*. I expect you want tea, *non?*"

She inspected the waist-high sunflowers. "Afternoon tea is one of my favourite times." One flower was taller than the rest. "Okay, I'm here. Surprise me," she whispered into its face. There was humour in that face and it appeared to smile.

When she looked up, the artist had already packed his materials into a shoulder bag. He gestured his hand towards a quaint newly-materialized village. "Welcome to Arles," he said. "My studio awaits. I hope you don't mind a bit of a mess. I have a painting there that wishes to speak with you."

Muffled laughter came from the field. *"To av speaks weez you,"* the sunflowers echoed.

Bash called back. "Okay, I get it. This is a nursery rhyme that's curiouser and sillier."

"Ah, *oui*, you are reminded of course, of my friend Monsieur Hatter, a kindred spirit of mine," Vincent said. "We both possess, shall we say, the infinite mind."

"My name is Bathsheba; I prefer to be called Bash."

He bowed and swept the air with his straw hat. "Mademoiselle Bash. I have been expecting you. I am Vincent." He winked and squashed his hat over a tangle of red hair. "But everyone calls me crazy."

"I suspected," Bash said, smiling. "I know your work very well, and since this is a lucid fairy tale from some Lewis Carroll childhood memory, a tea party would be lovely... *merci*."

Vincent handed her his painting. "It would help if you carried this for me."

"Delighted." Bash reached for it, eager to inspect an original Van Gogh masterpiece. It was a painting of the bedroom she had recently left, and Kit sat on her bed waving at her. Strange, but she *had* partaken of Charlotte's special tea as a nightcap, so anything could happen.

"*Bonsoir*," Vincent said, grinning. "I do believe we have a message to interpret and since two heads are better than one, I shall assist. The art of the studying of codes is a science."

Bash turned the painting to face Vincent. "May I introduce my brother, Christopher. He prefers to be called Kit. But you've already met."

"Yes, he is a most fascinating guest. He must join us for tea. Please, this way." At that, Vincent turned towards the town and gently pushed his way through the sunflowers. Each one turned their face towards him after he passed. *"Follow the sun. All hail our Sun King,"* they called in unison.

The sun-worshipping flower-children of Arles reached out to touch Bash with their gigantic leaf hands as she made her way, brushing her with their petals. Golden fuzz collected on her clothes and made her feel lighter than air. She floated an inch above the ground, drenched in sunshine. Kit chuckled from the painting. "My sister, the human honeybee, gathering magic pollen."

He envisioned the stalks of the sunflowers popping from the soil, giggling on tiptoed roots, straining to commune with the Egyptian sun god, the Aten. Immediately, a radiating fan of golden arms reached down against a sky of pure turquoise, and touched their eager upturned faces.

Vincent's paint-encrusted blue coat led Bash through several wheat fields to the outskirts of Arles and down a few higgledy-piggledy lanes paved with cobbles to an open square. A two-story house painted bright yellow, stood on the corner. A jaunty blue and white striped awning hung over an attached shop-front of Van Gogh's famous 'Yellow House'.

"I live here, you understand, but mostly out there," he said, gesturing to the countryside. He swivelled on his heels and directed her gaze to a café, kitty-corner to his street. "Or over there. You probably know it as the 'Night Café'. He fanned his sunburned face with his hat. "I get sunstroke all the time but that's the nature of the *plein air* art business, *eh? Your grand-mère, she once had a very important sunstroke when she was a leetle girl, as I recall.*" He squinted at his painting, now dry and mounted in a fancy gilt frame. It was a different bedroom scene that looked as if it had been made of wax and melted in the sun.

Vincent tapped the high-backed wooden chair in the painting. "That chair has been wanting to meet you two ever since I found it on my doorstep." His pipe puffed violet smoke.

Wonky tables spilled onto the square. An intoxicating aroma of soup issued from the night café. Pulling the street of leaning buildings closer together. A few casual customers lingered over coffee and croissants.

"By the way, it's 1888," Kit said, now outside the painting. He pulled Bash's arm. We can't stop to eat. Our window of 'downstairs' moonlight' won't last much longer. We're on a time-sensitive mission. Let's go." He nudged Bash with his elbow. "This is kind of fun, isn't it. Just like old times."

Vincent was waiting for them, filling his pipe. He leaned against his front door, studying the twins through a cloud of foul tobacco smoke.

Kit coughed. "Poo what a stink."

"You sound like Pigeon. I can just hear him," Bash said, imitating the bird: *Pooh to Jack and the Beanstalk... yellow sunflowers... state of the art...costs a fortune.*

"The real magic is upstairs. I can feel it," Kit said.

Vincent's studio was chaos but it smelled delightfully of art. At least a dozen wet paintings burst with the smells of turpentine and linseed oil. Every inch of floor was carpeted with drips of colours tracked into a wild carpet. Paint had migrated to tables and cupboards and spilled onto the curtains.

A red checkered tablecloth had been laid with blue and white china for two, and a single sunflower blossomed from a wine bottle wearing its own straw basket like a coat.

Sounds of furniture scraping across the second floor came from the ceiling. "Can we go up?" Kit asked.

"I'm surprised that chair wasn't already down here. You can hear its agitation. I'm going across to the café." He winked. "Take your time, *s'il vous plaît.*"

The sunflower rotated in its makeshift vase to face the rickety stairs. *"Take all the time you need, my dears,"* it said in Charlotte's familiar voice.

The first thing that greeted the twins at the top of the stairs, was a painting of Kit's throne-chair, in Vincent's definitive style. Bash checked his unmistakably bold signature 'Vincent' as close as she dared — seven crudely printed letters that cut a distracting diagonal swash of black paint over the lower corner.

"*Hmmn.*" She sniffed the surface. "Be careful. The paint's wet. The name Vincent was scrawled in large crude letters in a prominent place. He's got quite the confident signature," Bash said. "He may as well have added an exclamation mark after his name."

Kit stood back from the painting. "Well, this painting clearly never existed. It's wrong. The timing's off. I know the French were bonkers about Egypt, but Tut's tomb wasn't discovered until 1922, so Vincent never saw his throne. When's that? About thirty-five years from now?"

"Can you hear yourself? The *timing's* off? That's rich even for you, Professor Kiljoy."

"If I am supposed to be Bede's time traveller, and by the way, I'm not, then calendars are an important way to assess where and when we are? They're maps."

"Oh, for heaven's sake. We're not anywhere. We're dreaming. For goodness sake, we don't need a map. We're dreaming an illogical fairy tale for a reason. We're meant to play. Dream-sharing used to be fun. The real world is getting too serious."

"Says you. We live in a perpetual fairyland, and *that's* the very opposite of serious."

"You're being logical. Doing the math. We've been invited into a story, Kit, and you know as well as I do, that means we're supposed to pay attention. Now more than ever. Let the dream play out. Let it tell its story. Play along, and let's see where it takes us. Remember when we were kids?"

"You mean those innocent days when you called me your baby brother."

"Time's weird stuff. Maybe being three minutes older contains a lifetime of experience. So, please don't burst my lovely dream bubble. I'm enjoying myself."

Bash played her winning card. "A *real* scientist would see this through to the end in order to analyse it later."

Kit ducked his head in defeat. "Okay then, Professor Sunshine, here we are, visitors in a nutty art gallery. What do you make of this enchanting, *pardon the pun*, painting?"

"We don't *make* anything. We don't *think* anything, we relax. We look and listen."

On cue, the painting moved like an animated cartoon.

Bash grabbed Kit's hand. "Here we go."

XXX

ANIMATED CONVERSATION

The bright rectangle of pulsating colours beckoned them closer. Tut's throne, a square of sunshine yellow, rested on a sea of red and turquoise stripes that rolled like waves. Its juvenile angles were wonky, as if the chair had been squashed slightly so that it hovered over a trapezoidal floor in a room seen through the distorted reflections of a fun-house mirror. The artsy chair unable to occupy real space tipped forward, nearly unseating a white cat sleeping on it. Behind it, an overzealous decorator had split the backdrop horizontally in a garish equator. The upper wallpaper section of orange and turquoise stripes butted loudly against an emerald floor.

The cat slowly uncurled into Snowball, and yawned. She leapt down and trotted off, tail up, out of the picture frame. The green carpet was now long grass dotted with purple flowers. In Snowball's place, was Vincent's unmistakable straw hat with a jaunty sunflower stuck in its hat band.

Kit whispered an aside so the painting wouldn't hear. "Where's Rupert's sunglasses when you need them?"

"Shush. I rather like it. It reminds me of a tropical garden."

"The perspective is off, wouldn't you say?"

"Yeah, a bit like that Escher drawing you like so much with the impossible staircases."

"M.C. Escher was a scientific draftsman... a brilliant mathematician."

"Well, if your criteria is brilliance, I reckon this painting may eclipse black and white math."

The frame rattled against the wall to gain attention.

A small window showed a blue sky and puffy white clouds. The coat-stand from Kit's tower stood beside the throne-chair, considerably unstable, slightly leaning to the left from the weight of a red hoodie. On the wall to the right was Bash's blue clock with no hands. Both items winked out of sight and reappeared instantly with Vincent's hat perched atop the coat stand. Bash's blue clock had sprouted hands that pointed to twelve o'clock. It was clearly midnight from the night sky peppered with stars apparent in the window.

The painting grew darker into monochromatic blues. Tut's throne painting was displaced by a birds-eye view of Bede Hall, its maze, and Kit's tower, picked out by moonlight. The scene resembled a sleepy quilted landscape.

Unexpectedly, the throne winked back with its startling colours.

Kit blinked and took a step backwards. "I wish it would stop moving. I feel rather dizzy."

"That'll be from the paint fumes," Bash said. "They can be overwhelming. The paint is still wet."

Kit looked triumphant. "More toxic fumes! It's just like Bede. The smells are causing a loss of equilibrium. No wonder I felt weird. Is that why I'm here? Another ruse to get me to surrender? Are you saying I lack confidence? I'll have you know that I've acted with the truth of my convictions. I *am* confident. Confidant that you and the Twinters are wrong."

"Settle down. I can do that when we're awake. I didn't orchestrate this dream. It's the real thing. Give me some credit."

"This painting is not about you, young sir," a woman said, entering the room. "'Tis about the both of you, so ye might pay attention and stop yer yammering, else ye'll frighten the wee flowers."

The twins turned to face a familiar looking parlour-maid bearing a tea tray.

"Charlotte is that you?"

"Mah name's no Charlotte, Missus, it's Glynis. Glynis Findlay."

"*Um*… sorry, you look like a friend of mine."

"Master Vincent sends his regrets. He'll no be joining you fer yez tea. He says to make yerselves at home. And he'll see yez soon enough."

The word 'home' reverberated from the walls. Glynis curtsied and turned towards a different door. The blue door of the Winter Room.

"I'd recognize that chill anywhere," Kit said.

As Glynis passed through, into the hall, the doorway seemed to swallow her and close into a solid wall until Vincent's door shimmered into being.

"That's Charlotte all right. She's messing with us."

"No. I think it's the woman Charlotte *used* to be. Remember she was once a house parlour-maid when she was engaged to Parks. She lived in the Winter Room. Maybe she's used the portal to come here. Maybe she was Scottish."

"Or maybe she's just *skittish*," Kit replied.

The open door had ushered in a jarring cloud of floral scent that made Kit choke. Conflicting smells filled the room. The sweet fragrance of violets from the painting, met the odour of turpentine from the studio opposite, and mingled with the aroma of chicken soup wafting up from the kitchen, creating a cloying discord of savoury and floral.

"That's not violets you can smell," Bash said. "It's lavender."

Kit squinted his eyes in thought. "Two golden chairs. Why does that ring a bell?"

"*It's written in the prophecy,*" the yellow chair replied. "*Word for word. We are a lively pair for you to share. Each to each; side-by-side; back to back. Thinking chairs. Never parted. A communication device, no? – a telephone for long distances, if you understand me. A very long-distance line. Sometimes the mind alone is not strong enough to send or receive. Not even two minds or two minds with a single purpose. You have experienced this Monsieur Kit, have you not?"*

"This is where I leave the dream," Kit said. "No more funny business."

The chair spun slowly. *"No…please wait! I bring you a message to take heart. Time need not separate. Meditation is only one key. Banishment need not be forever. Listen to me, Monsieur Kit, but act like a true scientist and test what I say."*

Bash lowered herself onto the yellow chair. It felt weird to address it. "By now I expect you're long gone. That is, in *my* time," she said to it. "Old kitchen chairs rarely last one-hundred-twenty-eight years."

"Au contraire, Cherie. I am much older than that," the yellow chair replied. *"But this is my last incarnation as a chair. Mr. Clutterbuck, he keeps me in a back room of his junk emporium, in Bede. But I am so loaded down with books that I fear my seat will soon give way. Mademoiselle, please. I beg you to save me. I promise to serve you well. You will not be disappointed."*

Bash hesitated. "I..."

"Listen to her, a sunflower said from one of the paintings. The chair, she will save lives."

Kit's throne in the painting interrupted by hopping on one leg. *"When in doubt, follow Ra,"* it said.

"Jack knows best," the yellow chair said.

Kit lifted the chair testing its weight. "Can't you come back with us now?"

"Not out of history I can't," it said. *"But you already know this. Time can distort humans but humans cannot distort time. This is the first rule of time travel."*

"The second rule is to stay home," Kit said, carefully placing the chair in position. "Dream travel is much safer."

The sunflower piped up. *"Ma Cherie, the night train, he awaits. If you look into the painting of the 'Yellow House' you will see the train. Walk towards it. He is waiting in the station especially for you. Bon Voyage, mes amis."*

"Say goodbye to Vincent for us," Bash said.

"Tell him yourself. Or rather say hello. Vincent, SHE lives in Bede," the chair said. *"How else did you suppose I got there?"*

The door opened. Vincent was back with three glasses of something red that looked like wine.

The twins arranged themselves facing Vincent the way they used to sit when Lady Nan was about to deliver a story.

Vincent stared from twin to twin, slowly assessing them. "My brother Theo and I," he began, "we shared the love of art, yes? We wrote letters that passed each other in time but never surpassed in the understanding, *eh*? You understand? We were of one mind. One day after painting the sunflowers, I sat in this chair, knowing Theo would be impressed. I was, as you say, eager, to have his opinion. And as I pondered this, I heard his voice so clearly, I thought he had entered the room as a *surprisse*. But the *surprisse,* she was mine." He tapped his forehead. Theo was here, inside my head."

The second chair tapped its legs for attention.

"As you see, I have two identical chairs." He patted the chair nearest him affectionately. "This one, she brings me my brother." He gestured to the chair beside his bed. "The other has a purpose also. He functions as a table."

Vincent lowered himself onto the chair with a sublime expression and folded his arms.

"Mes enfants, I have learned two things. There are *spéciale* connections between devoted pairs of siblings, and there is an art to sitting."

Tut was piling marmalade on his toast when Bash breezed into the morning room and plonked down on one of the upholstered kitchen chairs with metal legs.

As usual, Kit cut his toast into isosceles triangles with one set aside for wolfhound Jack, riveted to the breakfast table.

Bash reached for the teapot. "Well, last night's dream was one for the books."

Kit downed his tea and clattered the cup onto its saucer. "A really *weird* book."

Tut looked from one twin to the other. "One of you better let me on it. It's lonely out here."

Blank stares and silence.

"Come on, at least spill a couple of beans. Mum's the word."

"You're not far wrong. It was magic seeds, actually," Bash said.

Kit waved his teaspoon in Tut's direction. "Apparently, humans can reincarnate as pieces of furniture. Who knew?"

Tut made a polite cough behind his hand. "Yeah, right… although, I have to say, that throne of yours is rather uppity."

Bash peeled a banana and cut it into slices over a bowl of cereal. "If it's true, maybe the opposite applies. Maybe furniture can rein-carnate as people. A chair for instance."

"Or a banana," Kit said. "It was only a dream."

Tut waggled his spoon at Kit. "That was no ordinary dream, kiddo. You two need to rethink it in the daylight and make a report to the Twinters. It sounds important."

Bash squinted her eyes at the ceiling, puzzling out a riddle. "The thing is, it means… it *suggests*… that Bede Hall may have been some*one*. A person who lived a long time ago. Which is how it can speak to Lady Nan."

Kit raised his head in a fake lightbulb moment. "Long ago and faraway in *Fairyland*… oh wait… don't we already live there?"

Tut speared Kit with his eyes. "Kit, you have to agree," he said. "That would explain a lot."

"It would explain that you're a pushover for a weird story," Kit said, tapping a large spoon on Tut's forehead.

Tut grabbed the spoon and set it down. "I'm saying that maybe it proves *you* have a closed mind."

Kit poured himself a bowl of cornflakes. "Sister dear, could you please pass me a banana. Which reminds me, methinks you're going to come back as a fruit basket in your next life."

Bash slid a banana down the table. "Better that, than a Petrie dish."

Tut stopped the banana from falling on the floor and handed it to Kit. "Or worse, something growing in one."

Mr. Clutterbuck's Junk Emporium delivered the yellow chair the following day, curtesy of Mrs. Hannah Johns. It came with a sunflower stem made of silk and a note on the back of a postcard with Vincent Van Gogh's 'Yellow Room' on the front. The message read: *Bienvenu Cherie*, welcome home my dear.

XXXI

THE LAND OF DÉJÀ VU

THE BEDE CHRONICLES
by Christopher Stratford-Smyth
December 2016 – Boxing Day… 9p.m.

The throne-chair did something.

It was a couple of days ago on Christmas Eve. It was no super big deal, other than I upset Jack. But I will never again question the intensity of Déjà vu. The chair jogged my memories into life flashes of life before my eyes. That wiping of the slate that's supposed to happen to human consciousness immediately before death. It was like flipping through a photo album of a particular Christmas I wanted to forget.

This visualizing thing worked too well. Jack was that unnerved, I let him sleep on the bed to calm him down. It occurred to me later, that the weight of an Irish wolfhound draped over my legs like a huge hairy paperweight would prevent me from having a real of out-of-body experience.

I sat in the chair and came in for a shock. And later, when I tried to process what had happened, every time I closed my eyes, I was seven again, floating and sinking in equal measure and felt the need to grab Jack as an anchor.

My first experience of astral travel, under Brooks' supervision, had been spontaneous and exhilarating, but the downside was it 'opened' my receptive abilities and primed me for the horrific sequel in the maze, and the subsequent journey to the future with Anna. I would have done anything to find my dad. Being twelve was a lifetime ago. Three years I'll never get back.

Every Christmas Eve, I reexperience an episode from when I was seven. The afternoon when I was left behind in a theatre after a pantomime of Peter Pan. I've never forgotten the horror of separation, walking in slow-motion through a fog of brightly-coloured coats, my life muffled behind glass where no-one could hear me. I had the odd sensation of being weighted down from lead boots while floating weightless at the same time. I was bodiless, looking down on the head of a boy where I'd once stood. I had enough time to realize the boy was me, but at the time, I was fast-disappearing into a small blue door in the ceiling. I recall thinking, Mum will never find me up here. No-one will ever find me.

Had the ceiling swallowed me whole or had I sunk into the quicksand of a red carpeted floor? I was no longer any 'where' that made sense. Even then, the thought dawned on me that I was between worlds. A premonition perhaps, because here I am, in 2016, facing a similarly uncertain quality of permanent invisibility.

Mum had an ironclad rule about expeditions. She made Bash and I promise to remain where we were if we were ever separated. That day in London, it felt like a lifetime before she reclaimed me, but it was half-an-hour. She hadn't realized I'd been left behind until she and Bash emerged onto Oxford Street, and it took time to wade through the crowds of milling theatre-goers and find a security guard. The theatre doors had been locked. Staff had scanned the theatre rows but hadn't seen me on the ceiling. Meanwhile I waited in two places at the same time.

Later, at home, I dutifully ate ice-cream to please my mother. She watched every bite with her lips set in a grim straight line, so fixated, she forgot to drink the sugary cup of tea to steady her nerves.

Clearly, she and Bash had experienced the same anxiety as I. Bash clung to my hand all the way home, and Mum plucked at her gloves on the short train ride to Livingston. Back home, her hands, scooping ice-cream, were as twitchy as Jack's paws when he dream-chased rabbits.

I wasn't sure if the ice cream was a reward for my obedience or to appease her guilt. To this day, I can't remember what flavor it was. All I knew, was Mum wanted me to have it and that I ate it for her even though it soured my already queasy stomach.

That night, I pushed my dinner away untouched and went to bed early with the excuse of an upset tummy that wasn't a word of a lie. I lay there with Feathers, a kitten then, no bigger than a sparrow, and held on to her as if she could save me.

The sensation of the bed dropping away and half-lifting out of my body was disturbing. I tried to clutch the sheets to keep from levitating but my arms wouldn't move until I reminded myself that gravity was a big deal and I was being a baby. Peter Pan was only a story about a boy who didn't want to grow up and flew to Neverland. But just the same, I made sure my bedroom window was locked.

I resisted closing my eyes as long as I could, but inevitably the undertow of sleep pulled me down through the theatre's red carpet into icy water teaming with fish with claws for fins. I swam up to safety, towards the surface, my arms flailing until I gained the sky lined with blue ceiling tiles. When it was safe to look down, all I saw was a gathering of theatre-goers pointing at a puddle on the spot where I'd formerly stood. That witch of a woman looked up at me and grinned. 'Bad kitty,' she said. 'Who's been a bad little kitty, then.'

I woke with a headache, clammy with sweat. Or so I thought. The truth is, I'd wet the bed. I stripped it before anyone knew, but I was mortified for months. If Bash guessed, she said nothing. She either kept my shameful secret or took pity on me. She was loyal back then. I still don't know for sure. I never asked, and we never discussed that incident from that day to this.

I spent Christmas Day, jumpy and subdued, faking seasonal joy for Mum's sake.

The thing is, I didn't just see things. Everything felt as real as if was I was there. I still had a bruise on my arm that I couldn't account for. And if it wasn't a lucid dream, the theatre must have been another time portal. Which begs the present obvious questions: does the chair have real abilities and have I been time traveling my whole life?

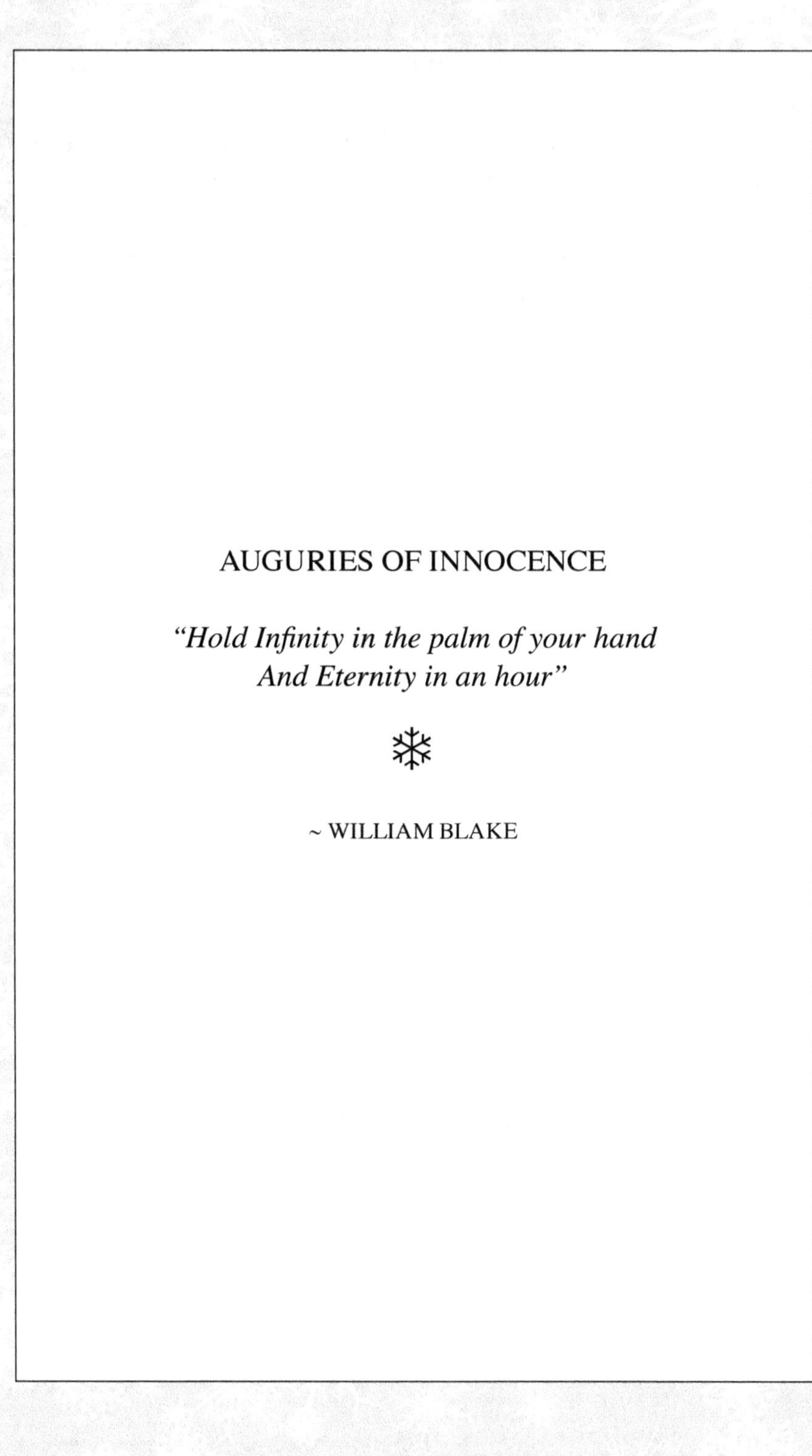

AUGURIES OF INNOCENCE

*"Hold Infinity in the palm of your hand
And Eternity in an hour"*

❄

~ WILLIAM BLAKE

XXXII

GOSWOLD & CO.

Bede Hall measured its progress, agonizingly slowly, one day at a time. It lay in-wait, battle-scarred and wary, tired after three years of chaos, almost restored by two years of plenty, but this latest year, already lean by the end of May, foreshadowed a war that could no longer be ignored.

The Hall drowsed between past and future, masking as a quiet jewel set in the English countryside, proud of its former glories and its recent position of refurbished wealth. But on the hottest days, the Hall succumbed to the mope of wilting. It slept as fitfully as its house-cats, with one sense constantly open to psychic disturbance.

The ears of the estate's trees, being closest to the earth, sent underground reports of every foreign vibration. Old dreams of grandeur were supplanted by flashes of the nightmare prophesy it was ordered to crush.

Bede Hall had held its position for centuries, conserving its energy as the earth shifted its axis and the earth's inner sun of churning magma aligned with its mother planet. The sundial, whiling away on solar time, awaited Ra's signal to release a payload of molten rock with the precision of a cosmic clock. Time drifted on a calendar – a brooding critical mass of destructive memories.

The full moon picked out its old Domesday boundaries: the Roman road to the south, the River Bede to the east, and a forest on two sides that once enclosed a deer park, a lavender farm, and an industrious monastery that initiated thriving partnerships with honeybees and apples. Bede's cider and honey had once been celebrated as far away as Brittany, even surpassing the healing properties of the European lavender grown for the perfume trade.

Bees still followed the trajectory of their ancestors from the orchards to the village hives, and birds taught their fledglings to navigate by the lines of footpaths etched into the fields below for five-hundred-years.

Thanks to its recent restoration, the row of mature poplar trees lined a freshly-graveled drive, but even though its Tudor maze was trimmed to geometric perfection, the natural landscape took precedence. Slopes and valleys settled, and groundwater filled outcrops of hollowed rock. Trees were allowed to dot the hills as if scattered like seeds, and yet, the manicured topiaries moved like a bizarre green herd in the moonlight patrolling the contours of a manmade lake. The tower of the Hall's first incarnation as a keep, had a splendid new roof.

A bright outline shone from the grass where the bones of the dismantled great hall had once stood. In the old days, it had held a hundred guests, feasting and dancing and making music, spinning the magic that eventually seeped into the stone walls and flagstones and collected under the eaves.

THE DAWNING OF THE AGE OF GEMINI
PANGEA – PLANET EARTH
175 million-years-ago

The sun settled to ground between the Bede pyramid and the standing stones of Pan, and slipped below the horizon. It was time to gather inside the great hall and face the task at hand that had brought a party of seers traveling by camels and ships and on horseback to celebrate the solstice and discuss the end of the world.

A round stone calendar made of star patterns, pictographs, and runes set on mud bricks, served as a low table in the great feasting hall of Bedea.

The magus, Goswold Mundi, a noted scholar of 'dead languages', had recently deciphered its temperamental symbols reluctant to give up their secrets. Goswold faced his fellows and bowed formally towards the calendar. "As you can see, my friends, languages may languish but they never truly die. Reincarnation is persistent."

Twin fires burned steadily behind him. He turned to lay a sacrificial bough of Rowan entwined with mistletoe on the sacred flames, and inhaled the smoke.

"This prophecy is immortal," Goswold intoned. "We can never destroy its roots, but we may forestall it a few millennia. I have translated only a portion of these runes. Disharmony foreshadows all. Pan suffers. The ancestors showed me many things in a dream quest. I see a double throne – twin seats of troubled gold for a child-king and queen, seated as one mind. A boy and girl lie under a tree of birds. The boy is unsettled… ill. The girl is vexed. They are too young. The sun is at its zenith. It sends a warning. Sadly, unheeded. There is much discord within a family. A feline will lead them. A singular word of dark magic is shrieked by a bird of many colours. I have yet to determine its meaning other than experiencing the scent of its sinister nature. The word is Ouija.

Goswold addressed the vapours gathering above the map. "We await this prophecy to reveal itself." When satisfied, he lifted his gaze to meet his followers. One by one, he acknowledged each with a nod, finally embracing them with outstretched arms. He closed his eyes briefly as if summoning a spirit before solemnly uttering his next words. "I fear we must prepare for an event that may destroy the world again." He raised a long parchment scroll aloft like a sacrificial sword. Atlas holding up the world.

In the ensuing silence, he lowered it with reverence and unrolled a map over the calendar. "A curse concealed herein is about to speak. We must concentrate with all due watchfulness."

As soon as it was exposed to the air, the central landmass cracked and buckled and moved apart like puzzle pieces floating on red custard. Some melted away all together. Others swirled and bumped into each other changing shape as land bridges disappeared and new mountains pushed up from the blue paint, bubbling like boiling water. An almost imperceptible wail of mourning arose from the map. A tiny dragon, painted in the lower left corner, lifted clumsily from the surface and screeched past Goswold's ear like an angry bee.

Every color of dark magic issued from it trying to escape but the mindfulness of the circle reduced it to a ball of lightning that darted off to explore the corners and crevices in the stone walls. There it found shelter in the deep carvings of mythological beasts in a cool marble slab that ran across the massive fireplace. It came to roost amongst the sphinxes and griffins and dragons, nesting there as if it was laying eggs for the future – a future generation whose duty it would be to eclipse the ancient curse. Goswold swayed with power, as entranced as his words that rang out like a spell: "Bedea shall know fire and ice and everlasting darkness!"

But by Bedea, Goswold Mundi meant Bede, and by Bede, he meant the world."

XXXIII

GEMINI CHAIRS

Bash, under the influence of Charlotte's Christmas tea, remembered more of the Vincent dream than Kit's vague recollection of French voices and a cloying scent of varnish. But he couldn't deny they had two chairs declared to be tools for amplifying the senses when their telepathic abilities were compromised by time. He remembered with fear how he'd called Bash from the future and barely succeeded. The chairs promised more: visions, sounds, and smells, as well as thought transmission.

Kit called for a controlled experiment in the Hall. Bash disagreed. "The proof is in the pudding," she said. "And to know for sure, you'd have to be time traveling."

Kit shrugged. "Tough. A controlled experiment is safe. And it's better than nothing."

At undisclosed locations, Kit's golden throne and a yellow chair named Vincent, waited like tin-can telephone receivers on the ends of a piece of string.

Tut was appointed moderator. Taraq and Anna would assist as 'tennis ball ghosts', flitting back and forth between the twins, relaying messages to Tut. No telepathy was allowed. The twins were receivers only. They were to sit and wait.

An overexcited Taraq flitted about the tower like a will-o-the wisp. "We're late. Tut's ready and Anna says Bash is tapping her foot in a temper."

Kit placed his hands on Taraq's transparent shoulders. "Calm yourself. They can't start the experiment without me."

"The throne must not be outside for long," Taraq said.

Kit saluted. "Duly noted. Taraq, old man, you're so much more than a fly on the wall, you're a buzzkill on the ceiling."

"I'm *not* an old man. I may have been nine-years-old for four-thousand-years, but I'm still only nine."

"Race you to the maze. It's time to play musical chairs."

Anna materialized next to Tut. "Bash is seated. Taraq says Kit is ready."

"Moment of truth," Tut said, holding aloft a stopwatch. "Tell them to sit tight and listen."

Taraq appeared in the maze. "It has begun."

"I'm sensing or maybe anticipating hearing a buzzing sound."

Taraq took up his usual spying position, from above, looking like a cloud wearing a white nightgown.

Anna observed Bash in the kitchen from behind a giant sunflower that manifested in her hand.

"Are you theeeeere?" Kit sent Bash, mimicking the wavery voice of a séance medium.

Bash held up one hand to signal she and Kit were connected. *"Tossssssseeeeeeer,"* she replied.

Anna and Taraq materialized next to Tut simultaneously. "They're sending each other messages," Taraq reported. Anna nodded. "They're arguing."

Tut checked his watch. "Taraq, try and keep Jack quiet. Both of you, remind them no telepathy is allowed for half an hour. We'll meet here in the library. Now go!"

Taraq shook his finger at Kit. "Tut says telepathy and no out-loud voices from now on."

"Mums the word," Kit said. "I'll tell you what that means later."

A puzzled Taraq pulled an imaginary zipper across his lips and floated above the maze.

Tut pushed Kit for details in the library. "Was it buzzing or tingling? A sound or sensation?"

Kit's comeback was honest. "Yes."

Bash made a strangled noise and gave Kit a look of disgust. "You know, for someone who takes science seriously, you…"

"Consider this a colossal waste of time," Kit finished. He straightened his shoulders. "I was, perhaps, anticipating but not expecting a sensation."

"Consider it an organic dial tone," Bash said, huffily, "and let's move on. It felt more powerful. Clearer. I heard Jack whining. I saw green walls."

Kit balked. Under the rules of experimental control, he'd never disclosed their canine companion Jack would be with him. Jack had whined every time Taraq vanished and growled at the empty space after he'd vacated it. "*Um…* I smelled something. There was a burbling noise." He closed his eyes to recall it."

"Coffee," Bash said triumphantly. "Vincent was in the kitchen. Mum had coffee percolating."

Kit threw his hands in the air. "Nice job keeping a poker face till all the data is in, Einstein."

"Well, for a *true* test, you would have had to actually been in another time."

"Let's assume, should that ever be the case, and I hope it isn't, our telepathic abilities will be okay. We communicate fine without chairs."

Tut smiled at Bash. "The test was promising," he said before turning to Kit. "But inconclusive."

Bash tossed her hair and dropped beside Kit. She stared ahead, her eyes unfocused, and took his hand. "Strawberry," she said, offhandedly.

"What?"

"It was strawberry ice-cream."

"I don't understand."

"That evening after the pantomime when you went missing."

"I didn't go missing, you and Mum did."

"Suit yourself. It was still strawberry."

A ghastly thought occurred to Kit. "What else do you remember about that night?"

Bash linked her arm in Kit's and leaned her head on his shoulder. "Nothing important. You're all right. Things happen, don't they, and no-one else needs to know."

XXXIV

THE ELEVENTH HOUR

DECEMBER 31, NEW YEAR'S EVE – 2016

Sooty heat still clogged the sky as moonlight struggled through a curtain of navy-blue smog.

Inside Bede Hall's night kitchen, Parks and Bash nursed mugs of cocoa while they waited for midnight. The only light in the kitchen was from the hearth where three cats formed a sleeping nest. Bash checked the window for the eleventh time and sighed. "Surely no magic could get through on a night like this. I can't see a single star."

"Magic is as magic does," Parks said. "The magic is between you and the seeds."

"It's all my fault. I'm too fidgety. We should do this another night."

"There's no other night quite like this one. That's how one must think on magic tasks. This night is the perfect time to leave childhood behind. Now or never. Restlessness fights every sort of magic. The transitions from one year's passing trine the next year's birth. It's been three years since you moved here. The three of three, the power of nine, and a triple moon has led you to this moment. Pressure will break the spell that keeps you doubting your power. I can wait. You can wait. Waiting is life.

185

"So, *no* pressure then."

"There's *always* pressure, ye ken? And there's always counter pressure. Wait on *that*. The art of patience is inside you."

Parks' weather-worn hands refilled Bash's cup with steaming cocoa but she pushed it away. "Thanks Parks. I've had too much sugar."

Parks smiled. "That's my lass."

A wave of affection passed from teacher to student and wove itself around them. Bash glanced at Parks and for a moment in the fire's glow his hair reminded her of leaves growing around a lined face the texture of bark. Then the impression vanished and he was Parks again, a sprightly grandfatherly figure. It was easy to forget Parks was a ghost with him being more solid in body and mind than any person Bash had met who was alive. The fact that he had fractured his death into several shades of himself meant he was stronger by tenfold. Every day the Stratford-Smyth family confronted Parks in a random phase of his former life, from a wee boy to the old age he never reached. His life, cut short in his twenties, grew exponentially with each incarnation. All indications suggested that growing up in the afterlife was no easier than in life.

Bash closed her thoughts. It didn't help that she was mad about Parks Six. *Am I in love with a ghost?* She could almost handle that. *But will he stay young as I grow old?*

Parks raised his head. "Do not despair, child. Six is his own man. Six tain't no ghost. I finally decided to reincarnate proper-like. He's real enough but he has my burdens to bear. He's a bit like my heir. Truth is, he evolved from me. No different than you from your ancestors. One of whom, by the by, runs stronger in your veins than the others. Six and I are especially bonded. Think on that too. Think on it now and remain patient. Even immortals grow too old for comfort."

Bash placed her left hand over the seeds in the palm of her right and closed her eyes. She was in love with Six. She had been, ever since he called her Miss and doffed his hat in deference. Her feelings for Six percolated inside her in a pleasant daydream. She lived in a perpetual state of anticipation for the sound of his voice and a glimpse of his powerful hands. Tonight she let the image of him digging the fields cleave to the comfortable ticking of the mantle clock until the ticking ceased and all she heard was the snap of an occasional log shifting in the fire.

Parks thoughts entered hers. "That's it, lass. Think on that. Hand-fast yourself to that." His deep reassuring chuckle resonated inside her body.

After what seemed an age, Parks touched Bash's cupped hands as if to wake them. "I reckon it's time m'dear. Now, take off your shoes. Tis the way of meeting the earth skin to skin – a child to its mother."

The night was as murky as before but the two trudged in silence in a trance of goodwill. Bash felt protected by a cocoon of her own magic, gestated and born from feeling true to herself. For a moment she had leaves entwined in her hair, and stood hand-fasted to Six under a clear moon.

The seeds glowed warm in her pocket. The two walked in silence. Parks had the same inner smile on his face. Harmful entities fled from their progress. She heard their wings scuttle into the air and felt a brief perfume of wind as they vaporized. But for a green vision of the goddess Chloris in her mind's eye, the electric charge beneath her feet made her want to run laughing into the forest.

When they reached the gate of her herb garden, the well-worn hinges made no sound.

A shaft of mauve light shone against their destination. The high brick wall echoed the hoot of an owl that cast its shadow over a precise spot. Parks' voice spoke in her head. "There are nine seeds. Arrange them in a circle a few inches from the wall. You want to be able to stand inside it ye ken? So, make the circle two feet in diameter."

"Shouldn't we dig first?"

"There's no need to dig. Mother Earth will feel the seedlings on her skin. She will do the rest. Take your place and keep still."

They waited. The seeds turned purple under the moonlight.

"Now," Parks said, "gently push them into the soil with your feet."

Bash applied a slight pressure with her toes and felt each seed drawn down by a natural force, sinking deeper into the ground. The owl returned and alighted on Parks' shoulder. Parks had taken on the aura of a young man in his prime. His old tweed coat and trousers resembled a cloak of leaves and the antlers of a stag grew from his hair. His face was Six's twin. He was Six!

"No worries, my sweeting," he said.

Bash startled from the unearthly sound of a fox screaming. She was alone in her garden. "SIX!... PARKS!"

Silence and the cooing of doves enveloped her.

The fog felt safe as a cloak. New thoughts gave her feet wings as she approached the Hall. *The seeds are sown. I'm no longer a child.*

Her room glowed with the same mauve light from the garden. The patio French doors were thrown open to take in the New Year. Her favourite armchair beckoned and she curled up in it, determined to savour the exquisite moment when Six had called her sweeting.

A moment later, she shook her head from the waking dream she'd been having, to find herself in bed. Dawn spilled into the room. Anna had left their rabbit doll, Pookie, on her pillow. She pulled it into an embrace and whispered Lady Nan's New Year's Day spell: "rabbits rabbits rabbits", she said aloud to the room, and with her duty discharged, she slept until the aroma of pancakes woke her at noon.

XXXV

HEAD'S UP

Kit's feet woke him. The heat of the room was so stifling he'd kicked his thin sheet to the floor. His forehead burned. Damned recurring dream. He'd been trudging through endless snowbanks again. Stamping life back into his frozen feet. And now his real feet were numb.

A chilling whisper crept under the locked door. *"Happy birthday, Kitty."*

"What? Who's there? Taraq?"

"A friend."

"My friends don't sneak up on me and try to scare me, Taraq."

"I'm a secret admirer. A very OLD friend."

Kit sat up and rubbed his toes. "Go away freak. I'm trying to sleep."

"What's the matter? Has the little kitty got cold feet?"

"Look if you're going to hang around, at least pass me a pair of socks will you. My feet are like ice. They're over on the chair."

"You need to toughen up, little kitty. Find your inner lion. Courage is as courage does."

There came a slight buzzing of insects. *"Don't you like birthday presents?"*

"Taraq, you know I hate surprises. Stop playing games, mate. We had an agreement. You weren't going to freak me out anymore. And I'm tired. Go bug Bash or Tut, it's their birthday too."

"It's not officially Tut's birthday."

"Well any day is as good as another when you don't know the date you were born, so he's sharing mine and Bash's. But you know this, so why are you..."

The words sunk in. His birthday was four months away. "It's a tad early and not very funny. TARAQ! SHOW YOURSELF!"

"Here is my gift," the voice continued. *"You will know fire and ice and eternal darkness."*

"Thanks, but you shouldn't have. I've already got those. Never mind, it's the thought that counts."

"Bash says you're a cowardly lion."

"She ought to know."

"You know little Kitty, you really shouldn't be quite so BASHful. She's not shy when it comes to bashing you."

Taraq knocked on the door before slipping through it. "You called?"

"Stop playing silly buggers. I haven't the strength."

"What did I do?"

"You. Just now. Acting like a ghost."

"I AM a ghost. Are you ill?"

"If having chills and a fever counts, then yes, I probably am. And what's that smell? It's a stupid time for Parks to be burning leaves."

Taraq picked up an envelope on the side table, and held it under his nose. "This smells of bad magic," he announced after a short sniff. "But it has your name on it."

Kit shivered. "Open it."

"It's a birthday card." Taraq announced. "There's a picture of the Great Sphinx on the front." He scowled. "There's a bunch of balloons tied around its neck. Very disrespectful." He glanced inside at the message. "It says, Happy New Year, Kit. May you know fire and ice and eternal darkness. And it's signed M." He looked up at Kit. "Very nice. Who's M?"

Kit rubbed a red bump swelling on his arm. "Not a friend, that's for sure."

A snicker echoed off the walls. *"I did say an OLD friend. But I meant many friends. Lots of NEW friends."*

Taraq's eyes widened. "It takes a lot to spook a ghost, but whoever that is... or was, it made me feel extremely unsettled in my bones." He glanced down at his transparent body. "Such as they are." He pointed to Kit's arm. "And *that's* a wasp bite."

"Did you see him? Or was it a her? What did... IT... look like?"

"To tell you the truth, I didn't look all that closely. I saw a dark cloud, so it hadn't fully manifested. It smelled of soot and ashes. But it was female. That much I *could* sense. And it's gone. I can feel that too. I reckon it's done what it meant to do."

"Right. To make you feel worse than you already do."

"How is that even possible? Man, I have *got* to get out of this place."

"But you can't go. You're the..." Taraq straightened with formal respect. "The chosen time traveller of the Hall of Reincarnations, and the only one who can save the planet from sudden..." he paused and took a deep otherworldly breath. "... from the fiery blast of a volcano and the ice of a perpetual winter."

"Call the others. This can't wait until morning. I think it's the sign we've been waiting for."

But all the time Taraq was gone, Kit planned what he would cram into his backpack when he escaped.

New Year's Day was having an effect on everyone's expectations. Wishes swarmed thick over Bede, floating like speech bubbles over everyone's heads.

Mr. S. was considering returning to Egypt after a three year's leave of absence, almost four counting his abduction by the black market tomb robbers in 2013. Rupert, his eldest son, who had developed a taste for Hollywood after being left in charge of hiring the Hall out as an on-location film set, fancied himself a leading man and set his sites on being a famous movie star, or at least, marrying one.

Tut, the latest edition to the clan, rescued from the dangerous streets of Cairo and transported to a land of 'afternoon teas with an assortment of cream cakes' that made each day feel like Christmas even if it did rain most of the time, hankered after the ingénue Imogen Banks, and promised himself he would talk to her if she ever returned.

Bash dreamed of Six declaring his undying love – an ironic concept in his family, all things considered. Kit accepted the Nobel Peace Prize for his ground-breaking resolution of the Bede lavender project.

Charlotte Findhorn felt it was time to put an end to a ridiculously long secret romantic engagement. Parks determined to train his champions using stronger tactics. The elemental faeries who resided deep in the greenwood, brought in the New Year by gathering at the base of the Rowan tree exchanging encouraging rumours as sightings of the Green Man were becoming more frequent throughout the dell.

Mrs. S would make less salads in spite of the weather.

And somewhere in Bede, Wilbur Tweedy, realtor extraordinaire in his own mind, signed on an imaginary dotted line, making Bede Hall his to develop or demolish. Meanwhile, his son Edgar, the Hall's trouble-making turncoat, pretended Bash was his girlfriend.

Another year had passed where Kit pushed aside icy thoughts and experimented with the Winter Room as if turning objects white was child's play, except in a sad way, it *was* entertaining. A fun trick, nothing more than a sleight of hand party trick. But an ice-age loomed behind the closet door. His terrible secrets waited there frozen in a box. Sadness and fear waited there, and stalling seemed the only way to approach what was going to be scary work.

Bede Hall prevailed over its estate as magician custodian, and when push came to a shove, it dabbled with controlling the weather. In fact, it was the elements of wind and water that marked its boundaries like an invisible fence.

Important humans dropped into the world of Bede after being summoned. Others, who visited by regular means, were rarely urged to stay. With the exception of the folderol of actors and crew, the Hall preferred the exclusive company of its family and minions. 'Needs must' deemed the new moving picture business necessary but it was decidedly '*old* business' that was raising alarm bells swirling into threats. It was the Hall's fervent wish for 2017 that the bank would grant his tenants a substantial business loan.

XXXVII

TOIL & BUBBLE

JANUARY 1 – NEW YEAR'S DAY, 2017

Tut popped a tape in the VCR just as the familiar theme music for the news blared from the television set, his finger poised over the record/pause button.

"Stand by. It should be the opening story. Dr. Brooks said to record whatever we could for tonight's meeting. Which means it's going to have to be at his place so we can watch it on TV a few times without causing a stir.

Ground footage of a steaming crater, aerial shots of steam escaping from a fissure, and an overall aerial view of an expanse of trees and scrub filled the screen... *This just in... tourists were interrupted yesterday when their campground buckled ... the warning of escaped gas from a nearby geyser appears to have saved their lives but the park is being closed until further seismic investigations can take place. And now we turn from Yellow-CHAIR National Park to a less disastrous report from ...*

Bash, crouched on the floor, sat bolt upright. "Hang on. What did he say? Tut, replay that last bit back. And turn the volume up full blast. I heard something in the background."

Kit nodded enthusiastically. "Yeah, I heard it too. But I thought it came from you."

194

"Nice turn of phrase, Bash," Tut said, manipulating the buttons. "Full blast it is."

The replay was normal. *And now we turn from Yellowstone National Park to other news*

Bash shivered and pulled her knees closer. "I could have sworn the announcer said Yellow-CHAIR National Park. It was quite distinct."

"We're both on edge," Kit said. "Look, the caldera only burped. It was no big deal. Besides, we know when it blows."

Tut shook his head, "Your yellow chair may be sending subliminal messages. You'd better keep a close eye on it."

"Anubis and Feathers are doing that. They're taking turns sleeping on it twenty-four hours a day."

"Remember Lady Nan said we're supposed to pay attention to anything Anubis does that seems out of the ordinary." She put her head to one side as if listening. "That message may be coming from the liminal realm."

"And where, perchance, would that be?"

"Liminal spaces exist between waking and sleeping and a few other semi-conscious crossover places like the enchanted entrances to strange worlds. The threshold of the netherworld for instance."

"You mean where Charlotte hangs out."

"I mean the maze."

"Yes, top notch, well done. Good for you," Dr. Brooks said with a sigh after viewing the televised tape. "But it doesn't matter now. There are more pressing items of business."

Parks shifted in his chair and pulled his cap further over his eyes. He peered sideways at Bash and then Kit and then settled on counting the leaves stuck to his shoes.

"Parks feels that... well..." the doctor continued.

Parks leaned forward and slapped his knees. "I feels it in me bones," he announced, and folded his arms.

Kit rolled his eyes. "I take it that means something not good?"

"Summit terrible and no mistake," Parks replied, his eyes squinting at a horizon only he could see.

"Are you sure?"

Bash laid her hand on Kit's arm and sent him a warning glance. Questioning her beloved mentor was a twin's entitlement gone too far.

Parks' stare bored into Kit's eyes. "It's in me waters, boy."

Dr. Brooks rubbed his hands together. "Well. That's it then. I have it on good authority that Parks' *waters* never lie." He smiled at Lady Nan.

Lady Nan nodded. "I've known Parks since I was a girl, and he's never exaggerated when it comes to the upkeep and safety of Bede Hall."

Over in the corner, Anna ventured to raise her hand but spoke before being recognized. "It means we have to go back in order to move forward. That the past creates the future."

Parks smiled at the young girl and nodded. "Out of the mouths of innocent children," he said.

Kit struggled to relieve himself of Bash's grip which was tightening by the second. "But the caldera was ... IS our goal. We agreed. We said that..."

Lady Nan's form flashed red. "We *said* that we would wait until Bede Hall told us what to do."

"And?"

"Dear boy. Parks is translating the Hall's instructions, if you'd only listen."

"You mean for all intents, Parks is Bede Hall?"

Lady Nan frowned without narrowing her eyes and her colour turned almost normal for a transparent ghost. "Not to put too fine a point on it, for the *time being*, yes."

Bash waved her hand for attention. "There's still new business. Or should I say the lack of it. I overheard Mom and Dad and Rupert discussing a bank loan to tide us over until a variation of movie magic' returns."

"And if it doesn't?"

"That's a whole different business. The cross-the-bridge-when-we-come-to-it sort."

"All the same, we need to order snowshoes and ice picks. No offense, Parks, but I beg to differ as to Twinter's priorities."

Bash pulled at Parks' sleeve. "I'm antsy about my seeds. Will they be okay, Parks?"

"Patience, child," Parks grumped. "They will or they won't."

Bash's face showed shock. "I… that is… I only meant…"

"Watch it Sis," Kit whispered. One New Year's Bash a year is enough."

"And if there were no Bede Hall there would be no time portal and no way for …"

Kit scrunched his eyes and waited for the axe to fall. He felt dread in his own waters. "You're saying there would be no way for me to time travel. Is that it?"

"In a nutshell, Einstein," Bash said.

Anxiety showed on Tut's forehead, his brow furrowed. "We could still use it for a while. We could stall them. But it won't come to that, will it?"

"I don't see how?" Bash said. "The first thing the developers intend to do is demolish the top floor and add bathrooms as a penthouse suite. There's even talk of a spa up there. Nothing but the top floor for a top guest."

"How do you know that?"

"Edgar."

"Him? He's a born liar."

Lady Nan fluttered her angry colours again. "Are we never to be rid of that troublesome boy. The Hall dispatched him a year ago… or was it two?"

"My informants tell me that *boy* is necessary. Best to let him do his thing," Charlotte said.

"Or we could let Rupert throttle him. He would you know. Without asking or giving anything away. Edgar broke his favourite sunglasses… so…"

"New Years' Day is cause for drastic measures. We rule nothing out."

"Not so," Parks said. "We rule out the caldera until we sort out what's coming afore it."

Kit raised his eyes skyward, "I daren't ask what."

"It's not always the same form."

"But I bet it's unpleasant," Kit said. "Isn't it."

Parks harrumphed in the affirmative. "Something untoward is on its way and it's to do with that older brother of yours. Although to be fair, not entirely. It's something that happened a long time ago. A curse that can stew like a volcano for thousands of years and then…" Parks made the gesture of a giant explosion with his hands. "Kaboom!"

"Thanks Parks," Kit said. "Nicely put."

"I didn't invent volcanoes, Master Kit. But I knows right enough what they do."

Tut leaned forward eagerly. "Can't we tie Rupert up or something?"

"In the old days, we could draft a fellow into the Navy. Volunteer him, like. Give him a few whiskies and then, quick as you like, he'd find himself aboard a ship, come morning. If only. All's I know is, he's going to create a dirty great hole and all hell's goin' to burst through it. Bats out of hell is nothing in comparison. Nothing! My trees are shedding their colours. The leaves aren't dropping but a forest of white trees is nothing to shake a stick at. The forest glades are too quiet and even the shade is hot. The fairies are noticeably more cunning. I have my eyes on a few of them. The youngens are the worst. Regular little thugs they are. Turncoats too. Too many cast spells before they're grow'd ready. Right little performers they are too, better than your actors that swan in here and pretend to be high and mighty." He scratched his neck under the stained kerchief he always wore. "And, worse of all, the rowan berries are withering as we speak. That's a bad sign, that is."

"Well, how soon is nigh?" Tut asked the room.

"Could be tomorrow or a month of Sundays," Parks said. "Or both."

Kit shook his head. Parks liked to make riddles. Conundrums, Bash called them. "Okay then, we have time."

Parks snickered. "That's the one thing we DO have. If, that is, we have the PORTALS. Otherwise, it's time that'll be having us. If you get my drift."

XXXVII

LEAP BEFORE YOU LOOK

FEBRUARY 28 – 2017

Bash sat cross-legged on her corner of a cloth spread on the lawn, held her lemonade up to the sun, and squinted through the condensation on the glass pretending to look at the sky. All the while her attention was focused on Parks Six, a short way off, mulching the soil around the rowan tree.

The afternoon sun shone relentlessly down on three sunhats having a girly visit on the back lawn of Bede Hall. Clementine Barton and Priscilla Collins, ever eager for an excuse to visit the Hall, languished, sun-tanning in halter tops and shorts on a bedspread.

The topic of conversation was boys in general and Six in particular, working across the garden, digging with his shirt hanging on the handle of an abandoned shovel planted in the soil. His bare skin, glistening of oil, made Bash dizzy. She cooled her face against her glass of lemonade and crunched an ice cube.

Clemmie rolled up her shorts for maximum exposure, Pris pushed her damp hair under her hat, and Bash applied suntan lotion to her legs, calling attention to the blue bandana around Six's neck. That's my best scarf," she said. "I lent it to him this morning. If he gives it back I'm never going to wash it."

"You missed your perfect chance with Six," Clemmie said to Bash. "Last year was a leap year – a golden opportunity to ask him..."

Bash made a strangling sound in her throat. "What? to marry me!"

Of the three friends, Clemmie was always keeping score. "Don't be daft. To go on a date. But did you *do* anything? Oh no, you gave up. The moment passed."

"He's too polite to have said no," Pris added.

Bash tried not to look annoyed, but she'd been challenged. "I didn't give up, I chickened out. It's not the same thing."

"Clemmie's right," Pris chimed in. "You've only yourself to blame." As usual, she was in awe of her two friends, and happy, if not stunned, to be one of their clique or in any clique at all. She craned her neck over the landscape, especially scanning the tower for any sign of movement. "Do you think your brothers are about somewhere?"

Bash replied with lackluster boredom. "Which one?"

Pris giggled. "Either one. Your brothers are hotter than this crazy summer."

"She's got a crush on Kit," Clemmie said.

Pris shrugged, good-naturedly. It was true, and she'd made it obvious for six months. "And you, hot pants, are gaga over Tut," she said to Clemmie, raising her lemonade in a toast to Bash. "So, now you know why we're here even though the movie stars have flown south for the winter."

"Which one of you was the bright spark who brought the bar of chocolate?" Bash said, licking melted chocolate off a bit of silver foil.

Pris searched her tote bag. "My mum's on a diet. She wanted rid of it. I brought ginger snaps too, but there's only four," she said, doling them out like playing cards, placing the odd biscuit in the centre of the bedspread.

Bash licked her fingers, resumed her study of Six's back, and replied like a robot. "The studio had no choice since they were scheduled to shoot snowy scenes. I'm pretty sure the production went to Norway." She took the last ginger snap and waved it in Priscila's face. "Women *can* make the first move during an ordinary year, you know."

Clemmie snatched the biscuit from Bash's fingers, broke it into three, and kept the biggest piece for herself. "Are you saying that living in Bede Hall is ordinary?"

Bash smiled to herself. *If they only knew.* "Bede Hall is just a place. A little grander than most, I grant you, but otherwise, it's just a home."

"Edgar says different. He says it's haunted."

"Edgar is an arse," Bash replied, popping her third of biscuit into her mouth. "You should take anything he says with a barrel of salt. He's delusional. Thank goodness my mother isn't taking in students anymore. He's a menace to society. He caused us a lot of trouble the summer he was here."

Clemmie winked. "He's got a thing for you. Now don't kill the messenger," she said after the haunted look on Bash's face. "It's a fact. He told me so himself."

Bash was about to launch into the reasons why Edgar Tweedy was the last guy on the planet she was, or ever would be, interested in, but she caught a message from the rowan tree. *'Parks said there was to be no more guests, Mistress Bathsheba. He's asked me to pass it on that he's not best pleased with young girls ogling the lads. These times is dangerous. Bede Hall is not open for curious eyes. We need to rally. Consider our gates to the public closed until further notice…. Oh, and by the by, Edgar Tweedy is a necessary thorn in our side. Do not dismiss his importance. Keep an open mind.'*

Bash shaded her eyes in Six's direction. The branches of the Rowan waved to her from across the lawn. *I'm in for it.* Whenever Parks called her Bathsheba or spoke indirectly to her through a plant, she was in deep trouble.

Clemmie adjusted the straps of her pink top. "You make a good point," she said pushing her portion of biscuit towards Bash as if awarding a prize. "You should eat this. You'll need all your strength. Six is over by the maze, doing something gardeny to the Rowan tree. Go on. Ask him out." She rolled over and stood up, brushing crumbs from her hands. "Last one to the lake is a rotten banana split."

Bash leapt up. "*Um*, sorry guys, the lake's out of bounds. Parks says it's too brackish for swimming. He only told me after you got here, and it slipped my mind. I think we should head into the village for ice cream."

Groans of protest assailed her. "Aw, I was looking forward to a lovely cool dip," Clemmie whined. "You promised."

Bash sent the Rowan a return message. *'I will get them out of here right away. Do you have any brainwaves for an excuse?'* The perfect answer arrived immediately, causing her to chuckle.

Bash stretched to show off her best profile in Six's direction, and spoke with authority. "Now that I think of it, that's where Kit and Tut went," she said. "I'll ask Six if he'll drive us.

XXXVIII

IN LIKE A LION

MARCH 1, 2017

The sleepy village of Bede nestled against the boundaries of its feudal lord's ancient estate protected by a fairy glamour until Bede Hall caught the bitter wind of the disturbance it had been dreading. It wouldn't be long before 'they' arrived. All they needed was an open conduit. So far, all the entrances and exits were patrolled by guards.

The first thing Bede Hall did when it sensed an otherworldly presence within its boundaries was summon the nearest wind to scan the grounds for intruders. As far as it could tell the village was safe. The source of the immediate disturbance lay clearly on the estate. It was only a precursor brigade on reconnaissance but it was ominous enough to take seriously.

The prevailing wind gathered its updrafts high over the surface of the lake and spread its power into two great wings of air. It dropped its tail to earth, skipping and sparking until it coughed once and popped itself into a search party of four eager twisters, sending each in a separate direction, to probe, listen, observe, and sniff for tell-tale signs of the otherworldly−disturbance of unwanted visitors.

The first whirlwind made a quick pass over the surface of the water, alarming the swans. But sensing calm other than the waking birds' distress, it spun off in the direction of the gates to check the security of the spells that held them impenetrable – a cyclone on a mission. It was looking for psychic footprints and claw marks. Imprints of negative disturbance that Parks called imp prints.

The second had the temperament of bottled lightning. It smelled the unmistakable whiff of panic and picked up speed, whirling itself into a cyclonic imp-finder.

The gentlest cyclone tidied the fallen leaves in the garden, where the once abandoned ghost-child Anna, known as Snow, had been rescued, before worrying its way into the walled enclosure where the sunflowers had gone to seed. It rattled the black pods once or twice and clinked a few loose roof tiles of Park's toolshed, making a pleasant terracotta wind chime sound, but nothing untoward scuttled out or showed its almond bloodshot eyes.

The sensible garden perennials huddled together for warmth, hugging a few spindly stakes, and the skeletons of sweet peas clung to a rickety trellis. Charlotte had warned them to stop their ears until she gave the signal to link with the topiaries. She called them the Hall's landmines as they were small half-buried sentinels that joined forces underground in a network of roots. Plants messaged below ground and water beetles, dragonflies, and bees swarmed the air. The birds came in waves like the tide, swooping in to clear the air of toxic vibes in a battle of wings.

The Hall loomed unstable while the winds searched for tell-tale signs of intruders. The purple wind sniffed out grimy fingerprints on the window ledges to Lady Nan's bedroom and the stairwell of Kit's tower. It checked the library windows, and examined the fresh claw marks on the French doors to Bash's bedroom.

After surveying the remnants of the bleak botanical graveyard of 2016, the intruder shook off its tracker and stormed across an acre of lawn, slamming into the windows of Bede Hall in an aftershock of pique and dripped down the glass. It seeped under the kitchen door as a chilly draught. Inside the kitchen it met the domestic scene of an old lady in a rocking chair and a canine creature, blissfully snoring beside the hearth. The miniature twister sucked itself up the chimney into a low-hanging black cloud that immediately imploded into a fireball showering the landscape below with toxic orange sparks.

Bede Hall's guardian wind, close behind, hoovered them up out of harms way and ejected them into the stratosphere. It sent a message to Anubis: *crisis averted, sir... some superficial damage to exterior buildings... threat removed... all clear.*

Below Bede Hall's silver grass, layers of ancient settlements sank heavier into each other's secrets. Bronze against iron. Roman mosaics crushed Anglo-Saxon bones between dark ages of red and grey clay strata laced with chalk pebbles as time crumbled against time. A determined mole nosed a pottery shard all night, upwards towards the sun, migrating to the surface, poking the shard's Neolithic soul into the rarified air of 2017.

Nimue's fairy hands hauled the heavy shard to the newly-formed mountain of leaves. Her wings strained to set it on top where it blended into the damp mulch of autumn compost. It was both a beacon and well-camouflaged. She polished its black glaze with a rose petal so Parks would sense it long before he ever set eyes on it, and by noon, Dr. Brooks would have it under a microscope and tagged it as a breakthrough of unprecedented discovery. Stone-Age pottery with the distinct imprint of Egyptian hieroglyphs: a winged scarab underneath a circle with a dot at its centre, the symbol for the sun god Ra, its rays of spindly arms with hands, designed to examine anything they touched.

Moonlit bedsheets billowed on a clothesline like pale blue sails. The occasional brisk flap of restless linen disturbed Jack's sleep, a grey stretch of fur languishing in front of the banked kitchen stove. A tremor of paws here, a gentle whimper there, a listening ear twitching away a buzzing sound.

Technically, it was a time of fallow for the countryside. The harvest was over. The winter waxed behind the harvest moon. Hot wind lassoed the branches of the grandfather oak, and tugged the tree trunk elders bending from the waist, creaking their knees, the ground beneath them slightly rolling when they flexed their toes in the earth. Their trapped roots incensed with the urge to roam, barely hung on.

Conversations between the topiaries, carried by the wind, invaded the dreams of the teenage 'Mistress of the Green', first daughter of the House of Bede, sleeping behind French doors on the ground floor.

XXXIX

HOPE SPRINGS ETERNAL

MARCH 20 – THE SPRING EQUINOX

To any outsider, the Twinters assembled in the red library held the air of another séance. Seven members were gathered expectantly around Kit who was perched on the edge of a padded massage table in the centre of the room.

"We look a bit like Arthurian knights seated at the round table," Lady Nan said.

"Red knights of the garter..." Pigeon chortled.

"I call this meeting to order," Dr. Brooks said. "First old... I mean, *new* business."

"It's all old business," Parks said. "Ancient, not to put too fine a point on it."

"It's all new business to me," Taraq said.

Dr. Brooks patted Kit on the shoulder and smiled reassuringly. "We've been waiting for the right time to interrogate Kit. The spring equinox holds special energies vital to the Hall's protection. I'm about to regress Kit in the hopes he will report the details of a dream he had a few years back that may be of significance," he said. "It's likely related to the recent postcard addressed to Bede Hall. Charlotte will then proceed with a session of hypnotic suggestion to reveal its depths. Let's be clear. The dreams of our appointed time-traveller contain clues, as do the visions of our..." he inclined his head slightly towards Bash, other initiate. We must be vigilant of all the twins' memories and especially their dreams."

He signalled to Kit to lie down, and handed him a feather, newly donated by Pigeon. "Look into the feather's colour and tell us what you see."

"Plummage alert," Pigeon squawked. *"Red alert...poo ahead."*

Kit held the parrot's long red tail feather between his fingers and twirled it slowly before speaking. A burst of red light swirled into a circle and he peered through it. "It was nine O-clock. One minute I was observing a Martian eclipse in my telescope," Kit said. "And the next, Mars pulsed three times and issued a menacing sound that freaked me out. I didn't see Bash anywhere, so it was a dream singularity. That's my name for dreams that are mine alone."

"Very *astro*-physical of you," Charlotte said in a droll voice.

Dr. Brooks scowled at her. "Shush."

Kit winked. "Well, it would be highly inappropriate if Bash and I shared *all* our dreams, wouldn't it."

Bash and Kit exchanged a smile and briefly linked pinky fingers in a gesture of solidarity.

Charlotte took a deep breath. "Kit. What do you see in the window?"

Kit squinted into the billowy red curtains that parted to reveal a deep window recess. "A china ornament of a fairy... Oh wait... it's moving!"

"He's ready," Charlotte said to the room. "Okay, Kit, visualize you're back in your Mars dream. Tell me what you see?"

"It's more what I hear."

"Explain."

"I'm in the tower. My telescope is all set to observe a Martian eclipse and there's this hellish shrieking coming from the stars. The constellation of Leo is an erratic string of red lights cracking like a whip and it's emitting a warning."

"How did you know it was a warning?"

"Well you do, don't you? You feel some things in your blood. It was like that."

Charlotte smiled. "This is good, Kit. It means you're intuition is working."

Kit squirmed comfortably, settling into his memory. "Mars began to rotate, flashing like a red light on the top of a police car. And you know how a police siren wails, well, this one sounded like maniacal laughter. Very high-pitched. Really creepy."

"Creepy? That's a tad *un*scientific."

"The light hypnotized me. A bit like that fairy light blinking on your windowsill."

"She's harmless."

Kit retracted his hand from Bash's grip and locked his fingers in a deliberate gesture to lock her out. "Some of them aren't," he replied softly, as if the two of them were alone.

Charlotte sighed. "That's very true, but not too many folk can tell the difference."

Kit closed his eyes and his voice changed. He spoke now from within a trance. "Like I said, it's in my blood to know these things."

"Who told you this?"

Kit was silent for a moment. His eyelids twitched in REM sleep as he searched his memories. He shuddered once and his body convulsed. "Oh," he said, sounding incredulous. "It was the Sphinx."

Dr. Brooks checked Kit's pulse and waved an open bottle of lavender extract under his nose. The tremors subsided instantly, and he signalled it was okay to continue with a nod to Charlotte.

"Do you mean Sage?" Charlotte continued.

Kit shook his head in disbelief as if amused by his inquisitor's ignorance and chuckled. "No, of course not. Silly woman. It was the *Great* Sphinx of Egypt – the *mother ship*, as it were. They're connected, you see. I thought of all people, you would know this. Parks knows."

Charlotte rolled her eyes at Parks. "Sage, the topiary and the Great Sphinx, or the Great Sphinx and Mars?"

"Yes."

Charlotte asked Kit a pertinent question. "Did you panic?"

Kit bristled, as if offended. "Scientists *don't* panic."

Charlotte smiled at Bash but held a finger over her mouth to command silence. "Then what *was* your science report?"

Kit swallowed and cleared his throat as if about to make a speech. "Mars began to rotate. As I said, I would describe it as uncannily similar to a flashing red light on the top of a police car. At first it emitted a hum but the sound morphed into a siren of high-pitched laughter. And then something odd happened. The 'Face on Mars' poster disappeared from my wall, and in its place was..." he chuckled again, "appropriately enough, a large black hole."

Charlotte looked positively gleeful. "Excellent. What else?"

"At first, I thought it was a window open to the night sky but it was a tunnel. I could see the edges of a distinct hallway with a pinprick of red light winking far off into the distance."

"I must apologize," Bash said. "I thought you were a coward."

Brooks sent her a warning glare with a finger over his lips to indicate silence.

Her words were echoed by Tut. "Me too. Sorry mate."

Brooks shook his head. He would have to insist on quiet in future.

"I woke up with that dreadful laughter echoing around the walls. My poster was back but tilted at a wild angle."

Kit unlocked his fingers, and reached for Bash's hand. "Not to worry. It was no big deal."

Bash squeezed Kit's hand. "With us, everything's a big deal," she said. "But there's two of us so it's nothing we can't handle."

"Kit gave a weak smile, his eyes still closed. "All for one," he whispered.

Tut moved to Kit's side and took his other hand.

"All for three," Kit said.

Tut and Bash joined hands. "a solid triple-threat to vanquish what's coming," Kit said. "I read that somewhere."

"It's going to be a right free for *all*," Dr. Brooks commented in a stage whisper.

Lady Nan shushed him. "Bash is right. It's nothing we can't handle," she said. "And there's a lot more than three of us when all is said and done."

Parks stood and crossed his arms. "I've got some topiaries to organize," he announced. "Charlotte, when you're done here, can you spare a moment in the maze." He coughed, blushing. "I have some *flora* business I need to discuss."

"I bet you do," Bash said, winking at Lady Nan."

Charlotte kept her eyes on Kit but her smile widened. "Wait, I'll go with you now. Judging by Nimue's glow on the windowsill, this lad's about to wake up."

The fairy's form flickered out like a snuffed candle with a gentle popping sound.

"Go ahead, do your worst. I'm ready," Kit said, his eyes staring at the ceiling.

"You did great," Charlotte said. "We're all done."

Parks gave a slight cough. "We've just gotten started," he replied. "Let's not paint too rosy a picture, m'dear."

Charlotte joined Parks' side, pried loose his crossed arms, linked her arm in his, and kissed him on the cheek. "Come on, you old goat. Someone has to be a diplomat."

"Yes, but roses have thorns for a reason," Parks said.

XL

LIFELINE

APRIL 1, 2017 – APRIL FOOLS DAY

"It was the Egyptians who started it," Dr. Brooks said. "With their Bast culture. Cats on pedestals cats, cat temples, cat statues, and cat worship. But it was what cats represented that was so powerful. It was the art of motherhood. You've all seen a mother cat and her kittens. Nurturing was a trait the ancient's revered enough to make the royal act of succession through the head female of a bloodline. Pharaohs could only rule after being anchored by feminine power. Cats were, and are, the power behind man's power.

When the magicians rediscovered the eternal time portals, it was by following a cat. They bred a royal line of cat priestesses. A line of that still configures to our present species of Feline Domesticus. This is why even male cats are called felines. A cat life-form is the key to unlocking the doors and various gates of the night as written in 'The Book of the Dead'. They prowl the night ride through the intestines of time in order to be reborn. Cats law.

"And so began the myth of nine lives and the rule of nine," Lady Nan said.

The teens listened spellbound. "What else," Tut said, keen on knowing more about the Egyptian culture he'd taken for granted as fairy stories.

"Animal life springs from lifeless matter," Brooks said. "As represented by the jackal who thrives by eating the abandoned corpses of ancient road kill. In other words, all food-chain deaths in the wild.

"*Ewww!*"

"Nonsense," Tut said, clearly proud of his heritage. "It's tidy."

Kit made a face. "Too bad Cairo doesn't obey the rules, then."

"Cairo is just..." Tut paused to remember the English word for busy.

"A right old mess," Kit finished. "About as far from tidy as a place can get."

"Full of … the commerce," Tut said, best pleased with himself."

"The black market is *not* commerce. The stealing and selling of precious artifacts is hardly sanctioned as fair trading."

"*Ahem.*" Lady Nan's eyebrows indicated she was losing patience. "When you're quite done boys. It's also time to explain further. Do you remember when I told you to follow Anubis if he made eye contact?"

The three teens nodded. Taraq slow-punched Kit's arm... "Told ya."

Lady Nan stopped until she had both boys' attention. "Stop messing about and listen to me. Our chief guardian was named Anubis for a reason."

Bash raised her hand, cautiously eyeing her grandmother. "Is Anubis a pharaoh?"

Lady Nan smiled. "In a way, yes. It is a perfect analogy. The Great Sphinx has the body of a wild cat to symbolize the same energy.

Bash couldn't help blurting a revelation. "A lion is king of the beasts."

"Nothing is coincidental," Lady Nan said in a loud voice. "A cat can save you. Anubis is the grand 'poohbah' of Bede's feline colony but Feathers is his queen from whom his power is anchored. Snowball is a special creature. She will have a great deal to do with saving Bede Hall and every one of us. We are fortunate. We have cats to thank for being here and for Kit's safe return from the time portal. Be aware, that cats understand everything we say."

Kit's expression changed to skepticism. Lady Nan and her stories. He'd almost believed her. "Then why can't they talk?

Lady Nan's face was stern. She wagged a finger at her grandson. "They *can* when they choose to, young man, so you needn't look at me as if I'm crazy. I think you'll agree that cats are perverse and act superior enough to remain aloof from our conversations. If and when it's important, you may be lucky enough to have a meaningful, even vital, conversation with one. Other than heaping constant inane praise upon them. Oh, they put up with it, of course, but ..."

"Can you? I mean, are you telling us... do you have conversations with Anubis?"

"Every day. Telepathic messages aren't just for twins, my boy."

The teens looked vaguely horrified, trying to recall what personal secrets may have been overheard by the cats.

Lady Nan heard their thoughts and waved them away. And well you might be concerned," she said, chuckling. "Cats listen and understand perfectly but they never judge. They love humans unconditionally. As the ancients discovered, they are supreme confidants, nurturers, and healers. But be forewarned, if you cross a member of the royal house, you will invoke the wrath of Sekhmet, the lioness goddess, with her dual powers of healing and destruction. Sekhmet is the power behind the Great Sphinx."

She surveyed the vacant expressions of her audience. "That said, all cats are guardians to a lesser extent. Some are extraordinarily so, even a few of the ones living with Miss Goodman in her cat sanctuary. They've been man's protectors through time. In your case, Bash, it was Feathers. And you acted perfectly. She tells me you displayed calm in Arles. Snowball is the power behind Sage. When there's no panic, the lesson being sent... and yes, Kit, there's always at least *one* lesson... a traveller hears with all six senses. Acceptance is the key to a safe journey. Panic, and it's harder to get home." She turned to Kit. "You are, I believe, familiar with this concept."

"Pooooooohbah," shrieked Pigeon. *"Pooh to g…g…ghastly Feathers… Pooh to CATalysts…. CATaclysmic… ghostly cats!"*

Feathers stretched in an abandoned chair and hissed at Pigeon. *"You just don't like that feathers are something we have in common."*

Kit wriggled uncomfortably and stared at the carpet, counting the cake crumbs he'd dropped.

Lady Nan's expression softened. "There's nothing whatsoever to be ashamed of. You were uninformed. Your first trip was spontaneous. I was unaware of it or there would have been more instruction. Parks knew of course, and he would have come to your aid if you'd been stuck. Mind you, that said, there are places it's too tricky to penetrate."

"Your grandmother is speaking of extreme distances of time," Brooks offered. "I think of Parks as unlimited with limitations. The reason being, that some limitations are necessary to preserve the balance of our time and space. If our portals are left unprotected, all manner of irrevocable damages are likely to endanger our future. And since the nature of our mission is to preserve the future and prevent a catastrophic event, it is crucial that he remains here in body as well as spirit."

Kit held up his hands for quiet. He glanced sideways at Parks and swallowed. "Excuse me for asking, but does Parks have a body? I mean a real one?"

Parks head lifted with touching dignity. "Yes Master Kit, sir, I do. Several in fact, as you've witnessed since you came here. Now then, you've seen me shifting tools and trimming hedges. I've eaten cake in your kitchen. It takes a body to do that. Mind you, it's a different body, right enough. Molecularly flexible is the only way to put it, or so Charlotte says. I'm sure there's a newfangled scientific word to explain it but that's in *your* future. So, it's *our* task to make sure that future happens, eh."

Kit opened his mouth to reply, thought better of it, and stopped.

"Speak up lad." Parks chuckled and slapped his thigh. "Cat got your tongue?"

Lady Nan smiled in spite of the seriousness of the lecture. "Out with it Christopher."

When Lady Nan used one of the twins *actual* names it was always time to pay attention and do as one was told, even on pain of a lecture.

"Is bravery part of that natural ability of ours or what?" Kit said. "How do you know... I mean, how do *I know*, that a different time-portal will be safe?"

"One never fully recovers from their first journey but it does get easier," Brooks said. "And for twins it can mean double the fear or double the courage. That's why it takes training. That's why you're undergoing an intensive program of mind control and ESP exercises. The two of you will need to be in constant reach of each other."

Kit sighed visibly. "I'm afraid to ask why," he said. "I know I've been designated as the traveller, so does that mean Bash won't be entering the portals? Ever?"

"I can see how you came to that conclusion," Dr. Brooks said. "And for the most part, that's true." He faced Bash. "Bash, you can still travel in dreams. And in many ways neither you nor Parks or Charlotte has any control over you spontaneously traveling. But, the Hall has set some liminal parameters in place as a first alert basis. It means avoiding the known locations, alone, where the portal dimension is thin: the maze, Bede Post Office, and the Winter Room."

Kit's anxious expression lifted after a brief fit of coughing. Dr. Brooks handed him a glass of water and tousled his hair to break the tension. The boy's legs visibly trembled and Brooks felt nervous tremors running from Kit's shoulders.

He squeezed Kit's arm. "We recommend that Bash leaves the traveling to your expertise. You may think one trip does not a traveller make but you would be wrong. The second trip will ease your fears. I suggest you take short trips to and from the Post Office. Bash still travels out of body in dreams. That can be nightmarish enough. As we've discussed, Bash's gardening skills literally ground Bede in order for your travels to be safe. It would be a lie if I told you there were never complications."

Lady Nan gave an audible sigh and nodded. "Sadly, drastic circumstances call for drastic measures," she said.

Anna's form flickered on and off in sympathy. "I've made the trip to Bede's past loads of times and I never got stuck."

Charlotte nodded, encouraged by Parks' telepathic message *'go on then, say what you're thinking.'* She blurted a worst case scenario. "But drastic measures *do* come with a degree of sacrifice... *um…* usually."

Lady Nan pursed her lips at Charlotte and hastily added. "Calculated risks, most assuredly. And it's no small thing to have a team like ours watching your back."

Kit smiled wanly at the touch of Anna's hand on his knee. His reply was a feeble, "Okay I guess."

Dr. Brooks rapped the table with a ruler. "As for an update of the Furies... there's no news, which is a *bad* sign. They're devilish clever with timing, so we remain on high alert. It's not as if they're going to go away. They WILL come. And when they do, they mean to flatten us. So you see, Kit, somewhere in the past is likely the safest place to be."

"As long as there's a place to come home *to,*" Tut said.

Kit was silent. There was no denying the truth of Tut's statement. "So much for boosting morale," he whispered under his breath.

Taraq, walking behind Kit, closer than any human could get, dissolved slightly into Kit's back and stopped unexpectedly, shouting for immediate hot-chocolate therapy.

Bash sent him a look of pity. "You do know it's 90 degrees in the shade, right?"

"You do know I'm *dead* and therefore unaffected by the weather, right?"

"Touché. It's easy to forget because all of you ghosts can look as solid as us livewires," Bash said. "By the way, is there a better word than ghost? I mean, specter and phantom are a bit off-putting."

"But you love to *off-put* us with words," Kit said. "Unless you've changed which means if we look up at the sky we should see flying pigs."

"Presence, apparition, shade." She made a point of staring at Taraq. "Poltergeist."

"Ghoul," Kit offered.

Bash rolled her eyes at Anna, whose form flickered on cue to make a point. "Ghost it is then."

XLI

APRIL FOOLS

APRIL 6, 2017 – Kit and Bash turn seventeen

Six grinned madly at Bash and extended both his fists. "Choose which hand. I didn't wrap your present. Grandad has no pretty wrapping paper."

Bash took a deep breath and tapped Six's right hand.

Six held out a small object wrapped in a strip of sackcloth. "It's a Luckinbooth," he said.

Parks emitted a low groan under his breath. He sighed and stared into the sun. "That's torn it."

The cloth hid a copper brooch, turned green with age. A motif of double hearts linked together like a magician's chain link trick.

Charlotte heard as Parks meant her to, and beamed at Six over Parks' shoulder. "Leave the lad to it," she whispered in his ear. "He hasn't got a clue, but neither did you at his age if I remember rightly."

Bash gasped. Delight reddened her cheeks. "What's a Luckinbooth?... What does it mean?"

Charlotte cut Six's reply short. "It's Scottish. A type of Claddagh. It's a symbol of *friend*ship. Hands across the sea and all that. And in this case, hands across Hadrian's Wall."

"It's old as Grandad I expect," Six said. "It came out of the earth as I was weeding the sunflower patch. Fair jumped out at me it did."

"Now I recognize it," Parks said. "I wondered where it went. Tis a family heirloom, that is, well, it was supposed to be."

"I didn't know that." Six blushed. "Finders keepers, Grandad?"

"And givers," Charlotte added. "Quite right too." She nudged Parks' arm. "Better given late than never I should think."

"All's fair in .... *um...*" Parks hesitated, lost for words. "Friendship and war."

"You're like family," Mrs. S said. "It's very old. Lovely and green for a green thumb girl."

The brooch emitted sparks from Bash's shoulder as she turned this way and that in the hall mirror to admire it. "I love it. Thank you thank you. I'll wear it every day."

"Friends forever," Six said. "Well, I'd best be off. I've got...*um...* that fence to mend."

Bash stared adoringly at Six. "But there's chocolate cake. You *must* stay."

Six looked to his grandfather for help and received a blank stare.

"A real friend would stay," Bash sweet-talked.

Parks frowned. *Please Odin, help the lad. She's already a wee minx at sixteen.*

Six reached into his pocket. "I almost forgot, Kit and Tut, we're friends too." He handed Tut a Roman coin and Kit a shard of red Samian-ware pottery. "Bede's garden is a relative gift shop," and paused to admire his own pun.

Bash sent Six a radiant smile. "I'll take a small piece of that cake now, if you don't mind, Mrs. S," he said. Bash took the knife from her mother's hand and cut a generous slice that came with a red icing rose.

"Charlotte squeezed Parks' arm. "The 'Book of Flowers' declares it's a *yellow* rose that symbolizes friendship."

Parks kissed her cheek and whispered in her ear. "I'm sorry I lost your brooch all those years ago, my love. Trust Six to find it at the wrong moment."

"There are no coincidences or wrong moments," Charlotte replied. "And besides, you named a lovely red rose after me, instead."

Parks tipped his hat. "All's fair in love and gardening, I always say. The Princess Charlotte Rose is my best work because of you."

Later, he took Six aside. "Listen, young pup, you want to be more sensitive, and by that I mean, more careful. Now, that brooch wanted you to find it, so I don't begrudge that it's yours. I bought that bitty trinket for Charlotte years ago when she was Glynnis. But did you realize that wee Bash has her heart set on you as some sort of knight in shining armour? It's an odd time to be distracting her with gewgaws. Women take more meaning from these tokens than we do. There's no telling what you've unleashed. And at this moment we've got all the unleashed energies we can handle. I suggest you keep your distance."

XLII

THE GREEN LANTERN

APRIL 7, 2017

Kit stood, grimly facing the friends he once counted as family, his legs apart, firmly planted against the barrage of questions he expected would follow. "In three years, the world is going to turn into a spherical ice-cube. And yes, I'm aware that's a physical impossibility."

"It's a paradox," Bash said.

"Whatever it's called, it's inevitable. Posh words won't make it any easier to figure out how we're going to resolve it."

"Since Bede Hall harbours a time tunnel to a future disaster, by the laws of physics, we can safely conclude it also contains the key to prevent it," Brooks said.

Lady Nan's eyes met Kit's. "The vital link is to be found in a time before Bede Hall was built."

"Egypt," Kit blurted. "It's the obvious place. We all know it, so you may as well say it." He snapped his fingers. "Just like that. Off you go Kit, to 'where the wild things are'… we'll keep your dinner hot while you're gone. Not very safe though, is it."

Taraq and Anna evaporated momentarily and rematerialized holding hands.

"You expect me to… oh, I don't know… time travel to ancient Egypt and fix everything, like it's some kind of tiddely crossword puzzle to while away an afternoon."

"Tiddely pom," shrieked Pigeon. *"The more it goes on snowing. Forever snowing. Forever bubbles."*

Lady Nan hugged her snow globe. "It's a worn-out cliché, but there's no time to lose."

Kit whirled on his grandmother and raised his voice. "But you and Pigeon have time to make jokes."

Brooks, enjoying a slump in his favourite armchair, stiffened and pulled himself upright. He leaned forward. "No-one is joking, Kit. It's a turn of phrase. You know your grandmother uses them for a reason. There's no need to get huffy."

Kit glared at Pigeon. "Yeah, yeah, the magic blah blah blah of living language. Spare me."

Pigeon flew around the room and set off a chain reaction with the other animals. Feathers cowered and hissed as he swept over her and swatted the air. Unicorn leapt from Lady Nan's lap onto the tablecloth and darted under a chair, dislodging a teacup on the way, the rattle of china startled Jack who issued a series of sharp whimpers in his sleep and began to twitch madly.

Pigeon, perched gargoyle-like on the roof of his cage, surveyed the damage and pecked furiously at the bars. Both cats grumbled to themselves as their fur settled.

There was a human scramble to right the rest of the tea things that had slipped dangerously close to falling onto Jack. The commotion roused Jack who stood half-awake and trembling.

Kit took advantage of the distraction, kneeling to hug Jack, and hid his face in the dog's fur. The comforting scent of fur momentarily stabilized him. *Fur is real. Jack is never a threat. Dogs are loyal. Jack is safe. Jack accepts the changed me, unconditionally.*

Kit slunk back to the sofa with a new idea. *Maybe Jack can go with me.*

Brooks, deciding to step in, made a move to speak.

Lady Nan silenced Brooks with her hand. She rose from her chair, tipped the snow globe into a blizzard, and placed it on the table in front of Kit. Inside it, a miniature Bede Hall was slowly dusted with white flakes. She rotated it to face Kit and sat beside him. "If you could be spared the ordeal, don't you think we would, child? But, you know more than anyone, there is simply no time to spare." She tapped the glass bubble. "*You* were the one who alerted *us*. Do you not see how certain words form a meaning*ful* circle? That is 'full of meaning'." She made a circular motion with her arms. "The hands of a clock trace an endless circle, repeating from one to twelve. Full circle. Solar time marks the epochs of the ages. The zodiac is a continual rotation of portents. You've said as much in your own words because you know it's your destiny. The Bede Prophecy was born in the age of Gemini. You and Bash are the foretold twins who must answer the call to exacting duties. And there's an end to it."

"Hopefully it's also a new beginning," Brooks said.

Fake snow settled on the miniature Bede Hall inside the globe.

Kit shuddered. He touched the glass with his fingertip and left it there. "Well, it's all very lovely to be cast as a romantic hero destined to save the world, but at least call an epoch what it really is. It's *geological* time. Name the Bede Prophecy for what it is – a winter prophecy, the curse of a blue door, or…" he pointed to Anna, "the dream of a lost child. Call it anything but *my* destiny."

Jack's low growls convulsed his body with a sudden bark.

Bash petted him. "You're upsetting the dog. Even Jack knows the caldera erupting is everyone's destiny. At least you get to leave and be spared slowly freezing to death."

Kit clasped his hands and dug a thumbnail into his index finger. *Don't cry. For pity's sake don't cry.* He stood and stretched, and headed for the door, but turned back to stare directly at Lady Nan. "I guess that's the bright side, then. Lucky me."

Taraq carefully detached himself from Anna's grip and rose to follow Kit. Jack responded to a nudge from Taraq and joined him.

"There they go, Kit's trained poodles," Bash said, her eyes raised to the ceiling.

Tut shook his head, Anna started to cry, and Ben lured Unicorn from under the chair with a piece of string.

Lady Nan sent Brooks a wearied look and rallied. "Chop chop everyone. I think we could all use a fresh pot of tea. Ben, be a love and put the kettle on. Anna, find Feathers for me, there's a good girl. I saw her go up the stairs. Cheer up now. Tut can you please calm Pigeon. There's a new cuttlebone in the sideboard. Bash, I think we need to have a word. In the library, I think."

"You're in for it," Tut whispered in Bash's ear. "Rather you than me."

"What did I do? How bad can one little word be?"

"Lady Nan's words are never little," Tut said. "No-one knows that better than you."

The library felt like an oasis. The scent of old books and polished wood smelled safe. Unicorn had managed to get there ahead of Lady Nan and sat in their favourite armchair. Lady Nan seated herself and waited for her granddaughter. Hiding under the great library table had been one of Beryl's earliest sanctuaries before the Winter Room had offered up its cool interior – the perfect retreat after sunstroke or a heated discussion. Insulated by books was one of the best places to think when under siege.

As a ghost, Lady Nan no longer suffered the headaches and fevers that beset her as a child or a fretful adult, but memories arrived just the same. It was time to take the twins in hand. They were moving apart at a time they needed to join forces. She automatically reached out to cuddle Unicorn who was already settling into a catnap.

Bash entered the room bearing the olive branch of fresh tea. She settled the cup near her grandmother and waited with mock humility, her hands behind her back. "You wanted a word?"

Lady Nan inclined her head towards the Bede dictionary on its pedestal. "You and I used to love finding words in there. Do you remember?"

"I do. We were best friends. I think Kit was jealous," Bash said. She lowered herself into the armchair opposite Lady Nan and watched Unicorn change colours. From white to blue to no colour at all. Her grandmother liked to take her time.

Lady Nan sipped her tea and tickled Unicorn into a purr. "I can't tell you the details, but Kit is plagued with... personal problems. Doubt mostly. Time travel devastated his confidence and ironically, it appears to be destroying his future. He's not the coward you think he is. His ways of coping are different from yours. Kit understands more than he lets on. And now, with all the pressure to revisit the fears that terrified him the most, he needs his best friend more than ever. He needs you."

APRIL 7, later

It wasn't the first time the golden scarab beetle in Mr. Stratford-Smyth's collection had behaved strangely but tonight it flashed like an emerald and emitted fiery sparks, turning the glass cabinet in Bede Hall's red library into a pulsating lantern. A plump brown mouse caught in the light glowed phosphorous as she scurried by on important business. Katydid paused to sniff the glass but scarpered in terror when something stirred on the scarab's back. For a moment, tiny transparent wings fanned the air before resettling, folding themselves tidily, readying for the call to flight. Her younger sister, Katydiddent was due to arrive for her shift.

Shafts of excited green light danced up the walls and shimmied up the chimney to escape into the night as a ribbon of lime smoke. Katydid reached the bottom of the curtains feeling anxious. "Relief watch approaching for lookout duty," she called up as she dug her first claw into the thick scarlet velvet. She shuddered when the green light made a pass over her route, turning it a shade of sickly brown. It hovered for a while to be helpful but all it did was turn a lovely purplish climbing wall into a dirty brown cliff. What omen could unhinge a mouse, privy as she was to all manner of unsettling traps and the unsavoury floor stew that accumulated in the abandoned stables?

In the far corner, the family's treasured globe, the size of an armchair, rotated noiselessly in its cradle until the moonlight shone on the shape of Egypt. A diminutive green pyramid pushed up in the Nile delta like a seedling in spring and throbbed like a heartbeat.

The library was rarely visited these days. Visited that is, by the living. White dust sheets draped the large overstuffed horsehair furniture, ironically looking more ghostlike than the actual contented ghosts who wandered through the walls.

When its residents were asleep, Bede Hall flapped its library curtains in a semaphore signal hoping Parks would decipher a message. Parks was an honorary member of the elite Bede Society – a secretive closed-mouthed bunch at the wordiest of times. The groundskeeper's senses were celebrated as extra-extrasensory. But then Parks had been tending the Hall's grounds since his death three-hundred-years before. It was the Hall's idea that Parks appear as later generations of himself every few years to remain above suspicion with the ordinary village folk. The subsequent incarnations, passed off as brothers, sons, grandsons, and nephews, were all named Stanley as a whimsical joke to amuse Charlotte.

Katydid scampered up the curtain as her second cousin Doolittle scooted down the braided curtain tieback, clinging to the tassel. "Katydiddent sends her regrets. She couldn't come," he said. "You'll have to put up with me."

Katydid nodded. "Did you see anything?" she asked.

The rope careened slightly. "Fellini is in fine form as usual, the rascal. Pretended to pounce on me, he did. Feathers is patrolling the terrace, the gates are rattling but there's no wind. I'll be glad to get to my bed."

A soft thud indicated Katydid had jumped the rest of the way.

"Are you all right?" Doolittle called down.

"Phew! It doesn't half smell strange down here. It's all... sooty," came the reply. "Nighty-night. I'm off to my bed."

Katydid peered across the lawn. Fellini, the topiary cat, raised his head in the mouse's direction and hissed. Katydid shuddered, there was no danger but still the green cat liked to sport with her, and it was always alarming. Feathers, Katydid's furry real-life concern stood sentinel on the stone steps facing the drive.

Feathers paused from washing her ginger fur and her hackles rose into spikes. Her ears perked forwards at the approach of an invisible stranger. Whatever was there failed to penetrate the iron gates. Feathers slunk back towards the cat flap in the kitchen door, heading for one of her regular hidey holes.

Mrs. Stratford-Smyth heard the hinges of the flap rattle, and intercepted her. "There you are," she said, scooping Feathers into a cuddle. "Come with me little madam. Where have you been, minx?" She jiggled the cat up and down like a fretful baby. "I've been calling and calling. It's long past time for your eardrops."

Feathers protested with a hiss. *Not now. I need to lay low and talk with my master.* Squirming failed to release her so she lashed out as nicely as she could.

"Scratching the hand that feeds you is no way to behave," Mrs. S declared, kissing the top of her head. Feathers was expertly wedged under Mrs. S's arm and unceremoniously swaddled into a blanket in her lap.

In a jiff, cool medicine filled Feathers' sore ear and flooded her with relief. But she had to struggle. It was cat's law. One didn't say thank you to humans. One didn't purr after medicine. It didn't do to let humans think they were in control. Some clawing action was expected. *Let me go!* It was a fair exchange for allowing them to feel all-powerful, besides, if you played your part well, one was rewarded with the inevitable cat treat. Yes, humans were easy to train. And it was well to remember that a complacent human often forgot the ritual of the treat jar. Small arguments maintained a dignified state of affairs between species. Feline supremacy required diplomacy, but today, Feathers squirmed away after her medicine, scrunched under the dresser, and refused the proffered tuna-flavoured 'sweetie'. She flattened her body as close against the wall as she could and closed her eyes. *"Master, something's at the gates,"* she mewed.

Danger lurked at the end of the drive and it was becoming bolder. Tonight she would have to station herself at the kitchen hearth. Chimneys were doors that could never be locked. That was the easiest way in for pesky elementals. Welcome guests were invited through the cat flap. Feathers concentrated on calming her fur but it wouldn't be tamed. Pesky failed to describe the malevolent entities she sensed. She couldn't remember a creepier feeling.

Feathers called for her daughter Snowball in a low half-growl. *'Come here immediately, there's danger.'* Snowball was almost fully-grown in size but not in experience. She was still perfecting the art of stalking with style. She had the silence of it down but not the stealth. Not the patience. She leaped too soon and her prey whizzed past her nose. Feathers was teaching Snowball how to hunt; her father, Anubis, was teaching her how to fight... two very different things – the way of crouching and pouncing and the art of leading with one's teeth and using the claws as a last resort. And a cat's secret weapon of shrieking in such a bloodcurdling yowl that petrified foes turned tail or wing, choosing flight over fight.

But Snowball's favourite lessons took place under the moon with Sage, the topiary sphinx, who recited tales about her Egyptian ancestors. Sage had accepted Snowball as a worthy student when she was only a few weeks old, and had even let her make a kind of sleeping nest in the leaves behind his left ear. But, in truth, Sage recognized one day soon, Snowball would be *his* teacher.

More often than not, Snowdrop could be found chasing ghost bees in the maze or sleeping in between the paws of her best friend, Sage, who told her stories of the Egyptian cat goddesses – the gentle Bast, known for her warm heart, and Sekhmet the warrior lioness whose fighting energy runs hot in every cat's brain. Because a cat's nurturing spirit is matched only by their warrior instinct to defend their position against all odds.

A Bede cat required a deal of experience in the bizarre events that unfolded as far removed from a normal countryside as 'things' could be. What was coming was nothing as easy as catching a butterfly. What was coming should not be cornered alone.

Mrs. S left a few tasty treats at the edge of Feathers' safety zone, but Feathers decided it was best to leave them for Jack. Wolfhound Jack would scarf them up like a vacuum cleaner, too fast to be able to taste them but he would thank her just the same. It was something the animals of Bede Hall did. They shared as friends because they were part of a second string of guardians in the employ of Bede Hall. But then, their master was Bede Hall itself.

From now on they were on high alert. Feathers let out a blood-curdling yowl. *Where was that daughter of hers? Whose sooty track marks led from the chimney and down the passage? And, come to think of it, where was Jack?*

The north wind delivered its payload of fighting energy into the maze, making a full circuit of its corridors and sallied from its mouth, stirring the topiaries into a frenzy. It prodded the sphinx awake. "Stir your stumps," it blustered, "The gates are somewhat compromised."

"Compromised or breached?"

"Sorry, I'm getting ahead of myself. What I meant was, the gates are buckling. They should hold for a while. But such relentless bombardment is bound to end in disaster."

XLIII
TUNNEL VISION

APRIL 8, 2017

Lady Nan, drifting in the garden, noticed the library window pulsing green. Two long flashes followed by two short ones and two more long ones declared an S.O.S.

Parks materialized beside her. "Evenin' Miss Beryl," he said, doffing his wool cap. For a few minutes they studied the Hall in silence as old friends, Miss Beryl Stratford-Smyth and the young gardener who befriended her as a girl. Even now, in the spirit world, Parks deferred to the twins' late grandmother, Lady Nan, as Miss Beryl.

"It's time," Lady Nan said, her voice breaking. Strong emotions caused her to shapeshift to a young girl and back again to the sprightly old lady she'd been at her death, shortly after last Christmas. "Hannah Johns says her sunflowers have gone to seed. The land lies fallow. Hail the dark ages approach."

It wasn't easy keeping track of real time but she made a calculation. It was likely October because she remembered attending Bede's harvest festival on the autumn equinox in mid-September. If so, she'd been in the spirit world for ten months. Hardly a separate realm, considering she was in touch with her grandchildren on a regular basis as the founding member of the Twinters. Were they ready? Three of them were barely teenagers.

"It's April," Parks whispered. "The times are all in a dither.

December is the anniversary of your passing." He crushed a freshly picked Rowan leaf and sniffed its juice. "I reckon we've got a week," he said. He thrust his gnarled hands into his shabby tweed work coat. "Well milady, we knew it would come. It was bound to happen with all those actor folk lording it about the place."

Lady Nan closed her eyes in order to see a slight brown haze rising from the grass. "You'd better gather your clan. It's all hands on deck I'm afraid. They're still here."

"No need to fear anything, Miss Beryl. They can't hurt the likes of you or me. Not anymore. It's the living we need to protect." His raspy voice carried out over his manicured lawns and flowerbeds. "Now listen," he said to the garden, "especially you topiaries. Stay calm. You anchor the energies of this place. Bash is, or will soon be, your mistress. Act like the guardians I trained you to be." He bowed before the green sphinx. "Master Sage, there's trouble afoot and no mistake but there's no need to look downcast, as always, I leave you in charge when I'm needed elsewhere. I'll have to be away." Sage emitted a low growl and held his head higher to sniff the wind like a true predator. His green tail twitched and thumped with a great rustle of leaves.

The swish of a bushy tail caught Parks' attention. He pointed to the smallest shrub, shaped like a squirrel, as yet pot-bound in an enormous urn. "And you there, Sable, you may be the youngest, but that doesn't mean you can race about after dark. When you travel, move slowly as you were taught, imperceptible to the human eye, or someone is bound to see you. Best stay in your pot until I or Sage say so."

The little green squirrel shivered its tail in answer and stifled a chuckle.

Down by the lake, the maze collected its energies to its heart and meditated on the past, the time it liked best. It was old enough to know what was coming. A warm breeze caressed the ghost cat sleeping on the small gravestone at its centre. Unicorn, 'Corny', could often be seen with Lady Nan's child-self, Miss Beryl, in their carefree years, playing hide and seek amongst the roses. Parks had even grown a catnip patch in Unicorn's honour that drew the present housecats Feathers and her husband Anubis into its spell. It lay fallow now, its harvest dried and stored in glass jars along with the summer's strawberry preserves and Mrs. S' special apple chutney.

The ominous mist swirling from the chimney churned into a small storm cloud and rolled eastward, hovering like a magic carpet over the maze where it dissipated into a phosphorescent fog. It slowly descended, clinging to the clipped hedge tops like a dewy spider's web. A small finger of mist detached itself and tickled Unicorn "Wake up," it whispered. "Lady Nan has need of you."

Kit's tower lay silhouetted against the moon. He'd taken to sleeping there whenever he worked late into the night on one of his experiments. He was a natural night owl which countered Bash's early-bird nature. Most days, Bash was up at dawn, weeding the garden in accord with Park's personal garden almanac.

One look told Parks that Kit was there. The boy's aura was intense when he became lost in science because although he was sleeping, he was always dreaming of a solution to save tomorrow. His dreams leaked through the cracks in the masonry and sparked the night with flickering golden trails like heat-seeking fireflies. His energy warmed the bricks of the tower into a beacon that only the ghosts could feel. There were quite a few of them now – never haunting but 'lingering with style' as Lady Nan like to say.

It was cosy at Bede Hall but troublesome things were ruffling the ether. It was time to hunker down, bolt the doors and windows, and post animal guards at all the fireplaces. The Hall was not without considerable power but what was coming would test them all. The twice-borns and the goddess Chloris would have to be summoned, and the young topiaries would have to grow up fast. Parks had much work for them to do. It had been many years since he'd had to summon the goddess Chloris, but needs must, and he would if he had to.

Little Unicorn arrived and rubbed himself against Lady Nan's legs. Parks picked him up and placed him in Lady Nan's arms. "Look who's come to see you, Miss Beryl."

Lady Nan relaxed visibly as she stroked the cat's fur. Parks spoke to her as if she was five-years-old. "You run along now, Miss Beryl, fetch your grandson, and take Corny with you," he said, "and I'll tell Six to patrol the boundary lines. He's got sharp eyes for all his cheek. No need to alarm the children but it's best they're inside. Besides, they're going to have to face the battle ahead for their parents' sake. I'll find Miss Bash. She'll be asleep at this hour. She rarely locks those French doors of hers but at least they'll be closed against the chill."

Bash was Parks' special charge. Like a granddaughter only closer because she was his protégé, gradually absorbing his wisdom and folklore of the plant kingdom, and he'd been her mentor with the fairies who were dashed tricky at the best of times. Parks headed for the kitchen. If he was lucky, after Miss Bash was accounted for, there'd be tea and lemon drizzle sponge cake and a snooze in his favourite rocking chair by the fire.

That reminded Parks of the missing time portal, essential to Bede's defence. Miss Bash would be the one to find it. Maeve of the fairies predicted this over a month ago. It had been more of a warning, and because of it he'd introduced Bash to the devas, the spirits of the plants, earlier than he'd planned, and begun lessons of how to harness the power of the seasons. It was time she had more formal training for the tasks ahead. He would have to send her to the 'society' for some extra guidance and hope for the best. Indeed, Ambassador Nimue of the Bede chapter of fairies, had recognized Bash's supernatural gifts from the moment they'd met. Queen Maeve had warned that the great goddess Chloris, more commonly referred to as Lady Flora would have to be called down when things got worse.

Miss Bash was special. She won people over with her charming way of using vocabulary beyond her years. Her use of fancy words impressed everyone except Kit who thought she was putting on airs and teased her mercilessly for being a walking dictionary until, that is, she corrected him in Latin that words never walk but they run together. "And you know what a sentence is, don't you?" she'd said smugly.

"Yeah. Being cursed by a pointless prophecy for eternity," he'd replied.

Bash shook her head. "Not even close. Charlotte says a curse can be a gift if you surrender to it. You're just fighting…"

"A lost cause. Yeah, I'm aware." He held his hands over his head. "Is this what you want? Does beaten into submission count? You do know, don't you, that I will most likely go. The pressure is relentless, but remember, giving in isn't the same thing. Tell Charlotte that."

XLIV

MAYHEM

MAY DAY – MAY 1, 2017

May Day seemed like one of those occurrences when aliens whisk people away from their wristwatches and deposit them further down the road wondering where on earth the time went. The annual ritual of bringing in the spring seemed dusted off from a box of old traditions stored in an attic. Without Parks in his tree costume, mingling as 'Jack in the Green', it was a pale re-enactment of better times and bittersweet memories.

But the afternoon heralded in an overdue straggle of a different festival. Movie pomp, slightly worse for wear by its absence, trickled through the gates of Bede Hall one trailer at a time. First came the trucks, and then buses and cars. Limousines ferrying their celebrities arrived last.

The circus was back in town.

MAY 2

Disappointment hung over the breakfast table. Kit stood at the stove stirring cheese into a pan of simmering eggs. "Bit of a fizzle," Kit announced. "It lacked lustre."

Bash toyed with her cereal. "Your omelette?"

"Very droll," Kit responded. "I meant, hurray hurray it's the first of May."

Tut, never quick to complain, sided with Kit. "Seriously, whatever yesterday *was*, it wasn't a real celebration without Parks. Surely someone else could have played Jack-in-the-Green."

"Nope. That role belongs to Parks."

Taraq watched his three friends from above, the ceiling stopping him from floating away.

Bash stirred her tea anticlockwise in slow motion with her eyes glazed. "It lacked..." she searched for a kind word.

"Panache?" Tut suggested with sarcastic eyebrows. "That IS your favorite word, isn't it?"

Kit chuckled. "The word to cover a multitude of occasions."

Bash glared at them with mock disdain. "A certain *je ne sais quoi.*"

"Oh, here we go," Kit said. "My fellow musketeers, *Mademoiselle Panache* has the floor."

"That certain... *something*," Bash mused. "The hearts of the villagers were elsewhere. Even Charlotte scored low on enthusiasm. Her May baskets were not her usual floral masterpieces."

"Phoned-in as some people might say of an actor who wasn't really trying."

"And speaking of actors," Taraq called down from the ceiling, "now that they're back, I have it on good authority that a certain girl is stirring up trouble as we speak."

Tut studied his eggs as if they would bite. "I'm happy they're back. I missed them."

"It was as if everyone in the village was distracted," Kit said. "The tension was like wading through quicksand. If you want to join us, Taraq, get down from there. It's distracting."

Anna and Lady Nan materialized at the table. "Dangerous ground," Lady Nan said. "It's a sign."

Taraq swooped down gracefully to shadow Anna.

"Parks is always right," Bash said. "The oppression was in the trees. It reminded me of that fairy tale where a curse lays over a palace for a hundred years. A frozen May Day."

Kit blanched. Frozen days were not amusing. Had he not made that clear. Flippant references to winters, especially magical ones, were counterproductive.

Tut poured himself a cup of lukewarm tea. "Doesn't mayday actually mean trouble?"

"Yeah, it's a ship's distress call," Kit said with disgust. "Apropos or what, eh Sis."

"I'm not entirely thrilled they're back, Bash said. Parks thinks they're a precursor to trouble. And somehow Edgar found out and is sniffing at the gates for his old job. It's unconscionable."

Kit slid his chair away from Anna. "Maybe that's why Parks went away for a while. Did he mention they were on their way? He must have known. He might have given the rest of us a heads up."

"Parks did warn me," Lady Nan said. "He's been hearing war drums from the rowans in the village, but he didn't want to alarm you. The hall has mixed feelings. It needs the income but money isn't everything."

Kit hummed the Marseille. "All for one and one for all. *La revolution!*"

"*Panache!... payback... bienvenue!*" shrieked Pigeon."

"Careful *d'Artagnan*," Bash said, "you're creeping Pigeon out."

"We were being observed," Lady Nan said, calming Pigeon with a stern look.

Kit waggled a finger at Bash. "I think the correct word is *absurd*, but yes, I did feel spied upon and not just by Edgar the leech, who, by the way, can't keep his beady little eyes off you."

Bash flicked toast crumbs in Kit's direction. "Ugh. Thanks for that. You *do* know there's a few irritating local girls who follow *you* around all besotted and drippy. Science must be sexy or something."

"What about me?" Tut asked. "Don't a few girls fancy me?"

Kit sniggered. "You wouldn't care unless it's Miss Snooty Nickers."

Tut thumped his fist on the table, making the cutlery jump. "Imogen Banks is *not* snooty. She's a star. Besides, I'm older and more street-wise than you."

"Hey mate, keep your shirt on," Kit said. "She's all yours."

Bash pretended to choke on her tea. She waved the sugar spoon at Tut. "You're not more *mysterious* than Kit, you just look more exotic, but you're excruciatingly shy. For some obscure reason, certain girls find that a magnetic combination. But this is the year for new things, so maybe you will take the plunge and actually talk to little Miss stars-in-her-eyes. This competitive thing doesn't look good on either of you. And Parks says we have to stay focused."

"I'm *not* jealous," Kit mumbled. "In fact, I could care less. We've got serious problems without getting bogged down in romantic foolishness."

Lady Nan put her arms around Anna. "There's something more sinister in the air than romance."

Tut hissed under his breath. "And I'm *not* a fool."

Bash stared dreamily out to sea. "The unknown is always a bit romantic, *n'est-ce pas?*

"So true. *Mmmmnnn.* Ooh, I wonder if Six loves me." Kit mimicked, fluttering his eyelashes. "I wonder if the world will end? I wonder..."

Bash narrowed her eyes at her brothers. "Morons. Six and I are just friends."

Taraq frowned and poked Kit in the ribs. "Why is she always doing that?"

"What?"

"Quoting French."

"She's not actually putting on airs," Kit said in a stage whisper. "She thinks the French are better than we are at expressing ourselves. I'm surprised there was no Latin. My sister is a bit of a stickler for panache. Which is French for sophisticated."

Tut resurfaced. "In other *words*, she's a wordsmithing geek. But in a nice way."

Bash grinned up at Kit. *"Merci beaucoup mon chéri."*

"Precise poo... perfectly excruciating... exuding plentiful piles of panache," Pigeon muttered to himself.

Kit leaned his chin on his hand as if he had all the time in the world. "Bash would you mind passing me *le compote au frais...* when you have a minute. No hurries."

Bash slid the strawberry jam towards Kit. *"Mais oui.* But of course."

"Mercy buckets," Kit said. "I just realised, this means Rupert will come home."

XLV

UNDER THE WEATHER

MAY 3, 2017

Sometimes it's impossible to see the world change. Outside the kitchen window the colours of the leaves of the maze's box hedges flickered on and off like dying lightbulbs. For a moment they looked pale blue – drained of green from midday stress. The dark ages had returned.

Kit slept in. He woke to the sounds of lunch being called, tangled in sheets that resembled the aftermath of a bedding war. The air snapped with sparks. Something felt different. *If I was psychic I'd say the world just shifted gears,* he thought, but the smells of breakfast made everything else irrelevant.

Mrs. S clattered a tray of poorly stacked dirty cups, and when a cup smashed in a tremendous crash, Anna disappeared in a tizzy.

Kit turned towards the racket. "Morning Mum. Need a hand."

"Chance would be a fine thing," she said, nodding her head towards Rupert lingering over a cup of coffee."

"No worries. I'll clear that up. Where's the dustpan?"

Mrs. S brightened. "Thanks Luvvy." She did a double-take. "Oh dear. Kit, you look like you've been in a fight."

Kit rumpled his hair into place. "I feel much worse than that. What's burning?"

Pigeon cackled. *"Proverbial…perfectly proverbial…poltergeist alert."*

Mrs. S spoke to Kit without looking up from the stove. "I let you sleep in," she said, before her usual good-morning, greeting. "Parks is back. The Hall's all of a tizzy this morning what with all the Parks' coming and going."

"Any idea why?"

Anna returned and dipped her finger in the pancake batter to stabilize.

Pigeon watched Anna smiling from the sweet taste. *"Pancakes and poncey parasites."*

Mrs. S scraped the burned pancake sticking to the bottom of a pan. "They didn't actually say. I think it was just a lot of talk about the weather. I gather there's a storm on its way."

"That's right up your street, Kitty," Rupert said, helping himself to the last rude squirt of ketchup that exploded from the squeeze bottle in a weak red spray. "We need more ketchup Mater," he shouted over his shoulder as if Mrs. S was his personal secretary.

Kit bristled at the despised name, Kitty – one that Rupert delivered like a calculated fork in the eye at every opportunity. One day he would wish he hadn't.

Mrs. S flipped the dead pancake into the waste bin. "An approaching weather front or some such. Something about a storm warning. All the Parks are batting down the hatches and it's an all-hands-on-deck thing. I leave the great outdoors business to them. I've got my hands full with the inside goings on. And there's such a to-doing with this movie business. They might have warned us, but apparently Bede's phone lines have been out of service for a week, so no wonder the phone was silent. We've still no dial tone. Your dad's gone to the village to report it. Anyway, it's a real hornet's nest. Cancellations and delays and I don't know what all."

"Well, I'm off to attend to my actors," Rupert announced. "They're being a tad stroppy about the local internet connection's disconnect."

Mrs. S eyed her eldest son coolly as he escaped past her, leaving his dirty dishes on the table.

Pigeon paced on his perch. *"Predictable…Piffle,"* he squawked. *"Here kitty kitty kitty."*

Mrs. S cleared away Rupert's leavings. "Rupert's left me with the lion's share of the bookkeeping, and it's a shambles, as usual. He's a stylish figurehead, I'll give him that, but he has no head for business, does our Rupert. Or clearing the table. Why you named him Boss is a mystery."

Kit upended the cereal box and was rewarded with cornflake dust. "He's bossy, Mum. He's an arrogant arse who treats his siblings and his mother like slaves. Did you not put that together? By the way, I'm adding Fruity-O's to your shopping list."

"I felt it in my tail the moment those wretched people arrived," Feathers said. *"And my ears are tingling almost as much as the twitchy telephone wires buzzing with parasites. They've gone all itchy-witchy. The lavender plants are out of sorts, too."*

Anubis stretched, tired after patrolling the grounds all night. *"Parks is having a word with them, now. And the topiaries are restless. Taking less precautions of being seen, and the rowans are busy sorting out the rest of the garden and the fairies are more flighty than usual, which is saying something. The time's ripe for you know what but even Parks thought we had more time."*

Up in the attic's Winter Room, Anna wiped a hole in the window frost and stared out with her forehead on the chill glass. From here, the gardens below had taken on their wintry aspect. The topiaries were barely recognizable under shapeless blobs of sticky snow. But Kit, as in awe as he was, wasn't fooled. It was an optical illusion. A decidedly impressive anomaly related to the Winter Room, but nevertheless, a shared hallucination from Anna's past and his future.

Kit spoke at last, keeping his back turned away. "Other than it's the best place to cool off, I called you up here for a reason. Consider it a truce. Please… tell me about your mother," he said. "How can I find her? … Please. Give me a clue. Give me anything at all."

Anna turned from the window, the tears on her cheeks frozen into pearls. "My mother was from Egypt. That's all I know," she said.

"Anything is good. Gosh, Egypt. Are you sure? Does my dad know her?"

Anna paused. "Wait I *do* know something else."

"Something else is good."

"There's a time portal in the Great Sphinx. I found it when I was called Snow. It's a way into the ancient past."

"That won't be necessary. I've no need to travel any deeper than I have to. I expect your mother will show up in due course. I have no need to visit Egypt again, except maybe to cool off. Bede's as hot as the Sahara. One visit was enough. But I have to admit, it was worth going there to find Tut.

Although friendly, not every villager welcomed the 'Hollyworks' entourage with open arms. But there were two factions in Bede. The normal folk and the twice-borns who looked normal but were decidedly eccentric behind their facades of shops and offices. Still, hundreds of years and several lifetimes had taught them much about clandestine living and keeping secrets. Hiding was best in the open and to this effect Charlotte sold flowers, Vincento Leoni, the chemist, made cough medicine and sold soap and toothpaste, and Dr. Brooks analysed the faint of heart.

Twiggley's tea shop was one establishment run by the normal sector. A hideout of gossip and sugar that thrived since famous actors occasionally dropped by to experience 'ye olde tea and cakes' of a rainy afternoon. Except the rain seemed to have abandoned the countryside even though there were plenty of dark clouds accumulating in the north and gales were reported along the coast, regular as clockwork.

If anyone stopped to notice, they would have seen the grass growing a darker green where it should have burned brown. It was not generally known Bede Hall's lawns were fed from below in an ingenious network of pipes that connected the lake to the roots of the trees and grass and plants. Even Mr. and Mrs. Stratford-Smyth had no knowledge of their new homes underground activities.

Of course, the Twinters knew all. Parks had given them a lecture as to his gardens' secrets as a few tunnels had to be patrolled for intruders small enough to filter via the air as particles of trouble. This job fell to the ghosts and the smallest guardians. The mice of Bede that lived in the 'Hall actual', were often the first line of defence. For now, the invaders remained as nightmarish premonitions – an intrusion into the dreams of the warriors of old and their new recruits who had been spared the full details of what lay ahead. Even Kit, who had been given the terrible vision of the forever winter, had no concept that ghosts worried as much as the living, and that death to a twice-born meant more than living twice, it meant immortality.

Bede Hall was an expert. Its old bones were steeped in intrigues and mysterious goings on. Bede may have been protected within a hostile era but now it was an endangered species. It worried itself to a frazzle. Even the last two years when it could relax and rest on its laurels, there was the knowledge of an army to come to end all invasions. The Hall sheltered in a corner of calm for a reason. When the time came, it would need all its strength to vanquish a war that would make the Viking conquests seem like a picnic at the seaside.

Formal flower arrangements were delivered to all the female cast, baskets of fruit to the males, and a homecoming-lunch was laid out buffet style in the actors' makeshift green room – a collapsible marquee structure with folding panels for walls. More than a tent but less than a building. Two sides were open to the air in the faint hope that a breeze would slip through the enclosure and bring relief to the actors already wearing uncompromising Edwardian costumes and wigs. Makeup artists wielding powder puffs hovered close by to blot foreheads and generally keep their V.I.P. charges from melting.

MAY 13

Groups of twos and threes drifted past the long tables and took their loaded trays of wilting salads and melting iced tea back to their trailers where the best sort of fans waited in silence. The fans who didn't ask for autographs but offered some relief from the cloying heat with spinning blades. Small air-conditioning units gave more relief, but stirred the script pages into a howling rustle of rogue paper, making it difficult to memorize lines.

A worried director sipped iced coffee in his canvas chair. Sadly, the words 'that's a wrap' had failed to grace the air for quite some time. With all the will in the world, actors with the best intentions of delivering award winning performances were becoming neurotic and superstitious. Beyond the disruptive heatwave, technical things were going wrong. Jealousies were legion. Toes and egos crushed beyond the norm, the tension, intolerable. Cantankerous cameras filmed takes not worth keeping. Lenses fogged, film melted, and lightbulbs popped. The curse hanging over the 'Curse of Pryde' was self-evident, and outside any individual's control. Events were fast disintegrating into a puddle of exceptionally toxic misfortune.

The crew were on hand to prove how invaluable they were to the creative process and put forward their claims towards the next project, and the cast were there to be professional and earn vast sums of money pretending to be other people – the public's darlings of the hour. Some of the executives had progressed from renting B&B rooms to buying small houses once it was established that the series was a resounding success. Some were so enamoured of English country life they harboured desires to stay on in Bede.

247

A sanctuary recluse holiday home, away from the hustle of Los Angeles in a place where they were treated with awe and respect as part of the magic business – the small fish living in a big pond situation being an exhausting and tedious existence of pressure and disappointment.

But living as a big fish in Bede Hall's duck pond was no better. All in all, it had been a terrible two weeks. The downward spiral seemed imminent. Things were falling apart.

Rupert addressed the green room, projecting his voice to the back of an imagined theatre, never taking his eyes of his 'catch of the day', his girl of the moment. "Attention! Morning everyone. I'd like to say a few words to set everyone at ease."

"You mean set*backs*," someone shouted.

Rampant agitation was palpable. Rupert regrouped and valiantly continued. His nervous chuckle response was not the best way to soothe the beast before him. For that's what they had become – a single angry mob of frustrated Americans… a monster with heatstroke.

Miriam paid Rupert no mind, preoccupied as she was, searching the ground, she clutched her throat, her eyes brimming with what she imagined was a fair representation of despair.

Rupert ignored the lukewarm reception and slapped his hands together with false gusto. "Welcome home *mes amis*," he shouted, a tad melodramatically. "I've laid on a special Bede Hall luncheon in your honour as an apology for the local disruptions which will be restored by the end of business today."

"A bit lavish for the hired help isn't it?" Miriam said through clenched teeth.

A quiet voice in the shadows murmured an audible aside. "Methinks the lord of the manor has killed the fatted calf to impress us peons."

"Don't be silly. *We're* the fatted calf. This place is in trouble without us. He's not kidding about the end of business. Management is not happy. We may be on the move again."

"Impressive."

Rupert beamed. "Nonsense. Circumstances call for a celebration. Nothing's too good for my actors."

"*Your* actors?" Hark who's talking. "We've been sold to the lowest bidder, lads."

"Hey Boss, can I have a raise?" a voice shouted from the crowd.

"Yeah, Boss. I haven't got enough lines," called another. "And there's no mobile signal."

Rupert sidled over to Miriam. "Lost something, Princess?"

"I could swear I put it on. I checked in the mirror not five minutes ago." She touched her neck again. "My heart-shaped locket. It was right here. I hope we don't have a poltergeist again this year."

"Was it gold?"

Miriam flashed Rupert a dirty look. "It's only silver but it's very important to me."

Rupert blushed but recovered. "I know just how to find... a necklace was it? but funnily enough it *will* take a poltergeist. How about a private séance in the red library tonight? You me and a few others? Tonight in the red library. Our family holds sessions quite regularly. It's jolly good fun."

XLVI

THE SCARLET LIBRARY

MAY 14

The special guest arrived early to make an entrance. Miriam Tripp surveyed the empty room and the candlelit table laid for two with a frown. "So, where's this group you mentioned, then?"

"Actually, there were only three others and they begged off a few hours ago. I hope it looks all right. I did my best to compensate."

"If I didn't know better, I'd say this looks like a setup for an assignation."

Rupert flashed her with a devastating grin. "Well, I wouldn't say no. But this meeting is meant to find your missing necklace. I have it on great authority that it works."

"Your family loses a lot of necklaces, do they?"

Rupert took Miriam's elbow and edged her towards the display cabinet. "Let me give you the grand tour," he whispered, guiding Miriam by the elbow. "These are ancient Egyptian scarabs. My father's collection. Extremely valuable. Thousands of years-old."

Miriam sniffed. "Kind of creepy. What are they, paperweights?"

"Basically, they're the first telegrams." Rupert pointed to the star scarab of the collection. "That green one is a heart scarab. It belonged to the Pharaoh Smenkhare." No response. "It's pretty much an invitation to mortality. It was buried inside his mummy wrappings. Placed where the heart should be. His real heart was removed and embalmed separately."

"Eww! Gross. I hope we can talk about more pleasant things."

The red library had been made over into a nightclub. The round reading table was set as if for an intimate dinner but the usual floral centerpiece was replaced with a Ouija board. Red pillar candles and tea lights twinkled on every surface. A bottle of champagne cooled in an ice bucket. Lady Nan's snow globe sparkled on a high shelf. All that was missing was a bowing waiter with a white napkin over his arm and violin music.

A small heart-shaped planchette the size of a small drinks coaster waited in the center of the board, angled slightly to point to the word NO.

Rupert seated Miriam in a plush armchair and filled two tall crystal glasses with champagne. He lifted his glass in a toast. "Here's to missing jewelry."

Miriam reached for the planchette and examined its underside. "No strings," she announced, with an exaggerated yawn. She rubbed the red felt base, all the while staring at Rupert with her eyebrows raised. After a moment she placed the planchette, red side up on her arm. She winked. "I reckon you're one of those heart on-your-sleeve sort of blokes. For you it's Valentine's Day every day when you've got a new conquest in your sights. Am I right?"

"You're confused. *I* think that *you* think that *I'm* a ladies' man."

Miriam positioned the planchette over her heart and smiled. "Right. And *you* think that I'm a lady."

Rupert cleared his throat dramatically. "Is anyone there?"

Silence with the exaggerated sound of a clock ticking filled the room.

"Anyone? Are you there?"

The planchette responded obligingly, gliding smoothly to the word YES.

"Spirit, we are here to find Miriam's missing necklace," Rupert said, winking at Miriam.

The planchette zoomed off the board, shot off the table and hit a wall of books on the opposite side of the room.

"Wow. Kind of melodramatic," Miriam said.

"Well you *are* an actress, so I'd expect nothing less."

Miriam took a sip of champagne. "You think *I* did that?"

Rupert retrieved the rogue planchette and returned to the table. "Let's do this properly, shall we." He nodded to Miriam. "Please spirit, tell us where the necklace is."

The words came swiftly. STOP WASTING MY TIME, MORTAL.

A dry fluttering sound issued from the heart scarab as it tested its wings.

"I apologize if we've… *um*… offended you," Rupert stammered. "We humbly ask for your help."

Miriam smirked, playing along. "Yes, spirit, we are exceedingly humble."

"Spirit. Where are you? I mean, are you in this room?" Rupert asked.

The heart-shaped pointer spelled out M...A...R...S – the red planet. The angry god of war.

"Oh, golly, you're a Martian," he said, grinning lopsidedly. "How interesting. Can you tell us your name?"

The planchette whizzed out W... H... Y

A slightly irritated expression passed over Rupert's face. "I was only being friendly. Hands across the sea and all that. Welcome to the planet Earth."

The point of the heart centered on the letter 'M'.

He gave a little cough of resignation. "Right. M for mysterious it is then."

The planchette spun erratically in a circle. Rupert and Miriam removed their hands, mid-spin. It hopped an inch off the table and landed upside-down on the word NO, still spinning but faster until it was a blur of red.

Miriam was delighted. She raised her glass to Rupert in a toast. "Brilliant. I was bored for a bit, there. Okay where's the magnet?"

Rupert gawped, horrified, jammed both hands in his pockets, and stared into the fireplace. "Look, Miriam, there are... certain," he hesitated. "Let's just say, somewhat *willful* presences in this house. Some wine should steady us."

Miriam was the first to notice her necklace draped over the library's doorknob like a pendulum. The heart-shaped locket hung open revealing a large letter M on one side and a picture of Medusa on the other. Miriam, suitably impressed, applauded Rupert as she would a magician's act. Her mouth formed an O of surprise. "*Très amusement.*" She tore out the offending image and handed it to Rupert. "Now, can I please have the picture of my mother back?"

Rupert looked over his shoulder in shock. "Someone's having a lark. Maybe someone from your props department. Someone jealous perhaps?"

"Roger Finch likes me but.... he couldn't pull off a stunt like this without help." Miriam checked her coat pocket. "Ah, there it is... this is my favorite picture of my mother."

"I had a wonderful evening. There's no need to go to such lengths the next time. Just don't take any more of my stuff. Okay?"

Rupert relaxed his shoulders and uncrossed his arms. "So, you're not surprised?"

"Well, it *was* a bit obvious, dahling. It's not rocket science," she said, fastening the necklace around her neck. "You fancy me and I fancy you."

"But we *did* find your necklace."

Miriam chucked him under the chin and pecked a brief thankyou kiss, leaving a red scar of lipstick on his cheek. "We both know it didn't drape itself on the bloody doorknob by itself."

Rupert's sheepish smile changed to hopeful. "Another damned poltergeist."

Lady Nan's snow globe started to storm. White particles swirled and turned black. The heart scarab unfolded its antennae and tapped on the glass.

"Breakfast tomorrow then?" Rupert said, reaching for the planchette. It skidded away from his hand to the word NO, and then settled on GOODBYE for ages, before it made it's ominous way to HELLO and began to spin madly, buzzing like a Martian wasp.

XLVII

A NEW YEAR'S REVOLUTION

MAY 15

Kit woke up thumpy-headed with an upset stomach. He didn't like to think that the shriek that woke him might also be fit to wake the dead. Not all ghosts were his friends, although to be fair, he hadn't met any unfriendly ones. Lady Nan, her brother Ben, and Taraq were exceptions to the rule of haunting by means of deplorable fear tactics. Not so for a few rogue fairies. Parks had been right to warn them of scams that seemed like good deeds. Thoughts of ghosts reinforced his assurance that benevolent reinforcements were on their way.

The dreaded name Megeara sprang to mind. Parks had made sure they were forewarned of her too. Kit had heard her once before in a nightmare he tried hard to forget. The voice was female albeit a throaty tone easily attributed to a monster rather than a human. For she had once been human, thousands of years ago. Parks would say no more and Kit couldn't have been more delighted. *'Let sleeping dogs lie is my motto,'* Parks had said, but then he'd added. *'Of course dogs are lovely creatures, so I'd best not go into the gory details. You children won't sleep a wink if I do.'*

The voice hissed inside his skull: *"Chris-sssssss-topher, the Sssssssphinx is waiting. Hissssssstory repeatsssss itsssssssself. Ssssssso sssssssssssssssory my dearest one."*

255

Megeara's voice came raspy in between ragged breaths as if she was choking down a particularly loathsome morsel. "Little Kitty. Did I wake you? Good morn to you. Did I ever let it slip that you and your friends shall know fire and ice and everlasting darkness."

The words resonated inside Kit's skull causing him to wince. He pressed both palms into his eyes to block the pain. Garish lights played behind his eyes and an aura spun in somewhere to his left. He covered his ears but the shrill screeching continued to ricochet inside his skull which now felt like a blown egg.

The accompanying odor of rotting flesh surrounded him. Cloying incense clashed with the smell of blood. For a moment he thought he might be sick. *This is only nerves. I can ignore this. It's a nightmare. I ate something bad.* He thought back to his last meal. A snack of toast with plain hot milk. Nothing untoward. No sugar. "You may have mentioned it in passing," he said being uncharacteristically flippant in the face of netherworld danger.

"That's right *little* fox. Fear me," the voice wheezed. "I bite and sting, no?" Fingernails dragged down the blackboard of the window pane. "False bravado is such a flimsy tactic, little fox."

"I don't understand. What's with the name little fox?"

"Does Kit not mean baby fox?"

"Look, whoever you are ... Megeara is it? We met before in a dream."

"I am *not* a who; I am a *when*. And consider this: I've been slumbering... gestating for too long. You could even say it's my birthday. But birth is exhausting and that makes me inordinately cranky. I've a need to stretch my limbs and flex my muscles." She coughed again and reeled in some strangled air for a few tense seconds. "Freedom is not as invigorating as I expected. No worries. I will soon get used to it, and when I do I will..."

Kit rubbed his temples and tried to stand. "Yeah yeah, I know... spread fire and ice and everlasting darkness."

Dizzy with nausea, Kit pulled on jeans and boots and several warm sweaters. He grabbed his ready flashlight stashed close to hand against a power failure. Even the Hall's new electrics were shaky and the storm was threatening to rip the roof off its foundations. He weighed the heft of the torch and brandished it like a weapon. "So, one question if I may be so bold. Why me?"

The entity cackled inside an intermittent hacking cough. "The sins...*cough*... of the fathers, dear boy." She cleared her throat but failed. Now she sounded hoarse. An old succubus hag with laryngitis.

"I'll have you know that my father..."

"Not that stupid archaeologist father of yours, you fool. Your *forefather's*. Ancestral sins gather strength the longer they incubate, little fox."

Over in the main house, Bash slept in a feverish state. Kit felt her whimpering in her sleep and shared a flash of her current dream. She was surrounded by a host of formless invasive creatures. He sent her a message: *'Stay put. I'm on my way. Don't do anything brave.'*

"Yes," Megeara taunted. "Your sister is far more courageous than you." She gave a wheezy chuckle and evaporated.

Kit raced across the dimly lit fog towards an intermittent blue light in Bash's ground floor window. It blinked on and off in sequence that Kit recognized as S.O.S – save our souls. He ran faster, mentally calling his sister. *'I'm nearly there. Hold on.'*

By the time he reached the French doors to her room, light played fitfully under the door as if it was trying to get out. Kit opened the door and something small and bright whizzed past his ear in a scent of roses. Too fast for a moth. It was Maeve. "Thanks," she called over her shoulder. "I'm needed in the garden. Can't stay. Bash won't wake up. Not all the way. Nimue is with her. Parks has summoned Charlotte. Back soon."

Even though he'd finally accepted the reality of fairies, they never ceased to startle him as much as that first time when one had landed near his cup of tea and introduced itself as Plum Duff and asked for a smidgen of bread and jam for his children.

Bash was sitting up in bed with her eyes closed. She opened one eye and motioned for him to be quiet with a finger over her lips. She was meditating at an extremely inconvenient moment. In fact, Kit was shocked that his sister was in direct communion of some kind, possibly with Megeara herself.

Nimue's fairy light twinkled over the mantelpiece and shone through the snow globe stationed there when she moved behind it. The effect agitated the snow swirling into a mini storm that echoed the howling winds outside, except, Kit noted with surprise that they'd been all noise and no bluster.

"Now that's what I call a tempest in a teacup," Bash mused, fully alert.

"I should be drenched," Kit said, feeling his hair. "It's a dry rainstorm, if you can believe it." He brushed off his clothes and a shower of grey particles sprinkled the floor. "It's raining dust out there."

Nimue's movements suddenly became erratic, fluttering helplessly like a bee trapped in a glass jar.

"Can you open the window for her," Bash said. "I'm nearly ready. Parks says we're to meet him in the Winter Room."

Kit crossed to the window and let Nimue out. Clearly the fairy was not buffeted by strong winds. Instead, she flew easily. The landscape wavered behind a cloud of smog. Raging elements that barely raised a flutter from a fallen leaf. "How on earth did you get wind of... I mean, *know* that?"

Bash stretched her arms above her head and hopped out of bed. "The rowan tree just told me. It's a bit hard to hear so I was concentrating when you arrived." She pulled sweatpants and a hoodie over her pajamas and tied back her hair. "What can you report?" she asked tucking her ponytail into the hood.

Something big was scratching to be let in. Kit marched to the door and gave it a good rattle. "I can report a ghastly conversation. It seems I'm the lucky designated receiver of messages as well as the token time traveler. "This is locked from the outside."

"Nothing token about it." Bash said. "You're the best chap for the job or it would have been assigned to someone else."

Kit paced from the window to the door. "This isn't a drill. It's the real thing, and it appears we're in a battle zone removed from the rest of the country. Boring old Livingston seems rather attractive right about now."

Bash busied herself stuffing food items into a rucksack. "It's like we're stuck in a glass bubble."

Kit swirled to face Bash. "Yeah... maybe a GLOBE of some kind." Visions of a bee caught in a bottle came to mind again, and Kit realized he had a whopping headache. His knees buckled. "I'm getting one of those migraine thingys," he said. "Why on earth are you taking an umbrella?"

"It's for you. Think of it as a weapon."

Kit grabbed it and approached the long flower patterned curtains that seemed to be hissing. The flowery faces looked angry and they were trying to speak. It took an effort to touch the fabric but he parted the curtains with the tip of the umbrella and stared outside, probing the air in front of him. Frantic barking came from the hallway. White light flashed through the keyhole and Jack burst in snarling.

"Fairies are quite handy aren't they? Bash sniggered.

"Good boy," Kit said, giving Bash a lopsided grin. "C'mon Jack, let's help the fairies save the world shall we."

He walked out the French doors waving the stick ahead of him swishing the air, cutting his way through an imagined jungle under-brush with a machete. The trees were still in spite of the howling winds. "It's foggy but nothing's moving," he called back. "I expected to see uprooted trees." Sassia was right behind me. I saw her talking to a band of mice. I think I may be have lost my grip on reality."

A few red leaves winked like rubies from the murk before he realized they were eyes. A swarm of dark figures swept past the window and were gone. Kit sensed glittering teeth and the sound of rustling scales. The trees remained frozen and blue-white in the moonlight that filtered down where the storm cloud pounded with thunder. The fog seemed caught in the far off tree-line that flanked the lake. It pulsated into patches of black and orange like a vast blanket chewed by moths. Black swirling shapes of red smoke could be seen strobing across the lawn. Wooly shapes flapped on the ground threatening to trip anyone in their path. And then a worse sound of cats fighting filled the night. Not battling each other but facing down a threat of sulphurous leaves that had amassed into a gross blob of rotting muck. Surely the din would wake the movie people, he thought, but the actor's trailers remained dark.

Kit reached into the dark to test for rain and recoiled after he encountered a hot handshake from something with claws. A large crow with a woman's face and teeth like thorns waivered into shape. Her death rattle voice – a hoarse cough thick with phlegm choked back a drooling red beak that formed into a smile inside a mane of razor sharp feathers sharpened like arrows arranged in plates of armor. Flakes of ash and small charcoal pebbles stung his face. The cloying musk changed color, from rust-tinged orange to brackish green and acid yellows sticky with sweat. Colors that Bash always described as dead or bilious or dangerously ill: grey sludge, slimy lime, and acid yellow. He ducked back inside after the hot fetid smell of rotting vegetation wrapped itself around his face. "It's still not raining."

Kit automatically wiped his hands down his shirt and left a smudge the color of an old bruise. "I had a bath. Where did this filth come from?"

Sassia, Nimue's twin, flitted down the chimney and landed on the bedpost, her wings quivering from green to white. "Bad times," she said, peering back up the flue.

"Sassia," Bash asked. "Have you seen Anubis?"

The fairy dipped her wings in deference as if to a queen. "He's with Feathers and Snowball, My Lady. Tut is bringing Pigeon. A rogue whirligig tumbled her towards the fireplace. She tried to curtsey in the air and crashed into the dressing table mirror.

Kit cupped Sassia in his hands and helped her out the window. "Take care."

Sassia's wings darkened as she threw him a determined look. "Yes Sir," she said, and launched into the storm.

Behind him, Bash had muffled her neck in a scarf. "Should we wake up Mom and Dad?" she said.

"It won't do any good, they won't believe this is anything other than a nasty bit of weather."

Down in the kitchen Kit warmed his hands on the banked fire just as the lights went out.

"Here," Bash said, holding out a tea towel filled with ice. "Put that on your temple. You look dreadful."

"Dread is the word," Kit said trying to lighten the tension.

More than ever, Megeara's chilling warning came to mind: *'Little fox. You and your friends shall know fire and ice and everlasting darkness.'*

The Winter Room seemed to expand like the Tardis with room to spare for ten entities sitting on the bed, two chairs, and the floor. Kit had forgotten the calming effects of it's tranquil bleached white interior.

Anna was calm as soon as Kit arrived. She stood by her old window and sent him a weak smile of hope that begged for attention. Kit heard the message but continued to keep his distance, "You're all right, Anna. Bede Hall's seen worse nights than this."

Anubis streaked up the stairs dragging a limp Snowball by the neck. He deposited her on Bash's lap and leapt to the windowsill where Anna petted him for courage even though his spiked fur flashed with cool sparks.

Feathers and Unicorn were already there. Tut arrived tangled up in Jack's leash with Pigeon on his shoulder, spouting: *"preposterous... pandemonium... palpable protest."* Taraq materialized, holding a glowing object in his hands.

The closet door creaked open and Parks showed his calm face. Remarkably sedate under the circumstances. He looked downright jolly. "Hello. Anyone thought to make tea or bring biscuits?"

"Lady Nan's in the kitchen," Tut said, "rustling up some refreshments."

A moment later the closet door opened again for Charlotte, and what appeared to be a small cloud of phosphorescent butterflies. It was Nimue and her clan, having escorted Charlotte's way by acting like miniature flashlights.

Dr. Brooks took the roll. Kit, Bash, Tut, Taraq, Anna, Parks, and Charlotte. "Beryl's making sandwiches with Ben. That makes ten of us plus assorted *ahem* 'butterflies'. Right. What's happened? Somebody start talking."

"It seems," Kit said, "that Rupert's gone and disturbed an old hornet's nest. And woken some creature named Megeara. She was having a major hissy-fit."

"I was in the library to observe," Taraq reported, proudly. "Rupert was holding a séance in there. Using a Ouija board no less." He opened his hands to reveal the golden scarab, snapping its front pinchers. "This fellow is ready for a fight."

Kit had the common sense to hide his immediate shock seeing one of his father's scarabs fully animated, and tried to ignore the implications as it walked up Taraq's arm emitting a clicking sound. "I'm afraid' so," he confirmed. "Rupert brought the stupid thing from the University. Apparently, it's a game to scare a girl into dating you or some such rubbish."

Charlotte translated for the fairies. "Oh, very heroic," she said.

"Introduce a peril and then save the girl when she's terrified out of her wits."

Nimue stifled a laugh. Her companions faked looks of shame. "We do that all the time. It works quite well... human's are so predictable."

Bash ignored their misplaced merriment as general fairy behaviour and referred back to the Ouija board. "Lady Nan refused to allow one in the house. She knew its negative side-effects."

"But we *were* expecting something," Tut said. "Bash, you called it 'sinister and untoward' whatever that signifies."

"There's nothing side-ish about the 'consequence' I just met," Kit said. "Although it did sideswipe me with a surprise."

Lady Nan overheard, entering the blue door pushing a squeaky trolley overloaded with refreshments. "Stupid stupid boy," she huffed. "Trust Rupert. What's he done now? Was it vanity again? Well, that's no surprise. I warned your mother not to spoil him."

Parks harumphed a few times and shuffled his feet, trying to appear indifferent. "'Twas," he grumped. "But no good comes of blamin' him. It was foretold, so I spect' he's only followin' orders."

Taraq stood formally and addressed Lady Nan with a bow before helping to pull the trolley over the threshold. "Your majesty, Ma'am, I was telling the others before you arrived. Rupert's been awakening the dead, Ma'am. He used a Ouija board. And it rather went berserk. A person calling themselves 'M' came through. It was female... not human... and not alive."

"Oh lordy. That's a can of worms not easily closed," Lady Nan said. "Stupid boy."

"M seemed stuck in a recurring loop of word salad," Taraq continued. "She said goodbye before welcome and then hello, and then goodbye again. She spelled words slowly. K --- I --- T and then repeated yes, no, and hello several times."

Kit was puzzled. "Why does she sound familiar?"

"I think it was Megeara," Bash said. "But I think she's actually the Ouija board. That's who Rupert unleashed.

THE BEDE CHRONICLES
by Christopher Stratford-Smyth

I'm a scientist. Once the phenomenon was attributed to the Furies, I did a search on the internet. Well, I tried. It was rather intermittent. The signal is iffy at best in Bede. It was a timely connection. In the few minutes it lasted I was able to gather a few grim details before the 'blue screen of death' popped up. Except, it wasn't blue. It was blood red and accompanied, appropriately enough, by a bloodcurdling scream.

I've had a few goes since, but whenever I type in the word furies the computer screen goes dead and begins to hiss. My phone vibrates across the table spinning madly even when its turned off. I removed the battery and still it buzzes like a demented hornet, sporting flashing orange and black stripes. Taraq is terrified of it and I'm jumpy. I'm as out of sorts as Bede Hall's landline.

Bash reports Bede's rowan 'network', supposedly immune to non-organic influences, is biologically offline which is odd because Parks says that trees exchange energy through their roots in a concerted effort to survive. My research backed him up. The scientific term is inosculation. Yet something has jammed the lines of communication, and it's not, as Bash believes, cellular technology playing havoc with vibrations that disrupt growth cycles.

The few key words that flashed in bold headlines were disturbing. I was in shock. The clash with Megeara winded me. My skin continues to crawl from insects I can't see. Shapes slither out the corner of my eye. I've learned that quaking in one's boots is a real thing. Not much else around her can be called real. My peripheral vision is haywire. Conclusive evidence notwithstanding, I have to assume I've entered a new stage of acceptance. Strangely, I miss the smell of lavender. No doubt, the stink of sulphur and rotting vegetation makes any floral scent welcome. My gag reflexes are getting a workout. Bash says, unpleasant as a compost heap is, it's organic, but I beg to differ. Maeve told me after the meeting broke up. It's pretty much toxic waste. Charlotte added her take on the matter the next day. She called the stench primordial soup from the earth's core which is scientifically as toxic as it gets.

XLVIII

THE GREEN ROOM BLUES

MAY 16

The ruckus began in the breakfast buffet line with a simple 'hey, save some for the rest of us, mate' when the bacon ran out. But the trouble began with the couple voted most likely to stay together for eternity. Charlotte mentioned someone with the unlikely name of Capability Brown, and Parks flipped out.

"I'll have you know madam, it was *me* who taught *him*," he said.

"If you say so."

"It WAS so."

The bickering escalated until a white light on Parks' shoulder intercepted a look from Charlotte and held up a piece of mirror to silence her.

Charlotte blanched from the light and shook herself. "We're doing it," she said softly as if speaking to herself. "Of all the times to fall apart. And over what? Some old 'Who's Who' of landscaping crumbled to dust? We're land-*escaping*, that's what."

Parks defused as quickly. "They're cunning little buggers. No two ways about it."

Several red sparks flew from their hair, formed a tiny ball and dropped to the grass where they rolled into a large urn belonging to Sable, the topiary that darted off frantically to rid itself like a dog with fleas. Sable only stopped when Sage roared and a puff of red dust flew up from his branches and imploded.

Lady Nan heard the altercation and relayed a message to Brooks. "It's started. The topiaries are awake and Parks and Charlotte are at each other's throats. So, we'd best be on our toes. If they've fallen out can we be far behind?"

The pandemonium soon spilled into the cafeteria tent and escalated into name calling. Insults were tossed about like a food fight: *You always think you're entitled to more. More close-ups, lines, more attention, and more bacon… some of us don't have to watch our figure… oh yeah? You're porky enough.*

Scripts torn into confetti littered the floor. There came a succession of trailer doors slamming. Women shrieked. A shrill catty voice cut through the general confusion and derided their colleague's choice of perfume that resembled insect repellent so no wonder she couldn't get a boyfriend. Within the domain of the 'company' there was no signs of instantaneous forgiving. The actors and crew bridled like hens and formed battle lines.

A massive surge of ego met the twins at the open flap of the green room tent. A free-for-all had broken out. It reminded Kit of a televised report of football aftermath. Gloves off, name calling, nail scratching with spite, eye gouging with attitude, a biting frenzy of bad behaviour. "We need to get Boss for this," Bash said, laughing. "He'll have to scramble to sort this lot. He'll see red. It may be worth coming back to watch." They left quickly and gave Rupert a sketchy message that he was needed urgently in the green room.

When Rupert entered unawares he was assailed by raised voices.

"You always get the best lines."

"I wonder why."

"So do the rest of us."

"Yeah well, you keep blocking my close-ups."

"It's a good deed. So the camera doesn't break."

"It pays to have *friends* on the inside."

"And which side of the casting couch would that be?"

"Ask Madam Tripp. She knows her way around the producers. Her daddy went to school with half of them."

Rupert made the tactical error of blowing a whistle for silence and was booed from the room. He took off his sunglasses in case they'd mistaken him for a nobody and whistled again, but his reward was a barrage of food scraps hurled in his general direction.

Several cars tore up the gravel and nearly collided into each other at the locked gates. Rupert waved his crushed sunglasses at the disappearing trail of gravel. "Well honestly. You're all philistines. Peasants. We don't need you," he shouted, brushing dust from his tailored Harris tweeds. He only had one word of derision left. "Actors," he said to himself. His best sunglasses would never be the same.

XLIX

SIBLING CHIVALRY

MAY 16

Tut thrust his face into Kit's. "You know, you could start an argument if you were the only person in the room."

Kit took a step backward.

"And," Tut continued, waving his arms erratically, "you've got a chip on your shoulder the size of a pyramid. Bash says you're always spoiling for a fight."

"Speak for yourself," Kit said, moving forward. "Once a street urchin always a street urchin. Bullying and thuggery are in your blood."

"Stupid boys," Anna shouted, suddenly appearing between them. "Grow up!"

Taraq put his head in the door. "There's a helluva 'do' going on in the camp. Let's go."

"I'm not being drawn into a fight. It's not my problem, mate," Kit said, his eyes levelled with Anna's. Her sudden demeanour of maturity rankled him. She was supposed to burst into tears. Tears were her default emotion. The fact that she was angry irritated him.

Taraq pulled Anna into a corner. "It's *everyone's* problem."

Tut woke as if from a trance. "Is Imogen there? Is she okay?"

"She probably started it," Kit said.

Anna shouted to Kit over Taraq's shoulder. "I hate you."

Taraq grabbed Kit and Tut by the arm. "Come on. You can fight it out later. Right now it's time to show your spines. Defend your homeland. Anna, you don't hate Kit. And Lady Nan wants you in the Winter Room. Go there and cool off."

Imogen and a palpable surge of unleashed egos met them at the entrance to the green room tent. The room buzzed like a hive stirred with a stick. For a moment the three boys stood dumbstruck assessing their next moves. "Rupert is supposed to deal with things like this," Kit said.

Tut gave a derisive snort as he searched the crowd. "Coward."

Taraq made a frightening shriek and dived into the melee, dispersing the crowd into small islands of hostility. Imogen spied them across the tent and made a beeline for the entrance.

Angry voices muted into a wallpaper of sound.

Imogen sidled up to Kit, amid a din of name-calling, eyelashes first. She moistened her lips, ready for battle. "You know, I've never been inside the Hall," she said as if nothing out of the ordinary was happening.

Tut placed his body strategically between them. "How can I help?"

Kit slightly put off, stared Imogen down. "Tut can give you the tour."

Her smile froze. "Another day then," she threw over her shoulder as she walked away.

Tut walked through Taraq without apology, stormed after her but stopped in retreat. His face was livid.

"What's got into him?"

"A girl."

"You mean that one? That touchy-feely one?"

Kit sent Tut a steady 'I'm ready to fight' look. "The very one."

Tut closed the distance between them, fists bared. "You bastard!"

"Hang on. *You* should talk," Kit said, "all things considered."

"Okay, guys. No girl's worth fighting over," Taraq said, taking up the position of moderator. "And I've heard that one. She's got her eyes on living in this house."

"Fighting FOR," Tut corrected. "And I'm not a bastard. I was an orphan."

"Oh yeah? How do *you* know."

"Masters," Taraq said, steering them outside. "I believe it's time to retire to the house. I suggest a pot of tea and some sugar. Lady Nan summons you both to join her. Be nice. Anna is with her."

The suggestion of tea as an intervention worked while Lady Nan was present. Egg sandwiches were distributed and eaten politely. Pound cake followed with fresh tea and chocolate biscuits. "This is all very civil," Lady Nan said. "I'll leave Anna in charge. Remember you're brothers under the influence of an intruder waiting to divide and conquer. See the bigger picture. And by bigger, I mean act mature." Her last words to Kit were meant to inspire solidarity. "Kit, you are Bede Hall's champion. Brooks and I believe in you."

Anna smiled from her chair. First at Tut, but when she turned to Kit she froze. Kit's eyes had narrowed into cruelty.

To spite his grandmother, no longer present to scold, Kit crammed an entire biscuit in his mouth and spoke with his mouth full. "You do know that Imogen is only interested in a genuine heir. Not a peasant."

Tut slammed his cup down hard enough to make Anna momentarily flicker out. "You're saying Imogen only wants an alignment with a *natural* son of the blood."

"I'm saying, yeah, she probably does."

Tut made a fist and pushed Kit to the sofa.

Anna ran around them whimpering. "Tut. Stop hurting him."

Tut delivered a withering glance over his shoulder. "Why do you care. He treats you like dirt. Back off, *Snowflake.*"

Taraq wove his way between them. "Young sirs. This is not you. You have been bitten. Stung. This is the poison talking. It's the emotional sting of killer wasps. You can't see them, but I can."

"Great," Kit shouted. "All we need is more fairies."

"Fairies don't smell like rotten meat," Taraq replied. "Fairies smell like flowers."

Kit turned on him. "According to Parks, fairies are also jealous by nature. Even the white ones."

Tut pushed Kit to the floor. "Maybe *you're* a fairy. You don't own Brooks, you know. He's allowed to help me too."

Anna moved to stand in front of Taraq. "Lady Nan believes in you." she glared at Tut, defying him to challenge her. "We all do."

Taraq squeezed in a belated request. "Kit, if you could spare a few minutes, Anna has been waiting to speak with you for a long time. It would be kind to hear her out."

Kit took a swipe at Taraq that momentarily surprised him. "You're wasting your breath."

He rallied quickly, reforming into a solid form. "But I don't..."

"Breathe. Yeah, I do know that. It was a joke, twit."

"Sticks and stones, Kit," Taraq chanted in an irritating childish singsong. "Anna cannot help who she is. Perhaps it's time to stop blaming her for your indiscretions."

Kit's anger turned to rage. "Don't you get it? You're an inanimate object, a figment of collective imagination. And so is Anna and your blessed throne. I was being cruel." He shook his head. "On purpose, you twerp."

Tut intervened to aggravate Kit. "He was just being a smart arse, Taraq. He likes to tease people."

Kit grabbed Tut by the throat. "If you have something intelligent to add why don't you just say it."

Tut wrenched Kit's hands away and cleared his throat. "You may be the biggest prat of all time. How's that."

"And Six isn't?" Anna chimed in.

"Anna, stay in the corner," Kit ordered.

"Where my sister stands or what she says is none of your business," Taraq shrieked.

"And speaking of business, Bede Hall is about to blow its roof. I suggest you save yourself by following your cowardly plan to run away."

Anna whimpered from the corner. "Are you going away?"

Kit faced her with an angry look. "You know I am. It's not a secret, now is it."

Mr. S. put her head around the door. "Lads. What's all the commotion? Is there a problem?"

Rupert was with her. "Kit. Who is Anna and why does she have to stay in the corner?" he said. "Is she one of the actors?"

Anna covered her ears with her hands. "Stoooooooop!"

Kit rounded on Rupert. "I don't work for you, clot."

"For the last time. Who's in some bloody corner? Rupert shouted. He scanned the room. "What corner? There's no-one in here."

Mrs. S retreated down the hall fuming. "I'm getting your father. This is a madhouse."

L

TWINNED TRIANGULATIONS

MAY 18

Kit waved his arms to get attention, and when none was forthcoming above the racket he raised his voice. "Someone has to take charge of this new situation. It's no longer a future event if you'll excuse the irony. And all of you know full well that I don't make time travel jokes lightly."

Bash, close by, was the only one to hear. "I feel as if we live inside the Bermuda Triangle."

"Well, that's a start," Kit said, clapping both hands above his head. "You're finally seeing Bede for what it is. Whatever's been unleashed, it's not from planet earth as I know it."

The discussions began again, louder than the first.

Kit stood on a chair and projected his voice towards Taraq in the back talking to Anna. "Heads up!"

No response.

Bash tried to hush everyone.

Finally, Kit bellowed loud enough to displace Taraq to the ceiling. "Look… it's not time to panic just yet. But one of us has to talk with this… this succubus thing and it's already made contact with me. So…. I'd appreciate some feedback. Anyone? Lady Nan?"

The room ignored him.

Ben, the silent one, blew a sharp whistle through his fingers. Despite the seriousness of the hour, he smiled, pleased with himself. "I was never able to do that when I was alive," he said by way of explanation. *Ahem…* "Shall we squabble or vote?" he shouted into the faces infested with exclamation marks.

"It's already a slam dunk," Taraq said, returning to the floor. "Dr. Brooks…"

"He isn't here? Kit said. "Or Parks or Charlotte? Neither of them answered my call."

Kit tried to curtail Taraq by grabbing his robe as he sailed past. "You know what?" he shouted after him. "You're no longer a wee buzzing nuisance on the wall you're an incessant buzzkill."

Taraq nodded. "Okay… so be it."

Lady Nan took her Queen Ankhesenamen form. "It's as I feared. Tension is escalating from strained to estranged. Even amongst ourselves. Look sharpish for sudden feelings of rage."

Kit turned on Anna, his eyes narrowed in frustration. "And you can buzz off too."

"Like that remark," Lady Nan said. "Thank you for making my point. Sometimes I think Pigeon has more sense."

Taraq returned in haste. "Don't talk to my sister like that!"

Bash moved a protective arm around the girl and raised her eyebrows in an accusation. *'Kit, use your loaf. Don't alienate yourself further by attacking Anna.'*

Kit ducked his head. "Sorry Anna. I'm all wound up." He took a deep breath and continued, "I think we should break into groups of three. Obviously, as I won't be here much longer, I'm the odd one out."

Taraq snickered.

Anna had the last word before the lights went out. "What's a slam dunk?"

LI
SCIENCE-FRICTION

MAY 19

Kit's legs were too agitated to stay within the confines of the biggest armchair on the planet. He stared mesmerized at the T.V., his arms around a cavernous bowl of popcorn, his legs dangling in space, twitching as if being tortured by random volts of electricity. Taraq could tell by the brown colour of the cloud surrounding Kit's head that he was about to lose it.

Tut, sprawled on the loveseat, taking in the movie with less intensity, slack-jawed from seeing it so many times. His legs were perfectly still, propped on several pillows.

The music swelled exponentially as the level of exploding lava on the screen surged higher, threatening to engulf science-officer Spock, descending into certain death. The music reached its crescendo. Mr. Spock pressed a button and turned the molten rock to cold grey stone.

Kit paused the movie. "Well, that's just perfect. Science-fiction does it again. Is there no end to the humiliation?"

Tut gripped a large cushion and threw it at Kit. "Hey, I was enjoying that."

Kit tossed him the remote. "Knock yourself out."

Taraq materialized between them as Tut pulled the tab from a can of pop and handed it to Kit. "It's only a movie, Captain. Get a grip. Here, drink some sugar to calm yourself down."

Tut pressed play but muted the sound.

"One minute I'm relaxing with the sublime escape of popcorn in a darkened room, a second later it's a reality show of 'this is your crappy life.' Or rather, this *isn't* your life."

Tut's eyes moved with the action on the screen. "You may be exaggerating. Only you would want to escape from escaping. Did you ever consider reality checks might also be opportunities."

"Ya know, that seeing red thing is real. That blood in your eyes deal is true. Megeara has hold of me. So, yeah, I guess it is an opportunity, so why is it that I'm furious with you for being an arse over a girl neither of us care about?"

Tut's eyes refocused cruelly. "Mind your own business."

"Bash told me it *was* my business. When I'm gone you may be the only one who can…"

"Couldn't happen too soon for me."

"Are we going to have to play that rivalry game again? I mean look at us. Megeara is like a virus affecting all of us. I've seen this scenario on the USS Enterprise often enough and it's the science officer's logic that rules the day, every time. So be nice to me."

"You hate science-fiction. But, like I said, it's a source of escapism from the need to escape escaping."

"Star Trek is different. It's science *and* fiction. At least it was a few minutes ago. A starship is a gentler form of time travel. It offers me that smartass paradox you just threw at me like a weapon. For an hour I get to daydream about traveling away from my life at warp speed, and I'm *not* the Captain. That's your fantasy, getting all the girls. It's certainly not mine."

Tut bristled at that. Kit knew him too well. "Well, excuse me, science-officer with the emotions of a doorknob." It was like someone inside him was saying things he didn't want to say.

For a split second, the sight and feel of the freezing doorknob to the Winter Room flashed in Kit's mind accompanied by maniacal laughter. "At least in a futuristic fantasy of trekking across the galaxy in 2223, earth was intact, the human species dodged every android and tsunami. But that scene rubbed my face in it. We've got to do what some bright spark wrote one afternoon for a fictional character. We have to do what Spock did. But we won't have a handy prop. There's no such invention as a cold fusion device that neutralizes volcanoes. That's careless science."

"You're jealous of Mr. Spock. How pathetic."

"As stupid as it sounds, it kind of adds to the sting of Yellowstone's guts, cooking under the earth, bubbling away with my name on it."

"Why on earth would you think that sounded stupid?"

Kit shrugged. He was beyond caring. He cared too much. Tut was no longer his friend. He wished they'd never met. "So, I'm supposed to just run madly into the big bad dark portal. No big deal for you, I guess." The thought made him queasy.

Words spilled every which way in Tut's mind. They tumbled from his mouth with appalling rudeness, hurting the only friend he'd ever had. The one who'd rescued him from a life of intolerable danger. A friend who'd generously shared his home and family. They'd become brothers. "Into darkness, my arse," he snickered. "I mean, use your noodle. Melted lava is red hot."

Kit looked about to burst into tears. The prospect was humiliating. He never cried. And now he was out of control. "My personal arse, actually," he said. His next words caught in his throat. "No one around here seems to appreciate that." He swiped angrily at the tears forming at the corners of his eyes. *Stop stop stop I am not going to cry. I won't.*

Megeara sighed in Kit's head. *'They all hate you. It's not fair is it.'*

Bitter words continued to spew from Tut's mouth. "Crybaby," he taunted "What a wimp." He heard himself as a faraway echo. "I'm not saying your trip wasn't scary but you got back okay."

"I am NOT okay, Mr. Sensitive!" Kit, shouted. *How embarrassing*. He buried his head in the crook of his arm and sobbed. His head throbbed.

"You're a disgrace," Tut sneered. "Some hero you're going to make." Tut, whose life on the streets of Cairo had always been shadowed by imminent death, tried to swallow a ludicrous thought but it issued forth without his consent. "Do you think I have a chance with Imogen?"

By now, Kit was out of control. *"Doorknob,"* Megeara whispered. *'Coward.'* Kit tried to shake her out of his head. "Get away from me. Get the hell out!"

Tut finished his drink, crushed the empty can, and tossed it at the T.V. "Sorry mate. This is *my* room. And I'll have your tower as well after you're gone."

Kit lifted a tearstained face, and managed to send Tut a look of abject disgust. "Mirror mirror on the wall, who's the stupidest git of all?"

Megeara shrieked in a full-blown headache of laughter. *'You are Kitty Kitty. You are.'*

THE BEDE CHRONICLES

by Christopher Carter Stratford-Smyth

MAY 19 –

I had a fight with Tut, Star Trek, and the universe all at once. I felt like a puppet reading a bad script. Tut either said what he's been wanting to say for a long time or he was affected by Megeara. Everyone is arguing.

My head hurts from crying. I had to. And in the end, I'm glad I did. I've been feeling sorry for myself and all that needed to come out.

I feel like an idiot. This documenting of events is important, but I can't escape that the similarities of writing a science log on the U.S.S. Enterprise is too ridiculous. But, There's nothing else I can do.

That said, the fantasy of a starship trip offers the pleasant day-dream of traveling away from my present worries at warp speed.

My nemesis, Megeara, turned me inside-out. She's turning everyone inside-out. I behaved like a jealous raving lunatic. Tut was no better. We scared poor Taraq. We've been his brothers who made him feel safe in his unstable state. He trusted us.

After staring incredulous at a paused screen, a freeze-frame of red and gold magma heat, it didn't take long for my fears to move back into attack position at the speed of light. There was my foe, volatile unstable waves of molten rock, cresting and crashing against time.

I despise wintry words, but there are no others that represent my level of horror. The truth is, I balked at watching the rest of the story because the remote froze time for me.

I was overwhelmed with jealousy when I watched Spock descend into a fiery pit of lava on a mission to save a distant world, armed only with a simple device. Science officer Spock, an undisguised hero whose casual logical and cool reasoning at the eleventh hour saves his sinking ship every week. I was humiliated by his cool head that rubbed my human face in his effortless triumph.

Spock, a stranger to guilt, has no sleepless nights. He suffers no regrets, and never hesitates to sacrifice himself for a friend. But he's fictional. I am real. Someone wrote Spock para-human attributes and gave him strengths that shield him from emotional fallout. He was awarded stoic Vulcan qualities at birth from an alien planet. He unflinchingly places duty above personal survival. I flinch all the time.

In fact, Mr. Spock is 'totally eclipsed' by logic, indifferent to pressure and human angst, and oblivious to emotional blackmail. Am I jealous? You bet I am, and Megeara planned that.

Unfortunately, time can't be paused like a T.V. show. Every day I flip from feeling sides-wiped to gobsmacked. I now know that the old saying of going from the sublime to the ridiculous is true because I envy Spock's title and emulate his simplistic style. And secretly, I covet his eyebrows.

Megeara read my mind tonight. No contest. She won this round.

LII

COWERING INFERNO

MAY 20

Kit's sneakers made no sound over the grass, they crunched over the gravel, and went quiet again on the worn stone steps of the tower. He hit the spiral stairs running, taking them two at a time until Taraq stopped him midway to the top. Taraq sat there cross-legged on the step as if he'd been waiting for centuries.

"Out of my way" seemed a ludicrous thing to shout at an apparition he could easily pass through. In fact, he'd walked through ghosts dozens of times after that first 'go on, I dare you' from Bash, years ago. He was a scientist, and scientists didn't hesitate to get their hands dirty or walk through a transparent person to see what would happen. Nothing ever did. Contrary to the movies, Kit never sneezed. The ghost never giggled once. Nothing happened.

"No Sir. I'm staying in your way for a reason," Taraq said.

Kit startled and steadied himself against the damp wall. "Taraq, I swear, the next time you do that I'm gonna kill you. You could give have given me a heart attack!"

Taraq, filled the stairwell. "Ah, then that would be another of your science experiments doomed to failure. I'm a tough nut to kill."

At first glance, Taraq seemed solid enough, but if Kit had had the time to look closely, he would have seen the faint shimmer of the tower's stone masonry through his friend's robes. Transparency depended on a ghost's mood.

Taraq stood meekly, brushed the creases from his long white Egyptian robe, bowed, and stepped aside for Kit to pass.

"The topiaries are on the move," Kit said. "I've got to see where Sage is."

"No need master. I've seen him at the gates. He's having a set-to with one of the fairies."

For once Kit brushed aside his distaste for being called master. "Bugger! which one?"

"One of the red ones," Taraq said. "Aren't those the ..."

"Devilish troublesome ones, yeah. Man oh man, why do towers have to have spiral staircases."

Slivers of anxious moonlight penetrated the window slits and slithered ahead of Kit like bewitched beams from a dying flashlight. The same shaft of light slunk behind him and formed itself into the shadow puppet of a demon and clawed after him. Taraq swatted it away as it tried to attach itself to Kit's heels.

Kit saw him out the corner of his eye. "What was that?"

Taraq grinned. "Just a trick of the light," he said. "Why are you so jumpy?"

Kit fumbled the padlock at the top of the stairs and practically fell into the tower room, dizzy, the muscles in his legs shaking, skinning one shoulder against the doorframe. Blue light spilled from the moon, illuminating the round space. He headed for the window but his feet became entangled in the legs of a tripod and he tripped, sprawling, breaking his fall with his wrists on the stone windowsill. "Ow!"

Taraq was already there, arms folded, waiting for instructions. "Steady on," he shouted, catching the telescope. "You're going to break something if you're not careful. Maybe your neck. I've never known a human as clumsy as you."

"There's no time for insults," Kit said, massaging his sore shoulder. He stepped aside from the window to give Taraq space. "Look down there!"

What Taraq saw in the garden turned him transparent. Sage, was limping towards his place in front of the maze and a small white cat lightly dusted in soot rode on his back. Suddenly, Sage's human head turned into that of a lion and let out a roar that left a cloud of leaves in his wake. The soot clinging to Snowball shrieked off in a tiny tornado that looked like a swarm of midges. Pure white fur glowed blue in the moonlight. Kit heard the cat purring all the way from the tower.

"I'll never get used to enchanted plants big as elephants, gallivanting about," Taraq said. "Especially not a sphinx. The Sphinx in Egypt is dignified. It never wanders off for a stroll down the Nile. Like I said, a true guardian never leaves its post."

Anubis and Feathers' daughter, Snowball, was introduced to Sage when she was only a few weeks old. Sage had accepted her as a worthy student at first sight and remarked: *you took your sweet time. I thought you'd never get here.* Snowball thought of Sage as her special teacher. He'd even let her make a hideaway in the leaves behind his left ear.

In two years, she hadn't grown much. But her feet had. She had extra toes. Dr. Fox called her a Polydactyl when he administered her kitten shots. Some cats are just small, perhaps she'll be extra smart too, he said.

Anubis had chuckled when Feathers recounted the story. *"Extra smart eh. My daughter is far more than that. Snowball is a genius. The joke is, those feet of hers are 'SNOWshoes'."* He preened, the proud father. *"She was born with the old magic. That's why Sage has taken her on as his apprentice. She'll save us all. You mark my words. I have it on good authority that she's primed for time travel and tip-top-ready. Lady Nan would appreciate that word magic… Snowball is 'reddy' for the red invaders."*

Feathers settled her tail by tucking it snugly under her front paws. *"It's lucky we have a few of our nine lives left."*

Usually Kit's first impulse was to allow the pleasure of his tower to sink in. Today, his eyes swept the room for anything out of place. It was easy for an elemental to invade the arrow slits and swirl inside the stairwell and worry the locked door.

It was chilly and damp, nothing out of the ordinary. The crude sliding panel in the ceiling was suitably secured with a hook. His second instinct was to open it and collapse on his cot for stargazing. The perfect spot for the occasional nap, and thinking through a problem.

Kit rubbed his arms and blew warmth into the tips of his fingers. "Phew, *stone cold* is a real thing." He stomped his feet and a puff of red mosquitos-sized fairies flitted around his ankles.

"Cold as a tomb," Taraq quipped. "Hold still, let me get rid of those while they're still small. They bite." He flattened them with a large atlas.

"Time to be serious," Kit said. "No more tomb jokes."

"I was just agreeing with you, master."

"I'm NOT your master. For Pete's sake. How many times?"

"Well, maybe I wasn't speaking to you. Maybe I was speaking to Pete."

Kit wedged his hands in his armpits for warmth. "Well, there's no-one else in the room."

Taraq spread his arms wide. "I am feeling..." he turned his head and shut his eyes dramatically, *"très desolate.* Extremely devastated and ravaged beyond shattering that you cannot see the huge elephant paradox standing between us."

"You've been spending too much time around my sister, but I get your drift."

"The thing is, master of none, there's no such animal as too much time."

"I admit, the movie busy-ness was a welcome distraction. I miss the 'circus' of them because I don't want to face the great *plan.*"

"Which is?"

"Dr. Brooks is about to tell us again," Kit said. "No doubt with some added details."

Dr. Brooks called the meeting to order. Before he finished, Lady Nan was on her feet. They watched her, knowing she was going to deliver an order or an ultimatum, not that there was much difference. "It's not like we're too late," she said. "We're perfectly on time. It's just that the sign we were waiting for has come earlier than anticipated. It's calling us to immediate action." She levelled her eyes at Kit. "And we have *people* to save, don't we."

"*Er...* Yes," Kit replied.

Lady Nan's expression softened. "I don't think everyone heard you, Christopher."

Anna shifted uncomfortably in her chair and turned whiter – the solid white of being dipped in paint. Even her chair turned white and a small frosty stain beneath her feet spread a chilly shadow that threatened the entire carpet.

Lady Nan reached knelt before Anna and held her face in her hands. "Come along Anna, we have to muddle through. We made a pact, yes?"

The girl nodded. A pink flush appeared under lady Nan's fingers. The pearls of ice on Anna's cheeks melted and then the white from the carpet receded and the colour returned to her shoes and up past the roses in her hand until she was her old self, albeit slightly tremulous.

Lady Nan clapped for silence. "I think Kit has something he wants to tell us."

Anna dematerialized momentarily and popped back wearing a summer dress imprinted with sunflowers.

Kit took one look at his grandmother's expression and decided to be brave. He moved to Anna's side and took her hand.

Bash made a choking sound.

"Anna and I have a little secret," Kit said. "It's going to sound weird."

Lady Nan nodded her approval. "You'll both feel better once it's out in the open," she said.

Bash gave Kit a shoulder hug. "It can't be *that* bad."

No, he thought, not as bad as the things he *couldn't* tell her. That she was going to die in the year 2021. "Bash, Tut, everyone, as you know, the year 2020 is the year of the explosion. What you don't know, is that Anna is my daughter." He paused to let the notion sink in.

Bash startled. "We… that is, you and I … that is, you'll be only nineteen-years-old in 2020. So, who…?" She looked from Kit to Anna and settled on Lady Nan. "Did you know about this?"

Anna found her voice. "I told her."

Bash searched Kit's face. He stood like a sentry on duty, eyes front, glazed. "Why have you carried this terrible burden alone all this time? I'm kind of angry at you. That's not what we're about. Twins law you always said."

"I'm sixteen and I don't even want a *girlfriend*," Kit said, reddening. "So, being a… finding out you have a nine-year-old kid when you're thirteen is a little creepy." He looked at Anna, clearly at a loss for words. "Anna, I'm not your father… yet. So, I feel awkward. And I have no idea who your…" He took a deep breath… "Who your mother is." He met Bash's eyes for a moment. "And that's not the *real* burden."

Dr. Brooks slapped his hands together with all too much enthusiasm. "Who's up for tea and cake?"

Lady Nan squeezed his arm. "I always find a cup of tea is the best cure-all for weirdness."

Bash responded first. "Oh, Kit and Anna. You poor things. But something wonderful is in your future, and in our present as well. We were a family before this revelation and now we're closer than ever." She giggled. "Goodness, I'm an aunt. And it's clear Anna survived the blast so that gives us hope." She clasped Anna's hands. "You lived for, what was it, three years?"

Lady Nan lowered her eyes, as Kit cleared his throat. "Well, that's the thing," he said to Bash. "You and I didn't."

Anna took Bash's hand. "And I'm still dying. I'm a time traveller. I guess it's in my blood."

LIII
SATIS-FICTION GUARANTEED

MAY 21

Bash, hands on hips, pulled another 'Princess Leia'. "Kit Stratford-Smyth, you're our only hope."

Kit gave the wall a sharp punch and rubbed his knuckles. "I'd just as soon never have my molecules scrambled again, thanks very much."

"Not even for science?"

"You are aware I'm *mortal*, right?"

"I'd go if I could."

"And I'd prefer to weed the gardens if *I* could. But you were born with courage and I ..."

"Got the brains?"

"I was about to say, I *wasn't*."

"And is Parks the Wizard of Oz in this story?"

"Sort of." Kit tried to make her laugh. "Well, by your admission, Charlotte *is* a witch."

Bash's eyes flashed daggers. "Then I guess that makes you Dorothy."

"The *good* one... the good witch. Don't excite yourself."

For a moment, Bash looked as if she agreed.

"No, of course Parks isn't the wizard," Kit said. "The wizard was actually a scientist. But you have to admit we've landed in a nightmarish fairy tale."

Bash pulled herself slightly taller than her full height. "*You* said space-time *was* science. Time travel was feasible, YOU said."

"Perhaps in the distant future. And yes, I did hear the irony in that statement."

"I guess we'll never know then because there isn't going to be a distant future, is there."

Kit conceded to save time. "I guess you *did* get the brains."

"And you have enough courage to be patronizing in the face of disaster."

Kit appealed to Bash's wordsmith side with no success. "Disaster means an ill-starred event. Don't you see? We're a pair of star-crossed muggins to fall for an ill-timed dream. Timing is everything and it's time to wake up."

The twins, genetically predisposed to stick together, continued to sleepwalk into a prophecy that pirated their closeness.

To Kit, it felt like walking the plank. He defaulted to believing the unbelievable. He acted willing and, if not all-embracing, he swallowed the compelling premise of the dark side of metaphysics. If reincarnation was even half-true, he'd probably have to die more than once.

Until recently, Kit never understood why everyone referred to him as old for his age, but lately, he had the sickening feeling that he was about to find out.

LIV

WE ARE NOT AMUSED

JUNE 21 – THE SUMMER SOLSTICE

A month later, Charlotte tapped her foot like an old schoolmarm. "In the old days, when druids were behind every tree, a rowan was called the PORTAL tree," she said. "Even Kit can't mistake the relevant symbolism. And this tree is a queen of the royal line from Lindisfarne."

Charlotte grasped the rowan branch hanging lowest to the ground with both hands and closed her eyes. It dropped away without an audible snap. She nodded to the tree. "Gratitude is mine Majesty," she said.

"You know, Kit tends to separate the words super and natural. He even blocks me out. I can still feel how tortured he is but I respect his need for privacy, so most of the time, more than he knows really, I don't push him. He won't discuss his time travel experience with me anymore and he avoids Anna. I try to give him the benefit of the doubt that he's being cruel to be kind, but there's something else. I can't reach him the way I used to."

Charlotte wiped dust from several leaves with a square of lavender cloth. "You two are growing up – a single tree that splits into two main branches. But soon, if Kit opens his mind, the pair of you will bond again."

Charlotte turned away from the tree and offered the branch to Bash, holding it aloft like a precious sword. "Now it's your turn. We need to find a small twig that's easy to carry."

"Find it? Why don't we snip a leafy bit from the end?"

"Because the rowan must gift it to you if you want her protection. Hold your hands over the end. Ask for her help. Be humble. Ask on Kit's behalf. The tree will do the rest. Hold onto the thought that it may save his life one day."

Bash cupped her hands around a small twig and concentrated until her hands tingled and a voice in her head welcomed her. *"Mistress of the green,"* it said, *"How may I serve thee."*

"Please help my brother return safely."

"So it shall be, remember me," the tree answered. As before, a portion separated gently. Soundlessly.

Bash bowed her head towards the tree, her hands still cupped around the twig that now fluttered like a baby bird. Formal words of thanks issued from her that, oddly, were not hers. "And so shall it ever be, majesty. I thank thee." She recovered and shook herself into reality. "That was weird. I wasn't me. But I was more me than I've ever been."

Charlotte beamed at her protégé. "Nicely done. No worries. There are many sides to your true nature. And you're really only waking up."

The two gifts laid side-by-side, glowed bright green and settled into the deep red colour of rowan berries before slowly paling to brown.

Charlotte smiled over the proceedings, herself queen-like. "There's one more thing. Fashion a small pouch for this amulet with your own hands. Use a piece of cloth from something you've worn. Tell Kit the truth, that he needs to carry this on his person."

"He doesn't believe in amulets."

"Find a way to convince him."

There was a loud rustling of leaves. Charlotte turned to the rowan and leaned her forehead against its trunk in silent communion.

"Mmmmn... yes, I see"... yes of course... I see.... thank you, maj-esty... I will." Her smile deepened. "This is extraordinary. Quite unprecedented," she said aloud to Bash. "Kit is one lucky young man. We require a second cutting. Choose a branch the circumference of your thumb where it meets the main trunk."

The new branch released as effortlessly as the first. To Bash's astonishment the end was hollow. Charlotte lopped off a slice half-an-inch wide with her ever-present pruning shears. Her left fist closed over it. When she held the raw end to the trunk with her right hand it rejoined the bark without a trace. "Always remember to receive offerings with your left hand," she said in her matter of fact 'teacher must be obeyed' voice. "And release with your right."

Bash nodded.

Charlotte nodded back. "Good. Now, hold out your left hand." She dropped the ring of wood on Bash's palm and folded her fingers over it before clasping Bash's fist between her hands. She closed her eyes, tilting her head as if listening. She shuddered and let go. "You're to sand the edges smooth, steep the ring in lavender oil under a full moon, and then rub it dry with rowan leaves. Take the leaves from the ground. They will be provided. And don't forget to say thank you."

Bash steered Kit towards the rowan tree as the sun set. "I brought you here for an important presentation. From me to you, an open-minded scientist. Can we do this?"

Kit spread his arms wide, staring up at the rowan's crown that resembled the underside of an umbrella. "Location location location," he said. "I'll listen but I can't promise anything."

"We were here not too long ago. That day of my choking and the birds swarming."

Kit looked blank.

"The day of the gravy?" Bash reminded him.

Kit chuckled. "Silly goose, of course I remember. What of it?"

Bash shook her head. "Exasperating baby brother."

"Yes, I recall that was also a topic under discussion."

"Just for now could you revisit your trip to the future with Snow."

"Her name is Anna."

"Okay... just for now, suspend your belief that I'm a nutcase. Denial doesn't look good on you. It negates all that portal panache of yours. The time-slip you experienced was real. You know it was. Not *how* it was possible but that it happened. Need I remind you that we live in an unusual place."

"I think you mean bizarre and weird. And I'm not an idiot. It isn't as if I'm unaware of what's happening. I prefer to separate the supernatural from the natural until I can examine... things."

"Super is a big word with you."

"Bash, you're not a nutcase, although it pains me to admit it, and I'm not blind. Of course I'm aware of the..." he paused with a pained expression "... *paranormal* anomalies of this place and what's happening. But I'm guarded. I'm conducting an experiment. Trust me. I have every intention of saving what needs to be saved."

"Oh, Kit, I've been thinking we were miles apart on this. I'm relieved."

Kit shivered. "I will be miles away soon, that's for sure. Cairo can be measured in more than distance. And don't think I haven't thought about ducking out of going." He patted the tree trunk. "So... this tree. Are you going to introduce us or what?"

LV

GOING GOING GONE

By mid-May, two things had shrivelled up and died. Maybe three. The summer solstice dawned innocently enough in spite of the growing tension.

The morning of June 21st began aggressively with the movie crowd fighting fit and by late afternoon, the director called out "That's a wrap, people. We're out of here!" The library set cleared in seconds. Rushing bodies headed for suitcases and cars. Snippets of anger trailed after the actors in mid-argument. Camera crew went into well-rehearsed high gear dissembling lights and cables.

Red dust assaulted Rupert entering the set as a massive headache between his eyes and bumped into Imogen. Her red fingernails looked dangerously poised for attack. "They can't fire me," she shrieked in Rupert's face. "I have a contract."

Determined to appear in charge, Rupert clutched his new monogrammed leather clipboard to his chest as a shield. "I'm sure I can clear this up. Wait here. I'll see what I can do."

Imogen had no intention of waiting and pushed past him. In case anyone was watching, he put on a concerned expression and briefly scanned an official looking production schedule as if it held the answer to everyone's problems. He opened the storage compartment attached to his executive model clipboard for loose papers and important notes, scurried after the director, headed down the stairs, and caught up with him at the massive front doors.

"*Um*... Just wondering. How long a break will you need?"

The director wheeled to meet Rupert head-on. His face was stone. "Forever wouldn't be long enough," he said. "That's us done. Colour us well and truly gone."

Rupert's plastered smile faltered for a split second but managed to reappear on his flustered face. It hung there a moment before his snazzy clipboard hit the side of Bede Hall. It opened, scattering several rolls of breath mints, a comb, an assortment of pens, and an extra pair of sunglasses on the front steps.

Rupert's carefully manicured world imploded. His body shrank for a second before his 'lord of the manor' temper ricocheted back, larger than life. "Bloody actors," he shrieked. He could act as well or better than most of them. "Peasants. And don't come back." Fast disappearing as they were, Rupert fired them in a satisfying sea of foul language. When his pulse returned to normal, he picked up his dignity, dusted it off, and headed for Wilbur Tweedy's office.

Unbelievably, one of the actors had already packed her things before the green room fiasco. As if on cue, her limo roared into life, gears grinded, and she was away through the gates like a career-seeking missile. If cars had emotions, this one seemed to be in the throws of a temper tantrum. The passenger was Miriam Tripp.

The car tearing up the gravel behind her was Rupert's.

The developing news sent shockwaves of cold hard realization through Bede Hall, almost as fast as it had with the production crew. The family kept out of sight in stunned silence as the circus folded its tents. The dismantling was one of efficiently orchestrated precision. Limousines, caravans, and trucks departed like a clockwork funeral procession, in order of seniority.

Professional to the last, a final clean-up crew raked the flotsam of torn scripts and empties. Parks, as vigilant overseer, pointed out areas they'd missed until all that was left was a chalk outline of a dead business in the flattened grass.

Bizarrely, the constant buzz of angry voices was actually missed. In a strange way, it had become soothing by its constancy. The background music building a dramatic scene.

All that remained was a free-for-all where the lawyers worked out the ugliest details. Word leaked to the developers, and a new show formed a circle around the Hall in a three-ring- performance bereft of compassion.

The second devastating death followed after the last truck rolled out of Bede for good. It was no coincidence that the same week on another innocent morning, Parks woke the household with ruinous news. There would be no early lavender harvest.

His voice rang out like a wartime air-raid siren. A blight had ravaged the entire crop of exotic French lavender. The truth sunk in days later. The shadow of a Twinters meeting was called to assess damage control. The war had begun.

There was a half-hearted attempt to pick up the pieces. The bank got its lion share first. It would take months to sort out the 'between the lines' details: which, if any, contract violations decreed compensation and which ones did not. Lawsuits hung in the air already toxic from the destruction of high hopes. Rupert had handled the original paperwork.

Mr. S looked over the files with bank officials and three lawyers. His excuses carried no water. Today, bank manager, Avery Merriman, a usually cheery sort, listened respectfully sympathetic. He forced his expression to be neutral but every now and then, he had to suppress the urge to sigh.

"I was out of the country when all of this began," Mr. S said. "Business isn't my forte, and I assumed all was in order from the legal documents. They were passed under my eyes in rather a blur. I wouldn't have noticed a mistake if they'd been chiselled in high relief and painted gold. Legalese is worse than hieroglyphics. More secretive creative evasion tactics in the guise of protecting the top of a business pyramid, carved in stone." He ran his fingers through his grey hair and thumped his fist on the table. "Jackals!"

"It wasn't your son's forte either, Cornelius," Merriman said. "He was eager. He mishandled a tricky situation."

"Bungled it is more like it," Mr. S said, pushing away the documents. One was particularly damning. A receipt for a bank deposit to Rupert's personal account. Rupert had signed a tentative sale agreement should the business fail – an unprecedented and greedy monster of a concept. He'd accepted a cash advance. A new can of paper worms would have to be contained and defeated. Its expiration date was yesterday.

Bash mourned over her once-prized fields, now a shrivelled desert baking under an unforgiving sun. She stared over a battlefield of grey shrunken plants. The only scent was the lingering horror of chemical warfare. Brutal designer-pesticides had seeped into the groundwater. They would pollute for years.

Kit kept apart from his sister's grief. In a way, he processed a more terrifying realization. There had been no mass hallucination. Botanicals couldn't be the culprit because the fairies that swarmed him said so. The supernatural events were real. He'd been cataclysmically wrong.

The library sweated from the stuffy evening heat that had collected all day. And if that wasn't stifling enough, the fan refused to cooperate. It's given up the ghost, Lady Nan mused without humour. She sniffed the fetid air. I can smell the furies in the curtains.

Lady Nan stayed in the room of mounting friction. A sweltering pressure cooker from the day's torrid challenges that had slowly mounted the stairs and created a suffocating arena for a dispute once expected to be short and painless.

She was hardly eavesdropping. She made no pretense of being there. It wasn't her fault the occupants couldn't see her or feel her presence. She stood defensively, behind her daughter's chair, and studied her son-in-law for signs of contamination. Husband and wife dynamics were all too familiar to her. So was the idiom 'curiosity killed the cat' but she was dead, and so she dismissed it as a perverse joke that, with even heavier irony, haunted her.

Neither Raine nor Cornelius were themselves. Neither could be under the circumstances, but in a strange way, her daughter was coming to life at a time when she might have surrendered without a struggle.

The cards were on the table – legal documents and letters and words that reeked of resignation and defeat. Barely twenty-four hours earlier the three of them had been cloistered with a smarmy straggle of smug developers flaunting cheque books. Their offers pencilled in pale numbers compared to the asking price of a few years ago. It had taken all her immense self-control not to materialize and upturn the tables, both read and metaphorical.

"I've listened carefully to your arguments," Cornelius said, heatedly. "But it's time to sell."

Raine briefly closed her eyes, breathed out a heavy sigh and sat up straight. Lady Nan placed her invisible hands on her daughter's shoulders. "I won't sell and that's that," Raine said. "Ultimately, it's my decision. So, there's an end to it." She moved to rise from the table and sat down again as Cornelius turned over his chair.

For the first time, she saw him livid. "I may have taken your family name when I married you, as against convention as it was, but I sure as hell didn't relinquish my commonsense."

"Why should you care?" Raine said in a clear emotionless voice. "Egypt is all that's important to you. You were hardly ever home."

Her poise unnerved her husband. He squirmed, momentarily speechless.

The old lady pondered this while her son-in-law regained his composure. This was essentially true. Archaeology kept his attention focused on the ancient past for months at a time. And when he *was* home, it was always a visit, noticeably felt as a short hiatus from his real life amongst the mummified passed.

Pharaoh Smenkhare, his prime subject of interest, was no passing phase. Cornelius had captured the man whole. In a way, it was an extraordinary second marriage of inconvenience. A long-distance affair, separated by three-thousand years of marital bliss. Raine was the odd third of the love triangle. She was in the strangest of ways, 'the other woman'. A housekeeper child-minder and a hardly a 'better half'. More like a runner-up in a fixed beauty contest. Raine's voice penetrated her thoughts. Her daughter was finally acting like a true Stratford-Smyth.

"We must preserve the Hall at all costs," Raine said. "It's our children's legacy. It's what my mother would have wanted."

"You do realize," Cornelius began, "that a fair chunk of change would have to be sacrificed if we waged a formal dispute or played hard to get with the developers. It's a game and they're shrewd players. They're not like us. They cheat. We'd be all right with startup funds from this place if we sell now. Properties in the south of London are pricey but within our budget if we act decisively. My funding hasn't dried up… *yet*, so I can go back to Egypt. It's no longer safe for Tut to join me but he can make a start on my book. The kids love London. This backwater can't be good for them. And you can be a teacher again in a real school."

Raine stood and faced her husband. Her voice was steady and devastatingly soft. "Backwater? This was my mother's estate and I will *never* sell," she said. "Is that decisive enough for you?"

Strangely, she was more beautiful to Cornelius in her stand of defiance. This was not the woman he married. He was taken aback, but some presence urged him to save face, so he said nothing, stormed from the room, and slammed the door.

Raine did not crumble. She squared her shoulders, collected the scattered papers into a file, and locked them in the desk.

Lady Nan felt her throat constrict. It was the same desk in which 'the captain' had locked away her key to the Winter Room, all those years ago. She could feel the ghost of it, there in the drawer, calling as it always had. She had never been proud of her daughter until this moment. It was true, she thought. Chickens really do come home to roost.

"I never wanted to be a teacher," Mrs. S said softly to the closed door.

LVI

THE FURIOUS SUMMER

JULY 1

Bash stared at the sky for any sign of rain using the techniques Charlotte had taught her. Parks had shown her how to squint into the blue for an underlying tone of yellow, but the air had no smell of rain to come. The hairs on her arms prickled with static electricity.

The gardens failed to shrivel due to Parks system of channelling water from the lake, deep below ground. The topiaries survived by swimming each night and absorbing water like sponges to endure during the worst part of the day. But Tut thrived, physically unaffected by the heat.

"I don't know where you get your energy," Kit said. "slow down. You're making us all look bad."

Bash gave Kit one of her incredulous 'you-call-yourself-a-scientist' looks. "Don't be stupid. He's in his natural element." That reminded her she was learning a lot about *the* elementals lately as part of her training. Parks called them *our* friends much the same way she and Kit had been taught to ask a policeman for help as children. Now that the truth was out, it was no longer odd to think of Parks as a child or a teenager or an old man. He was his usual sprightly self but then his element was ethereal with the ability to remain anatomically solid. At first, it was odd to think of ghosts as solid because Taraq and Anna still faded in and out when stressed. In fact more than half of everyone she knew were ghosts. The Twinters boasted five (not counting all of Parks incarnations) and goodness knows how many others 'lived' in town. And she couldn't help second-guessing everyone she met in Bede, too. They were a strange lot. Well, apart from the irritating developers who were all too alive and annoying.

Brooks had given them an intriguing but incomplete picture and Parks was obviously wary of divulging too much information too soon. When she pried, he laughed and said he was 'leading her up the garden path' for her own good. Then he would tip his cap and correct himself looking what she determined was the default image of chagrin, a word she loved. "It's for the good of the world," Parks would say, and that was meant to suffice. And because he was wont to appear mysterious, and in order to be evasive and open at the same time, he offered the Twinters a cryptic message: 'The mysteries of the villagers will reveal themselves when the time is ripe for apples.

Bash was relieved to know that the latest Stanley Parks, Parks Six, was actually alive and breathing in the most delightful way. Six was a handsome lad, tanned and perpetually smiling which made him quite the leading man when he'd sauntered through the movie folk oblivious to the effect he was having on the actresses. And whenever he showed her how to treat a plant just so, she felt dizzy in a most agreeable sensation.

Apparently the two village girls she'd made friends with, thought the same way when they'd visited the Hall. Charlotte had been far from amused. Her advice was: keep to yourself until the present situation is 'out of the woods'. Bash's excuse was that she wouldn't have sought new friends if her two brothers hadn't made her feel left out.

Charlotte raised her eyebrows at her in an accusatory expression that came with a lecture: "When are you going to accept you're not an ordinary girl? Do you think Parks and the Lady Chloris bestow titles on ordinary mortals? You were appointed 'Daughter of the

House of Bede and 'Mistress of the Green' for a reason. Distance yourself from these village girls. Seek the extraordinary folks in Bede Village and they will make themselves known to you. They are the twice-borns. One has already done so but you refused to see. When I use a term like 'out of the woods' it contains a twin message. One is obvious, that is to say, literal, and the other is subliminal. You must learn to tell the difference."

Bash had been both chastened and delighted. The word subliminal echoed the word liminal, one of Lady Nan's special words.

"It's Cairo hot," Tut declared. "Egypt dry. That first Christmas I was here was the happiest of miracles. I was cold but... you know, warmed by all of you. I remember that 'Jack Frost nipping at your nose' song and Bash told me how Parks was Jack-of-the-green as well as all the colours of Bede." A soppy smile came over his face. "And inside, in my new pyjamas, the fires roared me to sleep. I'd never had pyjamas before or a real bed for that matter. So it was all a bit of a marvel. It still is. But I'm happy to be able to help …Mum," he stopped awkwardly. It was still uncomfortable to use the word Mum quite so glibly, even after two years. "To help your mother."

Bash sighed and rubbed his arm. "She wants you to call her Mum. You do know that, right?"

Tut ducked his head and nodded. "I know. I am trying. Dad isn't easy either."

"No problem with Dad. I think he'd like it if we all called him Professor."

"I miss the snow too, Bash said to cover the moment."

Kit pictured the bleak view from the tower with snow so high he could almost touch its surface that reached barely a few feet under the highest window, and shuddered. "If I ever see another snowflake it'll be too soon."

The picturesque Christmas card Tut treasured, blanketed the countryside in soft flakes of warm ash. It was going to be a grey Christmas.

LVII

IT'S RAINING IT'S SNOWING

AUGUST 2

Kit thought he was still dreaming. It wasn't unusual for volcanoes to invade his dreams, and he was only too thankful that for some reason Bash rarely shared them. He leaned his back against the wall and closed his eyes, but as he counted to a hundred, Mrs. S gave a surprised shriek from the kitchen door that confirmed his fears. He rushed to her side, as casually as possible, still in his robe and slippers.

The lawns were pale grey and moving. A blanket of ash lifting and swirling low to the ground by a feeble wind.

"Mum it's not going to last. Somewhere in the world there's been an eruption and it's brought this ash here. It happens all the time." He examined the ground, thrilled to find the ash was thin. "Well, okay, it's kind of rare but it's nothing to worry about. This could easily blow away by lunch time."

"I'll make pancakes," she said. "That always helps."

Kit appraised his mother with a scowl.

She noticed and checked her words. "I mean, pancakes seem to start a day off quite well. Much better than cold cereal. I'll cook bacon as well." She turned abruptly, already smiling from the image of stirring a huge bowl of batter in her mind.

Tut passed Mrs. S in the kitchen passage. "What's Mum so happy about? I thought I heard her scr…" The sight of the lawns froze his speech. He gave a low whistle at the dark landscape. "Black sand," he said. "So, it's *not* a myth."

"It's only grey. You know about this?"

"I've only heard about it. It's an ancient curse. A myth from the beginning time. Before the pyramids when Egypt emerged from the mud as a small mound. Some versions call it fire dust."

"I wonder if it's snowing in Australia," Bash said, when she saw it. I'd better find Parks. This can't be good for the garden."

Bash was relieved to hear Parks making light of the situation. An ironic thought not lost on her, considering a certain 'dark times a-coming' had been the topic of several conversations.

"They're having a wee joke," Parks said, not too convincingly. "Now we can gird our loins. No more false starts. I smell pancakes. Your mother is helping in her way. Go easy on her."

"They?"

"I expect Brooks will call a meeting, right enough. All will be revealed, soon."

"Parks, will you join us? For once?"

Parks grinned. "I'd be delighted. I haven't had me breakfast and I fancy some pancakes."

"I meant the meetings."

"I know you did. I was trying to cheer things up a bit. From now on you can count on me being there. I was born for this day." He winked. "I mean, I *died* so I could *face* this day."

His words sent a shiver into Bash's morning. "Are you happy about this?"

"Zeus, no. But there's a relief to knowing something that was bound to come is no longer a threat. Ye can't fight a threat. But sure enough, we're called into battle." He checked the sky, seeming to measure it with his eyes with one ear to listen to the trees. He nodded as if he'd heard an answer. "Right, it's as grim as *that* is it," he said, scaring Bash with the determined expression on his face.

"Parks. I'm scared."

"Good. You're coming along. Fear is healthy at a time like this. Ain't no good sweeping ash under a carpet, as if one could. We've got work to do." And with that he stuck his shovel into the ground and rested on the handle. He seemed to be praying. Almost immediately, the Parks clan arrived with Six tagging along last. It took them the better part of the day to dig a deep pit at the edge of the tree line.

Bash was too upset to notice Six when she brought them lemonade. She watched the Parks' toil away as if she was somewhere else. "Parks," she said, when he thanked her for his drink. "Should I fetch Charlotte?"

"No need, she's already on her way." He handed Bash a large set of keys. "Let her in the gate and then be a good lass and bring these back to me, straight away. Straight away mind. Right?"

"Right as rain," Bash replied in a weak voice. Parks tried to reassure her by declaring it was 'early days' yet. He was right about one thing. Mrs. S was still making 'breakfast' at dinnertime.

Lady Nan showed herself in the kitchen and beckoned Bash to follow her. "Now, you're not to worry. There's a meeting tonight in the tower. Anna and Taraq will be there but for now they're doing an errand for me. It's all in hand for the moment. Tell Kit and Tut, and act normal as if nothing untoward is happening, there's a good girl. Your mother is easily panicked."

Bash smiled. "I think you mean pancaked." The look in Lady Nan's eyes erased her smile. "She makes pancakes when she's upset. You know, like your word game… panic… pancake? The laws of word-power? Parks made a joke to cheer me up, so I thought I'd…"

Lady Nan shook her head. "Your mother picks up on vibrations although she'd never admit it. Keep an eye on Anubis and if he makes eye contact with you, follow him. Do you understand? This is serious, but I appreciate your gesture to break the tension." She patted Bash's cheek. "Now, let's keep that to a minimum, shall we."

Bash stayed her grandmother's arm. "I do, except for one thing. What does girding one's loins mean?

The Hall wasted no time to call upon the North Wind's assistance. It vacuumed the ash from every leaf and roof shingle, freeing the chains of the twin's bicycles and swirled the entire morass into a pile raised into the sky where it was compressed into a black snowball that emitted a few angry red sparks. Parks & Sons buried it in their pit.

Charlotte and the fairies came and recited a cleansing ceremony over the grave of ashes. The moles and mice dug out the entrances to their tunnels. Mrs. S stopped making pancakes and made a roast with brown gravy for supper. The scarabs in the library reshuffled themselves into rows.

The Twinters called a meeting to circumvent the ruckus. Brooks made an announcement. "It's time to reveal the importance of a few villagers who will join us. Consider them Twinters. And yes, they know all about us and a great deal more. The historian, Clive Lucy, Nick Wardencliffe, retired engineer; and of course and especially, our friendly photographer-chemist Vincento Leoni for a start."

"I assumed the ash was a real one-of phenomenon as Mum and Dad saw it," Kit said. "But now I'm not sure. So, Parks, I defer to you. Please tell us what's going on in simple words?"

"It's the furies."

"The fairies?"

"Close enough I reckon," Parks said. "Jealous second cousins of the wee folk if you ask me. And when they get together all hell breaks loose. Good fairies can get downright nasty when push comes to shove. But bad fairies go one worse… they get malicious.

No good comes of them getting together. None at all." Parks stared long into each face in silence before delivering his final word. "Be wary of em. *All* of em. Ornery and persnickety fairies are... but the furies... they're out for blood. The furies are out to kill. Only two letters separate them." He winked at Lady Nan. "You know best how words contain magic. What are those letters called?"

Lady Nan smiled weakly and protested by holding up her hands in surrender. "Vowels."

Parks nodded with a satisfied expression. "Right. Things that rhyme with bowels as in the bowels of the earth. As in a caldera. The geological innards of churning poisons."

"I think you're being a little dramatic there, Parks," Kit said. "You've been around my sister too long."

Parks stamped his shovel on the floor for attention. "LISTEN! You can't be too trusting of fairies," he said. "They're the least cooperative of the elementals. They're supposed to listen to me, but do they? NO ... THEY ... DO ... NOT! Charlotte controls them easy-peasy, but I've seen too many botched shenanigans in my time. Give me the North Wind any day of the week."

Charlotte leaned over and planted a kiss on Parks' cheek. He blushed and turned into his younger self – a dead ringer for Six. Charlotte chucked him under the chin. "The truth is, the fairies are terrified of you, so they play games with you. They like to trick you.

For once it looked as if Parks was going to lose his temper with Charlotte. "My good woman, please tell these children that Furies do not play tricks. They kill, so let's not mince words for effect, shall we?"

Lady Nan manifested a book on Greek mythology, and held it aloft. "The ancient Greeks wrote about them."

"So... Stratford Smyth-ology," Bash said in a hushed voice. "Myth inside Smyth. You tried to tell us years ago about the laws of word-power. That's why you were upset when I was flippant earlier about the word panic."

Lady Nan softened. "Not for the reason you think. You've heard of Pan the nature god, well, that's where the word panic originates. Everything we do here is connected. Bede is the home of the great Pan… that is, it harbours Pan's energy. And now, as the Daughter of the House of Bede, so do you. It's a big responsibility."

"The thing you need to remember about the Furies," Parks continued, "is that they fight from the inside out. They get under your skin, up your nose, and inside your head where they plant toxic seeds. From there, your fear grows a harvest of trifling 'bothersomes' – pet peeves that blossom into full-blown mind-choking weeds. You itch with evil jealousy and fan frivolous complaints into tantrums. Humans can rage and storm emotionally and cause damage with consequences as devastating as any meteorological tempest."

"Fairies… furies… furious… furious fairies."

"Senseless hatred," Tut added, "and irrational anger."

Kit's face looked chalky. "And the angry red planet. Mars, the god of war. The face on Mars. I *defaced* it with a marker. Irrational fear. The entity 'M' is Megeara."

The name Megeara erupted a chorus of murmuring, but Parks silenced the room by shouting a single word. "Pan," he exclaimed. His next words froze his audience into submission. Parks' golden aura fanned around him like a cloak giving him the appearance of a giant in their midst as he delivered a chilling prophecy. "The continent of Pan has risen. Pangea is here. Time is upon us. The circle is full. The snake bites its own tail."

The gold scarab had its orders. Once it had rested inside the mummified body of its king, but between present missions it rested in its tray of purely decorative stone telegrams. Each winged beetle had conveyed a commemorative message, a wish, or a proclamation, sent by Pharaoh's chief scribe to sweep the populace with greetings and orders.

Now it was time for Bede's water beetles to take up the banner. They flew low and the local bees soared high. The mice were a lively forest carpet of activity, scurrying in a network of agitation. Even the fairies respected them.

Pharaoh SmenKhare valued the scarab enough to list it as one of the possessions chosen to accompany him to his afterlife. The message on its base begged him to live forever – the ancient equivalent of 'and they lived happily ever after.' The library's green glow quieted down once the ash was buried under the correct incantations. The scarab ceased to flutter, and folded its wings, powering down to conserve its energy, alert as a sleeping cat.

LVIII

BACK SOON

SEPTEMBER 22 – THE AUTUMNAL EQUINOX

The breakfast table was not exempt from emotional pressure. An invitation had arrived that set the proverbial cat amongst the pigeons. When the twins entered the kitchen, Mrs. S was shouting at their father, and slamming the oven door.

Mr. S brightened. "Morning children." He turned to his wife. "We need to take this to another room, Raine. The kids need to eat in peace."

The argument continued, filtering through the wall as if it were made of paper.

"You're not going to that dig again," Mrs. S said. "I forbid it."

"I'm considering it. The board has asked to meet with me. They're laying on a posh lunch at the Dorchester. They've even booked us a first-class room."

"It's selfish."

"It's what I was born to do."

"And it almost killed you."

"We could go together. It'd make a nice day trip to London. Clear the air. Do you not feel the pressure around here?"

"I do now. This is the last straw, Cornelius!"

Bash was hammering the top of her second boiled egg with the back of a spoon when Tut entered the kitchen wide-eyed. He gestured towards the dining room with his thumb. "What's going on in there? I don't suppose there's any pancakes going."

Kit snickered. "Not bloody likely."

"As near as I can tell," Bash said, "it's about some sort of fancy lunch in London. Mum is against. Dad is in favour."

"Pancakes aplenty." Pigeon shrieked. *"Peaceful pancakes."*

Tut put up his hand. "I'll go if she won't."

Kit kept slunk down behind a book on Mars and kept quiet.

Bash peeled away the shattered bits of shell. "It's not for the likes of *you*."

"What's *that* supposed to mean?"

"Street smarts don't count in posh hotels."

Pigeon edged to the furthest end of his perch and attempted to make himself as unobtrusive as possible by putting his head under one wing muttering about poo and posh.

Kit's voice came from behind his book. "You're scaring the bird. Keep it down. I can't read."

"Then you should have paid more attention in school."

"Ha ha. Very droll. I think you may have finally gotten the hang of the English language. That ought to impress Imogen."

"Shutup."

Kit lowered his book and sneered. "Ah. You HAVE got it down."

"I hate to be the bearer of bad news, but neither of you stood a chance with her, you know," Bash said.

"Like you with Six?" Tut said, sarcastically, immediately recognizing that he'd gone too far from Bash's expression of killer rage.

That's when Taraq arrived in a full state of righteous indignance and entered Bash and Tut's nasty contest, debating the pros and cons of the class system vs. street smarts.

But of all the sword clashing and sharpened teeth, the worst was Lady Nan momentarily manifested as the lioness Sekhmet. Brooks sent her a withering look and she immediately returned to being the nine-year old Beryl, holding Unicorn on her lap. "Sorry," she said, sheepishly in her child's voice, "I've always been able to control my other forms. Please disregard what you saw."

It was when the cats had a hissing fit over whose bowl was who's that Lady Nan called a halt. "This is what I thought would happen," she said. "A Bede cat-fight is the last straw. Mend your differences now. All of you. You'll need to be alert. It's going to get worse. Be on your best behaviour... even if it kills you."

"Was she talking to us or the cats?" Tut asked.

"Probably, the universe," Kit said.

Bash did a slow clap. "Spoken like a true ghost in the machine, Gran."

Lady Nan shuddered at the name Gran but she smiled genteelly and blew a handful of dry cornflakes at her granddaughter.

Pigeon's beak emerged from his red and gold plumage. *"Pecking order... Playful... Food fight,"* he squawked. *"I'm telling Mum. Play nice."*

Mrs. S haphazardly laid out a brown suit and a beige blouse on her bed, the first two items she'd come across in her closet. "I don't care what I wear. I don't want to go. Why on earth did I say yes?"

Bash looked on, horrified.

"This'll have to do. It's a situation of a country mouse visiting the city, I suppose. Maybe I can get out of it."

"Mum. It's about time you went out. Especially out of here. What with all the trouble. Have a mini holiday. Dress up. It will be good for you... and Dad."

Mrs. S slumped into a chair and started to cry.

Bash, completely out of her usual role, tried to provide comfort. "Everything will be all right," she said in a small voice.

Lady Nan materialized from the wardrobe mirror. "Goodness, she can't wear that! Raine never did get out much. She cared nothing for clothes. She's no fashion sense. Hemlines change; style does not. She was comfortable as a countrified drudge. She can't go to London in one of her dowdy outfits. We'll find what we need in my wardrobe. We're roughly the same size. She's slender and if she'd only stand up straight like she belonged in the room, she'd give the impression of being tall. As for elegant, we can't work wonders. For heaven's sake, don't let her wear that pale pink lipstick. It makes her smile disappear. She has decent lips. Let's get them noticed."

"She isn't smiling much these days."

Lady Nan's expression was vacant. "None of us are." She drew herself up to her full height. She was majestic even at seventy-three. "Never mind," she said. "Things pass. It's only a matter of time."

Fortunately, Bash had inherited her grandmother's jewellery and other personal effects and she had been able to persuade her mother to leave Lady Nan's room intact, as it had been on the day of her death. Lady Nan's hourglass and snow globe stood in places of honour beside the bed.

"It's morbid to keep a shrine," Mrs. S had said. But she hadn't put up a fuss. "You and your grandmother were always close. Not like her and I." She looked puzzled. "But then, neither are you and I. I wonder why that is. Keep whatever you want. It's a load of mixed memories for me. Mostly bad ones. The Hall is too large to miss one room. I leave it to all to your judgement. Ask Kit if he wants any of it."

Bash watched Anna bouncing on Lady Nan's bed from the corner of her eye. "I've already got the fairy bed, so I'll leave the room intact. I like to come in here to read. It's as if I can still visit her."

Anna's theatrics were no distraction to Mrs. S. The four-poster's bedsprings were silent and the bedspread stayed smooth and undisturbed. Bored, Anna moved to the dressing table and took the top off a jar of Nivea face cream. Bash glared at her, horrified, and retrieved the hovering jar and lid from mid-air. She sniffed the cream and extended it to Mrs. S as an invitation. "I can smell this cold cream in my room sometimes. Do you think maybe she's still hanging around… as a ghost. That would be nice, wouldn't it?"

"Hmmn?"

"I was saying that sometimes, Lady Nan's perfume is very strong in the library. Lady Nan used to call the sense of smell olfactory time travel."

Mrs. S snapped out of her daydreaming. "What? I wasn't listening." She surveyed the room, looking as if she were about to cry.

Bash glanced at her careworn mother whose posture always slumped in a perpetual persona of self-defeat. It was hard to believe she was Lady Nan's daughter. "I think panache skips a generation," Bash whispered aside to Anna.

"It's hot in Bede," Lady Nan commented. "But the weather station reports it's snowing in London. So, we'll find a dress and a jacket and pair it with some long gloves and a fur coat. Pearls work with everything. Your mother can use the coat as a travel rug if she won't wear it. Now, I know animal skins seem unethical for a place like Bede but it's part of an eco-system. Food chains exist. We all die. Death is natural."

Bash opened the curtains for light. "I'll get Lady Nan's makeup. She's got some super-red lipstick. It will be fun to do a makeover."

Mrs S cringed. She plucked at the brown skirt. "No Bash. It's not me. I couldn't wear red lips."

"Pleeese Mum. You can take it off if you hate it. Do it for Dad."

Lady Nan walked through her clothes hanging in the walk-in closet rather than pushing them aside. She chose a black silk dress and a short gold jacket embroidered with silver dragons cinched into three pleats at the back, added a choker of grey pearls and an emerald-cut hematite Dinner ring, and threw the lot in a heap on her bed. "Hurry child. Take these to you mother. Dear me, I feel like a fairy godmother."

Bash announced her mother with a theatrical flourish. "Presenting Milady Cornelius Stratford-Smyth." A red streak wound a string of light around her parents. She dashed over and waved it away.

Kit shared a look with Bash and attempted to help her. "You look nice, Mum."

Mrs. S beamed. "Thank you darling."

Mr. S raised his eyebrows and emitted a low wolf whistle in appraisal.

Mrs. S was far from flattered. "Oh, do be quiet, Cornelius."

More red lights zoomed about, ricocheting off the walls, and came to rest under the kitchen chairs.

"I didn't know our budget could stretch to new clothes. "This is why I prefer to live in the desert."

"It's okay, Dad. They were Lady Nan's," Bash announced. "I helped Mum throw something together. So it didn't cost anything."

Mr. S smiled at Bash. "Lovely darling. Well done." Even in an elegant suit, he looked like an archaeologist. All that was missing was his pith helmet.

Mrs. S brushed non-existent lint from her husband's shoulder, but Mr. S stopped her hand. "Raine, for heaven's sake stop fussing. We'll be late."

"I guess even the lint is imaginary around here," Kit said.

Mr. S plumped the sofa cushions, completely out of character.

"You're always in a dither," he said, pulling a beaded bag from behind a sofa cushion. He swung it by its strap. "What a marvellous place to keep a handbag. Have you got your shoes?"

"Back soon darlings," Mrs. S shouted, blowing a kiss from the car. She dabbed her eyes, red from the occasional burst of tears, and her voice threatened to break.

"Oh for heavens sake, we're only going for one night. We'll be back before you know it," Mr. S added. His concentration on the journey ahead was as strained as his wife's smile. He crunched the gears and put his foot on the gas pedal more heavily than usual. Mr. S was thrown back in her seat as the car leapt forward.

It left deep tire tracks in the gravel. Parks made a note to return and smooth it with a rake. Rather a long job as the ruts continued all the way to the gates. He shook his head and gazed miserably after the disappearing car. "And so the hourglass turns and events move," he muttered to himself. "Tomorrow is as tomorrow does."

The ransom note was not only stained with sooty fingerprints. It smelled of rotten cabbage. Someone had taken great pains to age a sheet of expensive parchment paper by holding it over a candle and then burying it in a rich patch of earth under a bad moon. The words wasted little time to state the furies were in control. There were only two demands.

Bede Hall must be sold to the developers. Mr. and Mrs. S would be released to Kit and no other. That was it. They were to accept the first deal offered and step aside. Failure to comply would end badly for Mr. and Mrs. Stratford-Smyth. Their little getaway might take a more permanent turn. And to reinforce their intent, the couple had been waylaid. Their new destination, being Cairo.

> *Bede Hall must be sold to the first bidder.*
> *Your loved ones are safe in Cairo.*
> *We will only release them to Kit.*
> *He must travel alone. Bring the signed deeds.*
> *Come to the Cairo Museum…alone! – M*

The note was folded once and sealed with the red wax impression of a wasp, wings outspread, and signed with an extravagant M.

It conspired that Parks found Mr. and Mrs. S' abandoned car in the middle of the road, not fifty yards from Bede Hall's gates. The demanding note was pinned to a red velvet cushion embroidered with a black border of wasps, left on the passenger seat.

Tut took one look at Kit's ashen face and volunteered. "I'll go," Tut said. "I know my way around Cairo. Kit will get lost… or worse."

"And you'll never come back," Bash said. "You're on some kind of hit list, remember? Besides, they've asked for Kit. He's got to go."

Kit waffled. "It makes no sense. The police will know what's best."

"They want you." Parks said. "You're the one who has to go. We're dealing with an alien entity. We can't tell the authorities that. The police must be kept out of this. You three are minors. Do you want to be taken away?"

"Brooks is our legal guardian," Bash said. "Mum told me ages ago before Dad was found."

Parks shook his head. "Once the police are involved they'll never let Kit go. This is Bede Hall's affair."

"I could go with him," Anna said.

"Better, it's me than Anna," Taraq said. "For the same reason Tut suggested."

Tut paced back and forth. "Taraq, Modern Cairo bears no resemblance to anything you remember."

Parks slammed his walking stick on the sundial for attention. "We have to advertise that the Hall's for sale. Now. There's no time for dilly dallying. We knew something would happen. This is it. The furies won't honour their claim, so we have to play their game for the time being."

Eerily, the amplified words 'time being' echoed off the sundial for over an hour.

LVIX

DEEP FREEZE

SEPTEMBER 23

The disappearance galvanized Bash into action. Only Lady Nan could stop her from calling the authorities and organizing a search party.

"This is strictly a family matter," Lady Nan said. "A challenge directed at Bede Hall. We're being tested. The Hall is being punished."

"Surely the police can search the airport if we report the car if we report it stolen."

"My dear child, your parents have been literally 'spirited away'. It's beyond the police or any other earthly agency. By now I'd have thought you realized that we live in a pocket of… let's just call it, misunderstanding. The rest of the world is asleep and we've awakened a curse."

"I'll kill Rupert if he ever shows his face around here."

"Rupert played into the furies' hands. He was a dupe. And now he's humiliated. It's in character he would return to where he feels most important. Remember, Bathsheba, this war has been stewing a long time. It is no coincidence that the future disaster Kit witnessed is aligned to a volcanic eruption. The furies rule over such calamities. I smelled their presence when your brother first reported his

318

encounter. Parks confirmed it. It's in the stars was all he'd say." She paused, smiling. "He still sees me as a little girl he needs to protect."

"I've always taught you to look between the letters of a powerful word. Disaster literally means bad star. And in this instance, the baleful influence of a planet. I'm sure you can guess which one."

"Bloody hell. It's never Mars! It's never bloody extraterrestrials!"

"Language Bash, language," Lady Nan admonished. "Be ever mindful of the words you choose. Words are deeds."

"Kit will be terrified. He's been on about 'the face on Mars' since forever."

"Your parents will only be found when the furies want them to be found. Take heart, often missing persons appear dazed at the edge of a forest clearing, unaware of passing time. That's the furies' way. Sadly, fairies have had to live down to that particular myth for centuries. And it is completely false. The furies have a lot of Grimms' Fairy Tales to answer for. That said, the sweetest fairies can throw a glamour as easily as any of the furies. But such drastic measures require a lengthy consensus to avoid a misreading of their sacred texts." She wagged a finger at her granddaughter. "However, when push comes to shove, I should be very sorry indeed, to be on the wrong side of a fairy's wrath."

"Charlotte's fairies have proved rather tricky. I remember that meeting when Parks told us to be wary of all fairies. It's easy to be overwhelmed by their presence."

"It's a matter of scent vs. odour," Lady Nan said. "The distinction between fragrance and odoriferous. Fairies emit an intoxicating perfume. Furies reek of a multitude of disgusting stinks."

Bash smiled at a new word. "Odoriferous," she repeated. "Even the word smells bad."

Lady Nan smiled at her protégé. "Other than the letters 'i' and 'u', the main difference between fairies and furies is that fairies never hold a grudge, they teach a lesson and go about their business. Furies take their name from the word furious – an explosive rage. A fury's curse is no small blowing-off-steam in a fit of pique."

Kit was in shock. Taraq stayed silent while Kit pulled out the meditation throne, wary of intervening in case of a further attack. The way his eyes narrowed could mean anything. But nothing good.

"I'm not going to hurt it," Kit said, facing the wall. "Give me some credit."

"You are too busy torturing yourself," I am here for you as much as the future."

Kit sat with his arms around Jack. "Why did they take them? They could have had me."

"And who is they? You don't believe in 'theys'. Permit me to say so, but I believe you are in danger of believing the very things you resist. Fairies."

Kit exploded with rage. "That's the ruddy problem. I DO believe them. All of them. I have done for ages. I just didn't want to give up on science, so I faked ignorance. And I've become so good at being arrogant and miserable that I don't like myself anymore." He gestured with his arms open wide. "I don't want to believe any of this."

"That said, there was one thing I never faked."

Taraq sighed. "Yes, I know. You are truly the worst coward I ever met."

"Thanks pal."

Taraq paused to study Kit's eyes and hesitated. "I think… you are most welcome."

"But doesn't being the *worst* coward mean that I'm brave?"

Taraq contemplated this as he dusted the throne for the ninth time. "Kit," he said, after some reflection. "You are the very BEST coward I know."

Kit bowed. "I don't *want* it to be true that I see fairies flitting and rowan trees pinching and chairs with lassos made of light."

A slow grin spread across Taraq's face. "That day…"

Kit was ahead of him and interrupted. "The one where I kicked the chair? Yeah, what of it?"

"You were kicking the light. Trying to get rid of the energy around your ankle. I thought you were upset with the chair."

"Was I that transparent?"

"Sorry?"

Kit shook his head and managed a faint grimace. "I was making a stupid ghost joke."

"You are then, happy?"

"Bloody hell, no. Making jokes is a ploy. To save face. I'm stunned at what's happened."

Taraq swooped around the room in a victory lap so fast Kit had to close his eyes. "Don't get me wrong," Kit said. "I *was* lashing out that day with the chair. But it was in retaliation for being *lashed by* a supernatural red string."

"And today you are cured. I am, as you say, beside myself."

"Don't be a numpty. Someone's messing with our emotions around here. I've had a conversation with one of them. The leader. I even know her name. But I've pretended to forget it."

"And you said nothing to the Twinters."

"That's correct because, nudge nudge wink wink, I didn't hear a word of it. Got it?"

"Almost."

"I'm not wholly unconscious, amoral, or immune to compassion. But I'm probably more observant than most."

"You lie more than most."

"I can't come clean with Bash. If I admit when I first saw the fairies she'll know I've been lying for ages."

Taraq looked up at Kit, still working on Kit's words. "So... you must lie to appear honest?"

"Basically, yeah."

"Master," Taraq said, his eyes full of awe. "You are the finest liar I know. You are..." he searched the sky for the right word. "You are a sphinx."

"And here's a conundrum. I don't want to time travel but I *do* want to time travel so I can go back and never open that damn blue door. I want to turn back time and stay here. Maybe I *am* a sphinx."

LX

KIT THE CONFESSOR

SEPTEMBER 23

Kit smoothed the page of his diary that had been creased to tear out. He reread his words and added two new ones in red capital letters that took up the height of three lines.

URGENT AMENDMENT
September 23

> I'm going over to the dark side. Well, my parents have. I've pretty much already gone, really. Taraq knows.
>
> Kidnap seems to be an ongoing theme for my family. Dad was verifiably kidnapped, and now both my parents have vanished. The ransom note read like a riot act, sealed with the same initial 'M' pressed into red wax as Bash's Christmas card.
>
> So far, I haven't announced my new status. I'm not even sure if any of the other Twinters would believe me. I put up that good of a fight.

LXI

THE RULES OF SOULSTICE

SEPTEMBER 24

Charlotte stood behind Parks and called for attention. "I have an important announcement to make," she said resting her hands on Parks's shoulders. "I meant to tell you on the solstice, but there was the distraction. So, two days late, here it is." She cleared her throat. "I was the original ghost of Bede Hall," she said shakily. I used to be Glynis. Glynis Findlay, that was. A housemaid. I worked in the stillery, mainly, but it fell to me to create all the formal floral arrangements for the house and to look after the houseplants. That kept me bumping into Parks on my flower-picking rounds. My room in the servants' quarters in the attic…" she paused to close her eyes and leaned her forehead on Parks. Her fingers tightened on his shoulders. "…it was the Winter Room." She took a deep breath. "Parks and I were engaged."

Parks reached up and took Charlotte's hand. And as their fingers met he became the persona of Parks 4. "I was twenty," he said. "I died on August 1, 1800, that time. And that's the beginning and end of it."

"Not quite the end, my love," Charlotte said. "There's always the future, isn't there Kit."

LXII

FALLOUT SHELTER

SEPTEMBER 25

Brooks had one spare room to the Hall's nineteen bedrooms. Besides, it couldn't be left empty or the developers would be all over it with measuring tapes and cameras. Valuable antiques were vulnerable, easily up for grabs and surely worth almost as much as the devalued estate, crumbling by the minute.

The Twinters were unanimous. Legally, Brooks was the teens' appointed guardian. Rupert had scarpered on his own steam and no-one assumed *he'd* been kidnapped. The papers presented by Messrs. Tweedy and Co. complicated matters with the bank. Rupert's signature, as eldest son, held some credibility on a sales agreement but wouldn't be binding until many months passed. People assumed missing weren't discounted for dead. Lawyers took a dim view of rushing into deals.

"For the time being," Brooks announced, "we will all be staying at the Hall. All ten of us. That way, the property is constantly monitored and the children can stay together. We must take the ransom note as a serious threat. I'm looking into a plane ticket for Kit."

Kit stood weakly. "I will be going to Cairo as soon as I can get a passport. Tut will brief me on street maps and customs. I've been there once and it was insane. We have no choice if we want to get

324

Mum and Dad back. Perhaps Rupert's idiot move will work for us. All the furies want is to see the house sold. His signature on a conditional sale may be enough."

"It won't," Parks said. "They want a fight."

"Don't they realize if they destroy the buildings it will be harder to sell. That goes against what they want."

"It's exactly what they want. To prolong the Hall's suffering. In the end the estate would either be sold for buttons or be left in ruins. Either way, we move out and the furies can harass the developers for sport. Complying bypasses the haggling and fighting and the psychic injuries. There's no fun in that."

"The upshot is this. Raine and Cornelius are alive. They can make short work of packing up and leaving. It's the subsequent demolition and degradation of the Hall the furies want most. We must assume Kit will find them in Cairo."

"But Mum and Dad have no idea what goes on here."

"They don't need to. They know that the writing's on the wall and that staying will result in less funds to begin anew somewhere else. The furies have no bones to pick with the family."

Parks stood and removed his cap. The others watched as his form passed through each of his incarnations until he resembled a stranger. "They want me," he said.

Brooks looked as if he'd had a stroke. Ben evaporated twice. Anna stared at the stranger and smiled.

"Panic stations," Pigeon squawked.

"I know you," Taraq said, and promptly turned as solid as he'd ever been. He bowed, trembling. "Master."

Parks returned to himself as if nothing untoward had happened. A few leaves rustled at his feet as if alive. "I didn't mean to startle everyone. I've been wanting to do that for a long time. Please, carry on. I promise it won't happen again. There's no need to be afraid."

Bash had been shrinking into the shadows, her eyes bulging. It couldn't be. She felt as if she resumed breathing after holding her breath underwater. "Parks," she said in a small voice. "Is that you? Are you the …"

Six stunned Bash into silence by shouting. "Shush. My great great grandfather needs no introduction."

Parks gaze travelled around the room at his clan. Parks 4 gripped Charlotte's hand, Six stared miserably at Bash. Parks 2, 3, and 5, newly materialized, stood shoulder-to-shoulder in decreasing order of age. Parks chuckled at a private joke. "All of us? None of us are here."

Ben sat next to his sister as the teenage version of himself. Snowball darted across the room and leapt onto the stranger's shoulder. Brooks stood to face Parks, his face ashen. "Then you're …" Parks held up his hand and silenced him. "There's no need, Peregrine. We've time enough for complications later. I will see to it that no-one here will remember what just occurred. But I'm happy you know at last. I was getting ahead of myself. For now, we must make a plan and keep to it. Charlotte's had a word with the fairies. They've got the developers in hand, so, that's one less enemy to worry about. Now… Raine and Cornelius are depending on us. But please be assured they're in the dark and thus sheltered from the full knowledge of what has occurred."

"They aren't the only ones," Kit said. And in the morning, Parks rash display of solidarity was no more than a distant dream of Egypt. The land he would have to visit alone if his parents were to be returned. Events had reached a precariously difficult state of affairs that set him directly between a hard decision and a hopelessly rocky situation. Refusal to cooperate was no longer part of the equation.

Strangely, this fact rather released him from a sense of being a poor sport. It was clear that he had to go to Cairo. There were no other options.

LXIII

DEVELOPING NEWS

SEPTEMBER // OCTOBER

The developers are massing like television Indians attacking a wagon train, "Kit said. "It's going to be a massacre. What chance do we have? The bank's bread is buttered, money-side up."

Nimue's wings fluffed up haughtily. "Let them come," she said.

Kit scoffed. "What are you going to do, wave a magic wand at them?"

Nimue stretched her form into a radiant glamour, twelve feet tall. "Ridiculous boy. You've been reading too many fairy tales. We're far more sophisticated." She reduced herself to the size of a butterfly. "I could have made you believe anything if I'd wanted to," she said. "Do you need another demonstration?"

"Ah, you're going to rely on *that* old stuff. Fairy abductions and all that. Parks said you had a plan."

"That 'old stuff' has worked for thousands of years, child. My clan learned it in Egypt when a magician's trick created us to amuse a bored princess. He had us emerge from a lotus flower on the child's palm, and from there we thrived. The Hall isn't the only one to boast time portals. We have one that's seldom used these days but, all things considered, I think it may serve us well."

"Can you make Jack's fleas disappear?"

327

"Splendid idea. Spoken like a true red-one."

Kit warmed to the plan. "I'm sure Edgar's dog would love a nice holiday."

"We intend to waylay the entourage as they pass through the western fringe of Green Lady Wood that encroaches onto the main road, in a tunnel-like… well, trap, not to put too fine a point on it – the junction where Dere Street crosses the Springwell Road behind the main road to Bede. Trespassers must be punished. And downright usurpers must receive the harshest punishment of all. We do try to *infringe* when we can."

Wilbur Tweedy led the three-car convoy with a grim smile of victory on his face. He was enjoying his future moment of triumph in splendid detail when he entered the section of shade from the sudden encroachment of Green Lady Wood.

The engine of his lovingly-restored Rover 2000 spluttered and the car cruised to a stop. The others pulled over. A gaunt man with a mustache had his mobile phone out, holding it up to the sun like an offering. "I can't get a signal in these damned woods. Never could. Desolate ruddy place. I'll drive on, shall I, and make a call for road service clear of these wretched trees, and be right back."

"There's no road service for miles," the third man said.

Wilbur Tweedy's face took fright. "Well, I'm *not* abandoning my expensive car in the middle of hell and gone for some yokel to steal, and that's flat." He sighed. "They might have built the road around this bit. It's only the edge of green. It's more like a thicket. Look, there's a field a few yards to the left. So inconvenient."

Mrs. Tweedy kept reading her book. The cover promised a steamy romance with a ravishing girl and a muscular male torso burnished with oil.

"It's a fairy dell or glade or something," Edgar piped up. "That creepy florist lady and the old gardener at the Hall both said so. Said I was to avoid it if I knew what was good for me. But I think they were trying to scare me after, you know, that time in the Hall when I fainted and couldn't remember what happened."

Edgar opened the car door and Nipper leaped into a biting frenzy, attacking the air, and summersaulting his Jack Russel body into a projectile with teeth. He ran in a wide circle frantically barking at the air. His jaws snapped at empty air but he growled as if he'd caught something.

"Shut that stupid beast up, Mr. Tweedy said, mopping his face with his sleeve. "The heat around here is getting worse. Edgar, make him stop. He's doing my head in."

"Something's upset him," Edgar offered weakly. "He hates Bede."

Mr. Tweedy tapped on the front passenger window and called to his wife. "Enid, it's far too hot to stay in the car. You'll boil to death, dear."

"Hmmmnnn?" Mrs. Tweedy replied, without looking up. "It's 2 o'clock."

"Good one, Dad," Edgar said. "Mum only told me this morning that she was reading a potboiler."

Nimue appeared in a clearing without making so much as a twig snap. A kindly old-dear conjured from the imagination of Edgar's childhood. "Whatever's amiss with your dog? Is he injured?"

Nipper went mad, yapping at her sturdy high-top shoes.

"Don't mind him, he hates boots," Edgar said. "We don't know why. He won't hurt you. Are you a witch or something?"

"Boy!" Mr. Tweedy snapped. "Manners."

Nimue chuckled. "I'm not a witch as it happens." She gave a deep curtsy, too deep for an old frail woman. "My name is Mrs. Nimue. I'm queen of the local fairies' guild… number 1066… the Rowan Branch." She pointed up at the rowan tree. "Literally."

Mr. Tweedy looked at his shoes. "I do apologize for my son. It's this heat."

Nimue spied the man trying to wave his phone into service. "You can use my telephone it's only beyond those trees. I expect a nice cup of tea and fairy cakes will put matters right. They usually do."

Tweedy spluttered much the same as his car's engine, and looked dubiously behind her. "Yes, well… I suppose that would be very nice. Thank you." He gestured to his comrades, forgetting his wife sweltering in her book. "Come along chaps, a land-line will do the trick."

"Tricks are what I do best," Nimue said, pointing to a path in the trees. "Just follow that track. I'll get your dear wife. But do keep your dog quiet if you can, I don't want to wake the lavender."

"Quite," Mr. Tweedy said, with glazed eyes. "One wouldn't want to do that."

The largest rowan in the grove sent a message to the Hall as old Mrs. Nimue turned all three car engines to stone. *"Trapped like flies in honey,"* it said. *"It was a joy to behold."*

LXIV

BLEAK SNOW

SEPTEMBER // OCTOBER

Anna traced her fingers around the open window of the tower and pouted.

"That's not a good look on any girl," Kit said.

"Father, I've only just found you, and now you'll be gone again."

"Please don't say that word."

"Gone?"

Kit chewed his lip. "No… Father."

Anna evaporated with sadness and materialized again in a shade of blue mist. Kit overflowed with guilt. Her life and death were his fault. "Anna, I want to say something before I leave. Listen carefully. This is hard for me to say."

"I'm listening."

"My mission in Cairo is to find my parents… your grandparents. But, I promise you, I will *also* find your mother. I assume she'll be about my age."

Anna nodded. "Oh, yes. Please. Kit, I'm sorry I don't remember more. My memories show up as passing shadows without warning and they go just as quickly. Lady Nan says they will only come when the time is right and that trying to remember is a waste of time."

"Time's tricky stuff. Whatever else happens, I don't plan to waste it anymore."

Anna brightened into the normal colours of a living girl.

"I've ignored you, pretending you're a ghost… because I saw you that day you died. The truth is people can die and come back sometimes, so, remote as it is, it's a possibility to keep in mind. I believe you've been a time traveller who has the properties of a ghost. Neither of us know the full extent of what happened the day we met. It was easier to think of you as deceased. You know, easier to dismiss… well, everything. It was a pretty strange experience. Ghastly in fact, and I freaked out."

Anna lifted her head and tried to smile. Instead, she flung herself on him in tears. "Do you really promise?"

Kit sat her down beside him. "It's not something that will be easy, and you know what a chicken I am."

"No," she blurted. "You forget. I know the future you. The last day I saw you was the day you went looking for my mother. You were determined and so brave."

"No need to remind me. I saw my frozen body on that trip."

Kit squeezed Anna's hand, relieved it felt warm and solid. "Anna, there's no need to cry is there? We have time portals. I can go back and forwards until all of us are safe. You have Taraq and your best friend, Rain… and Lady Nan. I forget sometimes she's your great grandmother. You have a family. You have me, and I'll only be gone a few days. Now chin up. You know the saying, 'cheer up it may never happen'. Well that's particularly true for us isn't it."

Anna brightened. "I will let Bash know if I remember anything else."

"Gosh, no, please don't. Tell Taraq. He can get a message to me. I don't want to upset Bash needlessly."

"Can I tell Lady Nan?"

"Of course. Obviously I don't know all the grim details. I'm so sorry I had to leave you behind. Maybe I had no choice. It was a gamble and all of us lost which is why I don't want to be responsible for anyone these days. But that's a poor excuse. Whatever it takes, I promise I will find your mother. I will go back and save you both. And one day we'll laugh at this horribly weird adventure that we had when time got muddled into such a mess."

"Kit, there *is* something I do remember. I've met the Great Sphinx. She's not what you call user-friendly."

"She?"

"Visit her while you're there. She is both mother and father to the world. I sense it is the mother you will meet."

"Oh great. Another trickster. I guess that's why he… *she's* so bloody great."

"Not exactly. Not like a fairy trickster. Her truth is all-knowing. Her decisions affect the bigger picture. She literally has no time for what she calls incidental insignificancies. Not the blink-of-an-eye lifetime of an individual player, sort."

"So, what should I do? Advise me."

"Bring her an offering of water. Don't pour it on the sand before her. Pour it on her paws. Stay humble. Make her laugh if you can. She's profoundly bored."

"Sounds like a regular egomaniac. The furies spring to mind."

"A plea isn't enough. Acting tough isn't enough. She sees through all that. But she's like any loving mother. She has a soft spot for her children and she can be moved to tears. She *wants* to be moved. All things puny and petty are vermin to her. Don't ever call her bluff. Move her to tears. Inspire her. She's eternally thirsty for human sparks and water."

Anna faltered. "I've been hearing the boy, again," she said.

"What boy?"

"A ghost I knew in my time. She touched the wall above the Winter Room's cot. "His voice comes from here. He's been calling me again. His voice is getting louder. He needs me."

LXV

HERE TOMORROW... GONE YESTERDAY

OCTOBER

Kit threw items into a suitcase without care. Taraq extracted them and folded them neatly. "I just want to go back to when it was good," Kit mumbled. "When science mattered. When things were simple. Normal. Mostly, I don't want to be a father before I've finished being a kid. I feel cheated. And I miss my sister."

"It's ironic, isn't it," Taraq said. "My future lies in the past. Dr. Brooks says a person can't undo awareness."

The suitcase was too heavy. Kit removed a history book and tossed it on the bed. "Everyone always said I knew too much for my own good. The funny thing is, I've been trying hard to be thoroughly disagreeable. And now I dislike myself."

Taraq placed the book on a shelf. "Yet your mission is to undo a chain of events that you can never wipe from your memories. You will always remember us, here. The rest of us will be asleep while you travel."

"I can't go back to undo something. But maybe I can find out how we can undo it here."

"One of these things must be true," Taraq said.

334

"You were never a teenager. Teenage-hood is a phase best left to self-indulgence. I will miss being selfish. I'm not the heroic type."

Kit read the note's hesitated greeting. It was as if Anna was in the room. Insecure, facing him, afraid but wanting to hug him.

Dear Father…for so you are and will always be
I've been hearing an old voice from home. Like Lady Nan, I have an invisible friend of my own. He was a boy my age. I never saw him. I only heard his voice. He never told me his name.
The thing is, he needs me more than anyone here. I've gone home to help him, and wait for my mother. I know you will find her. Keep her safe.
Maybe you and I will meet again. I hope there's still time.
Please say goodbye to the others for me. And thank Bash again, for Pookie. I took him with me to remember everyone by.
I've loved being part of your family.
Your loving daughter,
Anna

Back in the kitchen, materialized ghosts sat openly side-by-side with the living, having no need to stay in the shadows now that Mr. and Mrs. S were gone.

Pigeon began to pace on his perch, screeching and flapping with growing anxiety.

"Someone shut him up," Kit said, impatiently.

Bash threw Kit a dirty look. "Don't tell me you're missing Anna, now she's gone," she said. She scraped back her chair and rose to quieten the parrot. "It's okay bird. What's up?"

"*Pete's sake,*" Pigeon replied. "*P one and P two.*"

"Go on then. The floor is yours."

Pigeon pointed his beak towards the floor and cocked his head sideways as if listening to it with suspicion and carried on. "*Prince and Pauper,*" he squawked.

"I know that book," Lady Nan said. "I read it as a child, 'The Prince and the Pauper' by Mark Twain."

Kit leaned forward. "That might be a clue to Anna's boy ghost," he said.

"It was about two lookalike boys. They were identical and they switched places."

Taraq was the first to feel the throne's restless tapping, thrumming under his skin. He woke Kit with a stage whisper. "Son of Bede Hall, I think the chair is calling you."

"I heard something too. It sounded like sand blowing against the window."

"I need something to do. Shall I go to the tower and give the throne a polish?"

"Maybe I'll get over there this afternoon. Tomorrow is D-day and I have some writing to do."

Taraq winced and clamped his hands over his ears at the screeching in his head. "That won't do. It says to come immediately, and it's not exactly saying please, if you get my drift."

"When are you ever *not* drifting, Taraq?"

"That's what the Dr. B calls droll, isn't it? I assure you I'm well-informed as to ghost humour."

"Well, after tomorrow I won't be here to torture you."

Taraq had the throne gleaming. Or was it radiating. Whatever it was, it was different. Happier, if that were possible, with an added note of anticipation that Kit didn't share.

Kit went straight to it. No ritual. Without even the faintest possibility of emptying his mind. He sat down heavily, barely disguising his irritation, suppressing the urge to call out, what the hell do you want!

He felt himself pulled down into a slouching position as if he were melting. Not too terribly uncomfortable but nonetheless disquieting. Even more strangely, he didn't fight his body slumping into a balloon losing air. The word spineless was no longer an insult but a scientific fact – a pleasant feeling of floating suspended in a jar of liquid honey.

Lady Nan's oft repeated phrase, 'Patience is a virtue; have it and life will never hurt you' echoed between his ears in his grandmother's practiced tones of tetchiness.

Kit looked around to see if she'd manifested. An exasperated chuckle suggested she had, but that she intended to stay as much out of the way without interfering as a loving grandmother could.

He called up the memory of sand against his window and tried to push the image of blowing snow from his mind that arrived instead. Why did the future always interrupt everything? It was a waste of time. The snow remained as the wind died.

Kit stood on a blank canvass of white. As he searched for a landmark, faint blue parallel lines appeared underfoot. He caught a whiff of fresh paper. Immediately, a pen materialized in his hand. A red vertical line appeared to his left and beyond it, in front of a metal fence, a row of miniature potholes extended to the horizon. He recognized the fence with a start. Bright silver coils rolled in an even line. The post holes were perforation marks. He was standing on a blank page of his notebook.

Powdery snow drifted lazily over the toes of his shoes, and yet the temperature was baking hot. He tested the ground by walking in a circle. After a few yards, he turned to see if he'd left footprints. The snow lay pristine. He shouted a greeting that sprang from his lips and skidded sideways across the landscape. "HELLO." The word left the recognizable tracks of a toboggan heading in a straight line that gently veered right and left as it bumped over each blue line. A clear path with an invitation to follow. *Paths don't appear unless a dreamer is meant to follow, do they?* Kit took a confident step forward and sunk up to his knees in pink sand that was chill to the touch.

Someone called back hello or was it an echo?

"Who's in here?"

The sand swirled into a distant mirage – a human figure that shimmered once before it blew away as a small twister.

"I am."

"What do you want that's so urgent?"

There was a long silence before an answer came. Surprisingly close, beside him.

"Find me," a female voice said.

She was gone. But on the blue line nearest his feet were three familiar hieroglyphs inscribed with black ink, enclosed in a cartouche. Just as Taraq had said, there was no inference of please about the message. But neither had it been a haughty command. Not a request. Not an invitation. It was definitely an anguished heartfelt plea.

Kit jolted upright, back in the tower with Taraq's terrified face inches from his own shouting "What's a massive waste of time?"

Kit pushed him away, his hands going through Taraq's body. "Take it easy, mate. You're invading my space more than a tad. We've gone over the rules of etiquette, yeah?"

Taraq leaped back. Surprise and relief clearly obvious "Oh!"

"What's the matter, seen a ghost?"

"Look at your hands."

Kit's hands were slowly catching up to being solid. "This is *so not* the best time to be hallucinating. I need my wits for tomorrow. It's a brand-new-day for me."

"Master, you disappeared."

Kit stood and stretched. "You do get yourself worked up. I just nodded off. You could see I was here for goodness sake."

"No. You were completely gone for three hours," Taraq said. "The throne was empty."

Kit's stomach lurched with his old fears. He pointed to the handless blue clock. "See. No time has passed. No worries. Look, I've gotta split. I need to be alone for a while." He called out to an empty corner of the room. "And that means you too, Granny."

Lady Nan popped into view. "Christopher Carter Aloysius Stratford-Smyth. How would you like it if I started calling you Kitty?"

"How would you like it if you were spied on when *you* were a teenager?"

Her immediate disappearance was her answer.

Kit picked up his notebook and rapped it twice for effect. "I think I'm late for an appointment with my journal."

No-one heard the Winter Door creak open or felt the icy blast of blue ice crystals that swept down the main staircase into the kitchen where Pigeon restlessly pecked the bars of his cage reciting his variation of an old nursery rhyme. *"It's raining, it's snowing, the young girl is calling. She's bumped her head at the foot of the bed and won't get up in the morning."*

By first light, Pigeon's empty birdcage shimmered in a slick glaze of frost. A single red tail feather rested on Lady Nan's favourite chair. For a few hours, the stair banisters were painted white.

Down the passage, in Lady Nan's bedroom, Anna, whimpered inside a feverish dream. *'Is that you? I've waited so long. I thought you'd never come.'*

"*Patience child,*" Pigeon squawked. "You'll see him soon enough."

In the attic, a parrot's tail feather lay on the Winter Room's daybed. It sparkled, pure dazzling white.

All that day, variations of *'anyone seen the Pidge?'* echoed around the Hall.

Pigeon was gone. The bird had flown.

LXVI

FLY BY NIGHT

OCTOBER 29

Kit stared morosely at his packed bag. "I guess I always wanted to travel. You know, to Egypt alone with Dad. But it wasn't fun when we all went."

Bash snickered. "Are you kidding me? You're Peter Pan. You always said you wanted to fly. That's all time travel is, isn't it?"

"Serious jetlag, I fear."

"And you are definitely scared of growing up. I'll always be older than you."

"I don't think three minutes counts."

"Charlotte says everything counts in Bede."

Kit ducked from an imagined projectile. "And there it goes," he said. "Logic, straight out the window."

Kit said farewell to Jack and gave Taraq explicit instructions to keep the red fairies out of Jack's ears. Horrible pests. He rubbed Jack's shaggy head. "You're the only sane one around here old boy. Guard the tower for me and do as Taraq says. I'll be home in a few days and perhaps you and I can go off on our own for a bit."

Jack's baleful eyes wanted to believe as much as Kit. Kit hugged him gruffly after they'd played a game of fetch. Jack trotted loyally at his side like Peter Pan's shadow, and Kit had been extra generous with food from his plate at dinner.

The thought of flying drained Kit of steam. Everyone at the table was grim and silent until Parks went over the plan once more. "Remember. Megeara only wants the Hall, and she needs your mum and dad back here to sign it away. She's only trying to prove she has control, so this ploy is to scare them into a quick sale. However, it will mean you must sit your parents down and tell them the truth about me and your grandmother and your Great Uncle Ben, and even Taraq. For the… *ahem*… time being, there's no need to mention the Winter Door and Anna or the ice-age. The British consulate is your last resort."

"Eat up luvvy," Lady Nan said. "Charlotte and Bash made all your favourites."

Kit smiled weakly and took a bite of shepherds pie that tasted like hot cotton wool. He choked it down with a glass of ginger-ale, refusing a glass of Charlotte's homemade dandelion wine. Although, it might be a blessing to get on the plane sozzled under the influence of fairy dew or whatever concoction she was favouring these days. He was too wide awake. A distracting hallucination would be welcome. The prospect of leaving the ground reminded him of the day he floated over Bede when all the portal trouble started.

Kit smuggled his plate to Jack in plain sight after one or two mouthfuls. The thought occurred that if Charlotte *had* spiked the pie and mash with some active herbal ingredient, Jack would be seeing pink rabbits for days. Jack didn't allow his mood to eclipse his appetite, and had snorkeled it down. Kit retrieved a gleaming plate. "Enjoy your trip, mate," he said.

Charlotte stared at him from across the table, her glass of special brew raised in a toast. "Here's to everyone's safe return," she said, holding Kit's gaze. "Jack included." She nodded before releasing him.

Bash sent him a thought. *"My, what big memories you have."*

"All the better to miss me by," Kit replied.

On the day of departure, Tut, Six, and Bash held back at the front door after a brief checklist. Tut presented Kit with an armful of street maps and Bash reminded him of the rowan talisman followed by a stoic but overconfident "You're going to find them, Pigeon too."

"Good luck," Six called out.

Bash sent Six a grateful look. Her arms were around Anna who was sobbing. "He'll be back in a few days," she comforted. "It's only Cairo."

Tut heaved a heavy sigh. "It's only Cairo," he repeated.

Kit's hand paused on the car door handle, and scanned his well-wishers one last time, arranged as if for a family photograph. "Don't go growing up while I'm gone." His flip remark was meant to be a general goodbye of false bravado. But Bash and Anna nodded as if it was for them alone.

Anubis and Feathers fussed around everyone's legs. Charlotte seemed to be evoking a spell with her eyes closed while she held Parks' hand. Ben, now materialized as Lady Nan's big brother – twins age twenty-one and nine as only the afterlife could show them. The child Beryl, rested her head on his grownup shoulder. Taraq walked a respectful distance behind Kit and Dr. Brooks, flickering like a candle, and disappeared entirely when the car moved forward.

Lady Nan's old voice called out. "Let us know the moment your plane lands."

Parks waved and smiled with the others as he whispered to Charlotte. "Yesterday's another day."

Unicorn, now expanded to the size of a transparent lion, sat waiting to escort Brook's car to the gates. Jack howled and loped after the car but turned and limped back tail between his legs when Bash called him. He obeyed her much the same as Kit had, surrendering his will to his role of champion.

Taraq materialized in the back seat. "When in doubt follow the sacred texts of the Egyptian Book of the Dead," he said and popped quickly. Kit saw him running back to the Hall over the grass. "Thanks buddy. Look after Anna." Since Pigeon left she looked thinner, more ghostlike, no doubt from being a worrywort.

Kit felt in his pocket for the amulet as the plane left the ground. His left hand gripped the seat of his chair.

A voice from the window seat introduced a business suit issuing two words. "Nervous flyer?"

Not wanting to strike up a conversation, Kit removed his right hand from the amulet, linked his hands together in his lap and closed his eyes. "I don't like to travel, period. Don't mind me, I'm going to grab a catnap."

But even with his eyes closed, Kit saw the rowan ring and felt it tingle. A different voice entered his head *"Ah, smart boy,"* it purred.

Kit closed his eyes. "Go away Bash," he said, startling his neighbour.

The heat of Cairo was the same as Bede's December. But it was the noise that flattened him. The rowan twig reassured him, moving ever so slightly under his jacket all the way to the museum but once at the base of the museum's steps he put it out of his mind. He was in a dangerous foreign city alone, and the answers he needed lay behind the double doors that mocked him from the head of the stone steps.

LXVII

HOMEFIRES

OCTOBER 30

The Twinters gathered around Bash as if she was a shortwave radio. "I hear Kit," she said. "But he's not answering me." She smiled at Charlotte. "He's grown quite attached to his amulet."

Parks sat in quiet contemplation, his hand resting on Anubis' fur.

"Kit is exactly on-point," Anubis said.

Parks informed the others. "Anubis says that Kit's fine."

"Why can't he speak to all of us? A talking cat is not stranger than talking lavender plants."

"He will soon enough. Be patient."

Anubis stirred and hissed at the empty corner. *"I can see you. Look after Kit. He needs a guide."*

"I heard that," Bash said. "You were right, Lady Nan."

"Anubis *can* see Kit."

"And an old friend," Anubis said. *"Bash, relay to Kit to follow the cat he can see."*

"Kit, I can hear you. Follow the cat. He's your guide. I will get there when I can." She nodded to Charlotte. "I need the tea. NOW."

Charlotte poured a thimble-sized glass with red liquid from a thermos. "Swallow it all at once. You'll be safe. It's like taking an elevator up through the ceiling. Head for the moon and you won't go far wrong."

344

The tea tasted sweet. Bash's feet stayed on solid ground even as she seemed to fly out of her body. Dr. Brooks and Charlotte caught her as she slumped forward in her chair.

"Okay, sister dear," Kit said. "I'm going to assume you can hear me but I'd really appreciate voice confirmation. Anytime soon would be good."

It was a sobering thought to realize he had little control over events. He was hanging on to the tail of a tiger. He was prepped. Dr. Brooks told him as much. He called it instinctive investigation or in other words, to go with his gut feelings and not try to second guess everything.

But going with the flow sounded good on paper. He wanted to report back for further instructions. Back home, the Twinters were waiting for Bede Hall to make up its mind.

One thing was certain, he felt the presence of his parents nearby. This feeling buoyed him towards a successful rescue. On no account would he, or could he, go to the authorities. *No problem I have a rowan twig in my pocket.* The thought was ridiculous.

But several ghosts and a sentient building went part way to proving he was living outside the box. He was hardly a seasoned traveller, let alone a time traveller – a hat he had no wish to wear.

He spoke to Bash telepathically. *"Cairo to Bash."*

Nothing. No link. He was the missing link. *"I passed normal years ago."* Too bad denial wasn't his new best friend. He missed Tut. *"Come on Rowan, let's get this over with so we can go home, Anna. And, Anna, please help Pigeon, wherever he is."*

LXVIII

THE FORGOTTEN

OCTOBER 31 – ALL HALLOWS EVE

Kit shook the dizziness from his brain, squared his shoulders and faced the museum doors with mixed feelings of anticipation and dread. A lean black cat streaked past him and paused on the top step to look back at him with a silent meow. It gave him courage to continue. "Anubis?" he said to himself, "I think you may have a twin."

For no other reason than the cat was there, Kit felt compelled to follow.

When his hand touched the door handle, Mr. S's voice rushed past his left hear. "Kit, please turn back. Go home. Don't worry. We'll see each other soon enough. Now go!"

Kit shivered. "Dad, I'm here. Where are you?"

Back in Bede, the Rowan tree stood guard over Bash. Its charge sat in a trance, cross-legged in the moonlight, her back slumped against the trunk. Feathers sat in her lap, alert to every small movement in the silvery grass.

"She's ready," Feathers said to the tree as a familiar feline scudded from the maze as a blue mist.

"Ahoy Feathers," the cat called.

Feathers nodded hello. *"Unicorn."*

"Where are the others?"

The tree's boughs creaked above, weaving a protective spell over Bash.

"My husband and daughter are holding Kit's energy in the tower," Feathers said.

Unicorn arched his back and ran widdershins around the tree three times. *"Let's get to work then. We have an unpleasant night's work ahead. Sage is deeply troubled but he asked me to say the Great Sphinx has our boy in sight."*

"And Mr. and Mrs. S?"

"All we know is they're close by. Their signature energies are pulsating inside the museum."

"How's Kit holding up?"

The rowan rattled its topmost skeletal branches, flexing the smallest twigs in a crackle of sparks. The lowest branches dropped down over Bash, enclosing her in a hug. *"This one is sending Kit supportive thoughts,"* it said. *"But the lad is terrified. We all know how twins being far apart from each other unnerves them."*

Taraq's face materialized in the branches like the Cheshire Cat. "He's worried about being alone. He gets the night terrors of being trapped and abandoned from me. I tried to explain that being entombed alive was like falling asleep in a cocoon but I think that made it worse."

The hissing of a cat fight came from the shadows. Kit wheeled around, stunned. The museum visitors seemed oblivious. A black tail slithered around a glass case like a snake.

Kit called out. "Wait for me."

"Keep up then. I'm a busy creature."

The cat pawed at a pair of invisible sandals in the corner. *"Why are you here? Can't you see the boy's nervous. It's hard enough without you upsetting him."*

"SaRa needs this child to know what happened."

"It's already happened, so what good would it do."

The sandals took a step forward. "Sibuna, I never question my sister. And neither did Kit. He's going to need a guide."

Sibuna streaked away, catching Kit's peripheral vision. Again, Kit followed the black tail that left a thread of gold in its wake, never quite managing to catch up. The trail stopped at the foot of a reconstructed ancient wall. A sign indicated it was a wall fragment from the temple of Bast, 18th dynasty. The sound of scratching came from the other side, and Kit breached the velvet security ropes to investigate. "Come on Anubis old fella where did you go."

A single yowl was his answer. *"It's not much further, boy."*

The tail moved faster. Kit skated over the tile floor and skidded around the rows of display cases. By the time Kit caught up, the cat was sitting prettily on the pedestal of a tall statue of a female with a cat's head, washing its whiskers as if it had been waiting there all day. It's enormous black paws reminded Kit of boxing gloves.

Kit's hand shook badly as he reached out. "Hey kitty." Lady Nan had said to watch out for cats. Was this a sign? This cat had extra toes like Snowball.

The cat hissed.

"I don't like being called Kitty either. What's your name then? You look like a friend of mine named Anubis."

The cat blinked slowly and purred. *"Well spotted boy. SaRa was right."*

"Okay, Tiger it is." It was only then that Kit took in his surroundings. The air was oppressive and smelled of a dank fireplace grate. He was perspiring from the stuffy air and a ball of fear choked his throat. *"Bash are you here? Are you feeling this? What should I do?"*

"I'm right beside you in spirit," Bash replied. *"Feather's says that cat has an important message."*

"Feathers is TALKING to you!"

"Well, I'm asleep, Kit. So yes, she is. Listen to me. That sooty

smell means danger. And if you haven't noticed, everyone in there is moving in slow motion."

Kit paid more attention to the people around him. No-one was swarming the exhibits. They registered no excitement. They were shuffling in single file as if under a spell. A low mumble emanated from them, hanging suspended over their heads. Kit swore he saw speech bubbles appearing and popping like soap bubbles as their mouths moved. Overall, the sound was best described as muddy music.

"Bash, I don't feel safe," Kit said. *"Don't wake up and leave me."*

"I won't."

Kit dried his clammy hands on his jeans and wiped his brow with his sleeve.

The shape of a figure shimmered like the heatwaves of a mirage displacing the stone blocks in another section of reconstructed temple. The hieroglyphics carved into the facing wavered as if underwater. A man stepped from the anomaly, slowly materializing from his sandals up until a pair of piercing brown eyes locked on Kit with an expression that was either anger or fear. Brows knitted. He could have been from any era in his white robe but thoughts of Taraq came to mind.

Bash interrupted his thoughts. *"He looks like Taraq,"* she agreed. *"If Taraq was older. And that fabric is ancient. I can tell from the stitching. He feels harmless to me but he's definitely upset."*

Kit exhaled deeply. *"Yeah, me too."*

The man attempted a smile and failed. "You are Christopher, he said," without his words remotely resembling a question. "I have something urgent to show you. I hope you are as strong as SaRa said."

"I don't know anyone named SaRa."

"You will if we're careful."

"Why do I need to be strong? Has something bad happened to my parents? Do you know where they are?"

"They're here."

Kit breathed normally without feeling a sense of relief. "And you are?"

"I am Kha, SaRa's brother. Her twin. I must warn you. What you are about to see will shock you."

Slowly Bash materialized in a transparent state beside Kit and took his hand. "I'm here," she said, locking fingers. "We'll look together. I'll stay as long as I can."

"Welcome Miss Bathsheba," Kha said, bowing from the waist. "Please, follow me. We must go upstairs."

The twins elbowed their way past a hoard of new visitors who were now frozen like waxwork figures.

LXIX

HAUNTINGLY FAMILIAR

OCTOBER 31- HALLOWEEN morning

Kit hugged Bash hello and turned her around to face his new friends. "This is Kha and my pal, Tiger."

Bash held out her hand to shake, but Kha kissed the back of it with solemn formality. "That reminds me," she said, blushing, "I actually heard Anubis speaking tonight so I must be making progress. Parks said he's picky about who hears him. Anyway, Anubis said to follow the cat you could see. I doubt his name is Tiger."

Kit tousled Bash's hair affectionately. "You were sleeping. Cats don't talk."

"Yes we do," Tiger said, springing to Kha's shoulder. He blinked his golden eyes once, and spoke clearly in English. *"And she wasn't dreaming."*

Bash elbowed Kit. "You're not sleeping. Did you hear that?"

Kit took a step back and grinned. "I did."

"For now, while I can remain with you," Bash replied, "we should finish what you came for."

All the while Tiger and Kha led them past intriguing displays and doors, Kit strained to catch up. Both Kha and the cat glided much faster than walking. Bash stayed at Kit's pace although she could have accelerated to the speed of paranormal any time she

351

wished. There were times Kha disappeared around a corner and Kit had to break into a breathless run until he had his guides in his sights again.

Another staircase, longer than the first, wound around into a gallery that overlooked the second floor. It was here Kha and the cat turned left on the landing and waited for Kit to catch his breath. Kha pointed to the end of a long corridor. Tiger streaked ahead and disappeared into a maze of cabinets.

Kha paused at the entrance to the hall of mummies. "I hate this place."

"Why? Are you in there?"

His form wavered like a flag in the wind. "My heart is in there."

Tiger showed no such hesitation. His mewing echoed around the walls as he leapt onto the plate glass lid of a display cabinet at the center of the room.

Bash scanned the area. "It's strange that there are no visitors in here. Surely it's the single-most popular attraction."

"Not by half," Kit said. "Tutankhamen's golden mask is the Mona Lisa of Cairo."

"Sorry to disappoint, but it's his golden throne," Kha said.

Kit felt a tweak of homesickness for his tower. "I guess I'm not really surprised."

Kha kept his eyes fixed on Kit until he reciprocated, and their gaze was locked in a telepathic link. "Good. Keep focused and imagine how powerful Tut's throne, the REAL one, is."

Bash looked like a sleepwalker. "My yellow chair is the original article," she mumbled. "It feels alive."

"Kit, remember your sister's words," Kha said. "It requires authentic energy to connect through time. Certain objects are alive."

"Are you saying I should steal Tut's throne?"

"Don't be foolish. It's far too fragile to support the weight of even a scrawny boy."

"Thanks very much. You're a bit *thin* around the edges yourself."

The cat yowled his impatience.

"Tiger's calling us."

Kha cleared his throat and looked apologetic. "He says he approves of your name for him. But his name is Sibuna." Kha hesitated, avoiding eye contact. "He belongs to me."

"Is he dead?"

"Sometimes."

Kit felt he was wading through porridge. All the while Sibuna chased his tail in circles. But as amusing as he was, Kit was not in the mood for cat antics.

"Sibuna is not being playful," Kha said. "Nor is he trying to entertain you. He's sending you a message."

"Well, that's just great. I don't speak cat."

"I do," Bash said. "At least I think I do. Their messages are clearer when I'm sleeping."

"Then by all means, feel free to translate," Kha said, waiving her forward.

Bash's voice took on the intonation of an oracle. "What you seek is the invisible beginning of an ancient circle. You may briefly pounce upon a secret but never hold its truth for long. Standing still is a more favorable approach. Wait and watch before you leap. A cat's tail naturally covers its nose when it sleeps. This is the perfect time to bite and hang on. When in doubt, think like a cat. If you remember nothing else, remember that. There will be fleeting moments when you must catch your own tail. Take catnaps. When you need to travel, be a cat. Cats are natural time travelers."

"Yeah, well I'm traveling on a plane."

"You will indeed be flying," Bash said. That's the bigger picture."

"I should act like a cat when I'm on a plane?"

"Yes. Anywhere and everywhere. If you know what's good for you."

The case held two eighteenth-century royal mummies. Poignant sunken eye sockets stared blindly through the roof of their new coffin. Crumbling cheekbones... grimaces for smiles... and clawed fingers that reminded Bash of the Rowan twig in Kit's pocket. Black glue hard as rock held them together in a resin shroud. Red and white fairies looped overhead in a mad aerial display of dogfight energy.

Kit reached out to pet Sibuna. "Okay little tiger, where are my parents? What cat thoughts can you send me? Do you have a message from them?"

Sibuna's purring resonated in Kit's chest until he felt as big as the room. *So, that's what it feels like to be a cat.*

By now, the twins had positioned themselves facing Kha on the opposite side of the case. All three of them leaned their hands on the glass as if discussing a business deal over a boardroom table.

Bash blurted 'see you in my dreams' and blinked out.

"I sent her away," Kha said. "She's urgently needed at home. It's her responsibility to anchor things there just as your duty is to stabilize events here."

"Those red sparks over there. I know what they are. Are you one of them? Is Megeara here?"

Sibuna ceased purring and darted off, leaving the room entirely too silent to be endured for long.

"Now what?" Kit said. His voice sounded larger than life.

"Nothing… Everything. Megeara was here. She's gone. Her work is done."

"Very sphinx-like, but can you stop being so evasive. I've lived, pardon the expression, with an Egyptian ghost for three years and I know the signs of a perverse nature. So…"

"So?" Kha repeated. Round one is over and a new game begins." He pointed to the human remains. "Kit… look at them. Concentrate."

Kit took a deep breath. "On what?"

"These mummies are your parents!"

LXX

MUMMY AND DADDY

OCTOBER 31 – ALL HALLOWS EVE

Bash opened her eyes in Brooks' sitting room surrounded by anxious faces. The only expression that showed a measure of calm was Taraq, whose face was always white, but he was crying. "I tried to stay," Bash said in a small voice. "Kit's in a terrrible state. But I was called back."

Parks looked out the window with his hands in his pocket and counted the sparrows on Brook's fence. He tipped his hat to them. They waited on his command to leave. "I did that. I called you. I was under orders."

Bash sobbed. "He'll think I deserted him. And he'd be right. I did. Kha said to follow the cat. Oh, there was a cat." Increasing realization horrified her. "I abandoned my brother."

"Who's Kha?" Brooks asked.

Tut looked concerned. "I know what a ka is. It's a ghost. A duplicate of the deceased. It has its own temple, and relatives leave it food. Did you see Mum and Dad, I mean, your parents?"

"They weren't there. It was all a trick. Poor Kit. He doesn't like it there. He's terrified."

Kit accepted Kha's terrifying declaration without question, collapsing on the floor as if slowly melting, and grabbed onto a leg of the plinth supporting the display case. A drowning man clutching a passing plank of wood. Bash was no longer in evidence but he could hear her crying from far away.

The full impact of his next decision hit hard a few moments after the floor stopped undulating. A gauntlet had been thrown down by the furies and it was his turn to turn away or pick it up. Picking it up meant time travel. The caldera's importance faded into white sound.

Kha walked through the maze of tables and touched the corner of one at the periphery of Kit's vision. He gave its contents a sad cursory glance and ran his fingers down its length before evaporating.

The black cat strolled past and Kit took the opportunity to exchange the table leg for his warm body.

Sibuna allowed Kit to grip him in a life or death vice, and sob into his fur. *"It's best we go now. Rest assured, I'm not going to leave you."* He wriggled out of Kit's arms and stretched his back. *"Follow me,"* he said. *"We have someone to see. And kings don't like to be kept waiting."*

"I NEED BASH!"

"Your sister is awake. She cannot come with you but your connection is not entirely lost. it will get stronger with time."

Kit felt hysterical. "Time?"

Sibuna left the hall by a procession of leaps, streaking lily-pad-style from sarcophagus to sarcophagus, but waited in the corridor. *"You must carry me the rest of the way. The crowds will part for you. I will lend you my strength. Let me do all the talking. You will have your turn soon enough. Remain constant. It's best not to look back."*

LXXI

UNSEATED

"I have to talk to my sister. I need a phone. Right now. You won't know what those…"

"The boxes for communication over distance," Kha said.

"But how can you…?"

Kha bowed. "Ghosts may not grow old but we *do* evolve, Kit."

"So… to the nearest phone, then. You know this place inside-out, so lead me there."

"Tut's throne is faster. It's downstairs."

"Good. If a replica throne works in Bede, the real thing should be bloody brilliant."

"I've been told that it's bloody amazing."

"But all these people and the guards."

"They will see nothing. I will explain later."

The glass cage containing Tut's throne glowed from within, illuminated as if it were an aquarium on-stage prop for a magician's trick, lit by a single intense spotlight. But someone cut the power. The rest of the showrooms and corridors sputtered into the darkness of a cave. Kit shivered in anticipation. There was a shimmer of movement and a refraction of gold. The throne had shivered too.

The door swung open easily. Kit clambered in and sank his

entire weight on the delicate artifact. It held. There was no creaking. There was no buzzing of wasps. And after a few minutes of concentration it was clear there was no power.

Kha looked at Kit with trepidation. Clearly, he was nervous. "How do you feel?"

"Dethroned. Devastated. Angry."

"Thank you. I am satisfied? We can go now?"

Kit held Sibuna ahead of him, slightly aloft as if he was seated on an invisible cushion as Kha led the way through the choked streets to the Hotel Enigma. Car horns honked as if warbling underwater. The sun and moon hung side-by-side in a red sky.

Sibuna let out a bloodcurdling yowl.

Kit kept his eyes fixated on a vision of the hotel. "I feel like I'm sleepwalking."

"They're all dreaming"

"I don't understand."

"You will later."

The hotel elevator failed to respond when Kit pressed the button. The red number arrow stayed fixed on the number nine. It appeared to be frozen on the ninth floor. "I don't have time for this. I'm taking the stairs."

Immediately, Kit stood outside his room, key in hand, beside Kha.

Kit glanced at his watch. "How did I manage nine flights of stairs in under a minute?" Silence. "Right then, you'll tell me later, I suppose."

Kha held up his wrists to show they were empty of watches. "Sometimes there's no such thing as later."

The phone's dial-tone faded out. "Does nothing work in this wretched city."

"Everything works except you," Kha said.

"But this is a top hotel."

"Sir. This is Cairo."

Kha grabbed the chord and yanked it so hard it snapped like a whip. The severed ends were frayed, clearly permanently dead. "You don't need this," he said. "We have an appointment with a king remember? He will know what to do. Come, it's getting dark. *She* doesn't like to be kept waiting."

"A queen then."

"Sometimes."

Kit lurched from side to side, crashing into the hotel walls every few steps. The hallway was dark and sloped downwards. Its walls appeared covered in carved hieroglyphs. The damp passage smelled of wet plaster. The dim light of Kha's torch flickered ahead. Kit managed to speak. "Oh goody, the light at the end of the tunnel. Or should I say portal. I'm either out of my mind or dead."

"Why do you keep looking over your shoulder?"

"I'm avoiding a girl. My... *um...*" he took a deep breath. "My daughter's mother, actually."

"But, you have not met her."

The way became steeper. An invisible arm caught Kit as he slipped sideways. "I may have. I think she's here, somewhere."

"You haven't."

"You can't know that."

"You can stop worrying. She's not here."

Kha was too far ahead. Kit moved faster, tripping over loose stones that grew larger. His bare toe met the edge of a large dressed stone. "Where are my shoes?" The corridor hummed like hornets in a jar. "Kha, wait. I need to stop for a minute. I hurt my foot."

Kha's voice echoed back. "I've been waiting a long time. It's only a toe... you have nine others. And no, this is not the rule of nine."

Kit limped up to Kha. "Anna said her mother lived here."

"She did."

"How do you know?"

"I knew her... I know her."

"But..."

"She's my sister."

The light turned out to be the glint of gold far ahead. He saw a familiar flashback of Bede and his chair before he blacked out. Kha carried him the rest of the way. When Kit woke it was night and he was in the desert. The pyramids of Giza filled the sky like a mountain range designed by a persnickety mathematician. The air was chill.

Kit was ready for answers.

"Okay, then," he said. "It's high time you explained the streets and the sky and magic stairs. You said the people were dreaming?"

"We've been time traveling ever since we left the museum, Kit. The side exit was a portal. We're just traveling slower than the speed of light. It takes time to get used to it."

"Great another ghost with a tenuous grip on irony."

"It's, how do you say it? High time you surrendered."

"I'm a scientist. We don't surrender, we investigate."

"Ah yes, your crude investigations may catch up to alchemy one day."

"You're an alchemist?"

"In need of an apprentice. I believe you just volunteered.

*"Man says: time passes.
History says: time waits for no man.
The Sphinx says: man passes."*

❄

ANONYMOUS

LXXII

THE DARKEST SIDE OF THE MOON

MIDNIGHT – ALL HALLOWS EVE – Giza

"It was midnight when Kit stood facing the Great Sphinx. It was magnificent but inanimate. "So, this is the king you wanted me to meet?" he said to Kha. "We have an appointment with a sleeping lion made of stone?"

"The Great Sphinx is both king *and* queen. We shall see who greets us."

"WHO greets us? He shuffled his feet in the sand. Taraq had been right. In the fading light it was pinkish. "Now what? We wait for a clock to strike midnight or something?"

"Yes, we wait. We open our minds and we wait."

"You mean meditate."

"I believe you call it so."

"I have to tell you; it's not what I do best."

"No worries. It's what I do best."

The lights of Cairo blinked and went out.

And so," Kha said eerily, "we disappear behind the moon. We are no more."

The voice of a female emanated from the darkness. "It's all right, Kha. Leave the boy to me."

Kha fell to his knees and prostrated himself between the great lion's paws.

The Sphinx's voice rumbled like an earthquake in Kit's brain. "You have the look of your daughter about you."

Kit's fingers closed around the rowan twig in his pocket. The ring spun on his finger of its own accord. He kept his chin raised, hoping he looked brave rather than haughty. "Yes sir... *er* your majesty."

"You're a few seconds early, the Queen said. "But time is irrational."

"You were expecting me?"

"I ordered you to come, so, yes."

Kit took a step back and craned his neck to peer into the Sphinx's crumbling eye sockets. "We have met before. My father brought the family here to find the boy who saved him."

Silence.

The Sphinx's face transformed into the image of a woman. "And now you want Kha to save you?"

Kha's form shimmered into transparent of heat waves.

Kit's thoughts and images dissolved into his old winter dream. He remembered as if it was yesterday. "I was nine, Ma'am."

"That was the first time. There were three others. It WAS yesterday."

A gently purring came from the Sphinx's interior.

"You have a request for me. It is the same. You want to find your father."

"And my mother."

There followed a sighing sound of a dry wind. "Ah yes, Queen Ankhesenaten's child."

"*Um...* I think so. Lady Nan had mentioned something about reincarnation after she died. Smenkhare lives again as well. He is my teacher, Brooks. I bring you his respects."

"Parks said you would come."

"Parks!"

"What else did you bring me, apprentice of my apprentice?"

Kit scrambled towards his backpack, still in shock. Parks? The thermos containing sunflower oil was intact. He held it aloft with as much ceremony as he could summon. "My… my daughter sends you this gift. The flowers of the sun."

Kha materialized on the Sphinx's head, still in his submissive posture of worship. For a moment, he looked like Taraq intoning a prayer. "Do not keep her waiting, my brother. Conserve some oil for her tail."

"Ah, the scarab flowers. Anu has done well."

Kit sensed the Sphinx's delight as he poured the oil onto her stele. Her lion tail uncurled and thumped the ground into a small sandstorm.

Kit sprinkled a pouch of dried lavender. "My sister sends you these dried herbs, perfume from her own garden."

"You mean Parks' garden."

Kit pulled the twig from his pocket and placed it next to the other offerings. "And I bring you this amulet."

"I am well-pleased."

Kha sent Kit a smile and nodded.

"To find your parents," the Sphinx said, "you must enter the portal. There is no guarantee you can return. Time has a mind of its own. Is this acceptable?"

"Yes Ma'am," Kit said, looking askance at Kha. This little detail had been omitted from his briefing. No matter, he didn't want to be around for the future. But would his parents be able to return?

"Your daughter… she found you?"

"Kit stuttered a weak yes, overwhelmed with guilt."

"She is well?"

"No sir. She sleeps near death in a tomb of ice."

"All of you sleep near death in a tomb of ice. I asked if Anu is well."

"I… er… well, I haven't been, that is… she feels abandoned by her… father… by me."

"And you think time can erase your misdeeds?"

"What else would a time portal be for?"

"Silence child! Your gifts make me sleepy. Kha! Where are you?"

Kha, back in his original form, raised his eyes. "I am here My Lady-Pharaoh."

"Teach this one the rule of nine. Time is of the essence."

"Yeah, I never did understand that phrase," Kit blurted.

Kha sent Kit a silent reprimand with his eyes.

The Sphinx yawned and lowered her head to Kit's level. "Then it's high time you did."

LXXIII

KISS AT THE END OF THE WORLD

MIDNIGHT – ALL HALLOWS EVE – Bede Hall

Moonlight painted a faint grid over the chosen place and turned the black gate's iron latticework light blue. Gateway magic prevailed over the planting of the rowan seedling grown a substantial three-feet into a stout specimen, over almost a year. The Roman god Janus of two faces, the twin guardians of entrances and exits, watched over the ceremony with Six in attendance, who Bash had commandeered into digging.

The hole was a little wider than a post-hole but just as deep. Six held the tree upright in silence. He'd seen the ritual of covering before, performed by Parks. Timing was crucial and Bash was young to be presiding over such an important ceremony but Charlotte insisted it was her proving time.

A single rowan, infused with the vitality of the goddess's tree, would protect Bede from the worst of the ground intruders. At least those that crawled through gates. And this seedling had been decreed sacrosanct, bequeathed by the Lady Chloris from the holy precincts of Lindisfarne, and lovingly fostered under Charlotte's watch.

Bash knelt, spine erect as a priestess, taking a moment to settle her knees in the dark grass to listen and wait for a sign.

A barn owl swooped low and cast a brief shadow over the hole. "Now," it cried from inside her blood. Bash's hands cupped the loosened soil at the rowan's base, pushing and pulling it back and forth over the roots like kneading bread. Navy-blue soil was pressed into place and patted like a good child. The owl made another pass overhead to sanction the deed.

A stream of thanks surged from the rowan into her body. When its voice released her, she crumpled.

Six easily lifted her into his arms, and she clung to his neck. The scent of fresh earth mingled with Six's skin was intoxicating. She was sure she'd died and that Six would follow her after evaporating in the Parks' family tradition. She smiled at the prospect of being a ghost. If Six was with her, there was nothing to fear. Haunting Bede together forever sounded perfect.

Giddiness melted into surrender.

Six's warm mouth found hers. Years passed sweetly. A grove of hawthorn grew around them, clasping their branches above them, flowered, and passed into distant memory.

Liminal space quickened into honey time. Bash sensed a clearing and flashes of gold rings held over a glowing rowan branch. Entwined twin souls of mistletoe and ivy embraced a host tree. Ancient promises and lovers with green skin were being woven into a tapestry – the handiwork of the goddess. Lady Chloris's needle darted quickly to bind each to each, tying the knots of hand-fasting in a fairy bower. Birdsong and light infused them with the heady scent of a timeless summer.

The sound of a rusty hinge pulled Six to his feet. No breath of wind capable of shifting the wrought ironwork moved across the sky. The locks were secure. The squeal sounded again, closer. It made his skin itch. "Who's there?"

Silence.

"I'll have to get me granddad," he said. "Summits not right."

Bash clambered to her feet and clutched his shirt sleeves. "Stay."

He said nothing but cradled her head against him and patted her back. "It's all right, lass."

Six was going to disappear or she was. Perhaps, if fortune smiled, they could go together. All that kept them anchored to Bede was a handful of a rough cotton shirt that smelled of hard work, and the glistening beads of sweat on Six's collarbone.

The squeal of a gate hinge metal grating against metal hurt her teeth.

Bash recognized her own voice screaming from far away. "Please. Don't go."

Six relaxed. He smoothed the hair back from Bash's face, and pressed his forehead against hers. When he exhaled, it was a long, weary, sigh. "Pixie," he said. "You've been trying to enchant me for a long time."

"Wait for me."

His voice filled her mind. "I'm always here. No worries, girl. Now off home with ye and away to your bed. This business is done for the night."

Bash slipped into a waking sleep. She didn't feel Six go, but she knew he'd gone. When she startled awake her fists gripped handfuls of phantom cloth.

Blue fairies swarmed around the rowan like fireflies. Their voices teased Bash in song:

> *Planting kisses,*
> *Planting seedlings*
> *Planting wishes*
> *Planting dreamings*
> *Rowan rules*
> *What rowan please.*
>
> *Count on sixes*
> *Count on Kitties*
> *Count on breezes*

Count on teases
Moonlight gives
And moonlight fixes

Seize the seconds
Seize the hours
Seize the seasons
Seize the timings
Romance warms
And romance freezes

LXXIV

A PAPER TIME CAPSULE

MIDNIGHT – ALL HALLOWS EVE – Giza

Three-thousand years away, Kit felt Bash and Six embrace. Love blasted him against the side of the Sphinx and winded him. He steadied himself against the baking stone until Egypt stopped spinning. Jealousy melted into the kind of pain that only hate could match. The Furies mind games of torture intensified. His blood congealed into hard crystals like the brittle resins holding a mummy together. Rivulets of stone sweat blurred his vision. Beads of amber formed at the corners of his eyes. Kit screamed "Wait for me!" and felt his larynx tear. His legs grew heavy. Worse than turning into a plant, he was turning to living stone. An engraved smile stretched over granite teeth. His backpack felt weighted down with a small boulder. Mercifully, his right-brain filled with sand and shut down.

The words *I'm staying* died in his throat, but in any case, Kha wouldn't have heard him. He had gone ahead of him and disappeared. The renewed certainty of abandonment made Kit lightheaded.

The overriding dread of never seeing his parents again made him break into a renewed fever to climb. He hoisted his small pack higher over his shoulder, hoping the hourglass inside was faring well, wrapped in a soft hand towel, and concentrated. *The Furies are not going to win. This pain is not real. Breathe. I am not made of stone. My mind is open and alert.* There was no way to test if the rowan ring, resting on the weight-bearing hand above his head had been sabotaged, but he shouted to it so the Sphinx would hear. *All right Rowan old friend, here I am, wayfaring, so if it's all the same to you, I'd be truly grateful if you stepped in and did your stuff right about now. Thanking you in advance, Kit Stratford-Smyth. Over and out.*

The rowan ring made no perceptible response but Kit risked the chance of breaking his concentration to glance up at it, and felt it move a quarter turn. New strength flooded his right hand and spread into his arm. Its warm wooden heartbeat pulsed on his finger. It had defied the Furies. He felt like cheering.

More determined than ever, Kit clung to the shallow toeholds that made the bones of his fingers crack from supporting his extra weight. A narrow crevice, barely visible ahead, emitted a shrieking sound that put Pigeon to shame. He stretched out his ringed hand and a tanned arm, braceleted in cuffs of gold, pulled him inside. The rowan ring burned like blue fire. Three-thousand years away, Bash rubbed the corresponding cold spot on her finger.

BEDE VILLAGE

DECEMBER 21 – THE WINTER SOLSTICE – 2017

Sarah Goodman's cat colony lined up like bowling pins, perched atop a miniature version of Hadrian's great wall that marked the official border of her garden – the last cottage, at the end of the last street on the edge of the village. It was only due to the stone wall's position on a slight hill, that the cats had a clear view of the surrounding countryside. But they didn't need it to pinpoint the location of the House of Reincarnations. They faced north, as one, towards the cloud that hung over Bede Hall like a red umbrella.

371

Back in the Hall, Bash was desolate. Snow and frost were still happy distant memories. She performed her weeding in her green garden in slow motion. Six was on a secret mission for Parks, miles away in an undisclosed location. He could be anywhere. Two months had passed without a word from Kit. Another year was about to be born. The furies attacked randomly. They were overdue. The yellow chair looked cheerful enough in the rare patch of sunlight where it liked to dream but it was silent as far as two-way conversations were concerned.

Bash was separated from her parents *and* Kit, and she couldn't fully recollect their last dream together. Something about a cat. She felt disempowered. Too disparaged to ask Charlotte for a potion. She was alone but for the fairies who trailed her every movement and all three of the Hall's living cats that mewed underfoot, and the ghost of Unicorn, constantly in her way, hovering three feet off the ground, dreamily swatting at passing dust mites.

She thought back to Livingston where she and Kit had been born. The words living stone echoed in her mind with considerable force. It seemed a million-years-ago. And given the trickeries of fairies, maybe it was.

With that thought, Nimue appeared and spun a perfumed circle around her head. "There's something in the top garden for you Mistress," she whispered. "Parks wants you to come."

"The 'something' stood higher than Sage. A topiary elephant. Life-sized. Its trunk raised in victory."

"It's actually for Kit," Parks said. "It seemed fitting to honor the challenges none of us want to face. That is, for the time being."

Bash mulled over the phrase 'time being'. It was almost funny.

"It's perfect," she said. "Thank you. He'd be…"

"I only did the conjuring, mind," Parks said. "I had help."

Bash took a deep breath and smiled a shaky smile. "Charlotte's fairies?"

"No Mistress," Parks said. "It was Six who suggested it. He said to tell you that elephants never forget. He named her too. Her name's Memory."

Bash buried her face in the foliage of the elephant's leg.

Parks looked up at Memory, and gave her a nod. "She sees your parents safe in Egypt," he said to Bash.

Memory lowered her trunk and snuffled Bash's shoulder.

"I've never felt too sad to cry before."

"He'll be all right, my dear," Parks said. "They both will."

There was no time to dwell on sadness. There were things to busy herself with in the gardens, and for the time being, Bathsheba Carter Stratford-Smyth, Mistress of the Green, was thankful for the war.

V e r o n i c a   K N O X
a few   words   about me

www.veronicaknox.com

I've lived in the Findhorn Community of Scotland and turned an abandoned Scottish church near Loch Ness into an art gallery with painted 'floorals'.

I write surreal fiction: ART HISTORY DELIVERED IN GHOST STORIES under the name V KNOX.

I love highly-visual, multi-layered stories that reconcile historical facts with imaginative fiction… and deliver big surprises. I explore the creative inner worlds of autistic savants and master artists, and in one case, the unknown child in the Titanic cemetery. I explore the discrepancies between reality and lucid dreams, fish the depths of the subconscious, the afterlife, and reincarnation, the anomalies of parallel lives and dimensions, and the classic psyche of 'the ghostly lover'. I write time-slip situations that defy the logic I firmly believe in.

Studying for a Fine Arts degree from the University of Alberta led me to develop an imaginative take on art history that led to other untapped avenues for stories.

Inanimate objects are rarely bereft of life? Paintings tell me juicy secrets.

Italian Renaissance paintings hypnotizes me. Objects in a museum captivate me. A pair of baby shoes labeled 'from the Titanic' or painted portraits are frozen moments – snapshots of what was and more importantly, WHO was. I found a wealth of stories, hidden in plain sight.

The author on one of her painted 'floorals' – 2004

WHAT IF two children aboard the Titanic were meant to marry? What if a master painting was attributed to the wrong artist? What if the 'Mona Lisa' was Leonardo da Vinci's kid sister? Renaissance paintings had to be 'signed' in covert ways. Who left their definitive 'I was here' imprints in code?

I love words, so I was particularly delighted to learn that I am a serious pluviophile – a lover of rain. I proudly attach this attribute to my profile. It makes perfect sense of an idiosyncrasy of mine, that although I continue to amass a collection of extremely cool eclectic umbrellas, I prefer to get wet in the rain. However, as a great part of the joy of rain is the sound it makes (and for which there is no greater pleasure than walking under a fabric dome) to receive its full sensory experience I have one umbrella I employ after I get wet. It is emblazoned with the face of the 'Mona Lisa'.

I remain intent on listening to the ethereal echoes from objects in museums and the voices of the Italian Renaissance – the artists as well as their anonymous subjects and companions. I grant them second chances to air their grievances, tell their stories, and together we set the dreariest history books on fire.

Books by

V KNOX / VERONICA KNOX

'LISABETTA – a stolen glance'

'ADORATION – Loving Botticelli'

'I WAS THERE'

'WOO WOO –
the posthumous love story of Miss Emily Carr'

'THE INDIGO PEARL'

'PEARL BY PEARL'

'THE UNTHINKABLE SHOES'

'TWINTER – the first portal'

'TIME FALLS LIKE SNOW'

www.veronicaknox.com